Praise for the Hector Lassiter Series by Craig McDonald

"[The Lassiter novels] are compelling, thrilling and darkly humorous. Lassiter is a brilliant creation– a crime writer who learned his trade with Ernest Hemingway and the Lost Generation in Paris in the 1920s. He is also a man who seems dangerously prone to violent intrigue, doomed love affairs, tragic marriages and military campaigns (he's a veteran of the Punitive Expedition, World War One, the Spanish Civil War and World War Two). Lassiter witnesses history unfolding and, occasionally, has a role in shaping its course. With *Three Chords and the Truth*, Craig McDonald has crafted a remarkable coda to the series." —Steve Powell, *The Venetian Vase*

"With each of his Hector Lassiter novels, Craig McDonald has stretched his canvas wider and unfurled tales of increasingly greater resonance." —Megan Abbott

"Reading a Hector Lassiter novel is like having a great uncle pull you aside, pour you a tumbler of rye, and tell you a story about how the 20th century 'really' went down." —Duane Swierczynski

"What critics might call eclectic, and Eastern folks quirky, we Southerners call cussedness — and it's the cornerstone of the American genius. As in: "There's a right way, a wrong way, and my way." You want to see how that looks on the page, pick up any of Craig McDonald's novels. He's built him a nice little shack out there way off all the reg'lar roads, and he's brewing some fine, heady stuff. Leave your money under the rock and come back in an hour." —James Sallis

"Craig McDonald is wily, talented and – rarest of the rare – a true original. He writes melancholy poetry that actually has melancholy poets wandering around, but don't turn your backs on them, either." —Laura Lippman

"Experiencing the work of Craig McDonald is akin to experiencing a painting by Picasso, a dance by Baryshnikov, music by Tchaikovsky. No two people will experience it exactly the same, but everyone who does experience it will walk away richer." —Jen Forbus, *Jen's Book Thoughts*

"James Ellroy + Kerouac + Coen brothers + Tarantino = Craig McDonald" —Amazon.fr

Write from Wrong

ALSO BY CRAIG MCDONALD

Once A World
One True Sentence
Forever Is Just Pretend
Toros & Torsos
The Great Pretender
Roll the Credits
The Running Kind
Head Games
Print the Legend
Death In The Face
Three Chords & The Truth
Head Games: The Graphic Novel
El Gavilan
Parts Unknown
Carnival Noir
Cabal
Angels of Darkness
Art in the Blood
Rogue Males
Borderland Noir (editor)

Write from Wrong

CRAIG MCDONALD

First published in the English language worldwide by Betimes Books 2021

www.betimesbooks.com

Cover design by JT Lindroos

For Madeleine Blaise McDonald

CHAPTERS

"Art is the lie that tells the truth."

—Pablo Picasso

"Art should give us back the world that our living confiscates from us."

—John Wilson

"Character is plot. Obsession is motivation. The quest, whatever else it may appear to be, is always a search for self—a race against time to a blood-spritzed epiphany. When that light bulb goes on, the world goes dark. No happy endings."

—Hector Lassiter

COLT

(MEXICO, 1914)

The old man sprawls twisted on the cracked desert floor, surrounded by books. Their pages whip in the blast-furnace wind.

Wary, Hector Lassiter slides off his horse, slowly approaching the injured codger.

The old man has a full head of white hair and a thick white moustache rather like Paw-Paw Stryder's. Not sure the stranger's even alive, Hector calls softly, "Mister?"

Groaning, the old man raises an arm against the sun. His eyes slowly focus on reedy Hector. He rasps, "You didn't ride in on a pale horse, so I reckon you're not the Angel of Death, goddamn it. But hell, I'm an atheist anyhow."

Hector kneels by the injured man. "You're gonna be fine," he says hollowly.

The young man's head is at first haloed by the ruby sun at his back, rendering him a slender silhouette.

Gradually, the old man can see the boy's features more clearly.

The kid has the palest blue eyes, startlingly wan. He has dark brown hair and a nervous smile bracketed by deep dimples. Clean features; a handsome young face.

The boy's trying to buck him up, the old man knows:

"Listen, mister," Hector says, "both your legs look broken in at least two places and there's nothing around to build a sled. Figure best thing I can do is start a fire up close. Leave some fuel for that fire—maybe these books will do—then fetch help. Think I can be back before dawn with some men to get you out of here."

Wincing, the old man drops his head back on the hard sand. Eyes closed tight, he rasps, "Nah, sonny. Not just my legs. Back's broken, too. Everything from my waist down's an expanse of numbness. I'm old, tired, and there's no fixing me. I'm dying, that I know. Can feel that. Just sit with me, won't you, kid? Keep me company 'til it's over? Then maybe you could get me deep enough in the ground and some of these rocks around here over me so the critters don't gnaw me ragged? Don't scatter my bones?"

Hector's rattled by that prospect. Sensing it, the old man says, "Won't take long, expect. Sittin' with me, that is. Promise you, not much life left in this near corpse. Somethin' important inside got poked by somethin' else that's broken."

The old man manages a smile. "Funny. Thought I didn't mind dyin' alone. Seems I was very wrong about that. Your coming along is a rare piece of good luck. Good luck for me, at any rate. Not for you, of course. Very sorry you have to be burdened with me, sonny."

"It's not a burden," Hector says. "But you're sure I can't really help you? If I ride real fast, I could maybe make it back here in less time with a doc and—"

"No. Already too late, like I said. I'd have you chat with me, instead. Keep me company. Distract me from what's to come. Please."

"Okay..." The boy looks back at his restless mount; she keeps scenting the air, wary-like. "You want some water, mister? I have a spare canteen and—"

"Not thirsty like that. How old are you, kid?"

"Fourteen. Be fifteen past midnight."

The old man smiles. "Came in with the century did ya?"

Hector was born one minute after midnight on January first. He shrugs, says, "Guess that's so." That hadn't occurred to him before this old man's pointing it out. "What's your name, sir?"

The old man licks his lips, smiles crookedly and says, "Farquhar. Peyton Farquhar. My handle."

Hector picks up several of the books scattered around the old man, arranges them in a stack and checks their spines. They all bear the same byline: Ambrose Bierce.

Hector says, "Mister, no offense, but you don't seem to read too widely."

The codger laughs, but that soon enough turns into another cough. The old man wipes at his mouth with his dusty coat sleeve, says, "You're some kind of wicked wit, kid. What's your name?"

"Hector Lassiter."

"Well, I'll thank you not just for sharing your name, but also for so deftly putting an old man in his place, Hector."

Gesturing at the man's twisted body, Hector says, "What happened, sir?"

"Rattler spooked my horse," the old man says. "Calliope bucked, threw me. Then she fell and rolled on me. Broke my legs and back. Then bolted. That's okay, though. Really. Came south to die, truth be known. Just didn't figure it to happen like this. Figured more to be shot to rags. Something quick." He winks, says, "To be a gringo in Mexico, that's euthanasia." A sudden frown. "But I was wrong about that."

Hector's leafing through one of the books titled *The Devil's Dictionary*. "This Bierce must be good."

"Published plenty, anyway," the old man says. "Not that any of that means a damned thing."

"It has to mean something," Hector says, adamant.

"Yeah? You read a lot, Master Lassiter?"

"I read a lot, sure." Hector hesitates, then says it out loud for the first time. "I want to be a writer."

A wry smile. "A writer? Heh! Well, that does make this just about perfect. Maybe there is a God. And maybe he's a trickster. El Coyote."

Hector scowls. "What do you mean, sir?"

The old man shakes his head. "Never mind. I know all these books, and all too well. Got anything of your own along you might share with me?"

"Just the start of somethin', maybe. Hardly more than a few pages, really."

"Fetch 'em. Please read to me, Hector."

"Seems the wrong time," Hector says. "If you're really . . . you know."

The old man arches his bushy eyebrows. "Really dying? Really am. So, what better way to take my mind off matters? Fetch your piece of writing. Read it to me. Please. I really want you to."

Hector stands, brushes dust off his butt. He walks to his horse, rummages his saddlebags. Returning with a sheaf of paper, he plops down next to the old man. He clears his throat, begins to read, nervous sounding.

His story is about a young boy raised along the Mexican border; a young boy with a no-account father. The boy bolts home to try and hook up with the Mexican revolutionary general Francisco "Pancho" Villa.

That last certainly resonates for the old man.

"Met him," the dying man says. "Villa, I mean. Came down here looking for him. Drawn down here by *La Decena Trágica* and all that trailed out of it."

"What'd you think of Pancho Villa?"

"A terrible disappointment," the old man says.

Hector asks, "How so?"

"He didn't kill me."

Hector reads on; the old man finds the prose lean and simple and true. It tells the story in a strong and direct way, painting living pictures in his dazed and rather jaded mind.

But as the kid warned, his story doesn't end yet. "Still tryin' to think of how to close it off," Hector says.

"You'll find the right ending," the old man says, firm. "Hints of its proper end are in your story already. You just have to get used to reading your own stuff. Listening to it, so to speak. Do that, and you'll know exactly how to end her." He hesitates, says, "The father in your story, that mean son of a bitch, based on your real Pap?"

"More or less," Hector says. He frowns. "Why do you ask?"

"Because you're out here, alone in the desert on your birthday," the old man rasps. "Figure maybe you're livin' your story. A rambling orphan. A maverick."

"It's made up," Hector says, angry. "I made up all of it." He pauses, says, "Pa's dead. Paw-Paw's tied up with some business in El Paso through the end of the week. So, I thought I'd explore. Paw-Paw—he lets me wander. Trusts I know horses and trails."

"What precisely happened to your old man?"

Hector doesn't look up from his manuscript. "Shot him. Didn't kill him, though."

The old man's set back on heel by that. "You sound almost sorry you didn't finish off your paw," he says softly. "Why'd you shoot him?"

"He killed my mother. Found her with someone else and shot her. So, I shot him. Just winged him." A shrug. "State killed him for Mother's murder. Hanged him. In Texas."

"You should write that story, Hector," the old man says. "But only when you're really ready, I mean. When you can make it art."

"But that's my life," Hector says. A bitter edge to his voice: "It's real, not something I made up."

There it is again.

The old man says, "Hector, writers make up a hell of a lot less than you evidently think. The art is in the tellin'. We all use our lives. We oft times live what we write, then we write what we live. Nothin' wrong with that. Not for us." He thinks about it a further minute, then allows, "Might be a different story for those closest to us, mind you."

Finally arriving at it, Hector smiles, says, "You're a writer, aren't you?" Hector picks up a couple more books scattered across the desert floor. "You're this author, aren't you? You're Ambrose Bierce."

The old man searches the boy's pale blue eyes. "I am," he says. "But you don't dare tell anyone. Not ever. Came down here to disappear, son. It's important to me nobody ever know what happened to me. Swear you'll keep my secret, Hector Lassiter."

Hector nods solemnly. "I'll never tell if that's how you want things. Nobody will ever know about this. But why? You must have friends, family."

"This is well apart from them," the old man—Bierce—says. "I bid family, such as they were, adieu before I left. Wrote the ones I couldn't say good-bye to in person."

And friends?

Bierce has had none of those in his life. Surely not as he defines the term.

"This must stay our secret, Hector. You have to stand by this promise, always."

Hector says, "I will. Swear. I'll always keep your secret." He reads a few paragraphs of the old man's writing. Hector says, "Any tips for how I should finish my story?"

"Have me a notion how it should end, sure. But you do too, Hector. And it's your story, after all."

Bierce is intense now. "Told you how to end her. Listen close to what's already there. You've drawn the line in a very deliberate, certain way. Just have to follow it to its proper end. But you have to do that all by yourself. No true writer ever collaborates. He doesn't want help. Not down deep. You have to find your own way, one word at a time. That's what writing is. I know from what you've read to me that you're capable. More, and far rarer, you're worthy, son."

The old writer's words thrill him, of course. But Hector says, "All these books, your readers? Why leave 'em wondering what happened to you?"

"What they'd expect of me," Bierce says. "What they really want, though they may not know it themselves. You have to know your audience. Better than they know themselves, truth be told. This is the right way for me to end.

We all write against eternity, son. Even the ones who don't literally write. But some of us need that extra something to bolster our long game. To end in mystery is to maybe cheat death in the grander sense. See if my writing lasts beyond my simple living."

Hector isn't sure he understands what the old man means by that last, but he somehow grasps it's imperative for both of them that the old man is confident the younger writer really gets it. Hector nods, says, "Sure you don't want water, sir?"

"Dead sure," Bierce says. "But that bottle yonder there—please say she's intact."

Hector rises again, stepping wide around the old man's body. Deftly, he scoops up the bottle of Kentucky bourbon. "Not broken," he says. "Full to the brim."

"More rare good luck," Bierce says. "I am truly dizzy at tonight's windfall. Over the moon. You ever have spirits, Master Lassiter?"

"Never, sir."

"Well, you're old enough, and it is your birthday after all, goddamn it. And it's terrible for even a dying man to drink alone. Oh, and kid, we're fellow writers. Call me Bierce. That's an order. Now prop me up, won't you, Hector? Then won't you break that seal and we'll commence to murder this soldier together."

The young writer is dubious. "Won't it hurt if I move you?"

"As I said, kid, I'm dead already, tits down. Don't feel a goddamn thing down there anymore."

Hector takes his saddlebags off his horse and uses them to prop up the old man. He breaks the seal on the bottle and gives it to Bierce for a first drink.

The old writer takes a swig, passes it back to Hector. "Don't try and be a hero, kid. Just a wee sip, starting out. First one kicks like a goddamn mule."

Hector takes a tentative taste. Then he takes a second sample, far deeper—a fiery and savoring sip. He closes his eyes and feels the infusion of warmth that starts at the back of his throat, then bores down to his belly.

Suddenly, the colors of the world seem brighter. He looks at the bottle's label: Four Roses.

Sure. He could surely learn to like this, he thinks.

Bierce, closely watching, says, "You're a natural, Hector. So please do be careful, son. Many is the writer undone by that tarantula juice."

"I'll be careful," Hector pledges.

"Good boy. But please don't start bein' cautious tonight, sonny."

Bierce says, "Not to tell you your business, Hector, but was I you, while we talk and while it's cool and dark, I'd be digging my grave... If I were you, that's what I'd do."

Hector swallows hard. He says tightly, "You really think you're dying?"

"Thought we settled all that nonsense, kid. Yes, I am goddamn dyin'."

The old man holds up a long-barreled gun and it's a beauty: an 1873 Colt, the Cavalry model.

"If the Reaper doesn't come fast enough for me, I'll try and save you more trouble by doin' it myself," Bierce says. "Nothin' wrong with strategic suicide under proper circumstances."

He turns the gun in the gathering moonlight. "They don't call it a Peacemaker for no reason at all, you know."

Hector eyes the nearly vanished sun. "Let me get a fire going before I set to work. Gonna get cold fast, now."

"Please do that," Bierce says. "A last good crackling campfire would be very welcome. A comfort. And use those books as you need to. I no longer require them."

Taken aback by the suggestion now that he knows the books' relation to the old man, Hector says, "I will not do that. They're too valuable. There's plenty else to make a fire with." He sets to work doing so. As he gathers materials to burn, Hector says, "I'm sorry it maybe ends for you like this, Bierce."

The old man watches the young writer. This Hector Lassiter is like a colt, Bierce thinks—full of spirit and casual energy, all hearty promise and undefined boundaries.

So very enviable.

And himself? Bierce shakes his head, sipping more from the bottle. He's a thrice-stumbled swayback, too shot to put out to stud and just awaiting his hard-chased after coup de grace.

"Don't feel badly for me, son," Bierce says, raw-voiced. "Really. Had my ride and then had some more. You know what the definition of life is, Hector Lassiter?"

Looking up from a freshly crackling fire, Hector says, "Is this definition in that book there by your head? In *The Devil's Dictionary*?"

"Didn't make the cut," Bierce says. "Didn't know it. Not back then."

"What is the definition of life, Bierce?" Hector's decided to take the old man at his word: He gets out his trail plate and, getting down on one knee on the opposite side of the fire—where the old man will have a harder time seeing—Hector begins to claw a shallow grave from the desert floor.

It's tough going and the metal plate scrapes loudly against the parched sand.

"Life," Bierce says louder, "is a promise nobody keeps." He takes another swig from the bottle, trying hard to ignore the sound of the scratching and the boy's grunting as he works to carve the old man's shallow grave. "How'd you come to writing, Hector Lassiter?"

Hector pauses, drags a forearm across his damp forehead. "Writing helps me make sense of things, I guess. Only thing I can really do. Only thing I'm driven to do."

"Then for the love of Christ hanging proud in misery on his rugged old cross, do please push on after her, Hector. Do that without pity or second thought, for Christ's sake. That's the way it has to be—born to write and writing to live. Stay on that chase, son. Stay after that old whore hard."

Narrowing pale blue eyes. "You havin' me on, Bierce?"

"Not at all. Christ, no. Writing's been my life, all along my wicked way." Another sip of bourbon and fresh gravel in his timbre, Bierce asks, "How's that goddamn hole shaping up?"

Hector takes a breath, says, "Ground's pretty baked, but it's comin' along. Lot of big rocks around, like you said. Be enough protection from, you know... scavengers."

Even as Hector says it, something slinks along at campfire's edge. Coyote, he figures. If there's one, there is probably two, the other moving parallel in the dark.

The old man studies the critter's silhouette with disdain. Bierce says, "Those bastards are like too many critics, but without all their nose-in-the-air pretenses. You know what the definition of a critic is, Hector? That's a person who boasts himself hard to please because nobody ever tries to please him."

Smiling, Hector says, "That one in your book?"

"Bet your ass."

"And writing? There a definition of that in your book?"

"No," Bierce says, firmly. "That's nothing to be mocked. Not ever. Not the writing."

Bierce is quiet a time, then says, "I have one more big favor to ask you, my young and possibly my very best friend. After all you've done, it's too much to expect. But I have to ask. The biggest favor of all, I fear. Seems I'm not the brave, wicked old bastard I thought I was, Master Lassiter. May well need your help if this goes too slowly. Just not sure at all I can turn this old Colt on myself. May need you to pull her trigger, sonny."

Hector can't do that. There's no way he can do that.

"Just like puttin' down a rabid dog, or a horse with a broken leg," Bierce races on. "Mercy, not murder. You'd be doing me the greatest favor, kid. Giving the greatest gift."

Not wanting to argue with the old writer, Hector says, "Let's see how things go. Maybe you're wrong. Maybe you're not even dying."

"I surely am," Bierce says. "Just not fast enough. Fear I'll possibly need you to do this for me, sonny."

"I'll think on it."

The old man holds out the bottle. "Take a big drink, this time. It'll help. You know, for later."

Hector doesn't think that's so. And he'll never do it, anyway. But he accepts the bottle and takes a deep swallow. That delicious burn again.

The old man looks up at the stars. The sun's been down at least half-an-hour. He says, "Is it getting darker?"

Hector looks up from the long trench he's nearly finished digging. He gives the old man a closer look then says, "It's getting darker."

It isn't, of course, not that fast.

Hector quits his digging and crouches close to the old writer.

He can see it closing in on the old man, fast and hard.

Thank God, he won't have to cope with the writer's request to end him.

Bierce says, "Gun's yours, son. In payment for all you've done. Got her after the Brothers War. Lit off from Ohio, don't you know? A callow, starry-eyed kid, starved to fight in that one, thinking I'd learn something that might count. Figured to get myself a lot of material to write about. Well, I got all the material I could hope for, and more."

Hector says, "But you did learn something, too?"

"Meaningless... meaninglessness. Learned the definition of those words well enough, Master Lassiter."

"The meaninglessness of war, Bierce?"

"Sure. That, too." The old man seems to be taking more effort to breathe. "Life, too."

Hector says, "You're really saying that nothing matters?"

"The written word does. Makes the rest just about bearable. Least for me. Books can endure, Hector. Can't say that of much else in this mostly tepid world in my experience. You can keep those books, too. Or do the smart thing—burn 'em and keep yourself warm through this frigid-ass night. It is getting much colder, isn't it, son?"

"Yes," Hector lies. "We've already talked about this. I'm keeping your books. Mean to read every word. Not one is going in that fire."

"Getting' so much darker," Bierce says softly, slurring. "Must be nearly midnight. Happy birthday to you, kid. Happy death day to me." Groggy, Bierce smiles, says, "Symmetry in that. You can be the New Mister Me, God help you. Maybe you'll even get a story out of this dreary episode. Just remember, never use my name. That's critical. Instead make it your story one day, kid."

"I've promised to keep your secret," Hector says. "Happy New Year, Mr. Bierce."

The old author doesn't answer. Hector presumes to take the old man's hand. He holds it until the old writer's big mitt goes limp and just a spell later, cold.

Hector positions the last stone on the cairn.

Shivering, he moves closer to the fire. He opens one of Bierce's books. Hector reads on, rapt. He does that all night.

At first light, Hector finds the old man's horse, tethers it to his rented roan.

He repacks the books in the old man's own saddlebags. The beautiful old Colt Peacemaker Hector stows in his bags along with his evolving manuscript.

Passing by the cairn a last time, Hector sees a rattlesnake. It has strangely penetrating green eyes.

Likely, it's the viper that got Bierce killed. Before his horse spooks, Hector draws the ancient Colt.

He takes fast yet careful aim, firing from horseback, and cleanly blasts the head off the snake. The serpent's body whips wild a few seconds before acknowledging death. He strips the snake's body of its skin, thinking to maybe make a new band to replace the worn one on Paw-Paw Stryder's rugged old-hand-me down Stetson. The original band has shed many scales over the years.

Hector slips the handsome old gun back into his saddlebag.

A quote of the old man's he read in *The Devil's Dictionary* during the dark morning hours sitting vigil by the writer's anonymous cairn dogs Hector's thoughts.

"A person who doubts himself is like a man who would enlist in the ranks of his enemies and bear arms against himself. He makes his failure certain by himself being the first person to be convinced of it."

Very well. Hector vows he'll strive for the arrogance to create for always, even when he knows the words aren't quite coming together.

He will excel, at least, in never surrendering.

There'll be no indulging in self-doubt.

Another of the old man's quotes ambush him: "Death is not the end; there remains the litigation over the estate."

Smiling, Hector hears the old man rambling on:

"So, I end in mystery, Hector, because maybe I'm not writer enough to stay in print beyond the ruin of my sorry corpus. Need an angle. An edge. To simply disappear? That's a way to ensure my literary long game. Some might call it cheating. I call it strategy, Master Lassiter."

Quite the thinker, this Bierce.

This writer.

Hector dismounts, dons his rain slicker.

He's just settled back into the creaking saddle when the storm comes fiercely, the rain sheeting sideways, hard and fast across the hills of Juarez.

Hector sets off back toward El Paso, the driving rain on him all the way.

A DYING FALL
(SPAIN, 1923)

The Fiesta de San Fermín has already dissolved from discreet days into a seamless, wine-fueled always now.

Only the comings-and-goings of the sun vaguely mark time's true passage between each daily session of Corrida de Toros which the two American fiction writers take in with solemn fascination and reverence each afternoon, regarding the drama daily enacted within the ring as an elemental and heady expression of tragic art steeped in myth and ritual.

Hector is in the company of Ernest and Hadley Hemingway. He has barely slept between crowded, hazy and uncountable hours spent in the bullfighting arenas, afterward in the bars, and later still, gawking at exploding fireworks.

These rain down over raucous Pamplona, spectators *oohing* and *ahhing* at the light show while squeezing wine into their mouths from swiftly shriveling botas.

Dressed all-in-white, with a red neckerchief and black beret, Hem's gone fully native. Hem's gazing at a trio of cartels—bullfighting posters—pasted to the exterior wall of the Café Iruña.

Hector has stuck to his typical casual clothes worn during springs and summers in Paris—tennis shoes, cotton work pants, Polo shirts and light sport jacket when the sun sets and the dusty streets grow chilly.

Hadley is six-months pregnant, but as is her way, she's being the devout trooper for her newly-coined aficionado of a husband, inchoately embracing all that Hem loves.

Increasingly feeling like a third wheel as they've made their way toward Pamplona, several days ago, Hector accepted the lusty advances of an attractive freelance journalist from Madrid named Ana Marin.

There is no sacrifice in this: Ana is vivacious, pretty and exceptionally uninhibited in bed.

She is also a bullfighting enthusiast by her own description. One who was already tracking the Spanish bullfighting season, trekking town-to-town and penning write-ups for one of the smaller Spanish wire agencies.

But a day or two before Hector and Ana first coupled, the Hemingway party began taking on more camp followers of a sort.

These include a Spanish fiction writer and sometimes-journalist named Arturo Cabrero, and the man's fiancée.

Arturo's intended is a handsome widow named Isa Hidalgo.

Isa's daughters, ages ten and twelve, are also along for the entire heady experience it seems, despite the fact Pamplona during the Festival of San Fermin is not remotely child-friendly.

The action in the arena, where the girls are also a daily fixture in the stands, is visceral and fierce; frequently exceptionally bloody.

It's now ten in the morning. Hector, Hem and Arturo sit in the Iruna café, sipping café con leche and commiserating about the craft of writing.

Hector and Ernest are quite familiar with one another's works and aesthetic values. But neither's read anything by the older, apparently well-established Madrid-based fiction writer.

Correspondingly, the two young and aspiring American writers' and their fictional works are equally unknown to Arturo.

Discussing the challenge of endings, the Spanish writer vents his frustration about finding the proper climax to his work-in-progress.

"Endings are hardest, you will agree," Arturo says. "That's true if it is the ending of a short story, or a novel. Finding the proper bang as you Americans say to end on. And on precisely the right and even keening note? This is never easy, eh?"

Then Arturo smiles broadly, adds, "But the fact it is so hard? Maybe that is a gift for us in its way, yes? For if it was too easy, surely everyone might presume to write."

Grinning and stroking his dark moustache, Hem says, "Lasso and I were knocking this around the other night. The big ending has its place, sure. But not in every story, Art. At least that's my thought. Lasso's, too, I daresay."

Cupping his mug in his big hands, Hem says, "You see, Lasso and I have, each in our way, experimented with more of the dying fall sort of ending. Something understated as a climax. An ending that haunts the reader, even nags at him. But a far quieter curtain closer. Maybe even a vague denouement."

Hem smiles. "It should be a muted ending. One that keeps the reader hooked, thinking about the story, for some good time after the reading is done. Something in the end more powerful than the bombastic payoff that roundhouses the reader. Knocks him or her on their ass, but only for the moment. I think that sometimes we're all maybe too focused as writers on that knockout punch. As a boxing fan, I grant you, a TKO is a stunner when she lands. Sure as hell, I'll admit that's so. But those aren't the boxing matches that tend to linger in my memory."

Tearing the blunt end from a breakfast roll, Hector says, "I'm indeed tending that way more in my writing, too. The dying fall is a kind of Holy Grail. At least for now. The climax of choice for me."

"I shall think more on this," Arturo says, stroking his studiously tended waxed black moustache. "I have always gone for the jugular, I suppose you would say. Chasing what the French would call, *La phrase qui tue.*"

Hem is clearly already tiring of shop talk. He and Hector get plenty of such café chatter myriad nights in Paris, and certainly more than their fill around Gertrude Stein's salon, where both are frequently pestered-to-attend fixtures.

Stretching, Hem says, "Lasso and I are thinkin' about risking the run in the morning. You know? Bulls chasing the fellas through the streets to the plaza? The sprint before the fighting proper starts? You should join us, Art! Be a hell of fine time!"

This notion of his running with the bulls comes as news to Hector.

Oh, sure, Hem raised it as a kind of musing "what if" last night in his cups.

But Hector never thought Ernest was serious about risking one of these reckless, feckless and potentially lethal dashes—the crazy-ass sprint with half-a-dozen horned bulls pounding hard on heel.

Hell, plenty men have been mauled, even killed, making similar, crazed and drunken runs down through the years.

And anyway, running with the bulls is a sophomoric spectacle for the gawkers, to Hector's mind; carnival thrills for the drunken uninitiated. An obscenity peculiar only to Pamplona and that stands far apart from thc art and tradition of bullfighting itself.

Indeed, Hector has often wondered what fool in Pamplona first dreamed up the stupidity of having a bunch of hungover idiots race through barricaded streets with bulls charging behind.

Indeed, to Hector, a true aficionado, the idiocy of racing through the streets with bulls at your back has no merit and is a boorish affront to the ancient, mystical spectacle and fearsome ritual pitting man against bull within the sacred ring with the death of one or the other a certain climax.

Anyway, Arturo just smiles and says, "I haven't you two lads' youth on my side."

Hem waves a hand, dismissing that. "Youth we have in spades, sure. But I've seen you play tennis, Art. We don't have your legs or stamina, neither of us, of course. Lasso and I, we both got hit. Hit hard. Hit in the legs, in the Great War. Christ, without the rubber support I have around what's left of one of my knees, I'd still fall down just trying to stand up."

"I'll think on it," Arturo pledges. He does that with a smile and expression that Hector recognizes telegraphs, *This will* never *happen.*

And thank God, for that, Hector thinks.

Just then, the ladies arrive—Hadley, Ana, and Isa.

And the latter's daughters, Irena and kid sister, Ilda.

Hem gives his wife a fond bear hug. Hadley looks tired. In her present condition, she should be relaxing at home, Hector thinks, and not for the first time.

Very aware the young girls are watching them, Hector simply smiles and squeezes Ana's arm in greeting.

As he does that, Hector watches Arturo give his intended perfunctory Mayfair kisses and a fleeting embrace.

Then the older writer lavishes forehead, cheek and eyelid kisses on the two young girls. He bestows each little girl hard and familiar hugs they seem at best to tolerate.

Those latter hugs of Arturo's spark a twinge of unease in Hector—the result he thinks of something in the way they linger. The places on their too-young bodies where Arturo's liver-spotted hands familiarly fall.

Registering Hector's observation of all that, Ana leans in. She whispers urgently, "You see it, too! We will talk more of this . . . ."

Hector searches her eyes, but Ana is now seemingly focused on putting up a friendly social front.

First fetching extra chairs, then ordering lemonade for her girls, Hem says to Isa, You're just in time to talk your future husband into making the run with us tomorrow morning. You know—ahead of the bulls?"

Isa smiles, says, "Don't even joke! Art could probably do with some adventure. Something new to write about. But that's an absurd proposition." She waves a hand. "Anyway, you and Hector both walk with obvious limps—your war wounds. Regardless, even if you weren't both afflicted like that, and if Art was your age, it's still a stupid thing to do and a blight on bullfighting only this city has seen fit to inflict upon the sport."

Shaking her head, Isa said, "And people even die doing that, don't they? It's a crazy, pointless thing to do."

Hector passes his fresh, un-sampled *café con leche* to Ana. Fully on Isa's side, Hector says to Ana, "You're the bullfighting journalist, darlin'. What about that? How often do people actually get killed during these morning runs?"

Ana half-smiles, admonishes, "Héctor, the children!"

"They only speak Spanish fluently," Isa says, rather too casually for Hector's liking. "Their English? Same as nil."

Nodding and choosing her next words, Ana says in her soft and silky Spanish accent, "Very well. They've only kept records about any of that since 1910. Since then, nobody has been lost making the run. But plenty are injured every year. Fifty or even more, most summers here in Pamplona. And there is the occasional goring of runners. That can make you quite sick, or even worse later, from infection. The bulls' horns are filthy. Swimming in bacteria. And it is quite a long way to run with six hulking, horned beasts after you. The course is nearly a thousand yards, you should know."

Hadley shakes her head, says, "Hem, with your knee, you could and should never do that! And Hec, you still have problems from your war injuries, just as Isa has observed." To her husband Hadley says, "Stop talking nonsense, Tatie."

"Other than from any sort of responsibility, I'm indeed surely not much of a runner," Hector cracks to Hem's freckled-faced, red-headed wife. "That's too true. And I also smoke, and surely too much. Don't have the wind for such commotion."

Hector looks to Ernest, says, "And you have a child on the way, Hem. Can hardly afford to be laid up with some *herida* from a goring." Hector then makes the sign of the cross, and still trying to joke off the notion of joining the sea of idiots the next morning in the streets, he adds, "Or worse...."

But Ernest still isn't completely letting it go, jest or not. "We'll talk more on this," Hem vows. "A few more drinks of the giant killer, and I expect Arturo and even Lasso will prove out as up for it. If Art declares he game, you know you can't say no, Lasso."

Hector checks his pocket watch, says, "Only thing I know is it's only ten in the morning, but I've got to get at least a little sleep every thirty-six hours or so. If I don't, I'm going to fall over before today's cycle of fights. Going to grab a little siesta now. Reacquaint myself with the insides of my eyelids. They've been too-long denied company."

Ana says, "Could use some rest, too. We'll catch up with you all about one in the ring. Please don't let anyone steal our seats."

That's hardly a likelihood as today's tickets are very good ones for the *barreras*, or first row of seats.

Hadley winks at Ana, says knowingly, "Sweet dreams, Ana."

Bare and spent, Ana and Hector roll onto their backs, sprawling across the sweat-soaked sheets.

The shades are drawn against the sun, but the windows are open and the oscillating fans do little to drown the din from the street.

"So much for sleeping," he says.

Ana gives him a knowing smile. "You never intended that."

He reaches out, takes her sweat-slick hand in his. "Found out. I very much wanted to be alone with you. Guess I'm just not the hard-charging partier that Hem is. Or Arturo, to my surprise. Both are plenty happy drinking to dawn and beyond. Art maybe even more than Hem."

Invoking the elder writer's name finally brings them back around to her earlier remark about the Arturo's interactions with the children.

Voice going smoky, Ana says, "The way you looked at him as he touched those girls? The fury in your eyes? Your blue eyes' pale fire as you dwelled upon where he touched those girls? Tell me please, what do you really know about Arturo Cabrero?"

Hector picks up an ash tray, a box of matches and a cigarette. Adjusting pillows and sitting up more in bed, he says, "Never heard of him 'til he latched on to us a few days before you and I met. Still haven't read a word he's written. So, I'm just going on faith he's truly a writer of some reputation 'round these parts."

"Oh, he's an author, all right. As to reputation?" She wrinkles her pretty nose. "He certainly has one of those."

"You've read his stuff?"

"More than some."

"He's a good writer?"

"What does that even mean? A good writer?"

"You've read some of my stories. Where am I compared to Arturo? And be honest, please. Do that, knowin' I've got a thick skin."

"Not as good as you. Not even at his best. He's surely not as good as Ernesto. Cabrero is more... your English word would be notorious, I think. At least sensational."

"Sounds like I need to ask you far more about what you know about this man," Hector says. "Regardless how good he is as a writer. But he's popular here?"

"Not at all," she says. "Or not anymore. Far more the cult writer, now. Probably why he's fallen to journalism. His writing—particularly the early writing, which was much different than the more recent stories? Not for everyone. Not even for many, now. The subject matter is... how do I put this? Off-putting, to most. Certainly, I hope that's so. Much of the reluctance to read him now is fed by the old rumors some still know. Also, because of the resulting trial, although there was never any conviction through the courts."

"Rumors? Trial? No conviction? Jesus, tell me everything," Hector says. "Please do that, now."

Ana does that. Painfully. Protractedly.

Gathered up in his arms after, she asks, "What now, *mi corazón?*"

Seething, wanting to strangle Arturo with his bare hands, Hector says, "We tell, Hem. Then? Together, Hem and me? Reckon we'll hash out some sort of remedy for the sake of those kids."

At a quiet table, in an out-of-the way café, Ana sits between Hector and Ernest, fiddling with her wine glass while recounting her dark tale to the storyteller she calls "Ernesto."

"It was there in his first writings, for anyone who really wanted to see it, or knowingly looked, I suppose," she says. "Perhaps some writers are very lucky in that way. They are safely in the ground before their readers fully grasp what their favorite writer was truly saying in his writings. Not *modo manifestamente.* Not nakedly or obviously, of course. But what was shared between the lines, so to speak. You're both writers." A little smile. "You know what I mean."

Still more than a bit irked to be pulled from the bull-fights, Hem says, "You said he was arrested. Something about a trial. I suppose that all of that then shed some kind of dark backlight on his writing? That's what you're getting at?"

"Just so," Ana says. "Yes. Precisely."

Between the lack of sleep, the latest infusion of red wine, and his annoyance to be pulled from the arena, Hector can see that Hem's patience—and attention span—are severely taxed.

Hector says, "Heart of the matter, Hem? Based on his past history, he's likely marrying Isa to get at her daughters. Christ, I'm prepared to accept it as gospel."

Hem looks up sharply, his brown eyes darting from Hector to Ana, then back to Hector again. "All of this—us talking about this now—it all started because of the way he hugged those girls this morning, didn't it? I saw it, but didn't really see it, and goddam me for that. Blind in the moment. Shame on me for that. Too much of the giant killer, I guess."

"But you did note it, evidenced by your remarking on it now," Hector says. "Wasn't right, Hem. Crawled my nape. Yours, too, even through the fog of your hangover."

Ana cuts in. "And there's the matter of Marisol Lopez. She was Arturo's first-known wife of record. About ten years ago. Also far enough from here. That's to say, that to most people living outside of the Toledo area—where all this happened—it has been largely forgotten. If it was ever even known more widely. Now Arturo lives in Madrid. A new life there. Same as a world away."

Focus again wavering, Hem prompts, "Marisol Lopez…?"

Nodding, Ana says, "Yes. An earlier version of your friend, Isa. An attractive widow with a very pretty little ten-year-old girl. The child was Arturo's true objective. In time, that little girl told her grandmother what Arturo was doing to her, and even to her friends, when her mother wasn't around.

"And so, through the grandmother, the law got involved," Ana presses on. "Sides were chosen. Marisol sided with Arturo against her own little girl and all of her daughter's friends, who also had been 'interfered with' as the court documents phrased it. Very soon, the court case began to fall apart because the primary victim's claims weren't supported by her own mother."

Ana picks up the *bota*, squeezing with both hands to squirt more dry red wine into her glass. She drinks deeply, carefully choosing her next words.

She savors the dulling bliss of the wine, says, "In terrible desperation, obviously, the grandmother hired a man to take a shot at Arturo—to slay him. But the assassin accidentally shot Marisol instead. And the hired killer was promptly caught.

"*Abuela* quickly heard word the intended assassination failed, and heard of the arrest. So, she knew that she would be arrested, soon. Once that happened, Arturo would have an open road at the daughter. And her friends."

Squeezing the bridge of his nose, Hem growls, "Expect you're going to tell us *Abuela* killed the little girl and then herself, gently and swiftly as she could."

"Just so," Ana says. "Sleeping pills."

"And Arturo skated, unpunished," Hector says.

"More, he got a novel out of it all," she says. "But that backfired on him, in its way. That book sent people digging back into his earlier work to find any similar, dark subtext they missed on first pass. Close-readers focused on certain word choices in regards to descriptions of very young women or girls in this man's books and stories. They came to focus upon the sheer number of such young girls moving through his earlier works."

"And yet he still has readers here?" Hem curls his lip and says, "Can't see how that could be."

Ana says, "For one thing, many years ago, he changed the sorts of books he writes. But he didn't change his way of living, obviously."

Hem sighs. "Obviously, Isa needs to know all of this, now."

"We hardly know her any better than we do Arturo," Hector says. "Are you so certain she'll believe it all any more than that woman Marisol did in the day?"

Hem says, "This bastard now has a recorded history we can point to. There are his earlier writings. And we have Ana, who knows his history. She can tell Isa how it was."

Shrugging, Ana says, "Maybe. Yet I watched your friend Isa a while ago. She saw exactly what Héctor saw. What you noted, Ernesto. Yet she didn't seem bothered by it. Not a touch flustered. Yet Héctor saw that same thing and was appalled. It set off alarms in his head, and yours too. And Isa was the one on the receiving end of that cold, faux kiss of welcome this morning. Any other clear-eyed woman would know exactly what to make of that if it happened to her. Trust me on that."

Hem nods, says, "It's Marisol all over again, you're saying."

"Surely appears that way to me," she says. "And if you confront Isa with this, and if she ignores or dismisses what you say? What then of the daughters?"

"So, what do we do?" Hem cracks his knuckles, asks, "Really, what's to be done?"

She drains her glass again; this time Hector refills it. He does that even though he can see she's at least faintly drunk now.

He hopes that apparent condition explains Ana's next and rather remarkable statement.

"Look around—it's *el festival*," Ana says, dark eyes shining from the wine. "*La fiesta* and everyone is behaving very badly. If only some street thug was to simply walk up to this man with a knife, and if he then …?"

"Steady there," Hector says urgently. "That's likely how that luckless if loving grandmother started down her dark and bloody road to self-destruction."

Ana says nothing in reaction to that.

An uncomfortable silence hangs over the trio.

Hem eventually reaches for the wine skin, judges it tragically light and waves their *bota* in the air to signal for its refilling.

Hem finally says, "What if we really talk Arturo into making that run tomorrow morning, Lasso? Shame him into it? With his age he would surely be back of the pack.

And what if Arturo was to stumble? Even fall? What if the devil is left to serve as hindmost, to twist the cliché?"

Taking it as a grim joke on his friend's part—the kind of dark humor common to crime beat reporters, which, for a time in Kansas City, a young Hemingway was, Hector says, "Right. Sure. With our shot-up and bum legs, we'd be the more likely goners. Hell, doubt I could run across the street here, side-to-side, let alone cover more than nine hundred yards in the Spanish July heat. Not at more than a lethal limp."

"Oh, I wasn't suggesting we actually make that run," Hem said. "You're right — neither of us could do it. Besides, that fucking spectacle is an insult to everything you and I cherish about what actually takes place in the ring."

But Hem just shakes his head, grumbles, "So we'll think more on this. Think goddamn hard on it. We've defined the problem. Clearly we all agree something's got to be done. A solution will come to us. But for now, we should get back to 'em before Hadley, or Isa, or especially that son of a bitch child molester get suspicious about us being gone for so long."

The shadow of Arturo and his threat to the girls cast a pall over the day's *toros* schedule for Hector, Hem and Ana.

Eventually, Ana and Hector excuse themselves for another lusty, sunny siesta.

But the sinister shadow of Arturo tracks them to their bed, too.

Stretched out in their afterglow, bare and beaded in sweat but fondly holding hands, Ana says softly, "Part of me wants to think your friend was quite serious about tomorrow morning and the bulls."

Hector says—perhaps too quickly, and maybe too forcefully—"That's just Hem being Hem. He's scrupulous with facts in his journalism, but in casual social settings? In his fiction? Hem's frankly more than a bit of a fabulist.

"Take those war wounds he and Hadley mentioned," Hector charges on. "Hem was no soldier, you should know. Hem was declared physically unfit for combat. Instead, he ran a canteen for the Red Cross in Italy. One night, Hem decided to take his chocolate and cigarettes right up to the forward-most trenches. Hem did that very much against orders. Thrill-seeking, he got caught in a deadly firefight."

"And your wounds, Héctor?"

"I was a credentialed soldier. First hit came in Mexico, as a trooper, chasing Pancho Villa on horseback through the Mexican desert. Shot through the leg. My second wounding came a few months later, while a conscripted and terrified solider in a French trench."

"So, if I may ask, you have killed others?"

A long silence. "Considerably more than once."

Ana's quiet for a time; at last says, "Confess, I still rather hope your friend isn't showing off in some way. That he wasn't joking."

Some more cannon shots go off outside, signaling the next phase in the day's *corrida* schedule.

Hector says, "Please explain that desire on your part, darlin'? Why do you feel so personally and passionately about this man and lethal harm comin' to him? Why do you feel that enough to want to see this man slain?"

She turns to coil around him, despite the heat. She wraps a bronzed leg around his waist; clasps an arm around his shoulder.

Ana says softly into his chest, not looking him in the eye, "The story I told you and Ernesto about Arturo and his arrest? I know it so well because I lived it, Héctor. I grew up with Marisol's daughter. Her name was Lola. We went to school together. Sometimes slept over at one another's homes. Once, I was staying overnight with them at Arturo's hacienda, just before Lola confided everything to her grandmother. Arturo came into the room where we were sleeping that night. He did things. Mostly he did all that to his soon-to-be daughter-in-law. But he did things to me, too. Testing me, I think now. To see if I would balk? If I would scream or tattle?"

"Reckon I can imagine enough about that," Hector says icily, cutting off further description of any of that. "But how is he able to sit with you now? To pretend like none of that happened?"

Now Hector wants to tear Arturo apart, atom by atom, and to do it bare-handed.

"My name was different," Ana murmurs. "After the trial, I was sent away to live with other relatives. An embarrassment to my family, despite the fact I was attacked. Despite the fact I was a victim. So, now my name is different. And I'm an adult woman, now. No longer attractive to his kind. He has not connected me with Lola and Marisol. Of that I'm certain. And that's to my advantage."

Hector says nothing, just lets her keep telling it in her own time, and in her own way.

Ana says, "Ernesto? Too caught up in his zeal for the bulls and the festival to notice. But surely you must have wondered at my willingness as a bullfighting journalist, even one working freelance, to miss so many of the fights in order to make love with you? To simply spend time with you, my darling Héctor? With you I am more than taken. And the daily fights? I couldn't care less. I'm no fan, believe me. Have not even a flicker of *afición*. I especially detest what happens to the horses. Perhaps I too much identify with them. I hate what happens to the bulls, too. So I endure it by imagining the bulls and horses are that terrible man. I took this assignment only to get close to Arturo. You'll have deduced that by now. I do this for a paycheck because Arturo is stringing for another newspaper service, and it means I must go where he does."

Hector says, "And you and I? Since Arturo has been tugged into Hem's orbit, being with me like this frankly strikes me, at least a bit, as still more cynical strategy."

Her eyes flash and she grips him hard, fingernails digging in. "No! You stop right there, Héctor! I've come to truly know you. Became strongly attracted to you. Finding you in all of this, during my mission? You are a delicious and un-deserved gift, if also a dangerous distraction."

Already dreading the answer, he still asks, "Mission? Dangerous distraction…? Distraction from what mission, precisely?"

Ana lets go of his hand. "It took a long time for me to learn to enjoy being with a man after what happened to me, you should know. When I saw the announcement of this man's most recent engagement, and saw there were children again involved—saw their sex, their ages—it all came back to me, fiercely. I immediately started to steep myself in all the old poison. Poured over his older stories and novels again. And that made it all so much more raw. Reading his earlier writing deepened and worried old wounds. Stirred all my old demons. Made them horridly fresh."

"I'm so sorry for what happened to you," Hector says, searching her glistening eyes. "But you can't let that bastard own you. Mustn't let the past smother your present... Or rob you of your future."

"I know all that," she says thickly. "But then there was this one old short story of Cabrero's entirely new to me."

Despite the heat and sweat beading their bare bodies, Hector suffers a sudden chill. His resulting shiver inspires her to shiver back.

Ana says, "The little girl in this short story, and as she was described? The things hinted to have happened in that story to her? I'm sure it was all inspired by me. That night Cabrero violated me."

Her eyes lock with Hector's. "I'm sure all you fiction writers use your lives in similar ways. The good and the bad parts. Experience becomes grist. Perhaps us, like this now, will be something you'll write of later? Maybe I'll see myself in your fiction? But in a better, more pleasant light? Maybe it will bring back fond memories of what is wonderful being with you like this, in these otherwise darkest of days?"

"Many of us fiction writer do write about things that happened to us," Hector allows. "Some don't. Much, or sometimes all of it, we invent or imagine, you should know."

"Perhaps. Anyway, I have a different name now. I'm a grown woman. I know what Cabrero did. Most importantly, I know what a monster Cabrero still is. Right now. I've spent weeks on the *feria* circuit, stalking this devil. Watching him for signs he might somehow have changed. But of course he hasn't changed. Not a bit, just as you saw when he greeted the children. So? I've been working up the nerve . . . ."

Over dinner, Hem forcefully presses the case for this once-in-a-lifetime grand adventure—a frantic running ahead of the bulls after the day's first cannon fire signals the life-or-death race to the plaza.

Of course, Hem allows, he and Hector will be running only in spirit with Arturo if he dares do it.

Hem allows that the women were right the other day—Isa and Hadley—in their dismissal of the two young veterans with wounded legs ever making that morning run through the Pamplona streets with fleet-footed bulls fast behind them.

To Hector's shock—and growing mixture of fascination and dread—he watches as an increasingly wine-blitzed Arturo begins to warm to the prospect of making the deadly solo sprint.

But to what end is Hem pushing it? Just hoping for some act of God to find Arturo pounded under hooves or fatally run through by a filthy horn?

Even as he wonders at that, Hector figures he really shouldn't be so surprised by this turnaround resulting from Hem's focused, outwardly amiable campaign against the older writer's bloated, *muy macho* Latin ego.

After all, Hector has seen Hem exercise his masculine charm and charisma on many other men who should have known far better about fishing . . . About hunting, or boxing. Even about simple goddamn boozing.

Hem is the kind of man other men are ineffably driven to please—desperately so—and whose respect and affection they yearn to earn, regardless any risk to themselves.

Hector almost fell under that same spell a time or two when his friendship with Hem was freshest.

Even then, Ernest boasted a snake-charmer's gift for enticing others—most all of them male—bending them to his wild, potentially deadly whims.

As everyone, Ana included, toasts Arturo's vow to brave the six-in-the-morning running of the bulls, Hector's mind races in new and deadly directions.

Maybe he should make that run, too? At least in the early going? Trip and take Arturo down with him, right at the start?

Somehow propel Arturo under the thundering toros' hooves?

As previously suggested, an old Spaniard and two gimpy, Great War veterans aren't going to be leading anyone's parade—Hem's too right about that. It would have to happen very early in the run, and then Hector would have to and try and roll to shelter himself.

Once again excusing himself, Hector leaves with Ana on his arm to walk the channeled, claustrophobic gauntlet, to scope the terrain.

He does that with the notion of trying to pick the best and safest spot—far from any onlookers' lines of sight, if possible—in order to propel Arturo into the direct path of the bulls' cloven hooves.

Hector eventually settles on a particular place along the barricaded course. It's positioned squarely under an overhead pedestrian bridge where there can be no witnesses beyond possible fellow stragglers.

Fellow stragglers?

Synonymous with *Potential witnesses for the prosecution*.

Closely studying him, Ana asks, "Why are we here?"

Hector shrugs. "I was toying with being down here tomorrow with Arturo, if you must know. Weighing options, surveying the scene. There's one place where one might stage an accident, but it's too far from the starting point for me to attempt. Hell, we've just been walking, slowly, and already my leg is aching. I can hardly take another step without a strong limp."

Holding tightly to him, Ana says, "Thank you for thinking of attempting it. But it would be wrong."

Hector says, "As we've discussed, I've killed before."

"In self-defense, or mass combat," Ana says. "Doing what Hem joked about—what you seem serious about actually doing? It's a cold-blooded execution."

"You're right. Despite the fact he's a monster and did those awful things to you and to others, this would be entirely outside the law. Murder in itself. I reckon you should loathe me for even entertaining it."

"Please, Héctor! Loathe you? I love you for what you're willing to do for me tomorrow if it was at all possible. But it is not. But for even thinking hard about it, I love you even more now than I did already, because you were also willing to do this for me. To avenge me and all the others that man has harmed and even made die. That you'd do it for those two children. And those who would surely suffer next."

Wrinkling her nose, Ana suddenly says, "Maybe I could cut my hair. Dress as a man, and then *I* could run with him and . . . ?"

Hector senses she's actually quite serious about this, but tries to make a joke of it.

He discreetly squeezes her breast with one hand, pulls her close against him with his other hand pressed to the small of her back. "You'd never pull it off. Far too much a woman for that."

Ana stands on tiptoe; passionately kisses Hector.

She whispers in his ear, "Let the rest drink the night away. I just want to make love with you tonight. I would do that for just as long as you can stand it."

Hector says, "But what about Arturo?"

She pulls him closer, taking some of his weight upon herself and setting back the way they came toward their hotel. Ana says, "As Hem said, we've identified the problem. There are still days ahead of us beyond Pamplona. Something else may present itself to us as a solution, yes?"

Hector smiles wanly, trying to look like he actually believes that.

Five o'clock in the morning, July 10.

Arturo regards himself in the mirror. He's wearing the traditional white shirt, white pants and matching red neckerchief and sash tied around his waist. It's the garb expected of those who run with the bulls each morning in Pamplona during the fiesta.

But he is still not convinced upon making the run.

Arturo decides he'll get a feel for being down on the street ... see if anyone else of his approximate age is attempting the mad dash ahead of the charging bulls.

A knock. Alone in their room, Arturo moves toward the door.

Several rooms away, Hector takes a couple of belts of *Rioja Clarete*, then heads down to find a surely hungover Hem and Arturo Cabrero.

As they stand outside, awaiting Cabrero's arrival, Hector and Hem pass a bota back and forth, "Hair of the dog," as Hem puts it.

Handing Hector the wineskin, Hem growls, "Bet you the son of a bitch doesn't show. He may be a fiend, but he's not crazy like all these silly bastards who do this stupid sprint every morning. Ana's right… Isa too. This racing through the streets is an insult to everything you and I revere about bullfighting. This stupidity of running with the bulls that only happens in this goddamn town? Cheap carnival bullshit that stands apart from what matters. A desecration of a noble tradition."

Hector just nods distractedly, searching the crowd for sign of Ana, or of Arturo. "Where the hell is Arturo? I sure as hell hope the bastard didn't turn *cobarde* on us since last night."

Hector opens his pocket watch. If the run goes off punctually, it should take place in about twenty minutes.

Suddenly, Hector is seized by a sense of vague vertigo.

He's wondering at its cause when he somehow fleetingly loses his footing.

There is a low rumble, then from upper floor windows, there are mounting screams.

Church bells begin uneven then spastic ringing.

More people begin screaming and soon people are flooding from homes, bars and businesses, packing the streets.

The ground, Hector realizes, is bucking under foot.

It's a very strong earthquake. It thunders on for at least twelve seconds.

As soon as the ground stops its shaking, the skies open and a torrential rain begins.

Hem laments, "We're bitched, Lasso. No way the run, or the corrida—goes on today. Goddamn act of God in the other direction, I guess."

Hem's half-sarcastic aside about the Almighty will take on an eerie prescience as others will later declare July 10 to have been a kind of mini-Apocalyptic event, not just because of Pamplona's morning earthquake, but also based on a near simultaneous tornado in Zaragoza, Spain.

Also because of another storm, in Rostov, Russia, where a hellish hailstorm kills twenty-three people, pummeling them to death with freakish chunks of falling ice estimated to weigh two-pounds apiece.

Once the ground stops its shaking, Hector says, "I'm going to head back to the hotel. Get a coat and see if I can't find an umbrella."

And then he will go in search of Ana, Hector tells himself.

As he approaches the hotel, Hector sees several uniformed police officers out front, questioning people.

One of them is Ana, standing under an umbrella and being interviewed by a *Guardia Civil* officer.

Two men carry a stretcher out of the hotel lobby. A bloodstained sheet covers the body underneath.

Hector gets this hollow ache in his belly. He thinks, *For Christ's sake, please don't let Ana have shot or stabbed that rotten old son of a bitch.*

Hector approaches another Civil Guard officer handling crowd control. Hector says, "This is my hotel, and my friend is over there, talking to one of your colleagues. If I may ask, what has happened? Who is that they just carried away on that stretcher?"

The officer says, "Another hotel guest. I don't know the name and couldn't share it if I did. Not until we know proper notification has been made to family. As to what happened? An accident. The man was standing on the balcony with your friend. When the earthquake came, he lost his footing and fell over the railing. He was drinking, fairly heavily, despite the early hour, which likely contributed. That's all I know. All I can say. I'm sure your friend will soon be finished making her statement."

Ana seems engrossed in her conversation with the authorities; never a pleasant experience, not even if one is innocent.

As a registered guest, Hector is soon granted permission to return to his room.

As he makes his way through the lobby, he sees a distraught Isa Hidalgo in the company of still more Civil Guard authorities.

A hotel maid sits with the ashen-faced girls, trying to distract them with sweets.

So, it was like that, Hector thinks. It must indeed have been Cabrero's corpse he saw carried out; Cabrero's body now headed to the ice house.

He should, Hector supposes, go and offer aid or crocodile comfort to Isa.

But Hector doesn't feel kindly enough disposed toward her to do that. Not based on his presumptions about what this woman knew—and turned blind eye to—about Arturo and her daughters.

And Isa's girls in this time of tragedy?

They simply seem numb.

No tears, though.

Telling, Hector figures. Sighing, he climbs the stairs to his room on an aching leg. Any rain too often tends to make his war wounds throb.

He strips off his rain-soaked pants and shirt, changes into dry clothes.

Despite the hard rain, Hector briefly steps out onto the balcony. He gazes at the pavers below. His knees tremble a bit as he does that, because he has an innate fear of heights.

Still, Hector can see easily enough that if you fell—did that head first—it would be plenty enough drop to kill.

Hector hears the room's door open and steps back inside, closing the doors opening onto the balcony after himself.

Ana Marin looks sadly back at him, dark eyes wide and glistening.

Hector swallows hard, says, "Saw you with the authorities. They done with you? Finished with you for good?"

"Believe so," she says thickly. "They took my statement. The policeman said they will likely rule it 'death by misadventure.' An act of God, another said."

Hector thinks that term's getting quite the workout this bloody trip.

Ana says, "It was a long earthquake, wasn't it? Seemed even longer than it probably was."

Her eyes no longer meet his. "Bad as it might have seemed on the street, it was far worse up here. The building was swaying so terribly. I was holding tight to that railing to keep from going over myself."

"No more words about any of this," he says. "It's good you're safe."

Hector opens his arms and Ana quickly steps into them.

"No more words about any of it, darlin'." He hugs her tightly to his chest, says, "Not ever. Not unless you need to."

He strokes her back. "Today's schedule of fights is canceled, as you probably already deduced, or maybe even have heard. Because of the earthquake."

"I hadn't heard of course," she says thickly. "You know, Arturo had decided not to run after all."

"That doesn't surprise me," he says.

"I suppose that stupidity of the running of the bulls was also stopped by the earthquake?"

Hector says, "Yeah. Tragic, eh? Still don't know how anyone could enjoy that bloody act. And to perhaps even savor it?"

"Running ahead of the bulls, you mean?"

He kisses the part in her glistening, raven hair. Hector cups her chin, looking Ana in the eye.

"Of course," he says. "What else would I mean?"

"Ain't no Devil, only God
when He's drunk."

—Delta Blues standard

WRITE FROM WRONG (PUT-IN-BAY, 1927)

1 THE ISLAND

The street carnival nears its end under threat of a lake-effect winter storm.

Clowns and freak show tent attractions on last parade, most quite fearsome, spook sidewalk gawkers.

Wheezing calliope music and the scent of cotton candy are swept along by the equally freakish early autumn Alberta Clipper.

The stench of the carnival even reaches the lakeside station where a fresh load of tourists await one of the final ferries across to South Bass or back—mostly revelers hell-bent on a last crossing before the booze-soaked island shuts down for winter, consigning them to months of mainland Prohibition under the icier fist of the Volstead Act.

His back to the lake, a gaunt, tanned but older man argues with a woman. A long scar shows whitely on his forehead.

The scarred man thrusts a wind-whipped circular back into the gloved hands of the church woman who's just forced the flapping flyer on him. She's prim, plain and wholly committed to her cause.

The man says, "What you're peddling is very much not for me, dearie."

His eyes don't track, leaving one to guess which to favor while trying to meet his strange gaze.

With the ghost of a smile, he continues, "This is for me least of all, really. Now, move along, dumpling. You are, after all, wholly uninvited. You're also rudely interrupting a private parlay."

The scarred man rakes fingers through white, wind-whipped hair, grinning at his shorter, chubby companion.

The churchwoman stands her ground. "Sir, your eternal soul is worth a mere moment. Your friend's, too."

The scarred man raises a hand, hissing her to silence. He says, "Really, dearie, we're wholly uninterested in your silly, pious fantasies. Your faith is absurd ranged against this bloody reality we all must endure, and now in vast parts of this continent because of morons like you, without spirits." This last comes with a sweep of his arm.

He freshly appraises the woman, adds, "Why don't you find yourself some livelier, more gratifying hobby? This arid clerical bent doesn't become you at all. Does you no favors. Particularly not in light of all your other, not inconsiderable lackings."

He again shushes her as she starts to balk. The scarred man says, "A Buckeye fiction writer has—or someday will?—opine lonely women are the vessels of time. I'd add the pious of the sex must be the bloody corks stoppering those dreary vessels. My dear, from where I stand, you ooze oodles of loneliness and piety. Your added drabness?

It makes for a terrible trifecta! So, do please take your so-called Holy Ghost and shove the hell on."

The churchwoman's cheeks redden. Glaring, shaking her finger a last time, she snaps, "Devil!"

The scarred man cheerfully fires back, "Harpy!"

A gloved finger of hers, up in his face. "You're a terrible man!"

He leans in close, pretends to snap at her finger with his chops. He snarls, "And you're a sorry, Brecksterish bitch, fated to die, alone and begging."

Flinching, she somehow musters further courage. "May God have mercy on your soul," the churchwoman says, chin trembling.

This sparks a barking laugh from the scarred man.

She shows him her back, stalking off toward a new, quite solitary stranger.

Her next target of opportunity is smartly dressed; tanned and tall. A handsome, dapper and much younger man. His elbow casually rests on the rustic countertop as he stares dreamily off across the lake, smoking a cigarette and nursing a surreptitiously spiked iced tea.

Watching her go, then smiling at the fat man by his side, the scarred man with a dead eye says, "Feh! Even if souls were real, they're much too highly rated! You agree, Alphonse? Ever seen a soul? Confess I haven't either. Though, in a sense, I share that woman's obsession with the conceit. Albeit in ways she's incapable of comprehending. You and I both know folks same as sell their so-called souls for a song. They do that every goddamn day. On that note—"

A different woman, one married and standing close by the two men, heedlessly inserts herself.

This woman says to the stranger, "Faith! We have faith, sir. You were terrible to that woman. You treated her appallingly. Shame on you for that! You go and apologize to her, right now! You simply must do that!"

The intruding woman's husband clearly wants to be anywhere but by his wife's side in her moment of impetuous confrontation.

The scarred man grins. "Then I put the question to you, Madame. Shame and faith. Convince me they're more than fear-fueled affectations."

The scarred man shakes his head. "Show me faith in any form I can accept and, crucial this—that can be confirmed—and I'll accept your argument. But you can't do that, can you, Madame? You've already admitted it's impossible to literally grasp this thing you so claim to value. It's like stroking smoke or tapping a bullet in flight. All you truly have is faith in your faith, which makes for a doubly worthless intangible."

The scarred man says to his companion, "You of course agree with my appraisal, Alphonse? That's why we're still talking, isn't it? Well. I talk. You hang on my every word, trembling. Desperate for my judgment. Rightly so, given the stakes you perceive for yourself. Me? I need more than desperate leaps of faith and fairytales. Crave that thing I can touch hand and tongue to. *J'aime les sensations fortes.* I sense at least a dab of the same earthy and raging craving stirs even within you, Alphonse. Now let's see if I can't make the immaterial very material for you, but away from busybody, nosey bitches like this gold-digging, spent whore and hypocrite, with her breath mint-scented, lip-service piety and gin flask secreted between her long-neglected thighs."

The man with the head scar takes "Alphonse" firmly by the arm, steering him off toward the ferry station's refreshment stand as the second woman is left sputtering and glowering.

Alphonse says, "You're causing too much attention, Mister Krutch, picking rows like that!"

The scarred man—Krutch—isn't having that, not a smidge. "Picking rows? They came at me, as you saw. But there is something in what you say about going unnoticed. At least for now. I guess maybe your product got the best of me over lunch. I'm beastly when the horrors of the drink are upon me. The perfect devil when I'm drunk, Al. Best take that as a caution. Particularly given the availability of proper hard spirits on yonder island."

The tanned young man folds the departing churchwoman's flyer advertising a tent revival scheduled a few hours' distant into a tight little square. He slips the folded wedge of paper into his sports coat's pocket.

Hector Mason Lassiter has every intention of discretely binning the circular once politely out of the lady's line of sight. Comparatively young as he is, the world has already robbed this young man—a twice-wounded veteran—of any ability to believe as she does in some sort of engaged Higher Power.

At least in an interested God—some style of hands-on deity.

Hector is two-years widowed and recently returned from a not entirely successful, sorrow-drowning excursion to Europe. Too much booze, bullfights and nearly busted friendships littered Spain's summer circuit of ferias this year.

To the casual observer, Hector's been pondering the increasingly choppy gunmetal blue lake as he smokes and sips his drink, watching the whipping winds stir the lake's surface.

But Hector's actually playing spy.

He's stalking a man.

Hector squints at the approaching ferry, absently drumming fingers to the distant calliope music—presently a tinny merry-go-round rendition of "Darktown Strutters Ball." That soon gives way to "Our Director."

All the while, Hector's eavesdropping on others.

Listening in on the conversation of others is many a novelist's benign vice, he familiarly consoles himself.

A firmly established crime novelist—not a *mystery writer* (that loathsome label!)—Hector's ever on the hunt for any true-ringing snatch of dialogue. For an evocative exchange between strangers he might adapt for a work-in-progress, or save for some story yet to come.

Hector checks his pocket watch, then the level of his drink: Still time to savor and not shotgun his improvised, liberally spiked cocktail.

The two men who've staked out the stretch of "bar" closest him have clearly been at their bickering conversation for some time—the tall white-haired man with a scarred forehead and this smaller man, "Alphonse."

It's the most goddamned parlay, Hector thinks. It comes across as part philosophical debate or metaphysical salon talk, yet just possibly equal parts criminal conspiracy.

In Paris, in the early 1920s, Hector endured endless, similar philosophical ramblings in Gertrude Stein's flat during his apprenticeship as an author. But never did one of those Parisian parlor confabs percolate with such a palpable undertow of clear but unspecified dark intent as this exchange he's presently secret party to.

Based on the craziness of the oblique and portentous negotiation, Hector would figure the two men for simply being drunk if the ferry station bar served anything stronger than near-beer.

Some kind of queer collateral is at stake. But what exactly that is so far defies partly-overheard comprehension.

Also, maybe, like Hector, the two strangers are surreptitiously spiking their sweating glasses of tea and Coca-Cola with splashes of rum from hip flasks, just as Hector's been discretely doing while awaiting the tardy ferry to the notoriously and seductively wet Great Lakes island somewhere out there?

The tall man, the one who's been making digs at the recently departed churchwoman, as much as admitted he's already tight. He is also sardonic, and even mocking in his angles of intellectual attack aimed at his chubby friend, Al.

The scarred man's companion—a hammered-down, portly man with thinning black hair and a badly broken nose—is left frequently stammering and palpably, perpetually terrified.

Krutch lectures, "Stop dawdling, Alphonse. Christ on a crutch, it's far past time to fish or cut bait, as the mouth-breathing rubes 'round these parts delight in saying, and do so every time like it's the first time. Truth is, a creature like you desperately needs help from a creature like me. Particularly if you truly meant to cleave into the operation of that other Alphonse living off Lake Michigan, whom you aimed to edge out. But you've failed to honor our gentlemen's agreement. That was a fatal error.

"Because of your treachery, I've been forced to speak to that other Alphonse," Krutch continues. "Mr. Alphonse *Capone*. Snorky's most peeved at you, as I suppose you can already deduce. I know it's an unspoken thing among your Mafioso ilk never to go after families. But that other, Al?

"Mr. Capone now thinks an example must be made of you and yours. I strongly encourage you do the manful thing for your now-threatened family. You must really off yourself. Do it like a man. Importantly, you must do that fast. Before Mr. Capone comes after your long-suffering, much-cuckolded wife and those darling kids she squeezed out. This isn't idle palaver on my part, mind you. I'm directed to deliver this message."

The fat little man's face, already red—maybe from mounting blood-pressure, maybe from too much sun, or now, possibly even wind-burn—flushes a hue closer to true crimson.

He says, "For Christ's sake, Mister Krutch, keep your voice down, please! Be discreet, for Christ's sake!"

"Don't be daft," Mister Krutch says. "Look at them all. Local idiots and dullard summer tourists whose minds are elsewhere. All of 'em caught up in their silly, dismal little holiday plans. Carefully plotted itineraries for squandered time and tacky distractions from their drab, provincial little lives' tedious obligations. All of their focus is squarely on meaningless, last summer idylls, crammed in ahead of winter's icy blast. All so excited by the weekend stretching out before us. Most are probably going to the islands yonder to buy so-called grape juice."

Then Mister Krutch grins, waving an arm at the watery horizon. "Prohibition's mauled those islands yonder, yes? Hard times cut deeply into their precious tourism, which formerly was, in many ways, dependent on the wine industry. Vinos mostly made from the Labrusca grape which European wine makers yearn to render extinct."

The scarred man called Krutch—the man who is also Hector's secret quarry—slaps the fat little man's shoulder. "*In vino veritas*, eh, Alphonse? But not anymore! Not since those arid biddies in central Ohio like the one I just so deftly cut got their sorry temperance ball rolling a few counties south of here. Now, the nearly destitute Great Lakes winemakers have to secretly peddle their little jugs of unfermented grape juice.

"They truck in such sorry fare, along with clandestinely provided instructions for home fermentation," he continues. "But that do-it-yourself distillation is all so troublesome for the Average Joe who just wants an easy, solid drink that won't blind or even kill him. And our Old Average Joe? I say he wants that strong one, in a jiffy. Wants it ready to pour. And anyway, who can blame the poor, dry-mouthed devils? You've witnessed even my raging weakness for the stuff."

Krutch crowds in close to Al's florid face. "Hence our recent discussions. Our agreements you've recklessly—fatally—failed to honor. I've regretfully but necessarily fingered you to Mr. Capone. Now Mr. Capone's looming wrath is explained, if it still needed explaining. Isn't that all very much on target, Alphonse?"

"Please pipe down, Mister Krutch!" The fat little man urgently looks around again with crazed, imploring eyes.

Hector pretends to have all attention focused on the lumbering old ferry marred by peeling white paint. She's nearly into port, starting her turn for final docking.

Alphonse pleads again, "Christ, Krutch, some common sense, for God's sake! Hush! Someone'll overhear. Bring the Treasury Department down on us!"

Krutch shrugs. "So much easier in the end to leave it all to those crafty Canadians, as we originally agreed, wouldn't it have been? Let them take the risks up front? They're so practiced at whiskey running across the Great Lakes. Yes, those pesky Canucks have a nearly steady stream of Canadian whiskey successfully crossing the Erie, Huron, Michigan, the Superior and Lake Ontario—and nearly all the damn time."

A solemn head shake. Krutch says, "It's clear now your solo attempts to establish a foothold in the trade were always foredoomed, possibly even if you had honored our contract. Shame on me for believing in you, a critic might say. You've proven butterfingered as that fool, George Remus. Now we both simply have to face the consequences of our poor choices. Are you are going to do the honorable thing and fall on your sword? Or shall I tell Mr. Capone your family is to first foot your bloody bill come due?"

"Goddamn you, Krutch," Alphonse says, spraying spittle. "I said shut your goddamn mouth! I goddamn warned you against talking so loud! And what do you get out of this beyond what to you must be chump change?"

A shrug. "There's no financial recompense at all. Not now. And that's the crux of things between us, is it not?" Mister Krutch says, "Now, I'm merely protecting my bottom line... And reputation. I know you must understand that. We had a deal. You broke that deal. Now there are consequences. They must be equal to the stake. That means blood, especially with Capone in the mix. You see, the—"

Krutch's remaining words are buried beneath the clarion blast of the ferry's foghorn—unnecessarily signaling its frustratingly tedious, hulking docking has terminated.

Ticket-holders rise, gathering small bags and clutching at carry-on luggage. Porters ready creaking carts, sagging with suitcases and steamer trunks.

With pale blue eyes, Hector assays his fellow crossers.

These are a motley array of older couples, honeymooners and some comely women Hector's own age, some of these traveling in fetching pairs.

The last are targets of carnal opportunity, maybe, singularly or possibly even doubly. It is the waning days of the Jazz Age, after all. And unless you're an islander, you only go to South Bass to drink, party, or to slum while doing both.

But there is also Mister Krutch, this supposed fiend Hector's traveled half-a-world to find and having at last done so, to presently stalk and study.

This quarry of his? Hector first laid eyes on the man with mismatched eyes last evening when a nervous, lakefront hotelier over-energetically greeted the scar-faced man as, "My dear, dear Mister Krutch! Whatever can we do for you this time?"

That bit of coincidence—and was it merely that, just happenstance, but what else could it be, after all?—allowed Hector to at last acquire his potential target.

Hector's luggage is among all the other suitcases and duffle bags piled on the porters' squeaking carts.

Apart from his twin flasks hidden in either of his sport jacket's pockets—rum in the left, single malt whisky in the right—Hector carries a notebook containing the beginnings of a new novel. And just in case his own writing stalls on the little, likely-to-be bookshop-starved island, Hector also totes a copy of Herman Melville's criminally neglected novel *The Confidence Man* for after-work pleasure reading.

Broad shoulders and back to Krütch and Alphonse, Hector buttons his sports jacket, feeling the Lake Front cold coming on.

The wind mounts ahead of the forecasted charging Canadian cold front. Predictions are for damaging winds and perhaps even twisters.

It's surely been a crazy year for weather and more, with killer floods drowning whole towns along the Mississippi and tornadoes crushing vast swaths of St. Louis.

For his part, Hector just wants to complete this crossing before Lake Erie herself turns potentially deadly.

Hector fishes the pocket of his jacket for his pack of cigarettes and box of kitchen matches. He shakes out a Pall Mall and gets his latest coffin nail going, his back to the wind. Hector tosses the wooden match into the water where it sizzles and soon bobs as curious bluegill nibble at the sliver of charred wood, furiously but only fleetingly before deciding it can't be eaten.

The boat's boarding ramp sways under foot as six-two, hundred-and-eighty pound Hector steps from shore to ship.

An elderly ticket-taker smiles in apology; says to the novelist and a couple of close-by fellow passengers, "Look at that sky, won't ya? 'Fraid to say, liable to be an uncertain crossing, folks."

With a shrug and dimpled smile, Hector says to ferryman, "Honest to God, are there ever any other kind, old pal?"

2
THE CROSSING

Sleet begins falling as they at last set off after a final foghorn blast.

Standing on the bottom deck of the tall ferry, stationed just under the middle-deck's eaves, Hector stands just out of reach of the spray of the wind-driven rain as the ferry pushes out across the increasingly troubled lake.

The boat begins deepening rolls as it clears the breakers.

Hector smokes down the last of his cigarette, less concerned than his neighbors by the increasingly choppy waters. Hector owns his own boat—one he takes out on the ocean often, piloting her out into the "Great Blue River" of the Gulf Stream. Hector is consequently more calloused to bad weather on storm-swept open water than most of his fellow passengers.

Many minutes later, Hector spots their destination rising from the subtle curve of the lake.

The Doric column of Perry's Monument looms like a white spike above the relatively flat island. The tower—its base a long-languishing work in progress—nevertheless already eclipses the height of the far more famous Statue of Liberty, States away.

The stormy sky sports a menacing gray wash and the dock lights are already twinkling on, even though it's not yet four in the afternoon. In just the past few minutes, the temperature's dropped at least ten degrees, evidenced by mounting wind.

Two pretty girls standing shoulder-to-shoulder shiver, chatting and patting hair in place against the damp wind, all the while pointing at this or that sight on shore, talking fast, then laughing.

One, a tallish strawberry blonde, keeps makes lingering eyes at Hector. Pale skin, red hair. The gusty wind whips her dress at angles revealing the contours of pert breasts and shapely thighs. She stirs memories of another, a young woman named Hudson Leroux who briefly, piercingly passed through Hector's life and who claimed his virginity.

Whatever became of Hudson?

Hector's seriously debating whether or not to do something about this ginger beauty's flirting. Should he chase a carnal memory?

But even at a distance, the appealing redhead seems somehow needy—palpably starved for attention. And it is early hours, after all. There's a whole island of strangers ahead, some perhaps every bit as pretty and flirty as this one.

The ferry gradually turns again, drifting into dock at South Bass Island or "Put-in-Bay" as it's more widely known to tourists.

Mister Krutch stands sentry at the boat's forward-most rail in the cold falling rain, wind whipping white hair and pant legs.

Hector looks around again. No sign of portly Alphonse. Hector's certain he saw the fat man board with them.

Maybe Al went to one of the higher decks for a better view?

Maybe to escape Mister Krutch's brutal haranguing and mounting threats?

Hector could hardly blame the man, if so.

The foghorn sounds, again unnecessarily signaling their arrival to the impatiently attentive watchers on shore, tightly huddled under station awnings, awaiting their ride back to the mainland as the Great Lakes winter storm gathers fury.

Shivering children suck on fingers sticky with saltwater taffy and ice cream. Young and randy couples nuzzle, neck and pet in public a last time. Morals on the island are far looser than those on Ohio's other shore.

Some of these young lovers are probably also more brazen because of lowered inhibitions resulting from their first real alcohol buzzes, Hector reckons.

Mister Krutch, still very much alone in the mounting rain, waves to someone ashore. Krutch shoots the mystery person a damp thumbs-up. Krutch's head moves a fraction in Hector's nominal direction, although Krutch is faced squarely away from the novelist. Probably just coincidence, Hector tells himself.

So far as Hector can tell, his presence—and his intense, dark interest in Krutch—have so far gone undetected. Surely, Mister Krutch could mean anyone or anything on the boat with that opaque head bob?

Looking up at the sky, the author lashes himself for not bringing an umbrella as the already bucketing rain intensifies. And the rain is making his war wounds ache—this throbbing in his leg.

There's distant thunder too, echoing from the direction they've just come.

This seems a storm that will linger. Perhaps rage for days.

A stranger says to Hector, "Know just what yer thinkin', sonny, eyein' them clouds. Live here on this rock, seven months a year. Trust I damn well know. This here's kinda rain to stick through to morning, kiddo. Maybe two, three days beyond that. Maybe more. After a summer of near drought, comes a gusher."

The stranger's smile reveals missing teeth. He winks, says, "Hell, if my own boat was bigger, best believe I'd be pairin' up animals."

Stepping onto the pier in the pelting rain, Hector hears the ferry's ancient ticket-taker insist to another of the crew members, "Tellin' ya, sonny—thirty-four folks on, but only thirty-three off, goddamn ya!"

The younger crew member says, "A mistake. Has to be. We haven't lost one on a crossing in... well, ever. I've looked everywhere. There's nobody left. Hell, nobody else has said anything about anyone missing."

Inevitably, Hector again looks around the boat for Alphonse. Hector's cursory search again comes up empty. He hesitates, thinking about butting-in more squarely, but as quickly decides not to.

Hector surely doesn't want Krutch taking note of him. Not yet. He needs more time to investigate this scarred, white-haired man. Make certain about Krutch.

It's just possible his dead friend Tommy was wrong about what Krutch is all about—the unthinkable threat Krutch poses, not just to traitorous Great Lakes bootleggers, but to islanders like Hector's unthinkably recently dead war buddy.

Collar up and shoulders hunched, Hector scoops up his suitcases from the cart. He dashes across the sodden street to DeRivera Park—five acres of densely shaded green space fronting the bay and named for this island's long-dead owner.

The relative shelter of the big old shade trees spare Hector a complete drenching. From under the canopy of the ancient trees, he spots the Round House first. Its distinctive circular gray roof almost blends into the stormy sky.

The attached Park Hotel—Hector's immediate destination—sits just behind the circular building. He heads there to claim his room.

A battery of phone calls determined it's the only hotel on the island still taking on new guests this late in the season.

Behind him, Krutch trails slowly, seemingly oblivious to the weather and his soaked-through suit.

Mister Krutch whistles "Me & My Shadow" as he twirls a tippling cane, trailing Hector to the island's only still-operating hotel.

3
THE WOMAN

Concluding unpacking, Hector tucks his well-tended Colt seventy-three Peacemaker under his pillow. He fusses over the sheets and bedspread until just so, returning them to the state that his housekeeper left them.

He skids on a pair of khaki pants and black Polo shirt—something closer to his usual Key West togs—despite the driving rain and plunging mercury.

His skin is still bronzed from months of sun-drenched European ranging.

First came that bull fighting circuit across Spain with the *new* Hemingways—a vexed 1927 summer gauntlet with Ernest and, now, *Pauline* Hemingway.

Previously, Hector weathered the July feria circuit with Ernest and *Hadley* Hemingway, even as then-alleged Hadley-friend Pauline systematically and insidiously destroyed the first Hemingway marriage with her steady, unabashed stalking of Hem and undermining of Hadley. Even now, Hector regards Pauline as a kind of spider.

Fairly freshly widowed then, a hurting Hector sided with Hadley all along that bullfighting circuit of debauched Spanish towns in twenty-six, nearly murdering his longtime friendship with Hem as he stood steadfast by the soon-to-be-former first Mrs. Hemingway.

Hector's continuing devotion to Hadley further nettled the new, second Mrs. Hemingway during the summer's sojourn across dusty, drunken Spain.

And this time around? The trek across Spain seemed like chasing still-more-distant ghosts of happier times.

After saying his goodbyes to prickly Pauline and more than slightly irked Ernest—lingering on a time alone longer in Spain—Hector pushed on to Paris for a spell.

But he found the City of Lights still too full of memories of Brinke Devlin.

Hector quickly pressed on, settling for a later summer and early autumn in Venice, before heading back to the States to at last reunite with his old trail and Great War buddy, Tommy Breck, settled sometime back home in northern Ohio.

But that long-deferred reunion wasn't in the cards.

Before reaching Ohio, Hector learned Tommy had died, reportedly by his own hand.

Hector still doesn't believe that can be so.

Maybe, just maybe, this mysterious Mister Krutch is to blame for Tommy's death?

Hector surveys the mirror. He rakes fingers back through dark hair, stubbornly trying to best that untamable lank that falls in a perpetual comma above his right eye.

He thinks of the last person to make a dedicated run at the careless cowlick—the olive-skinned fingers of the delectable Maria Abandonato.

Maria's were early evening-into-late-morning campaigns conducted over leisurely lusty weeks, lolling in a tangle of arms and legs through a succession of Venetian *stanze d'albergo.*

If only Maria could have brought herself to venture out of her native Italy?

To sample his island at the southeast tip of North America?

In every sense but that of wanderlust, they'd otherwise so wonderfully clicked.

Hector clears his mind of such pointless thoughts. He pads downstairs to the enclosed patio to wolf down an off-hours meal.

The sun is low in the sky and so manages, at least for the moment, to teasingly break through the storm clouds. A lonely auburn beam seems aimed squarely at Hector, like some lighthouse's beacon.

Up the shoreline, construction crews bang away at the unfinished Perry Memorial.

A few solitary, stolid fishermen still toil out on the increasingly rough lake.

Hector shivers a little, at last conceding Indian Summer is suddenly, surely over. He's going to need something with long sleeves to wear under a jacket in a few hours. He figures to buy a fisherman's sweater to carry him through the chilly remains of the day.

Cormorants duck and dart through the mounting waves of the gun-metal lake, hunting perch or bass. Scudding gusts of wind send sea gulls flailing.

Hector is seized by the memory of how he half-awakened twice in the night at the careworn Port Clinton Hotel. It was there he first laid eyes on Krutch. Hector remembers being stirred from sleep by similar fierce winds darting like demons across the aged roof of that hotel, tangling wind chimes into knots.

Hector slips out his notebook and fountain pen.

He sets to work, guzzling more coffee and composing while waiting to order his advertised "breakfast-anytime" meal: eggs sunny-side-up, a thick slab of ham, bacon, home fries and crisp white toast with helping heaps of butter and apple jam.

It's a woman he's presently writing about.

Unfortunately—as all of Hector's fictional women seem to these past couple of years—this fictional woman sounds far too much like his late-wife in voice and attitude.

Yes, this made-up woman is also emerging with all of his lost-wife's distinctive mannerisms and quirky, ace fiction writer's way of pithily putting things, just so.

It's a vexing problem for Hector and, frankly, an increasingly alarming one, for nobody but that woman was ever like that woman.

Brinke is—was—a world away from the pretty if rather tawdry, round-heels store clerk he requires for his present short story.

He thinks about imposing aspects of Maria upon this new character, but no: his discarded-by Venetian lover is every bit as much a world apart from his present fictional needs as his late-wife would be.

Another voice, female, says from somewhere behind, "So sorry, Mr. Lassiter, but Lou, the desk clerk, says you're a great writer. His favorite. Lou loves your novels. But he's bashful. So, you get me."

A smiling young woman in a big, cozy cable-knit sweater extends a well-thumbed copy of Hector's first-published novel, *Rhapsody in Black*.

The book's dust jacket has seen better days. It's just three-years old or so, yet it already looks like twelve-flavors of battered, compulsively paged-through hell.

But Hector adores seeing such ragged wear in his books. The writer in him relishes seeing his novels ravaged to the edge of demolition.

Hector believes books of fiction are meant to be read and, better still, re-read.

Collectors could keep a few, uncut copies in pristine condition for posterity and secondary-market investment commerce.

But the vast press run of any book of fiction should be truly read, goddamn it, and done so considerably more than once, at least in his case. Hector's firm in that belief.

He certainly writes them with the hope knowing readers will delve into each title at least twice, detecting or at least sensing the layers and nuances he quietly, studiously insinuates into each novel. Books that some of the deluded dismiss as mere "mysteries" or disparage because they don't fit what too many accidental readers regard as the shallow, "mystery book" mold or still-more lamentable whodunnit genre.

To Hector's way of thinking, only dilettantes read truly well-written novels once—that single pass constituting at best a surface-read in books that are consciously composed and crafted, one true sentence after another.

It is a conceit perhaps, but if so, it's an intensely passionate one.

Hector believes he writes his novels deeply and he writes them well, with an honest craftsman's intent... if not always with sufficient reach.

Not yet, anyway.

But it's early days in his published writing career.

All athletes, he consoles himself, ebb with age.

But artists?

Writers, painters and musicians? They can improve. Ripen like sublime wine.

With a beaming smile, the pretty stranger asks, "Would you please autograph this one for Lou? It would pretty much mean the world to him if you did that, Mr. Lassiter."

She hoists a steaming pot of coffee in her other hand. "If it'll sway you, swear I'll handle it on my end and all your java will be on the house long as you stay on here at the Park."

Hector chuckles, sitting back in his chair for a better vista by which to view his comely waitress. She's tall and slender, yet boasts pleasing curves. Her hair is blonde and bobbed—has a profound yet natural-looking wave. The young woman has feline, green knowing eyes that invite reckless flavors of flirting. Her penetrating eyes also spark erotic wool gathering in Hector.

Already, Hector is smitten of course.

Okay, he thinks, *as grist for the fictional mill, this sultry young siren will do quite nicely, indeed. Sure, she will.*

Hector figures he'll just bend his work-in-progress to better fit this particular woman. It feels like a right move.

It strikes Hector as a long time since he's seized on one of those.

Hector hoists his mug. "Here's the thing, darlin'. This joint's coffee's tepid in every sense. I live far closer to Cuba than Georgia, far down Key West way. The extreme tip of Florida. Mostly drink our coffee black and wicked strong there. Who brewed this cup of crud?"

He's brazenly gambling it wasn't this fetching minx.

"That'd be Maitie Watts." Speaking softer, with a conspiratorial smile, she confides, "Maitie? Old as dirt and we both know what rain does to that. So, Maitie brews the house coffee weak for her own old and temperamental tummy."

His waitress flashes a bigger smile that freshly reaches Hector. "How's this, Mr. Lassiter? You write something real nice in this book—ragged though this copy may be—and I'll personally brew you a big, black and extra strong batch of coffee and all later consequences for drinking that brew are squarely on you. I'll even bring it to you in a steel thermos, piping hot. It'll stay hot as the seven hinges of hell, just as long as you soldier on out here."

Pulling her sweater closer, she shivers. "You're the only guest loco enough to eat outside, as you can see. Temperature's going to keep dropping. If you want to move inside, you need to do that real soon. There's maybe just four two-top tables left vacant in the dining room."

Hector lifts his pen and extends a hand for the beat up old copy of his debut novel. "You've got a deal. Not that you really needed to negotiate a trade, as I'm always delighted to sign a book for an honest fan. But do please go ahead on and serve me right out here, won't you, darlin'? Never have cottoned to crowd scenes. And, remember, just as you promised, black as you can make that coffee, and in that insulated thermos, please."

Hector pens a longish inscription and even draws a picture of a marlin for the desk clerk. He hands her back the book and again rakes that stubborn comma of hair back from his forehead. "You have me at a prime disadvantage knowin' my name and me not knowin' yours."

A thumb jabbed between her breasts. "Verity Chisholm. Very pleased to meet you, Hector Lassiter."

What an odd first name, he thinks, taking her now-offered hand.

But her grip is warm and strong. He figures Verity for being in her mid-to-late twenties; roughly his own age, that's to say. She boasts much more bosom than current fashion decrees pleasing and mystifyingly prefers.

Hector's tastes run against boyish, stick-like flapper figures. Hector craves curves.

Everything about Verity Chisholm is so far very much to the good in Hector's welcoming eyes.

Verity's accent? Vanilla Midwest.

If she's truly a dyed-in-the wool Ohioan—an honest Buckeye—Hector figures his usually subdued coastal Texas twang given more of its usually reined-in head might ratchet up his exotic appeal an extra notch or two. Hector invests his usually modulated Galveston accent with some added smoke to his natural baritone:

"Pleasure's mine, darlin'. And it's Hector, by the by. Mr. Lassiter—my old man? Soundly south of the sod. And now Verity, you're surely a lifesaver if you can deliver the brew you promise. And you are no interruption. *Gracias* in advance for the good and piping treat soon to come my way."

Verity says, "My God, you really are from Texas, aren't you? The biography at the back of the book said so, but you know how so many writers lie to make themselves seem more interesting?"

Hector surely does know how many writers do that, but that Verity would know the same is a fleeting puzzlement.

"Writers do often lie," he allows, studying her more closely. "Or many do. And those that do? They do that more than just about anyone else, I reckon." Hector smiles. "But for my part? I only lie between the first and last chapters. My author's biography, at least, is consistent with your first name."

She smiles sheepishly and nods. "Yes. That name. A story all its own. But not one to share just yet."

He says, "If not now, when?" He searches her pretty face. "Confess I'm on pins and needles. Why not later this evening? When you're on your own time?"

A little smile. "Maybe."

"You sound like you are from around these parts."

"Nowhere nearly as interesting a birthplace as Galveston, Texas, anyway." There's more than a little wistfulness hinted at.

She adds dully, "Seems like you either get off this island when you come of age—do that like a bullet, or maybe even a little before you come of age—or else you just dig in deeper. Then you die here."

Hector wonders what her mile-marker for "coming of age" is. Where does Verity see herself on the potential path to escape from here or surrender to that dark other?

He risks reaching out and briefly squeezes her hand, letting go before she can be expected to return the gesture, sincerely or not. Hector says, "Mighty glad you stuck it out long enough to warm me up at this chilly hour."

Searching his eyes, and seeming accepting of his fleeting touch, she says, "First time on the island, Hector?"

"Yes ma'am."

"You picked a pretty peculiar time to come," she says. "But you surely know that."

Her look and tone signals Hector she's convinced he has no grasp of any dodgy timing on his part.

Tourist season's same as over, he knows that much, at least.

She says, "Lots of shops? Already closed until next Memorial Day. You're cutting getting off this island very close. Weather moving in might shut down the daily ferry runs, any hour, now. Once that happens, and if the lake freezes over hard, deep and early, and unless you're some kind of daredevil who wants to hike a lake of ice, you could end up marooned here 'til long about April, or better. Lots of places are already shutting down because of the current weather. Signs are strong summer tourist trade's for certain over, and I mean starting now."

She narrows her bewitching green eyes. "Why are you here, Hector? And why just now, if I may ask?"

"Oh, just a kind of a research trip," he says.

So far, so true.

He pushes on, "Maybe I did cut it close, coming over this afternoon. Here to gather notes for a new novel."

For a fiction writer like Hector, just the simple act of living can honestly be called research, all the damned time.

He shrugs; toes further into somewhat benignly devious waters.

"To that end, I could sorely use a native guide," he says. "As time's growing short and doing that so fast?" He nods at the quickening lake-effect storm.

Hector asks, "When your hostess duties wind down, think you might show me 'round? Ratchet-up the pace of my education as all things in these parts further start to shut down for winter?"

Hector suddenly remembers to scope her left hand for what he increasingly thinks of as "claim" rings. He's sometimes regrettably tardy in timing his propositions against that elementary piece of any practiced lothario's due-diligence check for engagement rings or wedding bands.

Blessedly, this woman's slender, uniformly bronzed ring finger?

Encouragingly bare.

Hector adds for extra caution, "Unless it would maybe be untoward or misperceived to spend time together. Being a fellow islander, I surely grasp small-town gossip and life."

A shared smile as she pointedly checks his left hand.

Some widowers move their wedding bands to their right ring fingers. Hector instead chose to lock away his lonely wedding ring after it spent a fleeting stint of a few months dangling from a chain 'round his neck. Ultimately, it proved another reminder of enduring loss he surely didn't need, tangling in his collar and bumping constantly against his savaged heart.

He holds up his naked left hand, says, "Solo lobo, presently."

"I'm a lone wolf, too," she says. "And so…?"

Verity's very direct. Hector relishes that in a woman.

He says, "Let's think more on that, shall we?"

He nods at the nasty weather steadily escalating on the opposite side of the screened-in porch. "What fills the empty hours 'round these parts when winter really sets in and the island shuts down to all the tippling gawkers from the cornfields and plains and all points south of here?"

Verity shivers, as if recalling—enduring—a lifetime's memory of feckless December blasts.

She says, "Fast gets lonely. A shade scary, sometimes. For those who live here year 'round and the ones who stay on accidentally—usually that will be about one-hundred-fifty of us, any given winter, give or take a few—we're effectively marooned for months."

She crosses her arms tighter. "Lake Erie's mostly shallow as the Great Lakes run. Water warms and freezes fast. If you die on the island come the freeze, your body gets stored in the icehouse 'til the first lasting thaw. If it gets cold enough and you're still vertical? Then you can actually walk to the neighboring islands. But those islands are really just like here, only with even less than here, if you can imagine. Different faces, though. Long about February sometimes, that's not nothing."

Oui. Vive la difference, Hector silently concedes, thinking of his own island at the extreme tip of the Florida Keys during hurricane season.

Seemingly forgetting other customers, Verity pulls up a chair. She tugs her sweater closer again against the mounting chill. "Key West is where you live now. Just like your book and like you said, right? How's that island compare to this one?"

"Bone Key and here?" Hector looks around, taking fresh and romantically strategic measure.

He says, "Replace these big old pin oaks yonder with swaying palm trees. Stock some marlin and sharks in that water out there. Subtract any hint of snow, and I mean ever, and you're maybe just about there. Down my way, it stays warm pretty much year 'round. Hell, we don't even have furnaces or fireplaces in our houses."

Verity all but leaps on his description. "Do you realize you just said houses, not homes? Seems like a meaningful choice of words, if I might say." A little smile. "You being a writer and all."

"Shucks, you found me out. I'm frankly not really sure where home is, these days. Guess I have myself a tad of a roamin' disposition."

She smiles. "Whatever, it sounds past wonderful. In a few weeks, you just might have the first ice fisherman heading out onto the lake. Or at least working closer to shore in the early going. Until the deep ice of February."

She suddenly comes all-over glum, says, "Marooned? No exaggeration as a description of a winter here, you should know. Every year, at least a few first-timers go literally stir crazy. Sometimes do that in the worst way. By that, I mean the final way. Seems like at least one or two snap every year. Some get so desperate, they even try to drive across the lake before the ice is anywhere firm enough to support real weight. Couple maybe make it, somehow. Dumb blind luck, gotta figure. But more often than not, the ones who don't know the ropes just disappear to the lake bottom in their Model T's and A's. Not like you can go out on thin ice to find or recover the bodies, let alone the hole they and their car briefly left behind."

A long pause. She presses on, "Then there are the intentional suicides. 'Least one or two of those, every winter.

Mostly when the days are shortest. Or maybe when someone realizes they have something very wrong inside. Something getting worse and they know they have no access to the proper doctor for months and months."

Hector says, "Christ, you've got an airport here, yeah? Barring a serious snow storm or winter winds, planes fly in all sorts of weather."

"Airport's off that a-way," she confirms, nodding at a wall. "But not cheap. Especially if the weather's less than perfect. A sellers' market. And it's really got to be one of those dire medical emergencies."

She leans in on elbows, shivering again. "When the ferry and steamers stop making the run? Then you're wholly committed. So, you provision. Do that liberally, and do that diligently. 'Cause anything less can easily get you killed. You do that all tourist-season long, unless you're a fool. Just no making up for that lack of preparation later."

A hand wave. "For instance, you'll notice despite the demand for real estate, and some very crazy land values around here, there's still a lot of wooded acreage on this island. We need all those trees for firewood in winter when we're hunkering down and doing our best not to freeze to death. You said you have no furnaces in Key West? You'd be hard-pressed to find a building on this island that doesn't have at least one working fireplace. More often, several fireplaces."

"Maybe you should spend this winter on Key West," he says impulsively. "You did tout the appeal of variety, after all."

Of course Hector means that seemingly off-handed invitation as a feeler.

Punting further out, he says, "If you insist on working, could maybe set you up at the Electric Kitchen. Or, if you relish a rowdier joint, The Blind Pig."

She smiles, rising. "May get bawled out by my boss, despite that autograph, if I don't get back to it. You might get me fired and then I might really need one of those jobs down your way. Going to see if I can't whip up something strong and hot enough even for your palate. Something to rival that Cuban coffee you favor." Another little shiver, then, "And to keep you from freezing to death out here."

The sharp and steady drop in temperature has whipped the winds up to near gale-force strength. The wind strips the last of the browning leaves from the old-growth trees fronting the hotel.

"Sure," he says. "So, about you maybe also showing me around? Never answered me about any of that, you know."

"That I didn't," she says. "Get off work at six. Meet back here, 'round then?"

"Six o'clock it is."

She bites her lip, says, "But, no, let's say six-thirty, instead. Please? I'd like to dash home and freshen up. 'Least ditch this darned uniform. That be okay with you?"

"Perfect. Any preferences for dinner? Figure you surely know the best places."

"Your figure right of course. Still, let me think more on that. It would be real nice to go to a place I'll never go otherwise, you know? Now, let me see to that killer coffee. Black as sin, hot as hell."

"Fantastic." Already firmly in her clutches, Hector settles back in his chair.

He wonders again at her name, and what the teased-about story might be behind her strange but pretty handle.

Waiting on his better, stronger coffee, Hector idly gazes across the street.

Standing by a fountain, under the deteriorating canopy of the wind-whipped trees, Mister Krutch smokes a cigar, staring back at the Park Hotel.

For just a moment, Hector thinks Krutch actually winked at him.

But no, Hector decides. It's too far away and now far too gloomy to properly see anything even close to that.

3
THE SCARRED MAN

Just after five o'clock, the stormfront peaks. The howling wind ricochets off the roof, making the hotel's ancient beams creak. The Canadian Clipper flings spastic surges of muddy lake water over the banks and far enough across the street to lick the boundary of the downtown park.

Fierce weather.

Staring out the cracked window of his second-floor room, Hector smokes and watches the wind whip women's skirts and turn umbrellas inside-out. The wind also bends smaller, younger trees. The wind chases newspaper pages and freshly fallen leaves across grass and glistening pavement.

Watching straggling boats limp into dock through the gales, Hector feels a twinge of concern for the sports—and career-fisherman who've not reached safe port.

A distant dog bays back at the banshee wind. A strident voice carries over through an adjacent room's also just-cracked window, along with the stench of cigar smoke.

Female, the voice says, "Damned? Maybe! And so be it, if so! It's done now, either way! There's no point discussing it anymore. As you once said yourself, so many years ago, a deal is a deal!"

Hector frowns as he pours a little whiskey from his flask into a glass, taking it neat. He stows a half reread copy of proofs for his late-wife's last, to-be-posthumously-published novel, one for which he has yet to clandestinely supply its final, unwritten chapter drawn from her notes.

Then something smacks against the window, startling him.

It's a mourning dove, sent careening by the fierce wind. Dazed, it flaps spastically on the narrow ledge, then takes off again in wholly uncertain flight, dripping blood.

A hard, sheeting rain freshly glazes the glass.

Still standing at his window, sipping his legislatively forbidden hard liquor, Hector watches the storm build. He hopes it will ease, at least a little, in time for dinner with Miss Verity Chisholm.

Ah, Verity.

For the moment, the honey-blond island dweller seems the perfect antidote to his lost, raven-haired love.

Verity is fair where Brinke Devlin was so enticingly dark, in every sense.

And perhaps, most importantly, Verity is no fellow author, which seems still more to the good, presently.

Hector is feeling quite serious about all that stuff he's impulsively promised regarding finding Verity winter's work in Key West, if she for some reason actually wants to pursue that sort of thing.

But far better, Hector reasons, for the two of them to simply laze about that other island each day—his sultry Key that stands as America's southern-most point.

But only after he's wrapped up each morning's session of writing, boiling mere fleeting daily experience down to grist for potentially eternal fiction.

He'll do all the heavy lifting—such as it is—in terms of earning the bucks for eats and booze, Hector confidently assures himself—if this new beauty suddenly come into his fraught life will only let him do so.

Hector will write in the early morning, then knock off for a succession of days whose twilight hours will be deliciously murdered between the sheets with dishy Verity.

She can grow out her bob and bolster her Ohio island tan—all over, if she dares— across the meager beaches of Bone Key and on the deck of his fishing boat, "The Devil May Care."

Hector desires her hair longer so he can tangle fingers there as they roll as one across sweat-damp sheets.

But he's surely getting far ahead of himself with this idle dreaming.

After all, they've shared little more than a lingering handshake, and yet here he is, already moving her into his Key West cottage, in his mind.

There's no knowing Verity will go for something so lusty as "shacking up" in sun-kissed Key West, although her splendid body and something in the way she challengingly, proudly carries herself convinces Hector she just might go for such a pitch, once safe from the sight and provincial judgment of her tiny Buckeye island and its surely painfully-provincial neighbors.

A glance at his pocket watch. Still half-an-hour 'til they're to meet. Hector wonders if Verity would actually still try to get home to change clothes with this near monsoon at full roar. In its present intensity, the damned blow is almost like a Key West autumnal tropical blast. A mere few more drops in degrees, and the hard rain will be snow.

Hector drains the dregs of his drink and moseys downstairs, figuring to loiter on the hotel's deep, screened-in porch to be more directly one with the Great Lakes storm while he waits out the minutes for his date with Verity.

Standing just close enough to the screen to have cooling spray from the wind-driven rain graze his face, Hector closes his eyes and savors the scent of the thrashing storm, feeling the distant, delicious rumble of thunder deep inside muscle and bone.

Despite the early-onset arthritic pain it at times triggers in war wounds, Hector relishes the rain.

He loves thunderstorms, especially.

But he suddenly senses motion. He realizes another man mimicking his posture and position, close by the big window screens.

Mister Krutch.

Dragonflies cling fiercely to the screen to escape the gathering storm's fury. The bugs clutch to the wire grid with hooked talons, buffeted by hard gusts that set their transparent wings bending under the wind's bullying weight.

To Hector's disgust, Krutch begins systematically flicking at each long-tailed insect through the mesh, methodically dislodging each dragonfly's hooked feet, sending one-by-one off in wild, uncontrolled flight into the rising tempest.

The bugs call to mind that luckless mourning dove Hector fretted over, also left to the merciless wind.

The reeling insects flit away, as much tossed by the savage wind as actually flying. Hector imagines without the impediment of the screen between them, Krutch would instead delight in tearing off each of these creatures' delicate, shimmering wings.

Krutch smiles at Hector, says, "Beautiful, no?" His grin broadens. "The storm."

Hector says, "Sure. In a moody way. Savor a good rain. In doses."

So much for enjoying this storm alone. Hector heads back inside.

He's still not ready to confront this man.

Not before he knows so much more about Usher Krutch.

Hector slides into a lobby wing chair and spreads open a discarded newspaper.

The wags are still writing about Sacco and Vanzetti and the murderous duo's recent riding of state-mandated lightning, triggering world-wide riots.

Enough of that particular melodrama, he thinks. That sordid murder case is grossly over-covered and now very much a bore to the career crime novelist as the principals are dead. Disgusted, Hector folds and flings aside the newspaper.

A warm hand suddenly, firmly grips his shoulder. It gives him an intimate squeeze.

Verity smiles, says, "Afraid you'll have to accept me in work clothes. Couldn't slip away in time to change before the hurricane out there." She gives a wave at the door and the storm raging beyond.

Yet Verity's done a little something with her hair; stroked on some crimson lipstick.

"You're perfect," he says.

More commotion in the lobby suddenly, not tied to the weather. A man in a police uniform approaches the front desk. The clerk softly gives a number, one-door down from Hector's room.

Verity leans in, whispers, "Scuttlebutt? Woman is dead in the room next to yours. Pills, I hear. But also overheard there might have been a gun. Husband found her. Either way, likely a suicide, they say."

Hector nods. "Nothin' to be done about any of that now, yeah? Not by us, least ways. We eat here, then?"

Seeming a shade taken aback by his casual change of subject, Verity says, "Oh, Lord no. Not unless you're absolutely set on it. I spend way too much time in this place, as you can surely imagine."

She hoists an umbrella. "I have a place in mind. It's not far. Not too pricey, either."

"Please forget the price tag, darlin'," Hector says. "Take me where you want to go, typhoon or no. You've convinced me all distances are safely short."

Krutch is still alone on the front porch as they step from the lobby to brave the storm. He is still flicking at dragonflies' feet. Krutch smiles at Verity, says, "Miss Chisholm."

She murmurs back, "Mister Krutch."

"Who's this lucky friend of yours, Miss Chisholm? We chatted for a second, but your handsome beau never properly introduced himself."

Verity looks to Hector. He senses she's giving him the choice of offering up his real name.

If he's right in that reading of her intent, it's darkly telling in its own right, he figures. The author offers a big hand. "Hector Lassiter, vacationing Floridian."

A jerk move, Hector figures, but he decides to really give the bastard a tight grip. He's delighted as Krutch flinches.

Mister Krutch exaggerates a wary smile to offset his revealed pain. "Maybe Florida by choice, but that accent is coastal Texan by birth, yes? I'm widely traveled. Pride myself on identifying dialects… nailing accents."

Close in, Krutch's eyes perplex Hector, as they presumably perplex others.

Hector gives up trying to figure out which one is alive and in jiffy compromise focuses his attention on the bridge of Krutch's hawkish nose. Shaking the man's hand? To Hector, it suggests hefting a dazed small-mouth bass.

"Usher Krutch. It's my privilege, Mr. Lassiter."

Verity takes Hector by the arm, seeming determined to separate him from Mister Krutch as quickly as possible. She opens her umbrella, immediately fighting the wind's savage tugs at its fragile fabric.

Hector wraps an arm around her shoulders, pulling her closer under her umbrella's wind-jerked shelter. Out of the scarred man's ear-shot, he says, "You know him? Krutch?"

Verity says, "He lives here. Not at the hotel, I mean, but on the island. Somewhere. Or I think he does. Came over with the first wave. On the first boat. This season, I mean."

"Caught your meaning. Surely didn't take Old Usher for some immortal Pilgrim. You know the bastard's trade?"

"Search me. Kind of a mystery man. Creepy—even menacing—if you ask me. Although, by the same token, he's never been less than polite to me."

Hector mulls that, says, "If he has a place where he lives here, why does he spend any time at the hotel? Why spend time enough here for him to know your name?"

"He has a lot of lunches with people at the hotel. Business lunches, I guess."

She hesitates, at last confides, "Rumor is, Krutch might be, you know, in the Mob. Travels to Cleveland about twice a week, folks say. Sometimes to Toledo, too, which is where he's from originally. Or so I've heard. Once or twice this past summer, he went off to Youngstown. So, given those places he favors, of course rum and whiskey running are the big rumors regarding his so-called trade. That and the Mob."

Remembering the overheard conversation at the ferry dock with the since-vanished Alphonse, Hector says, "Might well be onto somethin', there."

"Can we not talk about that man anymore tonight? Krutch really is very creepy. And tonight?" She tries for a sexy smile and gets there, plenty easily for Hector's part.

"Sure," Hector says. "Please, forget I asked. Lord knows I—"

A gruff voice cuts in: "Excuse me. You are Mr. Hector Lassiter?"

Together, Hector and Verity turn under their shared umbrella.

The policeman standing framed under his dripping umbrella says, "Require a minute of your time, sir."

Hector is fairly certain whatever is to come will take well more than a minute.

But Hector nods, asks, "Do I have a choice, officer?"

The cop says, "Of course not."

4
THE POLICEMAN

The cop escorts Hector and Verity back to the hotel. Together, the two men press on to Hector's hotel room.

Leaning against a chest of drawers, another cop—this one the island's chief of police—poses questions.

Sitting on the foot of his rented bed, Hector smokes and answers each question honestly, if stingily. Cagily.

The police chief's a man of about thirty years named Booth Parker. Booth isn't particularly tall, but looks fit enough. Probably a formidable fighter, in-close, Hector wagers. Parker's prematurely graying brown hair is close-cropped; his uniform immaculate.

Parker says, "You're some kind of mystery novelist, isn't that right?"

Mystery novelist. That dreadful description again. Goddamn.

And in these backwater environs, Hector's probably already a prime suspect precisely because of his wrongly-presumed trade.

Hector says, "Just novelist actually. Sometimes screen-writer. Just a working writer, overall. And, because it's early days yet, and because a man has to live, I sometimes also do some newspaper work. Freelance, here and there. So, journalist, too."

A pause, then Hector adds, "If you can even call that last writing. I write all kinds of things for money. Writing's my trade. My only real, bankable skill."

The top cop says, "Walls in this place are thick enough, but there are gaps under common doors. Shared vents. Open windows, now and again, and the like. Maybe hear anything from next door in the past few hours, Mr. Lassiter?"

"You're talking about my neighbor that-a-way," he nods at the wall, "yes? Heard talk downstairs woman in that room died. Maybe from pills. Maybe a gun. Suicide, either way. Or, so go rumors."

"Where'd you exactly hear those rumors, sir?"

Hector thinks of Verity. No use dragging her into trouble with the cops for perceived motor-mouthing. He lights up a cigarette, blows smoke. "Lobby chatter. Hotel scuttlebutt. As to hearing much from that room, first-hand? Nah, I didn't. Not really—I just couldn't. Certainly didn't hear a gunshot. But I haven't spent much time at all in this pad. Mere minutes, really. Dropped my bags, then went out on the town, such as it is. This hotel? Just a place to lay down my head tonight."

Chief Parker said, "Strictly between us, was a gun killed your neighbor. Likely not self-inflicted."

Hector broods on his vintage Colt he hopes is still hidden under his pillow, all the while forcing himself not to look there.

God, don't let them search this room, he prays to a presumed-uninterested deity.

Parker drives on, "Probably dead from a derringer of some kind. You know? A sleeve pistol? Something small? I mean in every sense. Again, you insist you didn't hear anything like a shot, Mr. Lassiter?"

"Yep. Not at all. Maybe an hour back, I just heard a woman's voice, through a cracked window, like you say. Had my window open to let out the cigarette smoke as I took drags, watching the rain."

The cop eyes him hopefully. "They have an argument of some kind?"

"Not like I reckon you conjure," Hector says. "More a discussion, though the lady sounded especially emphatic."

A fifty-cent word that last one, maybe a word well above this yokel cop's head.

Just in case, Hector eases it back to, "Lady was certainly stating her case about somethin' to someone. It was a little heated. Mildly so. But nothing remarkable in the end. Nothin' worth leading to blows, let alone gunshots. Don't ask me who or what the subject was, 'cause I only ever heard her voice, and hardly much of that."

"What exactly did the lady say?"

"This will be a paraphrase you understand, because it wasn't much of a moment to my mind," Hector says.

Hector repeats his memory of her overheard statement about it all being worth it . . . Whatever *it* was.

"Suspect she was maybe talking about some kind of infidelity? You know, hanky-panky?" Now the cop is walking back his big words, too, so Hector is left supposing perhaps self-editing is catching, in its way.

"Maybe," Hector allows. "There was somethin' else, I now recall. Woman said it before the other I just repeated. Somethin' like, 'Damned? Well, so be it.'"

Hector pauses, adds, "And a cigar. Remember smelling the stink of cigar smoke over the scent of the rain. Very strong, very unpleasant. Live down Cuba way, so I know—this cheroot? Nothin' top shelf."

"She was Catholic, maybe," Parker says. "She had a crucifix on a necklace. Maybe there was some cheating going on. Maybe divorce was no option because of the church?"

"Maybe," Hector says doubtfully. The cop is clearly clutching at anything, absent . . . anything.

"You sure you didn't hear something that might have been a gunshot?"

The author—the crime novelist—in Hector has already gone to work on that one.

A small caliber weapon—which a sleeve gun certainly qualifies as being, and maybe with its muzzle blast further dampened by a pillow or a towel, say—could be astonishingly quiet.

A sad smile for Parker. "Sorry, but again, no."

Hector looks to the ceiling. "Between the rain on the glass and wind like a freight train tearing across the roof, I was lucky to hear what I heard. If I hadn't been standing at the cracked window, watching the rain, wouldn't have heard that much."

"Expect we're done here then, Mr. Lassiter. Do appreciate your time."

"All good luck with this bloody business," Hector says, rising and shaking hands.

"We could certainly use some luck," Parker says. "Between us, it's been a strange and bloody summer around these parts."

Hector is about to follow up on that admission, but Parker puts another question to him, first. "You aim to stay here long on South Bass, Mr. Lassiter?"

"Oh, Lord no," Hector says. "Surely hate to get trapped here for the winter, which I begin to think could be a real prospect inside a week or two."

"Probably at most." Parker pauses, hand on the doorknob. "Say, what did bring you here, this late in the season?"

"Mostly research," Hector says, telling the cop the same half-truth he handed Verity. "Stuff about lakeside rum-running and the like."

Let the cop assume Hector meant that research was for a book or screenplay. Hell, it could end up between the covers in some form like that down the road. Nearly all of

Hector's life ends up on the page, in one form or another, eventually.

"Then I might not be a bad source for you," the cop says. "Station's kitty-corner across the park, just yonder that-a-ways. I'm mostly there days and too many early evenings, too. If you find time to drop by before you leave, I'll treat you to a drink."

Hector smiles uncertainly. "You mean a real drink?"

A crooked smile back. The top cop says, "Prohibition mostly isn't here, as you probably well know by now. That's no reflection on me," he adds quickly. "Just the way we all like it around these parts. Hell, if I truly enforced the liquor laws? Frankly, this island would be worse than dead. A true ghost town."

South Bass is surely sounding more and more like Hector's Key West, at least in its stubbornly wet ways.

Parker says, "So, yes sir. Real firewater is what I pour. A heavy pour to friends. And no risk of blindness or cultivating St. Vitus' dance, after. Honest Injun. It'll be the real and the good stuff, Tex."

5
THE MUTUAL FRIEND

The storm has temporarily subsided as Hector spots Verity re-entering the lobby. She's taken advantage of the lull to make a dash off to somewhere to scrub-up and change into something slightly slinky. Her wavy blond hair's still damp from her fast shower or maybe more likely the driving rain.

A squeeze of his arm. "Sorry to keep you waiting. But thinking that talk you had to have might take much longer, and wanting very badly to wash off the day?"

"It's fine," he says. "Perfect timing really." She smells wonderful. He tells her so.

Verity says, "Everything is okay? I don't have to plot a jailbreak, do I?"

"Nah," he says. "And it was a gun. That killed my neighbor, I mean. Probably not suicide. But I'm not a suspect, so everything is just dandy, far as all that goes. Reckon we simply soldier on."

He steers her back toward the door, very aware of Lou, the desk clerk, watching them.

Verity still has her damp umbrella. He says, "Try this again? A clean get-away, this time?"

"Fingers firmly crossed," she says. "So, what did Chief Parker want to know?"

"Ah, all the predictable cop stuff," Hector says offhandedly, stepping onto the porch with her. "Did I hear anything? That lame-ass sort of questioning."

She again opens and raises her umbrella as they step into a softer rain. "And did you hear anything?"

"Nothin' useful, I fear," he says. He wraps his arm around her trim waist. She doesn't balk. The cold rain's ample cover for their lovers' huddle under her umbrella.

Verity rests her head on his shoulder. "Walk first, before dinner? Before the rain maybe gets harder again? Show you a few close-by sights and shops you'll maybe find useful? Rest of the island—which candidly isn't a ton, not at all—will still mean driving or renting a bike, weather allowing."

A romantic walk in the rain? More excuse to hold Verity close?

Better and better.

"Jiffy tour sounds a delight," Hector says. "Always dandy to have bearings in a new place. Good to know where the good drinks are as I'm getting the word from better than reliable sources this rock's not remotely dry."

"Golly, not a smidge," she confirms. "It's not simply right out there, for all to see, of course. But we're not talking speak-easy password stuff by any stretch, either."

"Get that sense," Hector says. "Christ, even the police chief was offering to bend elbows with me."

"Parker?" A husky chuckle. "Bet our top cop's starved for another man's man to pal with after a summer of want-to-be sports fishermen and drunken tourists from Cleveland and Detroit to contend with."

Hector checks their reflection together in a rain-glazed shop windows. For perhaps the first time since Brinke, Verity feels like coming home. They make a striking pair by gas lamp.

She adds, "Chief Parker? Good people. It's his first summer in the top spot, and not an easy one. Especially these past few months. Really pretty bloody."

There it is again, almost an echo of the chief's words. Hector says, "Elaborate on that, wouldn't you, darlin'? Bloody, exactly, how?"

"Bad things like that woman at the hotel," she says. "Violent deaths. This is two deaths like your neighbor in just twenty-four hours, if you can believe."

"Who's the other who died?"

"A man who fell off the very ferry you came over on," she says.

Alphonse, Hector supposes. "That one was a suicide, too?"

Verity shrugs. "People—tourists—would probably be more apt to off themselves that way going back than coming over, chatter goes. Maybe because they're depressed to leave all the dimming summer fun and this was a last blast of some sort? Or maybe they're still just drunk on island wine and feeling maudlin, so over the rail they go? Or maybe the island's indeed their last revel before who knows what bad thing's bearing down on them? No. Word is, this man had finger bruises on his throat and the blood vessels in his eyes were all burst. Throttled, then pitched over the side, I hear. Or so some say. Dead man was some kind of mobster, maybe even a bootlegger, talk is. Body washed up on Middle Bass."

Two dead.

Maybe by the same hand, and both of them spent their last minutes in some proximity to Hector.

To Hector, and, just maybe, to Mister Krutch.

Music reaches them from parts unknown: "In A Little Spanish Town."

Hector hopes the local police don't make that ferry connection, too. If so, he'll freshly be a suspect, and likely much more than a fleeting object of serious suspicion.

"There are still others," Verity confides, leaning harder into him as the pounding rain steps up its assault. "The worst—at least for me—was Tommy Breck. Tommy was a good friend. Tommy had so much going for him, in so many ways. If Tommy could go to pieces? I don't want to think about what that might portend for the rest of us.

The writer in Hector muses, *Portend*? Really?

A sad smile. With a deep tone of resignation, Verity says, "Trust me—Tommy's loss was pretty rough stuff for a lot of us here, Hec."

It's several seconds before that name consciously lands, and then it does so straight between Hector's eyes.

Tommy?

Tommy Breck?

Hector asks himself, did she really just invoke his Tommy's name?

The casually dropped name at last fully seizes Hector's attention.

Verity is closely studying him. Hector's sharp reaction seems to startle her. "You being the pro writer, I hate to resort to a cliché, but, Hector, you look just like you've just seen a ghost. My God! What's wrong?"

This woman knew his Tommy.

Well, that's not so surprising in and of itself, maybe, not on such a small island... so few year-'round natives, after all.

Key West? Much the same. Scrape off the sorry hordes of dayside-only tourists? You're left with comparatively few permanent islanders during the off-hours and the off-seasons—mostly merchants and fishermen.

But here? Where the ice locks you into a communal prison?

Where the few who stick it out year-long presumably become quite bonded, indeed?

Hector grants it all a few more moments of brooding, then takes the plunge:

"Confess, here and now, Tommy was a dear friend of mine. The oldest of those. Tommy's death is the true reason I'm here. You're right in that Tommy was certainly not the kind to hurt himself. Not in that sullen way. Tommy had every reason to do so years back, if he was truly so inclined. I talk of the Great War. After he was very badly hit by a mortar shell and left maimed in a muddy, bloody trench in France. Yet, Tom hung tight and he persevered. Tommy loved life too much to leave it without the most savage of shoves. I cling to that belief. I do that down deep."

Hector's turn to shrug. "And, so. Here I am. Tryin' to find what really happened to our friend. Figuring to find who really killed him and to see they pay dearly for it."

6
THE DUTCH UNCLE

"You know I've truly never drunk other than island wine," Verity confides. "If you're adamant on harder stuff, what do you recommend?"

Hector says, "We're having steak, so let's stick with wine. Decent and dry red wine, okay? But none of this local, sugary swill. Maybe later, if you hang in with me tonight, I'll introduce you to a *Cuba Libra*. Maybe, at the Roundhouse, after. Possibly even a *mojito*, if the bartender has the fixin's for that one. Mint leaves? Essential. Either way, talking rum as a base, but no acquired tastes there. Just softly sweet drinks you have to be a careful of 'cause suckers can sneak up on you like some silver-tongued, handsome demon."

Smiling as she browses the menu, Verity says, "Sounds a fine plan. First though, one of us has to talk more about Tommy. You knew him longest and best, so I volunteer you going first. Having said that, and knowing you both—Tommy better, obviously—have to think he had more than a few years on you, Hec."

"Several," Hector admits. "Years of life lived large. Lived hungry, by my reckonin'. Best figure if Mr. Webster's heirs get 'round to wantin' an illustration for the phrase *joie de vivre*, an engraved portrait of old Tom could stand just dandy for the cause. So, yeah, Tommy was older than me. Fought together, brothers in arms. First in Mexico, hunting Pancho Villa. Then in Europe. With his advice, native knowledge or simple survival instinct, Tommy must have saved my life a dozen times 'fore I saw eighteen. And nobody—nobody—understood and could direct war horses as Tommy could."

She wrinkles her nose. "Horses? As in cavalry? Could you really have been part of all that? Seems like cowboy movie stuff. Tom Mix and Tony! A distant age."

Hector nods. "Was just old enough to bury the noble trade, I suppose. Also have some nasty leg wounds from some very old guns of Mexican and European vintage to prove it. Tommy and I were horse soldiers together, first. In Mexico, during the Pershing Expedition."

Looking confused, Verity says, "The biography at the back of that book says we're nearly the same age. You'd had to have been—"

"Just a kid," Hector admits. "But a rangy and gloomy looking young buck. All glower and swagger, back when. Passed sufficiently to make the bloody cut after brazenly lying about my age. Had all the predictable, stupid boy's ideas about chasing banditos on horseback. Courting dark-eyed senoritas. Thank God Tommy was along for that crazy ride, especially in the early going. Like I said, I'd likely have been dead inside a week without our Tommy watching over me."

Hector's startling blue eyes seem vistas away as she freshly appraises him.

Something in Hector's expression reaches Verity.

Hector Lassiter is a man of action but still somehow a dreamer, that most rare of combinations, to Verity's singular mind.

The-still young century's nearly annihilated the last of the mavericks that Hector Lassiter stubbornly—if unconsciously—embodies.

In a kind of daze, Hector rambles, "Tommy and me? Campaigned down into Mexico. Later home and back into Texas. Eventually—too soon—we were shipped over to Europe and those goddamn French trenches. Lice, rats and death. Then Tommy and me got hit. Both got hit hard over there. I was the nearer miss, in that sense. Merely shot through a couple times. But Tommy's leg got lost. Blown clean off. I knotted off what was left with my belt and somehow carried him on my back to an aid station. Saved Tommy's life, that rare time. I finished out the war in the Italian Red Cross, driving ambulances. Spent a few years in Paris after the war learning how to really write. Gertrude Stein, Ezra Pound and Scott Fitzgerald? My Holy Trinity. My early champions and teachers, if you've heard tell of any of 'em. Long 'bout age twenty-five? Came home. Married a great woman. Fellow writer. Got my own boat and heard Tommy had his own charter outfit here on Lake Erie. Tom and me? Spent couple years swappin' letters. Pledging each other one of us would visit the other's best fishin' holes, soon."

Hector stares at his hands. Eventually, raw-voiced he confesses, "Not fated to happen. Ended up widowed, then suddenly had the time. Tom and I were startin' to talk sincerely about dates to meet up. Then a few days ago came the word...."

Hector bites his lip.

"You know the details about what happened to Tom, Hec?"

Verity asks it carefully, giving him room to dodge, he figures, just in case, case-hardened though he may seem, he doesn't want to stare too squarely into that abyss.

"Only from some news clippings, via a service," Hector says. "And a couple of third-hand accounts, through even more uncertain channels. We'll get to what really happened soon enough, expect. As you were here, I mean, and so know best. I have questions for you now, as you'd expect. You said you knew Tommy pretty well, before his end?"

Hector can't credibly put these two acquaintances of his together, certainly not romantically.

And, at least in the early going after the loss of his leg, Tommy the former tomcat, steered clear of all female company, even casual brushes not apt to lead to the bedroom—considering himself too-damaged goods, and in his blackest studies, even "a goddamn, one-legged freak."

Of course, Hector railed against all that, but to no effect in the early going.

But maybe in time Tommy again ventured down carnal paths. But not with this woman, Hector figures for some reason to which he can't lay meaningful foundation to beyond proven horndog instinct.

Verity is clearly doing her own thinking as she sips her red wine.

She's acquiring the taste Hector reckons, truly convinced it's her first glass of really good red *vino*—not this sickly sweet and sorry thin, locally produced sugar water the island grape-growers truck as wine.

Hector figures he'd have to guzzle a case of the lake grown stuff just to get the faintest intimation of a soothe. A buzz might take a vineyard.

"Tommy was a good and loyal friend," she says at last. "A life advisor, of sorts, at least at times. Tom was my unofficial, older brother who would cool the heels of many a fresh customer who was starting to get too busy with his mouth or hands."

She shoots Hector a sheepish look and says, "Sometimes he was less an honorary big brother and more a Dutch uncle. But I have to confess, I was probably deserving of that approach, those times."

Hector laughs. "Sounds about perfect. Old Tom was my Dutch uncle a time or ten, as well."

His laugh's echoes too quickly die out. There's a long silence. Hector at last says, "It's true he hanged himself?"

Verity's fingers stroke her goblet's stem. Glumly, she says, "That's how they found his body. He lives—he lived—in an old boat house down by the marina."

Hector says, "Hear he left a note. At least all the newspapers my clipping service found said it was so. Having said that, I surely know enough about the newspaper trade not to take any of that as even close to gospel."

"There was a note left," she confirms. "Written in his own hand."

Hector's baritone grinds to gravel. "Well, goddamn."

Verity sips more wine. She closes a warm hand over Hector's. "I know exactly how you feel to hear it. Believe me, I looked for something that felt wrong or didn't ring true. But I came up empty-handed." She squeezes the bridge of her nose, says, "Or mostly I did. But who am I to question the authorities?"

"Authorities. You mean the cops? Hell, they're not immune to mistakes." Hector pauses, her words still sinking in. He repeats softly, with emphasis, "Do go on, Verity. Please do that. What do you doubt?"

"There are little eyebrow-raisers for me. They make me question some official findings. Chief Parker has his doubts, too, to be fair."

"You have Parker's ear?"

"More like breakfast small-talk stuff. Not even so much with Parker, as others around him," she says. "Everyone comes through the hotel for breakfast, more often than not. Especially come winter, or even about now, when we're the only hotel around still up and running. I expect I fill nearly every one's coffee cup, any given day, at some point when the cold truly sets in. Some that I hear things from report to Parker. They share when they shouldn't. Anyway, Chief Parker? He has his doubts, too."

"Do tell, please."

"For one thing, the words in the note didn't fall right to my ear, or to Chief Parker's either." She looks around for possible eavesdroppers, then whispers, "Thought is, Tommy was maybe forced to copy something down. Maybe even to take a kind of, you know, dictation?" She shivers. "Isn't that a terrible thought?"

Copying. Dictation.

The prospect indeed crawls Hector's nape.

It all seems at once creepy enticement, and yet, a too-far reach.

But the part of Hector that can't accept Tommy as willing victim of suicide is eager to cling to one or the other prospect, regardless how outré it may otherwise seem.

Verity says softly, "The bigger issue, at least so far as Parker says, is the way Tom died. The rafter they found Tommy hanging from was at least twelve feet off the ground. There was no ladder found and no chair on earth that would get you anywhere close to all the way up there, the chief said."

Hector's pale blue eyes widen. "So how could Tommy have possibly done the deed? That's the cop's logic?" It's not really a question on Hector's part, rather, a crime novelist's extrapolation.

Verity nods. "There was a flight of stairs up to a small loft, but no banister on those stairs. Even if Tommy got up there, then he'd have had to shinny out on that very rafter about ten feet to reach the point where the rope was found tied off.

"So, thinking is," she continues, "without a banister? With only one real leg? None of us who really knew him can figure out how Tommy could ever have made the climb to make the final jump, let alone engineered the rest."

Indeed. How could an older, one-legged man presumably not thinking clearly manage all that?

She smiles sadly. Hector muses from her rather dreamy look she's maybe starting to feel the wine.

He says, "You know, of course, Tommy moved pretty well for a guy with only one leg on even ground. Just seeing him walk like that, if you didn't know about his lost leg, you'd maybe never know, right? But for all his nimbleness on flat earth, even Tommy couldn't have made that climb you just described, you're right enough about that. But I'd still like to see for myself the place where it happened."

"I'm sure," Verity says. "You know, even if he had somehow managed to get up there, he'd have used a sailor's or fisherman's knot of some kind on that rope. The chief insists on that anyhow, and I agree."

Their waitress interrupts. They order perch, fresh steamed vegetables and—rather reckless or possibly even strategic this, depending on your point of view—a bottle of true and dry Sauvignon Blanc.

Alone again after their server goes, Verity says, "How much can you stand to know about, well, you know? I mean Tommy's passing, in real detail? This part is sort of gory, I guess. But also possibly quite telling."

Hector is immediately all re-sharpened attention. He says carefully, "Think of what I do for a living, darlin'. Think of my military record. Maybe it says less of me as a person, but I'm not in the least squeamish. Even about my dearest ones. And I was an ambulance driver, during the bloodiest ever of conflicts. Do go on, please. Anything could be very important to me."

"Of course." She briefly touches his arm. "You're a man who's been places. Who has seen many things." She steels herself with another swig of what is to Verity, very heady wine.

She says, with a hint of a slur Hector detects, "Tommy's neck wasn't broken. The coroner ruled Tommy was strangled. And that knot? Those knots at both ends of the noose? Amateurish, the doctor and Parker said. And they were no real known knots to speak of. And the end that was tied to that rafter Tommy could never have gotten out to in the first place to make such a sloppy knot? That part of the rope was cut off just above the amateur knot, as Doc Phelps described it.

Hector starts to speak but Verity raises a hand. He can see the wine's glisten in her eyes, now.

"But there's more, Hec! Several feet of the rope were actually missing. The remains were found about one-hundred yards from the scene of the suicide. The found-end of the rope's remainders were clearly cut with a knife."

Now Hector's seething. "And still it's a suicide on the goddamned books? Holy Jesus! That's a crime, all itself."

But of course, his outrage at the official verdict aside, Hector immediately grasps Verity's darker drift. Someone who didn't know that Tommy lacked a critical limb seemingly staged an impossible suicide scenario.

Tommy's killer never expected anyone to question the obvious, to actually doubt the suicide scene.

If the local officials are right, person or persons unknown hoisted Tommy to his death. Then they improvised a tardy knot and cut off the excess, figuring evident suicide would preclude a deeper search for the rest of that rope, subsequently discarded far too haphazardly.

Whoever faked Tommy's suicide was also clearly nimbler than the murdered one-legged vet could manage on his best day.

It is strangely comforting in its way to know a life force like Tommy's was indeed seemingly too strong to simply snuff itself out in a tragic spasm of despair.

The older vet was clearly slain.

Hector's more convinced than ever of that.

Considering it all, moving puzzle pieces around to try and form a coherent criminal narrative, Hector says—trying to do so nonchalantly—"The local heat, er, the police that's to say, and Chief Parker, they surely clue you into an awful special lot, darlin'."

"Didn't get this all from Parker, I told you. Really, not any of it. Mostly know what I know in pieces from others who report to the chief."

Hector mulls that. "You read that suicide note of Tommy's? In person?"

Verity shakes her head. "Sorry, but of course not. Just heard it described."

Hector thinks more, says, "Let's backtrack, a tad. You grew up on this island, you said."

She traces the damp rim of her glass with a fingertip. The crystal makes a haunting trill as she strokes its edge.

"Mom and Dad owned a winery in the day—hence my name," she says over that eerie trill. "From *in vino veritas*? In wine there is truth? But Veritas isn't a very good girl's name, or even a man's. So it became Verity. The wine business was real good for a while, you know? Until Prohibition. The Volstead act. It was going to be the family business and my inheritance. But my folks were just too honest to break the law, even in the gray ways like so many do now." A hand wave at the rest of the island. "The family business? Went belly up. Did that hard."

"Sorry," Hector says from the heart. "Still, have to ask, though frankly this question is very much about you. Verity, have you ever been anywhere that isn't—you know—here?"

An embarrassed shrug and a terrible admission through oblique implication: "Summer trade's so important to this place," she almost whispers. "It's everything, really, Hec. But once the ferry shuts down, it's Quitsville on roaming if you're still here. At least until the thaw comes around these parts. Even then, it's all prep again for the following season. I've just never quite put together the nickels to escape an island winter."

Jesus Christ. Verity has been precisely nowhere.

That's what she's toeing-around admitting to nomadic Hector, the consummate wanderer. Her indirect revelation horrifies him almost as much as her disclosures about their mutual friend's seeming murder.

Verity's horizons have so far been bound by this postage stamp island's nearly beach-devoid perimeter.

What a ghastly revelation! Hector is truly appalled. Yet he's increasingly and quietly excited. There's a world for him to gift this enticing young woman.

Yet, surely during the still-good years, her parents might have arranged something. Perhaps a winter with some far-rambling, trusted relative? One who lived anywhere else than on this small dab of honey-combed limestone cast in the middle of a middling so-called Great Lake that's actually so shallow that any-given icy winter makes it a prison for its most stubborn natives.

"In tribute to Tommy, I'm covering your expenses," Hector says firmly. "At the very least, you and I are on the last ferry off this rock together as this season closes for keeps, please? Say yes, and we'll start in Key West, Verity."

Hector takes her hand in his. "But that's an island, too. So, we'll soon enough push on once hurricane season dies down. Cuba will be next. Another island, sure, but bigger. More exotic and even more sultry. And one that can be left near on anytime, and at will. Then we'll head back across the Gulf of Mexico to Galveston where I was born."

With glistening green eyes, she squeezes his hand harder; begins to rake a thumb nail back and forth across his palm.

He says, "From there, we'll rent a Chevy. See the heartland. Spend a weekend or maybe more in New York City. From the Big Apple, we'll take a liner to Europe. Paris, first. Then on to Madrid and Milan. Anywhere you've heard of and most fancy seeing. I'll warn you now, once we hit Italy, if we do, I'm apt to likely bore you with war stories of me and Tommy and my other writer friend, Hem. But I promise to have you back here in time for summer's first boatload of tourists. Promise that even if I have to bring you here on my own boat. I mean, if, after all that, you want to come back."

The look on Verity's pretty face is a curious mixture of excitement, happy fear and blatant skepticism—as if perhaps Hector's maybe cruelly having her on.

Her green eyes shine with what he regards as equal parts anticipation and challenge.

"You have to know what you're promising is beyond my dreams, Hec. I'm prepared to say, yes, immediately. If this is really a true offer."

She bites her lips, says, "But know that if it isn't, it's possibly the cruelest thing anyone has ever done to me."

"Christ, it's no joke," he says. "And there are no strings, darlin'. Swear."

Verity says carefully, "Strings could be an issue. I mean expectation of something like that. Best to let life take its own course, yes? Anyway, a trip like you're talking about? That must cost a small fortune. It's impossible."

"Not at all. I'm having a great business year and, whole truth be known, darlin', Key West is just goddamn lousy with vivid ghosts whom I desperately need to drown with a positive ocean of new, good memories."

Ghosts. That's the closest thing to an outright lie he's thrown at this woman.

Really it is just that single, obvious and too-potent specter, of course. The specter an anonymous but fetching legion of nubile tourists in and out of his Key West brass bed have come nowhere near laying to rest in Hector's heart and head.

Brinke Devlin's ghost.

"Candidly need some new and happy memories of my island," he murmurs.

It seems to him Verity is owed a frank sense of the immense grief he combats every day on Bone Key. The terrors of loss that wrench him from sleep too many nights, damp and screaming. "All that good memory building is also on me, of course," he adds.

"You're really serious about this?"

"This will happen if you're game, Verity. Our biggest issue is getting you a jiffy passport. Does this place have a post office? It has to, right?"

She searches his face. "A passport is doable."

"So, are you really up for this?"

Verity squeezes his hand. "You swear this isn't some cruel joke, Hec?"

"Swear. You're entirely right. I'd be a monster to tease about something like this and not deliver."

"You would indeed." She squeezes his hand harder. "Very well. Two for the road."

After dinner, to her palpable frustration, Hector insists Verity drop him by the police station for another confab with the chief of police.

Verity relents, allowing how she wants to tidy up her place before possibly having him over for a single nightcap—a last drink that will be followed by "a dropping off at your hotel, of course."

Of course.

"And please, don't mention me or what I've told you about what Parker or especially his people have told me," she says. "Not yet. Don't want to cost any local cops their jobs for being indiscreet. Soon enough, I figure the three of us will sit down together and talk all this out. Then I can confide to him if needed how I filled you in."

"Mums, the word," Hector vows.

As he approaches the station house, Hector sees Usher Krutch, clearly much the worse for drink. The old man's scarred forehead is pressed to the wall of the police headquarters.

Suddenly doubling over, Krutch becomes violently ill.

Hector squints in distaste.

When he sees he's been seen retching, Krutch snarls back at Hector, standing there with a clear look of distaste, "Don't you dare judge me, Hector Lassiter!"

Krutch says apparently apropos of nothing, "You're not the only one to know loss you know!" Krutch is sick twice more, then he sobs, "You don't what it's like to have your only child loathe you!"

Hector's immediate impulse is to shoot back, *Holy cow! You have a kid?*

But Hector holds his tongue, reaching for the door handle of the police station HQ.

Krutch shakes his head, dragging a sleeve across his mouth, "I apologize for being like this in front of you. But without the balm of drink…?"

Instead of rising to either bits of seemingly self-pitying bait, Hector just nods. He says, "I have a pressing appointment with the police chief. Do you need me to have someone come out and assist you?"

Krutch holds up a shaking hand. "No. There's no help for this."

Upon entering the police station, a still rattled Hector plops down across a battered walnut desk from the chief of police.

Hector white-lies to Parker, "I quite recently learned through various locals you and I reportedly shared a friend."

Many minutes pass; secrets are shared.

Hector stubs out a third Pall Mall and winces again at the piece of paper gripped in his hand.

He at last passes Tommy's apparent suicide note back to Parker.

"Hell yes, it's bogus," Hector declares. "Tommy's handwriting. That's for certain. But the words are all wrong, just as you say. For one thing, *regret* was never in Tommy's vocabulary."

After bashing around more dubious points about Tommy's apparent last letter, the two men brave the rain now verging on sleet, stalking two blocks to the hulking, decaying structure in which Tommy was found dangling from that dubiously knotted-off noose.

Staring up at the span of timber Tommy could never possibly have reached, Hector says, wholly unnecessarily to his own ears, "You're absolutely convinced it was murder?"

"Absolutely," the chief says. "No damn question. I see you're sure of the same."

Parker looks Hector in the eye. "But as to the who? The why? I am not on firm ground yet. Hell, not even close."

Hector thanks the cop for his time. Shaking hands and renewing his pledge for a discrete drink together, perhaps the next day, the two men say goodnight.

Just before the door closes, Chief Parker asks, "By the way, how'd you know I know Tommy, again?"

Hector says, "They say it's a small world. If that's true, then this island is same as the tiniest world of all, yeah? Some of the folks here and there I've talked to said you and Tommy were friends, too."

The chief grunts. "Right...."

His hand on the doorknob this time, Hector thinks of something else, inquires, "Any more on my hotel neighbor's suicide?"

"In a manner of speaking, yes," Parker says. "The husband's dead now, too. Apparently shot himself out there in the park, just yonder."

Pointing, Parker says, "His body was found sitting on that bench just there, facing the lake. Fella did the deed directly across from the window of the room where his missus...."

The chief makes a funny face. "Anyway, sorry bastard left a note, of course. Not knowing him, I can't speak to that letter's authenticity. Least not yet."

7
THE CABIN

Verity drives an old Model T that, like its pretty owner, Hector suspects has never known a non-South Bass Island stretch of road. That epiphany freshly and deeply depresses the novelist.

Her car is presumably a parents' hand-me-down jalopy, but still runs. Car also has clearly stubbornly endured the pitiless lake-effect winters, but at least keeps them out of this round of inclement weather.

As Verity drives Hector around her island—first end-to-end, then side-to-side, all the while giving him his island bearings—she describes more of the island's recent and mysterious deaths.

Most of them seem convincing, though no less shocking, suicides. Or Verity says officials at least ruled them acts of self-annihilation.

Two others were clearly violent deaths, but they are down on the books as "robberies gone wrong," she's heard.

That should be easily enough confirmed the next time he crosses paths with Parker, Hector assures himself, smoking a cigarette and tapping ashes out the cracked, passenger's side window into the bucketing sleet as he listens to her tales of myriad island demises.

Making a last turn onto the curving, lakeside road running past the site of Perry's Monument, Verity says, "That's about it, as our tour goes. That's all of the public, tourist face of this place, anyway. There are a lot of long, twisting private drives and hidden roads, but most of those dead-end at some island merchant's private house. Or a sports fisherman's place where they escape the tourists. Those roads are mostly posted private."

With a slight air of unspecific uncertainty that Hector wants to think foreshadows something pleasing, Verity says, "Rain's picking up again. Suppose I should get you back to your hotel before some robed, bearded man with a staff starts pairing up animals?"

He laughs, casually draping an arm across her seat's back, fingertips just brushing her shoulder. "Second time I've heard that joke on this island," he says.

Verity's smile back isn't discouraging. He cups her shoulder with his hand. She checks the rearview mirror. Traffic of any normal sort is no problem at this hour—the last of the ferries have fled back with the cars they carried over, and roads are now nearly empty, even this early in the evening.

She pulls over to the near non-existent shoulder; sets the parking brake. Verity nods at the lake. "This is my favorite view. Other than from my backyard."

"Beautiful," Hector says. "But your backyard's view is somehow better?"

"Much."

Something hungry in her eyes encourages Hector to lean in. He does and she pulls him closer, faster. They kiss, warmly and softly at first. Their kiss lingers, goes very long, then grows hungrier. Verity uses her tongue first. Panting, she finally breaks it off.

Hector says, "But my tour's not complete. You haven't shown me your place." A smile and he says, "You know? Your private view? Eclipsing this one? How can I leave this place, never having seen it?"

For all he knows, she might still live there with her folks.

If so, he's decided to roll those dice. Hector will, if necessary, ruefully endure some game of bridge or rum five-hundred with the geezers, or whatever.

Or maybe just some conversation with her folks—a wistful talk about all the harsh vagaries and vicissitudes of running a lackluster winery in the feckless, misguided throes of the goddamn and increasingly vexing Volstead Act, perhaps?

She seems to think about it, then Verity smiles conspiratorially. She says, “You’re right. You should see it all. You should surely see everything.”

Verity turns around in her seat and deftly executes a three-point turn.

They drive on through the mounting icy rain to one of those intermittent, marked “private drives” she spoke of.

This one is a long, mostly-straight gravel path extending into a vaulted canopy of old-growth trees with trunks so thick they leave Hector staggered by their diameter.

Somewhere under one-hundred yards in, the wooded tunnel gives way to a clearing. A small, New England-style cottage whose dimensions and overall look again faintly echo Hector’s Florida home at last emerges.

But Hector’s house fronts a municipal street and affords just a sliver of ocean view.

Verity’s home is lushly tree-shaded; the slope of its scant backyard subsides into a private, sandy beach with a panoramic lake view.

At height of summer, it truly must be beautiful here, Hector thinks.

But he’s missed the summer by enough to compromise most of that beauty.

Now, something about the view of the still-gathering storm across the gun-metal gray, wind-whipped lake is downright harrowing.

The lyrics of the old Celtic song, "In the Bleak Midwinter" drift through his mind.

And yet, still out a-ways on the lake, there are scattered boats piloted by intrepid or more likely very desperate fishermen determined to make last nickels to see them through winter.

Or hell, maybe they're just drunk.

It must be beautiful in the summer here, surely, yes, Hector tells himself again as he looks around.

And during the all-too brief Ohio autumn?

Then this would likely be a fine scene for crackling bonfires and deep talk over mulled and spiked hot cider, or smoky berry wines sipped while huddled close, anticipating a night of lusty love-making in Verity's cozy cottage.

But in the full-throes of February or March?

In actual winter, Hector figures, Verity's would variously be a vista of still-grayer, choppy waters or an endless jumbled horizon of pitiless ice that would blind her when burnished by a glaring winter sun bringing no heat.

Lonely.

Harrowing.

Possibly even quite depressing, knowing one had only the island's last working and open restaurant and grocery store to venture into for months on end.

Then, the oh-so bleak midwinter would equate to a view that might literally kill.

A mild stroke or an appendicitis attack could also be a life-threatening event if there was lake-effect winter weather to impede those pricey and fragile little planes taking life-saving wing.

Hector feels a fresh chill at the prospect of becoming trapped on this island through the palpably looming winter months—possibly confined on this island with Tommy's presumed killer.

Even with a potential hidden assassin subtracted from the mix, Hector can't envision "wintering" months on this rock.

He's far too much the rambler.

Hell, even as a child, Hector abhorred boundaries. It's too true what he told Verity earlier—Hector has a rover's unquenchable disposition.

She saves him an awkward question with a head bob over a shoulder and offers, "We're on the very last point, this side of the island. My folks lived down a similar drive, about half-a-mile down the road, but across the street. Same as a world away, in a sense. But, they're both passed anyhow. About a year ago."

"I'm so sorry to heart that."

A mere year? That timing: Hector knows from wrenching experience that loss is still fresh enough to hurt plenty.

He looks around some more. "This place is all yours?"

"All mine," she confirms. "I love it. Or for at least three months a year, I do. Maybe five, during a mild-weather year."

"It is very beautiful. I love it, too."

He truly does, or at least his vision of what it must be in the better spring and summer weather. He says, "But winters? They must be almost a nightmare. Truly doubt I could tough it out for the long-haul."

They kiss again. She's the aggressor, once more. Verity uses her tongue again, quite knowingly.

Hector intuits it best to let Verity relax all further boundaries between them. It's hardly a sacrifice as she not prudish or bashful in the least. He relishes watching this sensual, but too-long confined and cloistered woman cave into her cravings.

Might that be the very essence of their next few months together if they come off as Hector has planned? His continued marveling at and savoring of Verity's introduction to the wider, wilder world?

For the first time in longer than he can almost bear to admit to himself, Hector has at least a mid-range plan for his life outside of the daily, driven writing that dependably distracts him—keeps him tethered to a wicked world robbed of Brinke Devlin.

After kissing her deeply again, Hector whispers in Verity's ear, "This year's icy blast, I pledge again, you'll be spared enduring. I'll even help you close this place up for the season. Batten her down. Do that with real relish. Then we'll spend the coming winter chasin' the warm sun, close to the Equator. The Great Blue River—that's what some down my way call the Gulf Stream."

"But are you really serious about traveling together like that? Even to Europe? Really?"

Verity looks at him again like it might be a cruel joke, or a flighty promise on which he might too-easily renege.

"With all my heart, darlin', I swear it's so." Hector says with a little smile, "Promise that with my head and my heart."

"Yet we hardly know one another," she says.

But then Verity adds, "Though I suppose we have a while in the hours ahead to see if we can endure one another's company for more than a single rainy afternoon. Tell me, please. How do you like your eggs, Mr. Lassiter?"

Hector's delighted by the promising, passionate phrasing in that oh-so loaded question.

"Sunny-side-up, as you know because of your day job. A perfect breakfast includes just those sorts of eggs, bacon or ham, home fries and killer black coffee, just like you gifted me a few hours back. Maybe freshly squeezed orange juice if it's remotely doable here. And I can even help with all that. I would relish doing it all for us. I like makin' breakfast."

He searches her eyes. "But you're under no obligation to make that breakfast or for us to even do that together. You just drop me at the hotel later and—?"

"Under no obligation," she repeats, cutting him off. "You're a writer, so you know more than almost any other that words mean things. I don't have to do anything. You're right. Under no obligation. None at all. I surely know that."

Her fingers trace his lips; jawline. Verity says, "But I want to, Hector. I want tonight with you. And I want it like that. And I so want that wonderful, oh-so-long trip you've promised me. I crave all of it. More than pretty much anything else in this world I've ever wanted."

She presses pulsing palm to his cheek. "And I frankly crave something else from you, too, Hec."

Despite his mounting affection for her—and certainly his swiftly escalating lust to bed her—there's this flutter in his gut.

"Whatever I can do, of course, I will," he says with thinly masked trepidation.

Her fingers go to work at his damn cowlick. Hector thinks of all the ones who've tried and failed to tame and been bested by that thick and stubborn lank of stray hairs.

Verity says, "All these wonderful places you've promised me? I must believe they're full of memories for you, just like Key West is, as you've already confessed. Some of those memories are probably quite painful."

"Can't deny it, particularly having pretty much already conceded it so," he says. "Covered a lot of ground in my time. Maybe too much."

"It's okay," she says. "We'll make new good memories everywhere we go. I sense it's an honest aim of yours in all this, and I'm happy to oblige. But I need one thing more from you. I believe you think I'm some kind of locked-away innocent. But that's not so. Not exactly. At least not the innocent part."

"I actually think you're an old soul," he says carefully, not sure where she's headed or maybe even on the verge of potentially confessing.

"Maybe older than even you can imagine," she says. Her teeth tease her bee-stung bottom lip.

He kisses her first this time; their most passionate kiss yet. He closes a hand over her breast. Panting, she presses it there harder with her palm, also urging him to massage her with his other hand. He does that; savoring the heat and force of her body's striving against his fingers between her thighs.

Close in, he whispers, "You said there's something else you want from me."

He braces for it.

"Yes," she says, playfully biting his chin. "You actually touched on it already. It's simply this... for now. I know you're widely traveled. But in this time we'll share together, you have to promise to make a point of going to at least a few places that are brand new to you, too."

Hector intimately caresses her, slower. Harder. He murmurs, "Yours is surely an old and knowing soul, as I said.

Yes, Verity, I can well promise you that. Something I'd love to do, in fact. I've always been an explorer. Often wonder why I even still own that Florida house."

Nodding at her place, he says, "This island's brand new to me, for starters. That beautiful little house yonder? Certainly somewhere I've never been. How about if we start making my new memories, right there?"

Hector points at a random window of her distant house.

She closes one eye and views along his index finger like it's a gun sight. "You're pointing precisely at my bedroom, Hec! Must be fate? Unless you're maybe gifted with second-sight?"

Verity kisses him fiercely. Now her hand is between his legs.

She says, "Yes. Let's start making those memories. In that very room. Let's do that now, darling."

8
THE NEWSHAWK

It's an hour before dawn. As is his custom, Hector rises early.

He writes longhand in a small pocket notebook for an hour, then dresses and prepares breakfast for two.

The scent of the sizzling bacon, the eggs, and the aroma of the strong black coffee he's brewing in a second frying pan—coffee he prepares trail-style, hearkening back to his Punitive Expedition days chasing Pancho Villa—spur waking-up sounds from the bedroom.

First there's the squeak of bedsprings. A brass headboard groans. Then there's the sounds of a deep yawn and a shower's spray.

Verity appears just about the time he's ladling eggs and still-sizzling bacon onto twin plates.

Her naturally wavy hair is damp again. It will stay shades darker 'til it dries. She's wearing a short flannel nightgown and big, warm woolen socks. Otherwise, she's showing a lot of leg, bronzed and freshly shorn of the nearly invisible blonde down he felt under his passionate caresses last night.

There's even an adhesive bandage where she nicked her knee with a razor. She gives him a sheepish grin, says, "If I'd known where we were headed last night, I'd have taken care of these sooner."

He winces at her nicked knee, says, "Hope it was worth it. 'Cause your stems were already past sublime. You were plenty perfect before."

"Oh, yes, it surely was worth it," she beams. "Or will be. You are worth it. And you better be again. But only after we eat. Unless you maybe have better places to be this stormy morning?"

"I'm precisely where I want to be." Hector passes Verity a plate.

Her nostrils flare a shade. "Smells delicious." She pours herself some coffee, sips. "This is how you like it? Really? This might raise the dead."

"A desert-acquired taste. How me made it back when we were chasing General Pancho Villa, the so-called Lion of the North, across Mexico. Coffee made in a skillet. Consequently, extra strong."

She opens the icebox and uncaps a bottle of milk. "Please forgive me. I'm still fond of my stomach." She dilutes the pitch-black coffee to butterscotch brown.

"Like I said, an acquired taste damn few have acquired." He takes a seat opposite. He's having his java bitter and black.

"I was more than a little thrown to wake up and find you gone. At least until I smelled all of this."

So, she missed the fact he left far earlier, to write. It's going to come up eventually, Hector knows, probably sooner rather than later, so he says, "Didn't leave, as you can see."

Hector takes her hand briefly and squeezes. "I'm an early morning writer, when at my best. Typically go about five to ten in the mornin'. If you sleep in, you'll likely find me back in bed, spooned up against you as the Florida heat sets in after the usual Key West morning showers. Be like I never left our bed."

Our bed.

Well hell. He means it. Goddamn if he doesn't.

"Sounds a dream, Hec. So's waking up to this scrumptious breakfast."

Verity rakes nails across his unshaven jaw. "I'll see to the dishes. You shower while I do. After breakfast? We'll fetch your bags. I can save you hotel costs while we're here on South Bass. Unless of course you want—you know—a little more freedom? Places to roam closer to your writing desk? It's not like I have a fully stocked bar or live music like the hotel, of course."

Hector scoots his chair around; leans in for another lingering kiss.

"If that's really a serious offer, I'm moving in with you, pronto," he says after. "But only if it won't hurt you with the townies. We can ride into town together in the mornings and you can drop me along the way somewhere far enough from your workplace for appearances' sake. As long as I have a notebook, pen or pencil, and walkin' 'round money, the wide world's my writing den. I'm not like stunted, superstitious writers who need the same chair, the same desk, or a certain kind and number of pens or pencils laid out to stir my muse."

Hector's pale blue eyes flare. "And, you can trust, I'll be doing so much more than just consigning words to paper. If Tommy and all these others were indeed murdered or pushed to self-destruction? The son of a bitch did it? He or she's going to pay, all the way up. Then they'll pay plenty more."

Hector takes her hand, raises her wrist to his lips and kisses.

"I'm a writer," Hector confesses. "If revenge can indeed be made an art, then I bring a level of creativity to that task wholly my own. One well beyond that of the humdrum tribe. I'm a crime novelist. I'm patient. Diligent. A plotter in the truest sense. Studied in the art of revision and honing a sentence or paragraph into a dagger of the mind. I will never stop seeking who killed Tommy. When I'm sure who it is, I'll bring to bear every darkly creative spark within my grasp in that moment to shape an end to the person or people who killed our Tommy that will exceed any misery Tommy experienced and I will do all that with unfathomable, exponential degrees of inflicted suffering unimpeded by even a flicker of compassion."

Solemn-eyed but shivering, Verity says, "I believe you, Hector. I utterly do. But how are you going to set about this bloody task?"

Hector sips his bitter, trail-style java. He recalls suddenly it was Tommy who taught him how to prepare coffee in such a manner—to prepare it right.

After a bitter sip, Hector says, "Krutch seems right enough a place to start as the weather's clearly intent on stepping up her game and he's on my extremely short list of suspects. So, I need to be fast, too. No way the two of us are getting stuck here on this rock with Tom's killer for the winter. If time doesn't favor me getting Tommy's killer this season? Then I'll strategically retreat. You and I will run, together. Let the devil take the hindmost of those left on this cursed island. I'll bide my time. Seek justice at a time and place of my preference."

He hesitates, amends, "That said, legally, they do have to make at least one more ferry or steamer run here-and-back, don't they? By law, don't they have to do that?"

Verity's tongue teases her lips. "Sorry, darling. Not sure about that. It's more of a moral than a lawful thing, I suspect. A matter of conscience on the part of the ones running the ferry lines. Who'd want the guilt of cutting seasonal workers or tardy-to-leave tourists off from their families for months, or maybe, forever?

"And there's still plenty of provisioning to be done for those aiming to stay on," Verity says. "We're lucky it was a pretty dry summer. Otherwise? There might be flooding on top of everything else to cope with, presently. There've been occasions this time of year when most of the island was cut off even from other parts of itself by flood waters, and so winter provisioning doesn't happen properly. Makes for a desperate and even potentially deadly few months for many until the ferries resume crossings again in the spring."

"I was browsing over a picture book from your library," Hector cuts in. "Photographs of these ice boats used during winter sports in these parts. You could get out on one of those, couldn't you?"

"If the ice was thick enough, maybe," Verity says. "If the ice was smooth. But more often than not? Gale winds sweep across the lake. They drop the temperature, fast. When that happens, waves are literally frozen in time. Then you can't even safely or easily walk across the frozen lake. You can't possibly stand up on the ice, let alone try to traverse it. But if it was flat and thick enough, we might even drive this car to shore. Maybe do that all the way to Sandusky or Port Clinton. About once every five years, you get a freeze like that. When it happens, they mark a safe path. Usually about mid-February it comes. But it's such a rarity, Hec. Nothing to pin hopes to. A scary drive to make, too, always fearing the ice might give way under you."

Hector curses vulgarly to himself.

Middle February?

As Hem would say, *Too bloody fucking long.*

Perhaps subconsciously, Hector finds himself mimicking the look of a native islander as winter further charges in.

He purchases a cheap, island-knit black fisherman's sweater with black leather patches at the elbows he pairs with a black T-shirt and gray flannel work pants. He stows his dress shoes in favor of the battered, ankle-high black work boots he prefers when not in a sport coat or something more formal.

Before returning to the island's last functioning hotel, Hector took Verity up on her offered shower, but resisted offered use of her razor. He's been down that bloody route enough times to know any lady's razor often as not leaves a man's face looking like a crime scene.

He checks out with the hotel clerk; stows his bags in Verity's locked Ford for the eventual trip back to her cottage once her shift ends.

The rain's stopped for the moment. But the sky? Still gun-metal gray. And the cloud ceiling? Oppressively low.

Hector ducks into the hotel lounge, curious whether Krutch might be loitering there again.

Coming up empty, he crosses to the park with its ancient black cannons pointed toward the bay. Hector next ventures onto the ferry dock to see if Krutch might possibly be there. Perhaps to meet some other boat, coming or going?

Again, no.

Hector wanders back across the park; heads back to the police station.

Chief Parker knows little enough about Usher Krutch.

The cop allows Krutch is a suspicious enough candidate for a "possible perpetrator," as Parker puts it. Superficially, that scar on Krutch's forehead doesn't make the man seem any more innocent.

Nor do frequent trips to notorious Ohio mob towns including Cleveland, Youngstown and Toledo.

Parker admits all that, even as he spikes Hector's coffee with a dash of proper and potent Canadian whiskey, smuggled in across the Great Lakes.

But there's no real evidence, circumstantial or otherwise, to support any of his suspicions, Parker also concedes.

Hector's in fact about the only person other than the chief to express any out-loud doubts about Krutch, however tenuous.

"It sure feels like there should be something there," Parker laments. "Gawd, but it does. But so far, I can't even figure out where Krutch hangs his damn hat, nights. Not sure he even has a base on this island. Every question I put to hotel managers comes up empty. My best guess is Krutch has either quietly bought property through some phantom business titling, or else he's holed up in one of the island's unknown numbers of bed and breakfast places."

The cop sips his hopped-up drink, hazards, "Or maybe he's on some adjacent island, come night? If he's coming and going on each day's first and last boats, Krutch might even be on the mainland, somewhere. You know? As night falls? Say, Sandusky? Port Clinton?"

Hector flares up a cigarette. Through a haze of smoke, he says, "You get a lot of suicides or strange deaths in either of those cities? If not, I'm doubtful of the murderer—be he Krutch, or some other—calling either of those places home."

"No deaths like the ones here," the chief says. "I've checked. My other problem? I don't have so much as the blush of an excuse to justify putting even mild questions to the son of a bitch. Any kind of unofficial fishing expedition might send Krutch into full flight."

"Then expect the best option is for me—wholly unofficial type I am—to ingratiate myself more directly," Hector says. "Come at him socially and go from there, yeah?"

Hector expels twin streams of smoke into the light hanging above and between them.

"Trick may be finding him again," Parker says.

Hector shakes his head. "Have this suspicion he'll find me." Hector weighs that further. "If not, if Krutch is some kind of roaming sadist and repeat killer, then regardless of inscrutable, presently unfathomable motives, he should certainly be where people can best be found—places rich with targets of opportunity."

That should necessarily focus most of Hector's search on the main commercial strip fronting the park and, beyond there—around the bay and its boat slips, he figures.

Hector first wanders downtown bars, then restaurants. Lastly, the increasingly empty hotel lobbies along the strip.

Soon enough frustrated, he turns to tourist sites. Hector visits various commercial caves and gem caverns. He drifts through their attendant gift shops, though they seem decided long-shots with tourism petering out so fast, and considering the kind of time it would presumably take to finesse a just-met man or woman in such a place into snuffing out their life.

The police chief seems skeptical that latter scenario really describes what—if anything—has been going on with Krutch or whomever is maybe triggering the island's suspicious deaths. The top cop is palpably dubious an emotional sadist could actually succeed in sowing seeds of mass self-destruction across little South Bass.

But crazy as it sounds, there is a precedent in Hector's admittedly rarified experience.

Not so long ago, Hector intrepidly determined to exterminate a cult of similar such maniacs in Paris. A clique of nihilist artists who'd succeeded in making self-destruction creative validation—a form of exceptionally bloody and ultimate personal artistic statement.

Maybe, like so many dubious European fads and vogues that eventually leapfrog the Atlantic, the *Nada Coven* and its bloody siren's song of violent, public self-destruction is tardily asserting itself in the Americas?

Tired of ducking in and out of soft speakeasies—increasingly wary some commiserating bartenders or vendors grousing about that same stranger in town, sneaking in and out repeatedly, yet never ordering drinks might make him for a Treasury or "dry agent" and so a candidate for a length of rope or weighted drop off some private boat's side or lonely pier—Hector gives up making his already twice or three-times repeated searches of such previously visited sites.

And the nearly-deserted tourist traps?

Christ's sake, if he has to endure just one more imploring postcard or mural emblazoned with the motto "Don't Give Up the Ship!" Hector thinks he just might have to eat his Colt—do that entirely of jaundiced self-volition.

Down a side pathway not far from the Roundhouse and his recently forsaken hotel, Hector spies a sign for the local newspaper office.

The one-man band newsman—a ferret-faced young entrepreneur named Marcus Trapp—helps Hector empty a flask of Canadian Club, then, with increasing and reckless good cheer, exuberantly opens his files and photo archive to Hector.

It proves to be a kind of dark and bloody goldmine.

There are twelve local potential suicide scenes by Hector's reasoning. At least seven of them by Hector's fierce reckoning are palpably staged.

Hector leaves the newspaper office with a sense of another casual but possibly useful alliance having been cemented. Hector now has the top cop, a key waitress and the town's newspaperman in his network.

If he bonds with tiny island's only local barber, he figures he'll have the rock's gossip chain well and fully secured. Craving hot coffee and a simple lunch, Hector ducks in out of the just-returned icy rain that keeps trying and just fails to become snow.

He's chosen an old pub whose warped wooden floor is strewn with peanut shells. Ceiling fans stir dangling strips of densely studded flypaper and kick around the island air that always smells of fish.

Hungover vagrants rise and leave park benches in DeRivera Park as lighting suddenly flashes across the lake, and low, deep booms of thunder rattle bottles behind the bar.

The quickening chilly rain sweeps in, gusting in driving sheets off the lake. A waitress rushes to close the door as the rain blows in so hard and deep as to reach the nearest diners and the drinkers.

Hector claims a high-top table, far from the lashing rain's reach.

At the table to his right, two old fishermen nurse alleged near-beers.

One of the men is dappled with brown blotches of the sort Hem romantically dismisses as "benign" skin cancer.

This codger, missing front teeth, lisps, "Tellin' ya, first *sh*now on the ground, and *sh*ticking, mind ya, by next week. I clo*sh*ed down the Lizzie May. Pulled her from the water la*sh*t night. Bet the ferry *sh*ervice*sh* pack it in even before first *sh*now."

A baleful look at his drinking companion. "Have I ever called it wrong?"

The other old man shakes his head in confirmation of his lisping buddy's chilling record of accuracy on such matters.

Hector thinks, *Christ! I've got hardly any time left!*

He emphatically does not want to spend a winter trapped on South Bass, even if it promises to be one spent mostly warm and tangled in the arms or gripped tight between the slick and striving thighs of Verity, who has already somehow proven pleasingly and enthusiastically worldly between the sheets for one with such extremely limited horizons.

The other fisherman sports an unruly crop of yellow-white hair. His face is deeply bronzed, but his wrinkled neck is white at its deepest folds.

This old lake dog says, husky-voiced, "Closed my boat down three days ago and—" he reaches across their peanut shell-covered table top and taps the other on the chest, "—and I'll go you two days better on that ferry closing this year."

This still more aggressive prediction punts Hector into a state of near panic. Goddammit! Hardly any time is left until he's surely trapped here.

Killer identified and brought to book or not, Hector figures he best soon get himself and Verity on one of those last ferries back to Port Clinton, or else face marooning for the full and claustrophobic winter.

He eats only half his sandwich and picks at a pile of homemade potato chips in a morose and edgy mounting sulk, washing it all down with half-flat Coca-Cola and staring out at the lake often, as though it might somehow suddenly start vanishing into a haze of blinding snow flurries and confining ice.

Gun metal storm clouds brood over the gray horizon.

The falling barometer and dipping thermometer draw more dire predictions from the freshwater fishermen.

Hector settles up and leaves before the old islanders can further damage his all-but decimated morale.

9
THE MONUMENT MAN

Collar up and head down, Hector steps into the icy storm that soon enough has his eyes tearing.

The boat slips located near the far side of the park seem about a third emptier than just an hour ago.

The summer people are commencing their swift exodus—the most intrepid stragglers finally fast fleeing 'til next spring.

Just as soon as the ferry operators detect their margins in a steady freefall, they'll surely give a scant twenty-four hours' notice—maybe thirty-six if Hector is really lucky—and promptly shut down dependable service until balmier spring weather asserts itself in April or, much more likely in Ohio in recent years, sometime in May.

After hours of stubbornly hitting the same stingy number of bars and hotel lounges, the island seems to Hector alarmingly smaller.

The last of the most-intrepid tourists wander his way, a sextet of middle-aged couples. All of them look fairly flustered. The women are wan and clearly deeply shaken as they fulminate under their wind-whipped umbrellas, held tightly in their respective, elderly husbands' trembling, white-knuckled hands.

One of the older women says, "Horrible! A horrid way to die! Nearly four-hundred feet up we were, the ranger said."

She shudders, pledges, "I'll never, ever get it out of my head. Seeing what was left down there. I'll never forget it! And that sound when he hit the ground? Not, ever! Oh, my God, but I need some good wine! No! I need good Canadian whiskey! A double. Neat!"

Her mates seem to agree it was suicide.

They even more heartily agree about finding real hooch to drown their memories.

Hurriedly, Hector takes a bead on the tower where a crew daily toils to finish work to the base after a construction cessation that kicked in circa 1915, or thereabouts. Or so he's read.

Suddenly, more than ten years later, it's seemingly some madcap rush to finish the damn job.

Hector half-runs, half-walks through sheets of cold rain toward the great gray spike meant to memorialize Commodore Perry, who famously—allegedly—implored his men, "Don't give up the ship!"

It isn't a particularly long distance to the tower, but the stretch seems to increase as the rain's pitch picks up. That's an unpleasant prospect for a man with no umbrella or a car—and no sheltering trees under which to take cover once he has left the park to cross the long expanse of open field to the memorial and what is suddenly a crime scene.

Three police cars are parked in front of the memorial—Model A's with law enforcement stars painted on their doors.

A couple of unfamiliar police officers and some presumed volunteers keep at bay a sparse number of soggy gawkers.

Construction workers and state park rangers hold up sodden sheets, trying to obscure view of the remains of the deceased as cops go about their work of scraping up the leftovers.

Chief Booth Parks spots Hector as the rain gathers greater intensity.

The top cop gestures to approach with two fingers, leading Hector into the interior of the monument, out of the needle-sting rain.

Hector's grateful for more than the simple shelter. He has a terrific fear of heights. Just looking up at the top of Perry's Monument, even from below and squinting against the rain, set his stomach to fluttering and knees trembling.

Inside the monument, Hector's more himself. He observes a total of four opposing entrances lead to this common, vaulted chamber. Under the floor are buried the bodies of sailors from either side of the war who fell in battle.

"How'd you already hear about this, Hector?" The top cop's voice reverberates within the gray stone chamber.

Hector waves a hand. "C'mon? When you die this way? Swan dive off a public monument on this postage stamp island? Word spreads muy pronto, Chief. Caught some tourist chatter from alleged witnesses to the deed."

"Well, there you go again . . . ."

Hector says, "What a terrible way to cash out. What was left of the poor son of bitch?"

"Nothing we can lift. I'm going to go topside directly and look around in a minute. Come along?"

"Oh, Holy Jesus, no," Hector says. "Goddamn hate heights."

Parker nods. "Got that sense. Figured I was seeing you get vertigo lookin' up at the top on your approach. Your Florida tan vanished for a bit. You walked like a drunkard."

Hector asks thickly, "Who exactly is dead?"

"Not a tourist," Parker says. "Lonnie Cap. Island's only barber. His wife took the boys and left on the first morning ferry to winter at her folks' place in Des Moines. Claimed she simply couldn't take another winter stuck here. Said another cold spell on South Bass would find her putting a gun to hers, and to their children's heads. We found her note in Lonnie's pocket. Guess he just couldn't face a winter without his family. And, of course, he couldn't follow and lose his livelihood. Who can really fault him for any of it in the end?"

Yet, the chief sounds skeptical about the cause of Lonnie's apparent suicide.

Rightly or wrongly, his family certainly will dismiss the dead man for a weakling, Hector figures. And so much for the possibility of adding the local barber to his network of spies.

Parker says, "Not much left to share at this point, Hec. May know more, later. You want a lift to someplace? You could probably ride in the ice wagon to the doc's downtown with the body if you're not squeamish about that sort of thing."

"Maybe." Hector says it doubtfully, far more inclined to loiter for an eventual ride back with the chief.

Booth points at a uniformed officer. "Yeah, I wouldn't want to accept that lift, either. That officer's name is George Samuels. Tell him I promised he'd see it done if you asked for a ride back in one of our cars to wherever you want to go."

Parker shakes Hector's hand, says, "Heading up now. Sure you don't . . . ?"

"More than certain." Hector turns back toward the rain, brooding on this stranger's last terrible seconds—hundreds of feet of free-fall, then that unimaginable slam against the unyielding concrete—bone pulverizing and organs bursting.

He wonders if you do indeed stay conscious all the way down.

Probably it's so, the cynic in Hector's inclined to believe.

A chilling prospect, all its own.

Hector also wonders if the dead man's wife and children have been caught up with? Delivered word about what their abandonment has apparently precipitated?

Will the barber's widow feel at least an inkling of guilt?

When the kids get older, and learn of the thing Mommy chose to do that seems to have tripped Daddy's tragic trigger, will they turn on her?

Will the kiddos possibly nurse a resentful grudge 'til Mommy's own demise?

Of the island suicides Hector has studied, this one seems on surface to possibly be the most likely to have occurred without assistance or to have been provoked by some sinister, outside force or particular figure of dark intent.

Before he steps out into the rain, Hector shakes out a cigarette, fires her up.

A new voice inquires, almost mockingly, "Tragic, yes? A terrible, even ghastly way to die."

The voice is half-familiar but slightly distorted, echoing as it does off the vaulted ceiling and all the stone. Yet, Hector can tell the voice is coming from behind.

The hardboiled novelist in Hector fires off a glib remark even before he can turn to see the voice's source.

Hector says, "Short of dying in your sleep, is there truly any good way to go, old pal?" Then he flinches to see Usher Krutch standing there, even though Krutch's identity was half-consciously anticipated.

Krutch is silhouetted in the entryway opposite Hector. Hard rain falls at his back. Mister Krutch crosses the antechamber with echoing steps to stand close by Hector. He eyes the novelist's cigarette.

Taking the hint, Hector shakes out a fresh smoke from his pack. Krutch thanks him, then lights the coffin nail with his own kitchen match. Krutch flings the spent match into the rain. It lands in a puddle with a sizzle.

"I've learned some more since we last stood somewhere, staring off through just such a rain," Krutch says. He smiles, and when he does that, for the first time, Hector realizes the man's writhing facial scar suggests a wriggling leech.

A memory: That last time at the hotel, and the damp screen ringing the porch. This man with his pale, wormy scar above his wandering eyes, carefully and deliberately torturing storm-ravaged dragonflies.

Wreathed in a halo of blue-gray smoke, Krutch says, "It's Lassiter, isn't it? Hector Mason Lassiter? The author, yes?" A wicked smile. "The crime novelist?"

"Yes, and yes," Hector says reluctantly. Hector doesn't offer a hand to shake and in fact shoves his dominant right hand—his non-cigarette hand—into his coat's right pocket, wrapping his fingers around the taped roll of nickels in there. "What brings you here, of all sorry places, Mister Krutch?"

A frosty smile, then smoke out both nostrils. Krutch says, "Probably the same thing that brought you here. Intimations of tragedy? But now I've seen same as all there is to see. I'm heading back downtown, directly. Take you for a ride, Hector?"

Surely this man must know how that last question's loaded phrasing resonates for a crime novelist.

Or perhaps not. Either way, Hector smiles, says, "That'd be swell of you."

They step into the storm that's still dampening a recently poured expanse of concrete.

Hector squints in the rain at the pavement. He frowns, and then Hector shivers.

There are what appear to be fresh hoof tracks in that newly-poured concrete—prints of cloven hooves.

10
THE RIDE

Mister Krutch gets his car in gear. "The Park is your hotel, yes?"

The rain peppers the bug-sprayed windscreen.

"That's right," Hector lies. "Only hotel now still up and running. Buy you a coffee or some tea there? Payment for the lift back in this damn monsoon?"

"Kind of you, yes. I would quite like that. I'm fascinated, I'll confess, to hear more about the writing life. Took me a time after our introduction to remember exactly why your name rang bells. Feel like I might have a story—a book—in me. But I wager you hear that a lot."

Yes. Oh, Christ, yes. If he had a goddamn nickel for every time? But instead, Hector lies, says, "No. Hardly ever."

"You're just being polite," Krutch says. "I've known a writer or two in my time. So I fancy I know what the writing life is like, in key ways. And I know how few lives that are lived by other than artists and fiends are honestly compelling."

Artists and fiends?

Honestly compelling?

Hector shakes his head. "Hardly. Every life is a story of some sort, in the end. Take that one back there that just ended in blood and, presumably, in final and abject terror. But what were you really doing there? Surely it wasn't just grisly interest—not in this weather. Word is, you're some kind of businessman, though I confess I haven't heard a specific trade named. Anyway, I would have thought you'd have gotten the tourist traps and the island's biggest landmark out of the way in your early going. I mean, as much time as you seem to spend around here, according to locals."

Hector eyes the interior of the car. It literally looks lived in. So far as he's noticed, rental cars aren't an option on South Bass. He's convinced this must be Krutch's own car.

Maybe it ferries over, each morning and night, just as Chief Parker theorized. Maybe it's Mister Krutch's mobile bed?

Or, maybe it stays on the island somewhere? Perhaps in an overnight ferry-affiliated parking lot, just like the one now housing Hector's Chevrolet, far across the troubled lake?

Hector sniffs. Krutch's Ford is rank with the stale stench of cigars. Hector measures his memory against the odor of cigar smoke that drifted over to his room from the scene of his neighbor's presumed suicide.

Could surely be the same, Hector decides.

"Oh, I heard about the tragedy and felt compelled to look, despite the rain," Krutch continues. He stares straight ahead through the rain-streaked glass, hands steady on the wheel. "I assume that's your reason for visiting, as well. I mean, what other reason would you have? We all savor a gruesome rubberneck as we drive by a crash scene, much as we like to kid ourselves we don't, yes?"

Hector nods. "Can't deny it's so. It's that old and sorry side of human nature, I reckon. But in my defense, you must also consider my trade. For me, it's a kind of research for the books I write. Visiting crime scenes, I mean."

"Crime scenes? But that at the tower was a suicide, I heard."

"Self-murder isn't a crime?"

Mister Krutch shoots him a smile. "Now you're getting philosophical. Confess, I'm just not that deep a thinker, Hector."

"What is your trade, if I might ask you directly, Mister Krutch?" A smile, "Seems only fair as you seemingly know my occupation."

Krutch's tone suggests boredom. "Investments, more or less."

"Stocks, say? Life insurance?"

"Closer to the latter. But I'm mostly retired. Already made my scratch, so to speak. It's all really drab and tedious stuff in the end. Paper shuffling. Particularly compared to what you do for a living, Hector—the life of the artist."

"Hell, I just make things up."

Mister Krutch isn't having that. "*Au contraire, Monsieur Lassiter.* I fancy a good thriller and first read one of yours in French translation in Paris. It was December of 1924. I was so pole-armed I sought out the original English version in February 1925, in a bookstore in Miami. *Rhapsody in Black*. I loved the original—the *English* version—far more. That French version? So much lost in translation, as the cliché goes. I confess I savor intrigue—from safe distance, of course—as much, if not maybe even more, than the next poor devil."

Krutch cranks down his window a further crack and flicks his nearly spent cigarette into the rain as he drives on toward DeRivera Park. "I was so taken, I actually traveled further south from Miami to Key West to try and meet you there. But you were away."

Lucky me, Hector thinks.

Krutch says, "I was reading *The Times* this past Sunday. Saw a review of your latest. Have you seen it?"

Hector hasn't. He knows his publisher's clipping agent will stubbornly rectify that in time, despite Hector's stern warnings not to send him book reviewers' clippings, be they thumbs-up or down.

Krutch presses on. "The reviewer did some digging and declared your novel is really rooted in fact. He says you live what you write and write what you live. Brilliant! Wonderful! And I expect you can get some hearty publicity mileage out of that little bit of fawning criticism, yes?"

Christ. Hector really needs to think about that one.

And goddamn that *New York Times* reviewer, whomever it was.

Hector somehow resists asking Krutch what the cursed book critic's overall verdict was. He says, "I rarely put stock in any critic's bloviating. Those who can write fiction? They do that. Those who can't? Some too often become imitations of critics. I make up plenty of my fiction, thank you very much. Anyway, who could truly live the stuff I write and long endure? In the end, it's just that all accomplished fiction writers are exceptionally practiced liars."

Krutch laughs. "Again, wonderful! Really terrific! And you said that last without a whiff of irony! You are indeed a remarkable creature, Hector Lassiter."

Krutch steers his Ford curbside; sets the parking brake.

They set off on foot for Hector's former hotel.

A sulky hostess seats them next to the front window where they can storm– and people-watch.

"Obviously, the tourist season is all but over and thank God for that," Krutch drawls. "No more long waits for drinks and food. No more crowded sidewalks, thick with tipsy tourists. Elbow room, at last!"

Hector is at least partly surprised at the assertion. "Really? You'll be staying on here 'til the thaw? You mean to winter here?"

Krutch's left eye, the one Hector has all but decided is the dead one, wanders. "Oh, definitely. Frankly, I adore the starkness of this place in winter. Or I fancy I shall. Relish the prospect of this band of us, brothers and sisters, soldiering on together 'til winter's end. A shared test of character."

That makes chilling sense. If Krutch is some kind of mass killer, he can step up the intensity among the brave few who dare to winter on this isolated rock. Hector scowls. "Is that really what you would call it, Mister Krutch? A test of character?"

"Adventure might be the better and the right word, since you press. I relish the starkness of this place in winter. Or I tell myself I will. One never can know how one will respond 'til one must respond, after all. Isn't that your own experience, Hector? Don't you agree we discover our truest selves in deepest peril?"

Rubbing his jaw, Hector say, "Now you're the one going to the deep places. And, anyway, plenty in these parts seem to be faltering in the most bloody of ways. Doing that before winter even takes hold."

An arched eyebrow above a hard to read but very thin smile. Krutch says softly, "Indeed."

Krutch's smile turns feral. "We can agree the weather will really do little to change any of that? Rarely can depressed people be dissuaded from self-destruction. We are, like the stars, fixed in our courses. We delude ourselves we really have choices. Down deep, we know otherwise. God, after all, has His master plan."

Mister Krutch crosses his arms, leaning across the tabletop. "And you, Hector? Won't you be staying on through spring, too? I frankly savor the prospect of sharing this island with you. Soldiering together through this winter's certain to be fierce and icy blast. I relish sharing the adventure with you. To see the story that will inevitably result from our icy privation. The novel provoked from within the man who lives what he writes and writes what he lives."

"Afraid that's very much not my plan," Hector says. "I mean to be gone in a day or two, tops."

"Really?" Krutch scratches his chin with a polished, pointed thumbnail. "I confess sincere disappointment if that somehow proves out. Seems to me a writer—a solitary creature in the purest, most pitiless sense—would relish and savor the solitude for creative work promised by a winter spent here. Certainly, a devoted fan might expect one such as you would also relish all the plot complications ice-bound life on a remote island might afford a writer of thrillers, especially."

Hector shakes his head. "I have my imagination. I'm just a storyteller—the form of artistic expression an acquaintance rightly called the lie that tells the truth. I hardly need to spend a sorry goddamn winter here to fire my muse. Was born on the Gulf Coast. Galveston, Texas, to be precise. Survived a mammoth hurricane that same year. I came of age in Revolutionary Mexico. Survived that, too. Live much of my life now in Key West, as you noted. Neither place has ever seen a snow, so far as I know. I'm not too likely to set one of my books in a damn snowbound wasteland, precisely because I savor the sun. Love the fragrance of sun-kissed female flesh and the earthy, fishy scent around the docks. The smell of the ocean and her brine. Hell, even the aroma of all that damn suntan oil the tourists down my way seem to favor more each year."

A new waitress approaches: Verity. The ghost of her musky perfume evokes lusty memories in Hector.

She manages to conceal her reasonably-expected shock regarding Hector's table mate.

Hector requests black coffee, fairly sure to be disappointed in its intensity unless Verity takes an active hand in its brewing.

Krutch orders a glass of ice water. He persists, "You really don't mean to stay on, Hector?"

"Really, I don't," Hector says. "Speeding off here in a few days. Frankly finding there's just not terribly much research required for a novel on the Great Lakes bootleg wars and the Italian mob's efforts in that direction. Unless you somehow maybe know something I don't? Seems I came to the project with knowledge enough to craft the story I imagined. This trip has proven a redundancy, research-wise."

Hector accepts his coffee from a returned Verity. "As to where you'll weather the winter, I hear you might have a little place of your own here on South Bass?"

"An enterprise I live above, actually," Krutch says, sipping his ice water while inspecting Hector's face over the rim of his glass. "But I confess I had no idea anyone knew. It's up Catawba Avenue. Sits above a vast gem cave. It's mostly a side enterprise a flunky runs. You know—conducting tours?

Selling little bits of crystal chipped from the cave's walls? I live on the second floor, above the gift shop and museum."

"Folks say it pays to diversify," Hector says. "I should maybe work on that. Have all my eggs very much in one basket."

"A risky way to live, indeed," Krutch agrees. "One setback—" a sharp finger-snap "—and poof!"

For the first time, Hector notices the man's nails are unduly long—manicured to sharp points. "Then the wolf is truly at the door," Krutch says. "Then things become desperate. Rash courses of action inevitably ensue. Eventually, perhaps, even thoughts of self-destruction."

And so here they are again, toeing around the subject of suicide.

And Mister Krutch has brought them back to the somber topic.

Telling?

Hector thinks more about the sort of psychology that must spur a killer yearning to drive people to destroy themselves. A homicidal trickster, of sorts? A prankster sadist?

Hector glances out the window and his eyes seize on a dark vision.

A flock of motionless seagulls line the top rung of a park bench out front. The ivory birds stare at the two men, eerily still and unblinking.

There's something deeply unsettling to Hector in that sentinel avian-tableau. Something unnatural in the birds' fix-eyed gazes.

But Hector is decided: no guts, no glory. It's time to follow Krutch's apparent lead, doing so with icy calculation. He says, "All these suicides? You knew many of the victims?"

A frosty smile. Krutch shrugs. "I still must balk at the word victim being used to describe a suicide. Self-murder being a choice in the end."

"But you're the man who just a few minutes ago said there are no choices in life."

"Touché. I frankly think the planets rule us perhaps as much or more than God. I will concede I'm an astrology buff. You are a Capricorn, I believe. Just like our fabled Savior. Ambitious. Disciplined. Among the most determined of humans. And, as your classical, given first name indicates, a kind of anchor. You also value reliability and purpose as character traits."

Hector arches his right eyebrow. "And your Zodiac sign?"

"Oh, I grew up in an orphanage. No records of delivery. Nor of birth, alas. . . ." A shrug. "But yes, I daresay I knew all of them—these people you call victims. Though many I knew just maybe in passing. No pun intended."

Now Krutch contemplates the birds staring back at them. "A very few I knew rather more intimately. But, yes, to your earlier question, I daresay I was acquainted with nearly all of them, to greater or lesser extent. She's such a scant island, after all."

Hector sips his coffee, weighing next words. Seconds tick by.

Decided, Hector says, "What about Tommy Breck? Tommy one of the ones you knew intimately?"

Fresh interest sparks Krutch's gimlet gaze. "Thomas was somewhere in that gray gulf between a casual and intimate acquaintance. You knew Thomas, as well? In what context?"

"A very dear and longtime friend. Fellow combatants in the so-called Great War and elsewhere."

"Then I am very sorry for your loss, my young friend. I, too, have lost brothers while at arms. You came here to pay respects to your friend, didn't you, Hector? In addition to book research?"

"Sure. That's precisely why I'm also here."

Krutch says, "Apart from loss of hope or maybe because of some terrible disease Thomas might have learned he had—something painful and incurable, say—what other possible circumstances could there be involving his death?"

"Since you ask? The circumstances under which Tommy died are impossible," Hector says, blue eyes studying Krutch's far darker, deep-set eyes.

"Impossible?" It is clear from his expression that Krutch's interest has spiked.

"Utterly impossible," Hector presses on. "Tom's death was staged. It is, therefore, an obvious homicide scene. I'm convinced Tommy was murdered. I mean to find out who did it."

With the tip of a finger, Mister Krutch traces the rim of his sweating glass of water. The glass begins to make a strange trilling sound. Hector is struck by some nagging sense of frisson he can't lay claim to.

Krutch says, "Seem to recall the newspaper reporting your friend left a note."

"Best believe I'm far more attuned to words than most others because of my trade," Hector says. "Oh, it was Tommy's handwriting in that last note. That's for sure. But those were definitely not my friend's own words in that last letter. We corresponded, robustly. The voice was all wrong in that last note. But it's the way Tommy died that's the real capper, for me. That's the tell, to use a poker term."

Krutch claps hands, says, "Forgive me a certain awkward bit of delight, but this is just like one of your novels! And just look at you go! Rightly raging at your friend's bitter fate! Clearly hell-bent on avenging him. It's the very pulp novelist I've read so much about who draws on his life to inform his art, just as that *Times'* critic, Boucher, observed!"

Hector immediately balks. "This would never read like it lived. Not a lick. And anyway, whomever killed my friend appears to have lacked a critical piece of information about Tom that brought down his killer's house of cards. Gave lie to his suicide scenario."

"Still more fascinating," Krutch says. "What precisely was this tell, as you put it?"

"As arranged, Tommy's seeming suicide—" Hector slings some extra salt in his voice for that last word "—would have required accomplices. Even then, it never could have come off as presented."

"Elaborate on that, please." Krutch says it with equal parts fascination and derision. "What exactly was amiss?"

"Tommy was a survivor of many bloody and terrible campaigns," Hector says, meeting Krutch's unwavering gaze. "But the Great War? That melee cost Old Tom most of a leg. Cashiered Tom out of service for keeps."

Hector gestures at his own leg. "Tom left the military maimed. Yet he could still cut a straight and manly figure. Worked hard on masking any tell-tale limp. If you didn't know about his lost leg, you wouldn't *know*. But, you see, despite his agility on level ground, Tommy could never have made the climb his death by hanging required. Never have shinnied out on a timber to hang himself like a handful of fools now wrongly declare he did. Not in so-called real life."

Krutch says, "If you are right about this, his death still seems to me like something torn one from of your stories or books. And all the more compelling for that. Surely you must see that."

"Reckon we'll all see about all of that, and in short enough order," Hector says. "You've heard my story about Tommy. Tell me, how'd you and Tommy cross paths? You don't strike me as much of a fisherman, so figure it couldn't have been from a charter."

Verity picks that moment to freshen their drinks. Krutch winks; Verity averts her eyes.

Closely watching her fill his glass, Mister Krutch says, "I'm more of a fisher of men, maybe, if that's not too grandiose a way to put it. Or at least that was so when I was more at my other trade."

Hector prompts, "You and Tommy …?

"No angling for actual fish between us, you're surely right about that. More like partners in elbow-bending, now and again. I've a fondness, I confess even an occasional over-fondness for drink, as—and I apologize for my sorry state the other night—you have observed first-hand. Though I knew him not as well as you, clearly, I think you'll allow Tommy was rarely a moderate drinker."

True enough. A lonely boat's foghorn forlornly echoes across the park grounds. Hector abruptly catches himself focusing on the bewitching twitch of Verity's departing rump.

Krutch catches Hector in his lustful glance, smiles conspiratorially. "Lovely, isn't she? Quite possibly wasted on this drab, so tiny island. One sincerely hopes she finds a good and worldly man who can help her escape the sorry gravity of this rock. Two or three more years? Just a few more winters, lashing at her luscious ivory skin? I fear she'll be flirting with a flinty, weather-worn spinsterhood."

Absurdly unlikely.

Clearly correctly assaying Hector's mounting irritation—and further irritating Hector for the realization—smiling, Krutch says, "Our neighbors be damned. I demand a proper smoke."

Krutch snips the end from a cigar with a little handheld guillotine. As he prepares his cigar, Krutch says softly, "Presumably, you didn't know more of the island's suicides? Acquaintances, like Tommy, I mean. Yet, just as presumably, you might suspect foul play in those cases, as well?"

Now Hector leans forward on crossed forearms. "One might presume."

Of a sudden, there's something electric in the air between them. Something Hector can't quite define, but it is there. For his part, Hector feels painfully taut with the tension mounting between them. He winces at sudden spasms in his lower back.

Grinning, Usher Krutch is once again wreathed in a halo of rancid smoke.

Unable to meet Krutch's nasty gaze, Hector watches Verity far across the dining room, serving others. But her green-eyed gaze is very much directed back at him. She moves to the counter, beginning to wrap freshly washed utensils in black linen napkins, all the while maintaining her focus on Hector and Krutch as her hands go through the familiar motions.

"Presumably, you think these aren't crimes of passion or somehow driven by money motives, Hector?"

"There's no evidence to support either of those theories, except maybe a sadistic passion on the killer's part for control and manipulation," Hector says, striving now to look Krutch in the eye; not blinking. "Perhaps some ecstasy derived from driving men and women to kill themselves?"

Krutch taps the table with clicking fingernails. He says, "Dear Lord, your feral artist's mind! What a wonder it is to watch in its wild works. What a chilling but fascinating creature you've conjured! The rational part of me, the part that doesn't want to see more of my friends and neighbors driven under the dirt by such a devil as your storyteller's mind has whipped up is appropriately spooked by this figment you imagine."

Then Krutch shrugs. "By the same token, the tiniest sliver of me, the part that savors books like yours, thrills a bit at the notion such a fiend could actually stalk his way through this drab old world!"

Warming to that notion, Krutch says, "Confess I relish the notion of such a creature and you dueling across an icy wasteland like the one bearing down on the two of us. A dance of death with maybe two hundred stout, Midwestern souls in the balance? What a novel or moving picture that would make, eh?"

Hector fights an urge to take the man by the throat. His impulse is to throttle Krutch, bystanders paying witness be damned.

If Krutch is indeed the killer Hector imagines, this scenario Krutch is enthusing over is no passing fancy. It's more akin to an admission of dark intent or sinister mission statement by Usher Krutch.

In the moment, Hector again feels a decided urge to take Verity by the hand and run. Board the very next ferry to the mainland.

Bone Key: There they could idle away the weeks amidst sultry months of rum drinks, bowls of conch chowder and countless hours of Verity Chisholm, naked as often as possible, sprawled panting, spent and sweat-beaded in his Key West bed in after-glow.

Hector imagines her velvety skin moving slickly against his.

Mister Krutch stands and shallowly bows. "I'm frankly quite attached to myself. Wouldn't want to be talked into a noose or into downing a bottle of pills. So, no hard feelings, but I hope this scenario—this theory of yours—is only that, Hector. A dark fancy in no way wedded to reality. Now, to coin a phrase, I really, and in truth, must go and see a man about a dog."

Krutch offers no hand to shake before he takes his leave. "It's truly been my privilege." A lupine smile. "Do hope our paths cross at least a few more times over the next couple of days. Before you can escape from South Bass. Next time, let's do share a proper, or still better, an improper drink. And let's let that one be my treat."

"Let's do that very thing," Hector says evenly. He watches Krutch exit the restaurant. The now snow-rain mix has stopped, but probably only for a brief time, Hector imagines.

Krutch crosses the street in the glistening dark.

A man is standing in the wet grass under a presently unneeded umbrella. Krutch stalks toward the stranger at a fast pace.

In his other hand, the short, rather portly man indeed clutches a dog leash, at the end of which twirls and dances an increasingly frantic wire-haired terrier.

As Krutch draws much closer, Hector notices the dog grows increasingly still.

As Krutch stands before it, the dog bares its teeth in a sustained growl.

Animals—dogs, especially, Hector muses, *always sense the worst amongst us.*

11
THE GRAVE

Hector is momentarily startled as Verity slides swiftly into Krutch's vacated seat. "I'm on a break," she says. "Learn anything from that awful man?"

Hector turns his attention back to the street, but Krutch, the stranger and the dog have vanished. He looks left-to-right; back again. His vantage point offers a near end-to-end vista of the park.

It seems impossible the two men could cover so much ground, so quickly. Surely, the old-growth trees must be blocking his view of the pair?

He says dully, "Anything new, you mean?" Hector frowns. "Not so much. Just more like a vague sense of confirmation. A dance. Our Mister Krutch surely loves to front himself as the thinly-veiled fiend."

Verity considers that. Hector watchers her; feels a fresh urge to bed her.

Krutch is right about this much: Hector has to get this woman off this dab of rock and across that glacier-cut lake—get her out and into the big wild world where she can truly live and grow as the free spirit she's palpably if unconsciously raging to become.

Verity says, "You do still suspect Krutch?"

Hector squeezes her hand. "More than ever."

Hector borrows Verity's car. Despite how much he loathes Fords, Hector rambles the rain-slicked streets in her heap until he sees the road sign for Catawba.

He signals a left turn to nobody and starts up the rising, sometimes dipping road. On the right, he sees a white building called The Casino. It promises a bar, restaurant, second-floor dance hall and, underneath all that, "Perry's Cave." The latter hid a freshwater source that nursed Col. Oliver Hazard Perry's men back to health after they were sickened by the lake's tainted waters.

Across the road, two more cave complexes are touted—Mammoth Cave and another promising a glimpse of the world's largest geode.

The "Mammoth" operation is more in keeping with what Krutch has described. But it looks closed, while the other two are still open for business.

There's no sign of Krutch's car around the Mammoth lot, either.

But there is another thing about the place that seizes Hector's attention: A dog leash dangles from a porch rail.

But no dog in sight.

Pull over? Park and poke around some more?

If Hector's caught doing that, it will make it clear he's coming at Krutch directly.

And unless Krutch is perhaps taking trophies of some kind from his victims, what can Hector hope to find? The very point of these seemingly staged suicides seems to be to hide the fact they are indeed murders.

Hector drives to road's end, turning around at a cliff-side dead-end. He doubles back. When he passes the Mammoth facility again, the dog leash is gone.

But there is still no sign of dog or a car.

Hector continues back toward the downtown.

The police station is on the left. Hector palms into its lot. He finds Booth at his desk.

The island's top cop pours two cups of passable coffee Hector presumes to fortify with splashes of whisky from a flask.

As he does so, Hector says, "Hope you're not gonna say something about being on duty, 'cause this is good and rare stuff. All the way from the Scottish Highlands."

The cop sips, thanks Hector with his eyes. He says, "Honestly? This is lately how I keep doing the damn job." He winces, holds up a hand. "I know. Not a sustainable strategy."

Booth takes another pull, says, "Still working on it, but I don't think that barber jumped off the tower. Despite early claims to the contrary, some tourists backed down on really seeing anything, when strongly confronted. So, no real eye-witnesses up top. The ranger was on the other side of the tower, so his view was obviously blocked. Despite the pulping the body took on impact—hell, I've still got guys with hoses out there mopping up because even all this rain isn't getting it done—we can tell the fingernails on both of the man's hands were broken, some to the point of drawing blood. I found scratches on the ledge that look fresh and filled with desperate intent to hang on there. There was also a shoe print on the back of barber's jacket. Right there at the small of the back. I'm fairly certain he was forced—hell, kicked—off the tower."

Hector is seized by images of winged insects flicked loose into punishing winds. He frowns. "If the man fought back, even tore his nails trying to hang on from falling, why didn't he scream to get the ranger or others' attention? Hell, I'd expect him to scream all the way down if his heart wasn't in the leap."

"Hell, me too," Booth says. "But his slayer slit Lonnie's throat first. Guess the killer also hoped a three-hundred-plus foot fall would cover that bit of carnage, just like that shoeprint. But it didn't. After all this was over, our mystery man or woman seems to have slid into an elevator. Somehow evaded or merged with the few tourists and history buffs braving the weather in and outside the monument. Hell, maybe he even stayed on. Stood among the gawkers, watching the aftermath of what he'd done."

The cop shoots Hector a look. "On that note, my fellas say you caught a ride back toward town with Usher Krutch, who was spotted there."

"I did get a lift from him, yes."

"Gutsy. What can you tell me?"

Hector describes the ensuing discussion and the precious little possible new information he drew from Krutch. He ends with, "You know this cave?"

Booth sighs. "Island is riddled with caverns, caves and tunnels, they say. A crazy honeycomb down there. Heard tell of maybe thirty or more caves you can actually stand up in. Even travel in a real distance if you're brave, have sufficient flashlights and know the paths. For the moment, most are probably packed with hooch and vino. You know, nature's natural wine cellars?"

Indeed. Hector suddenly craves a deep goblet of strong red wine. Something Spanish and very dry. Vino to dull and maybe even quiet his overplayed imagination and nerves.

"So, what next, Hector? You up to sticking around through winter to help me duel this devil? Surely would welcome the assist."

"Not sure yet what's next for me," Hector says. "But I swear I'm not spending winter here. Figure I have at best a couple more days to nose around before they burn all the boats, so to speak."

Something Krutch said suddenly ambushes Hector. "Where'd they bury Tommy? Occurs I'm past due payin' respects."

"Tommy's grave, it's in a private little old cemetery," Booth says. "Because it was judged a suicide, Lady of the Sorrow's couldn't touch it, or him, of course. Tom couldn't be laid to rest in hallowed ground."

Booth gives him directions. "Such as it is? Local fisherman took up a collection to pay for the headstone. Tommy's affairs, much as there were any of those, weren't so much in order at the time of his passing."

"Hardly surprising," Hector says. "Particularly if Tom didn't see his end coming so soon. Wars were over for Tom. Or so he thought. Let's try to stay in jiffy hailing distance going forward. Oh, and by the way, there's a man and his little pet terrier I think may have gone missing. I frankly fear for both of 'em."

Rustic. The charitable word Hector settles on to describe Tommy's gravestone.

Twenty—twenty-five years, tops—and Hector figures the weather will have made short-work of the letters shallowly carved in the headstone made of too-soft, down-market sandstone.

It indeed sits on seldom-traveled, unhallowed ground—not that Tommy, the embodiment of a lapsed Catholic—would care about any of that.

A check of his timepiece. Still an hour before her shift ends and Hector is to pick Verity up at the hotel. He wades through sodden leaves to her Ford; cranks its creaking engine.

Graveyards always seem forlorn to Hector, yet this one seems especially gloomy, giving way to weeds and bullying forest.

It would also be a dandy place to inter Tommy's killer, Hector decides. Hell, where better to stash a body than a derelict graveyard?

At last nearing the gate and passage back onto the road, an imposing, moldering tomb catches Hector's eye. Then it fills him with dread.

The name and inscription, worn to near illegibility above its rusted iron gate that bars the stone temple's door, reads:

Julius Usher Krutch IV
1620-1_ _ _
"Be sober, be vigilant;
because your adversary the devil,
as a roaring lion,
walketh about,
seeking whom he may devour."
—Peter 5:8

The date of death, Hector reckons, surely long ago eroded to invisibility.

Time crawls as Hector counts the minutes 'til he'll be reunited with his lover. Over a glass of non-lake red wine at the Roundhouse, he at last cracks the spine on Herman Melville's neglected, largely unknown novel, *The Confidence Man*.

But the book steadily stirs in Hector yet another ineffable sense of *frisson*.

Still, Hector reads on, having told the desk clerk where Verity can find him.

"Like Hawthorne on hop," Hector thinks, jotting off an unofficial and unsolicited blurb for the long-dead other author's lesser-known novel in fountain pen.

Verity's voice from behind: "My God, now Lonnie Cap has killed himself?"

"That's a bracing way to announce yourself, darlin'," Hector says, stowing Melville's book.

He slides over to make room on his side of the booth for Verity.

Lowering his voice, he says, "Lonnie was actually murdered. Throat cut and a boot to his back to facilitate his fall. But that's strictly 'tween us."

Hector frowns. "An extraordinarily courageous kill. Long elevator ride or stair climb up there, then back down, and so every chance to be noticed and later made as the perpetrator. So, I'm thinking the killer must not have gone up there with the actual intention of slaying that barber. Not in that place. Unless . . . ?"

Verity helps herself to his hardly touched wine. He gestures it's all hers; orders himself a whiskey soda. When it's just the two of them again, Verity repeats, "You said, unless…"

Hector repeats, "Unless he's addicted to risk-taking. Lord knows, he's sloppy and lacks attention to detail in others of his killings. If anything, they seem to be getting looser and louder. Killing on boats out on the water where you leave yourself little or no room for flight? Killing on the top of high towers that lure tourists like flies? That's courageous. Or reckless. Shall we call the latter thrill kills?"

Increasingly, Hector fancies he indeed faces a fiend in search of kicks and challenges—one who actually views killing as a game or gamble.

And the killer may indeed envision some mano-a-mano with Hector across a finite arena of ice-bound rock populated by trapped and increasingly paranoid and frenzied victims.

Hector drums fingers on the table in a fast beat. He takes the plunge. "Part of me thinks we should maybe be away from here tomorrow. Day-after at the latest. Cut out before the killer locks me in here for the winter with him."

Verity says, "You really believe Krutch is not only killing these people, but that he truly means to trap you here?"

"Bastard same as said so."

Hector recounts his discussion with Krutch; Verity hangs on his tale.

He finishes, "Going to toe-to-toe with a blood-simple psychopath across five miles of what seems to be near hollow rock? *Mucho* fuel for nightmares. Surely you can fathom that?"

She squeezes his hand. "Of course I can. And I don't think less of you for wanting to run away. I want us to run away, too."

Run away?

Hector suddenly can't get around that phrasing of hers. He immediately wishes she'd put it differently. Now he very much feels a coward.

Hector says, "It's not so much running away as biding time. Unless Krutch crosses the ice, he'll be contained here."

"Yes, of course. But contained here with people I care about, Hec. Far-fetched as it sounds, I'm afraid those who sail over on the first ferry come the spring might find an island of the dead."

Chillingly to Hector, that doesn't strike him as a far-fetched possibility.

He says, "Honey, this killer may or may not be increasingly reckless, but unless he's caught red-handed, your island cops are flat stymied. Krutch is already a soft suspect, yet can't be hauled in without risking a lawsuit for harassment or false arrest."

"Okay, then let's think about the other side of this," she says. "You've already made progress in just a day or two, Hec. You've all but directly confronted Krutch. He at least suspects that you suspect he is likely a killer. And now we know where he lives."

"And him knowin' makes me—and by extension, maybe you—still more the target," Hector finishes for her.

He quickly holds up a hand as she starts to speak. "Which is not the real worry, far as *I'm* concerned. It's a sadly familiar role, if you want to know the sorry truth. The bigger concern is I'm staying with you. I'm very much taken with you, too. So now I have two hearts for Krutch to target. You're likely a victim, if for no other reason than simple cynical strategy on his part. That can't happen."

Verity says, "But just a couple more days and you might have him, especially working with Chief Parker directly. The boats to mainland will run at least another week if the weather improves just a little. Just maybe even run for two more weeks. You know, Indian Summer? The snow flurries have been letting up almost two hours, now."

Hector smiles and strokes her cheek. "Yet the mercury continues to plummet. And I know a couple of local salts proud of past predictions who'd beg to differ on your timetable. They've declared two days, tops, before the ferry services stop dead."

"Okay, that might be a fair point from those sorts of sources," she says. "And I've been talking to Lou about you. Now I know far more about your life and reputation as a man's man. I know you would never run from a fair fight."

Verity closes her hand over his, stroking its back with her thumb. This look. He finally registers she changed her clothes. Doffed her waitress togs in favor of this fetching frock clearly designed for a night on the town. Glad rags.

"Trapped on the ice with a madman? Months waiting for him to maybe strike at you directly? That's too much to ask of anyone." She smiles and squeezes his hand. "Besides, you've promised me Florida and Texas. The Big Apple and Paris. Barcelona. I can hardly wait for us to start."

She gazes out the window. The sky is the color of an ugly bruise, blending into the lake. "It does begin to look like winter already. That's more like a January afternoon sky."

The more Hector thinks on it, the more he wonders at it. Jesus, how do these gritty islanders survive a winter on this little patch of ground, even absent a blood-lusting wolf harrying their fold?

Hector is freshly agog. And he increasingly realizes he might have to include some form of claustrophobia along with his fear of heights on his growing list of innate terrors.

Key West is tiny too, of course, but barring the occasional hurricane, the ocean is always an easy ticket out in any direction. Hector can put out from Bone Key in his boat to Cuba, to Bimini . . . to adjacent Keys or run up the chain of islands to wicked Miami to exercise his legs and libido.

Winter on South Bass increasingly suggests to Hector a kind of real prison sentence, even if Usher Krutch—perhaps the freshest generation to carry that family name?—is at last dead and buried in that half-ass Potter's Field across the island where Tommy and at least one Krutch ancestor presumably rot.

A vast ziggurat of lightning flashes over the marina and the hotel lights briefly flicker. An instant later, glassware and window panes rattle from the chasing thunder.

"There goes your improving weather," he says. "And maybe the power with her."

"I was going to suggest dinner and some dancing at the casino, but I think this is only going to get worse," Verity says. "I saw my car's out front. I hope you won't think I'm some kind of wanton, Hec, but I'd really just like to get a nice dinner-to-go and get you alone at my place. I especially want to do that if I might need to say goodbye to it soon. Can you cope with that? A quiet evening alone together? I have a phonograph. We can still dance and not waste...." A downward glance at her saucy dress.

Hector can surely cope with all that.

He says, "Sure, we'll just get a couple of menus and—"

But sudden icy rain and high winds keep them pinned down in the Round House, where they opt to eat their dinner rather than to take it to-go.

After another hour of intense precipitation at last abates for a time, Hector takes her hand, says, "We can't waste your dress on private dancing. Sorry I'm a little under-dressed, but we should still go to The Casino. At least squeeze in a slow dance or two."

Hector takes the wheel of her despised old Ford, circling around DeRivera Park, then once again heading up Catawba toward The Casino.

As they pass by Krutch's suspected base, Verity leans over for a better look through the rain streaked glass. "Dark and no cars... no dog," she says redundantly.

Standing in line to enter the dancehall, they overhear a greeter opine to another patron, "This Saturday? Absolute last crossing this season. Ask me, this might be the White Hurricane of thirteen, all over again. Figure soon enough, we'll have full ice and it'll lock in place through the New Year. Should I put you down for evergreen duty?"

Hector says softly to his island lover, "What in God's name is evergreen duty?"

Verity squeezes his hand. "They use discarded Christmas trees to mark the safest path for the ice boats you mentioned earlier. They race them, and even move some goods with them if the ice seems thick enough to bear the extra weight."

She runs fingers back through her rain-kissed hair. "Maybe we should be packing, instead of dawdling here. When everyone is saying the same thing—the weather is closing in like some hound of heaven—we're surely fools not to listen. Seems something dumber than stubbornness to deny it."

"Christ, don't get me started," Hector says. "I'd leave tonight if the ferries were still running' at this hour."

Hector suddenly sees the familiar vehicle hulking yonder. He nods in its direction, says, "Look over there, but subtle-like. That's Krutch's car. Makes sense he'd be this side of the street if he's truly what we think he is. Has to go where people are to find fresh pickin's, right?"

Hector sees no sign of Krutch standing in the falling drizzle with them. He lets go of Verity's hand, says, "In case he hasn't yet fully linked us, you and I can't be seen together like this by that man. You know that."

A tone of real disappointment: "So you're saying dancing is scratched?"

"At least in this joint," Hector says. "But there's an opportunity here, right now. I'm going to sneak in, make sure he's indeed in there, and try to do that without Krutch seein' me."

Verity scowls. "And if he is inside and doesn't see you? Then what, Hec?"

"You get in your car right now. Stay low, out of sight. Watch that door. Hopefully, you'll see me come out and cross the street to search his house. If Krutch comes out of this place, let him get to the far side of the road, then you give a couple of short blasts of your car horn to tip me he's coming. After you hit that horn, you best duck way down in case he goes looking for the horn's source. One other thing, Ver—I've stowed a gun under your front passenger's seat. It's my second, back up gun. It's ready to fire. Just cock the hammer and point her like a finger. Don't worry about aiming more than shooting for the center of the chest."

Wide-eyed, she murmurs, "I'm terrified now, you know."

A forced grin. "Me too. I'm going to step right into hell's own mouth over there, maybe."

"What if there is someone else hiding in there, Hector? Say, the man with the dog? A Krutch accomplice?"

"Look's far too dark. Too empty looking. I say it's a worthwhile risk with the weather clock running out on us." He manages another smile. "Don't worry darlin'. I do this kind of thing all too often. The man who lives what he writes, and writes what he lives, you know? That's what the critics call me."

His smile dies on his lips. "Or so I'm hearing of late. Not sure I trust the source, not even on that bit of silliness."

12
THE CAVE

Head down and shoulders hunched, Hector dashes across the street under stinging ice pellets.

He figures he has perhaps twenty minutes of useful natural light left him, critical light he's counting on penetrating unclean windows as he has no flashlight and can't risk using one if he did. Not with the owner of the house just across the street and positioned to possibly spot the flashing and splashing of artificial light behind dusty interior glass.

Hector skirts around to behind the house, losing footing a time or two on uneven, sodden ground—a kind of welter of small sink holes that perhaps intimate the crystal caverns of uncertain stability deep underfoot.

The backdoor has a simple lock Hector overcomes with a sliver of flexible metal retrieved from his sports coat's interior breast pocket.

If Mister Krutch really has anything to hide, he's surely doing it on the cheap in terms of security as Hector's simple shim easily pops the latch.

But the corroded hinges groan.

Hector winces as he eases through the narrowest crack he can manage. It's a crazy to risk with no flashlight and just this impulsive leap of faith he'll somehow actually hear a car horn's warning blast across this distance and the blanketing hush of the drilling-down rain.

But maybe if Krutch catches Hector in the act, Krutch won't shoot him as an intruder, Hector kids himself.

Instead, Krutch could simply strategically press charges.

And wouldn't that be the perfect trap?

Have Hector securely jailed as the ice locks around them.

Then drop those charges and see the author released for their ensuing duel to the death across an island winter. Or, Hector's eventual perceived suicide.

Or, maybe, the local authorities won't arrest and prosecute Hector for trespassing and burglary since he's been operating under veiled or at least implied color of authority in some respects these past couple of days.

Hector moves softly on boot-toe across an empty mudroom. All the while, he curses the creaking, badly bowed floorboards.

He finds himself in a combination kitchen-dining room, also devoid of furnishings.

Hector creeps around the first floor of the house, braving empty room after empty room, finding only cobwebs, mouse skeletons and the attendant stench of rodent decay.

There are no signs of use in most of this place; Hector's footprints are skin-crawlingly lonely on the dusty floors.

A flight of stairs invites, but the steps are also badly bowed, so there'd be no getting up there quietly.

Even more tellingly, there's a discouraging layer of undisturbed dust making clear nobody has ventured upstairs, not for many, many months, at least.

So much for Krutch's claims to be using the second floor as his living quarters.

Hector thinks he hears two distant horn blasts.

His already pounding heart steps up its spastic beating.

Dashing back toward the mudroom, he hears the outside bottom step creak under settling weight.

If Krutch notices the fresh footprints in the dust, Hector decides he'll rabbit punch the man into unconsciousness before he can be recognized.

The backdoor creaks open; Hector's hands are already slick with nervous perspiration. There's a tickling at his groin and underarms.

Hector's lungs already ache from withheld breath.

A moment's hesitation, then another door groans open.

That second door must have been obscured by the open back door in the confines of the tight little vestibule when Hector made his forced entry.

The creak of more stairs; the sound of these rotting steps descend into a softening echo.

Yes, Hector decides. The sound of the footfalls grow softer with each step. They are indeed headed downward.

With the cellar door open, a new odor reaches Hector—a far stronger stench of decomposition, and from something far larger than the stray dead rodent.

This smell irresistibly sparks in Hector horrific memories of the European trenches and stink of his fallen comrades rotting around him in the mud or suspended on barb wire strung across No Man's Land.

Shaking, struggling to tamp down his rising gorge, Hector counts twenty, then moves as slowly and quietly across the dusty kitchen floor as he can manage.

A cool rush of foul air hits him the face as he approaches the revealed staircase descending into the caverns.

Hector gags, despite himself.

A distant dangling light bulb barely illuminates the length of the staircase to its top where Hector now stands, trembling.

The bulb doesn't provide enough light for Hector to see the landing far below.

Hector believes he can hear low moans from down there.

But surely that's just his overworked imagination?

He squints down the stairs, braced to see a grinning Usher Krutch staring up at him, possibly leering over the barrel of a rifle.

Instead, the long and empty staircase yawns back at him, fading into gloom.

And, dear Lord, is that violin music he now hears?

It surely is. Hector places the piece. Giuseppe Tartini's "Violin Sonata in G minor."

Go down there? Hector can't bring himself to do that.

The smell of decomposition seems strongest from somewhere down in the gem caverns—now all but overwhelming.

How in hell can Krutch descend into that stench without becoming violently ill?

Fighting his rising nausea, Hector eases out the back door. Remembering the creakiness of the porch steps, Hector instead leaps onto the wet grass.

He lands slipping and sliding; almost loses all footing.

Outside now, with at least a single door between them, Hector tells himself he'll get away clean.

Blinking back a light hail, Hector breaks into a flat run, gratefully sucking in the bracing icy air.

He rounds the corner to the front of the house, gains the front yard and puts on still more speed.

Verity stands in the hail on the opposite side of the street, shielding her eyes and searching the gathering gloom.

When she sees Hector, she waves and then—and this freshly terrifies him—his new love frantically urges Hector to run faster!

Hector hears—or at least imagines he hears—the panting of some hound close at his heels.

Yet Hector is afraid to put on any more speed, fearful of slipping on the wet turf or of tripping or slipping in some sink hole and breaking an ankle or destroying a knee.

Now Verity is wide-eyed, frantically pointing at something behind him.

A shaft of light envelopes Hector. He instinctively freezes; turns.

Hector begins to move backwards even as he does so, realizing he's still in range of a shot from a long gun.

The light comes from a storm cellar door at the front of the house.

Silhouetted in the square of light is Mister Krutch.

After a terrible, derisive laugh, Usher Krutch calls out, "Now we see how it truly is! Go ahead and run, Hector! Flee like your life depends on it, you writer! But know it's impossible to hide from me on my island riddled with all her tunnels, caves and caverns. I might just pop up tonight in your new girlfriend's storm cellar!"

Hector's heart pounds.

It is open war between them now.

Realizing that, Hector doesn't care how it looks to Krutch or to Verity.

He lays on more speed as he races across the slick street, half-expecting the lightening-like burn and lagging thunder of a gunshot that doesn't come.

13
THE STORM

Verity drives as Hector, clutching his Colt, turns in his seat, watching for any pursuer.

"I was horrified when he crossed the street—on foot, mind you," she says. "He never went near his car which is still parked in the Casino lot. He almost ran across the street, like he knew something was up in his place. When I hit the horn, he half-turned, trying to see which car's horn honked. Then he really ran toward that horrid house. I think he instinctively grasped the horn blasts were a signal."

Hector just nods, dry-mouthed, yet soaked in sweat and rain.

"Maybe we should hide out tonight somewhere," she says. "I could park on an out-of-the-way private drive. There are hidden streets as I told you. One's only the most-knowing locals even realize exist. We could sleep in the car. Or, we could hoof it back to town. Check in at the—"

Hector isn't having any of that. "Would cost you precious packing time. Anyway, we can't be sure he even really knows where you live, right?" He squeezes her shoulder. "We have a gun. I'll stay up the night. Your coffee will see to that."

She shivers. "I knew this island was peppered with caverns and caves, just as he says. A real honeycomb. But it never occurred to me they might also all connect in some way. That they might open into crawlspaces or into root and wine cellars. Now I can't shake the image of Mister Krutch crawling around down in those holes like some murderous mole. Tunneling into and popping up in a basement or storm cellar and…?"

And…

And?

Yes.

Hector lies. "His threat surely can't be real about caverns actually stretching between your place and his. That's miles of cave to navigate in darkness even if it were so, and I'm sure it isn't. Hell, do you even have a storm cellar?"

"No. Not a basement, either."

"And that's to the good," he says. "Our other alternative is to pack fast and find some old salt to take us across tonight. Get our travels underway, pronto."

"Not a chance with this weather," she says. "We'll still find no takers, whatever the offering price."

The icy-rain pounds down as they turn at Bayview and Catawba. Hector points at the sign for a five-and-dime store. He wants to get some cigarettes and a couple of other items. These include a knife to back up his Colt.

He pledges to Verity, "Won't be more than two minutes. Think we're in the clear, but just in case, watch our caboose."

"You must know it wouldn't take that long for him to follow us down here," she says.

"It sure will if he tries to do it in his car," Hector says again. "I let the air out of two of his tires before I crossed the street to search his place."

Hector buys a couple packs of Pall Malls and a razor-sharp, eight-inch fishing knife with a cork grip and a bag of unshelled peanuts.

As he checks out, the clerk eyes his shops' flickering overhead lights. He says, "Ya maybe want a carton of smokes, instead? If I lose power, you lose cigarette access, bud."

"Nah. Leaving here tomorrow. Even I can't smoke 'em that fast."

The proprietor says, "Ya won't be leaving tomorrow unless you have your own boat. All ferry service is cancelled for at least two days for the weather—the weather we have right now, and what's still coming our way. That's official. Word came an hour ago."

The store-owner points out the window into total darkness with a crooked index finger. "Was a water spout seen just yonder there two hours back. You're lookin' at two more days at least before ferry service is up again. Sure you don't want that carton?"

Hector grimaces with an acid stomach; reaches into his pocket for his roll. "Reckon you have something there, after all."

Standing in her kitchen, nursing a glass of wine, Verity says, "Your worst nightmare's coming true. Trapped. At least for now, and for unknown numbers of days."

Hector just nods, says, "You really don't have a basement or wine cellar, right?"

"Now who's spreading fear and borrowing trouble?"

"A bad joke. Whistling past the bone yard humor. Sorry."

"Not funny at all, Hec."

Hector can't disagree. He says, "Sitting on the water's edge, even overhanging it a bit as your cottage does, I expect it's all solid limestone underfoot around your place. No hills around, so likely no connecting caves. Other than by boat, the only approach to your house seems that long path back to the main road."

Looking agitated, Verity studies him over the rim of her glass. "So, what next? We sit up in shifts with your old Colt and my loaner gun until the powers-that-be let a last ferry deliver us from here?"

Hector shakes his head. "I think we pack you up and ready your place for a season's shut down. While we do that, we just stay vigilant, within reason. At the risk of putting too-fine a point on things, here's how I figure it. If this man is innocent of what we think he's been doing, he'd already be here with Chief Parker in tow to press charges against me for trespassing. But he hasn't done that.

"On the other hand," Hector says, "he hasn't raced here for a last confrontation, either. I do think Krutch delights in throwing deep scares into people. And I think Krutch was very honest hinting he relishes playing a long game against me, for whatever reason. For now, Mother Nature and God seem to be in cahoots keeping me here, just as the bloody son of a bitch wants it."

Hector sips his wine, mind racing. "In other words, Krutch is in perfect position to bide his time."

"What is his long game, do you think, Hec?"

"Reckon it's his usual gambit, but stretched out still further. Trap me here for some icy dark months. Wage psychological warfare on me 'til I crack."

He sighs. "Confess, I am a bit hung up on that image you put out there of the first ferry arriving a few months from now. Her crew finding an island littered with corpses. Countless suicides. At the rate of two-or three-a-day, Krutch just might pull off that bloody feat before the ice opens up again. He might take out the whole population before Memorial Day. Can you imagine those headlines?"

"That's a horrid thought." She smiles softly. "And the worse for it because it was originally my vision."

Hector at last confides to her of what he smelled in the house—that boundless stench of something—a lot of somethings—rotting.

Ashen, Verity drains her goblet and holds it out for a refill. "We need cases of this stuff, I think. And you've ruined me for island wine with these European red wines, I'm afraid. All the local wine seems too pale and fruity now."

"'Cause they are. This island stuff? Swill." Hector pours her more true Spanish red.

"With wines, it pays not to hew to the lower shelves," he says. "Just falls to me to not jade your palate, but rather, too cultivate it. We've got entire countries of wine for you to sample ahead of us. The grapes of the world."

Her kisses her, savoring the taste of her mouth and the wine on her darting tongue.

"How about we get you out of those glad rags," he says.

"I thought we were going to dance?" But Verity's heart doesn't seem in it. And Hector doesn't want to risk burying the sound of anyone creeping around outside under music.

He smiles, fiddling with her buttons. "Nothing saying you have to be standing up to dance."

Her fingers grasp the bottom of his sweater.

They quickly strip one another. Hector carries Verity to her bed. As he kisses his way down her torso, she groans huskily, then lightly rakes nails down his scarred back. "You know I'm going to enjoy this more if your gun is in easy reach, Hec."

"Sound reasoning," he says.

Hector rises, padding back to the kitchen. Then he remembers his bags of unshelled peanuts—a singularly planned purchase. Hector slings the still-shelled nuts across the front and back steps. Naked, he circles Verity's secluded house in the drizzling rain, slinging peanuts under all of her windows, too.

His bag at last empty, Hector slides back inside and towels off with his discarded sweater. Colt in his right hand, he returns to the bedroom.

Verity's waiting naked atop the sheets, her curves accented by deepening shadows in all the right enticing places.

She says, "Second time tonight you've scared me with a too-long wait, Hec. You really need to stop that. What kept you?"

He gently sets his Colt on the side table beside her big and ancient featherbed. The bed's brass headboard creaks as he stretches out alongside her, a hand on her belly, tracing its curve to the shadow where Verity's thighs meet.

"What I was up to," he says, "was a last, peace-of-mind security check. Be damned if I'm letting all this spooky stuff get in the way of us now and here, like this."

Hector's mouth finds Verity's. With his knee, he gently parts Verity legs. She rises, arching her back to join with him.

Verity surprises Hector with certain requests growled in his ear; husky, urgent demands she puts to him between mounting groans.

Hector's also slightly more than surprised by several things she presumes to do to him.

Sometime around two in the morning, mutually exhausted and trembling, the lovers fall into deep and dreamless sleep.

For the first time he can remember, Hector sleeps through his usual early-morning writing hours.

The scent of Verity's cooking eventually awakens him. Hector rises; quickly showers and dresses.

A lingering good morning kiss.

As Verity finishes preparing his eggs—sunny-side-up, just the way he favors them—Hector slips out the back door to nose around.

Some of the peanuts have apparently been carried off or fretted over by the island's black squirrel population—empty and fractured shells abound far from where Hector originally strew them.

Of the remaining nuts he left scattered on the front and back steps? Conspicuously intact.

Moving around the cottage, padding from window to window, Hector finds much the same thing—the only evidence of the shells being disturbed mostly likely attributable to critters.

But then he reaches Verity's bedroom window.

While the shells there are largely intact, most are deeply embedded in the sodden ground, as if restless feet have ground down upon them.

Hector brushes the shells off the front and back steps. There's no value in further scaring Verity with thoughts of some potential Peeping Tom—or worse—whom Hector can do nothing about for the moment.

14
THE PRIEST

Sitting under the back-porch eaves, well out of the rain, watching the storm whip the waves, Hector says, "It's already a kind of torture just to see those other islands out there, so close, yet they might as well be the moon. Knowing you can't even reach 'em, let alone anything beyond. Have to admit, it is an intense storm. Not sure my boat back home would sustain against those waves and she's built for ocean travel."

Bundled up in a cable-knit sweater and pea coat—today and tomorrow she says are her days off—Verity sips coffee. She says, "It's too often the way with Great Lakes storms. They come up fast and are wicked fierce. They say that's again owed to the shallowness of Lake Erie."

He wonders aloud, "So how best to pass time, now?"

"Even if the weather permitted sight-seeing, you've pretty much seen all the worthwhile landmarks," she says. "Given what you've done to my body, I'm going to need time to recuperate. We can't spend all day and night in bed, heavenly as our time there is."

She strokes the back of his neck. "You were talking in your sleep last night, you know." She inquires carefully, "Who is Molly?"

Who *was* Molly would be the appropriate phrasing.

Dreaming of that other pretty, voluptuous blonde and in this setting?

Telling?

He says, "Molly was a young woman I knew in Paris a few years ago. She fell in with a wicked crowd. A kind of death cult. Killed herself. Straight up suicide, right off a pretty old Parisian bridge. The Seine was rarely and thinly iced-over that night. You can see why she'd be on my mind."

She hesitates, says, "You were lovers?"

How to answer that in any meaningful and shorthand way? How to explain what they'd fleetingly, intensely been to one another? There is simply no gracefully explaining that. Hector changes the subject. "There's maybe another solution to all this, you know."

"All this being *what*, exactly?"

"Krutch and his chameleon killings."

Verity pulls him closer. "Just from the tone of your voice, I fear I'm going to hate this."

"Me too. This thought I have, it's simple, summary execution. A strategic slaying, committed for the good of the community. I'm a veteran a couple times over, after all. Wouldn't be the first time I did society's sanctioned bloody bidding. Just another righteous campaign, in that sense."

Verity scoffs. "Crazy talk! Those other times you were in uniform. Killing under color of authority. You were under direct orders and I hope you hated what you were directed to do."

She stops touching him, instead wrapping her arms tighter around herself. Her teeth begin to chatter. "This thing you're describing would be more like cold-blooded murder. Justifiable killing almost, if there can really be such a thing. But really murder in all but name. You'd throw your life away like that? If you think this island will be oppressive in a few more days, imagine your maverick self locked in a prison cell in the Ohio State Penitentiary until you're an old and spent man. Or until you were put in Old Sparky—you know, the chair?"

Hector sighs, says, "Wouldn't be aimin' to get caught, for one thing. And, even if I did tend toward this course of action, and I'm not saying I do, I need to be certain about Krutch. That stench from his basement aside, it all's still just suspicion and circumstantial evidence, if getting stronger by the minute. 'Least for now."

The smell from the cellar freshly ambushes him with its memory.

Hector well knows that stink; knows what causes it.

How much proof beyond that does he require?

Hell, the man has already threatened them.

Verity leans back into Hector, head on his shoulder. Then she echoes his thoughts. "You're really not certain about that yet? Not after all this crazy talk he's thrown at you? That insane place he's living in that reeks of rotting cadavers?"

"I might be all but sure," Hector says. "But I'm also more than a bit convinced he must have some sort of a partner. Probably more than one."

Lifting her head, she searches his robins-egg blue eyes. "Why do you say that?"

"Krutch is a tall man. Bastard's got some heft to him. But he's older and I have more sheer muscle in my favor and I'm pretty sure I couldn't hoist somebody built like Tommy a good twelve feet or more off the floor. Not all alone, I couldn't. Hell, I doubt Chief Parker and I could do that thing together."

The wind shifts, gusting the rain in under the porch roof's protection.

They rise, seeking shelter inside.

Smoothing rain from her forehead, with his thumbs he says, "Let's go into town. Wander around whatever's still open. At least confirm nobody else went to their reward last night."

Peering through the rain-streaked windshield, on a kind of whim, Hector asks, "Turn right here, please."

Scowling, Verity complies, steering into the parking lot of Mother of Our Sorrows Catholic Church.

She says, "Now? Here?"

A beat, then she adds, "And you're Catholic?"

"Technically Catholic, yes," he says.

"Technically?"

"I have... questions. Certain doubts the war didn't ease. But I look okay on the books. What about you? I've seen a Lutheran place on this rock. A Baptist church, too. Bet good money there's a Methodist church tucked away somewhere."

"Wasn't really raised that way," she says.

Hector kisses her hand, says, "Gonna see if I can find the priest."

"For confession? You feel we've been that wicked?"

A smile. "Not that. This is more an instinct I can't quite explain. A hunch. Least ways, this feels like a right next move, somehow."

"How about if I wait this one out? Confession time, from me to you. My family's former enterprises and the church haven't always, well.... Let's say we haven't always blended."

Suddenly thinking for some reason of rank communion wine, Hector says, "Sure."

On the other hand, it's probably better he have the padre to himself. He says to Verity, "My spare gun is still under the seat. You remember the drill? Anything odd develops out here, hit that horn, yes?"

"Best believe it!" They kiss hungrily, then he slips from the Ford.

Hands in pockets, head down against the rain, Hector dodges and jumps over expanding puddles. From somewhere across the street, he hears a record playing; recognizes Jim Jackson's "Kansas City Blues."

He tugs on the church's front door; Hector's pleased to find it opens to him.

Immediately, the old, familiar and near-suffocating scent of incense seizes him, dragging him back to earliest childhood.

An older man of perhaps forty has his back to the door. He's dressed in a cassock and fussing over something at the altar. Hector softly clears his throat.

The priest turns, smiling inquires, "May I help you?"

"Hello, Father."

The older man has smart gray eyes that quickly appraise Hector. He stuns the author with his next words. "I've wondered when we should actually meet, Mr. Lassiter. I'll confide right here, I've seriously thought of reaching out to you. I'm delighted we've at last come together. But you won't be needing that here, I hope."

He gestures at Hector's torso. Hector looks down and sees his coat's gapped, revealing the butt of his holstered Colt.

Half-smiling, Hector says, "I should hope I wouldn't, yes," he says. Then he asks, "How on earth do you know my name, Father?"

"Booth Parker is a church member," the priest says. "I'm something of his ear." He hastens to add, "Not in a confessional sense, mind you." A pause. "I'm sorry about your friend Thomas. Sorry I couldn't, well...."

His unfinished sentence hangs there awkwardly.

The priest gestures at a front pew. They sit down alongside one another.

The priest says, "If you and Booth don't succeed in proving Tommy was actually murdered, perhaps in a couple of years I might quietly be able to have his body moved and...?"

That would be some consolation, Hector supposes the priest supposes. He says, "Much appreciated, Father. But, on the other hand, dead is dead. And I suspect Tommy's well-past caring where his bones wound up. More importantly, sounds to me like you know there's a killer loose on this island."

A deep sigh. "I know all about that. And of the suspicion centered on the man Usher Krutch. I assume canny precaution drives you as a private citizen to be walking around with that vintage Colt. She's a beauty. A Peacemaker, isn't she?"

"She is. And you know guns? That surprises me."

"Guns, cars .... Baseball. Even a priest needs a few hobbies. I also hunt."

Hector turns that over. "So what do you think about all that's happening here?"

"I'm inclined to agree with you and Parker. Four of these who passed? Members of my congregation. I've known them for many years. Counseled at least one regarding other ... call them matters. These were not self-destructive people. Not any of them, Mr. Lassiter. If you pressed me, I'd venture these four weren't even driven to suicide by Krutch or some other. I think they were strategic victims, but for specific, maybe even for mercenary reasons."

"Do tell?"

"One owned the property I hear you've recently attached to Krutch. That parishioner of mine—Mr. Samuel Cove—had plans and funds to open a restaurant above the cave running under the property. He was going to open a bed and breakfast. Then he was dead and somehow Krutch held the title to the property. I should insert here now, our mutual friend Chief Parker can't find a corresponding bill of sale or legal transfer of title."

So maybe Mister Krutch is *willing to kill for straight-up profit, as well as for presumed pleasure*, Hector thinks.

Krutch would hardly be the first, if so. Hector not so long ago ran afoul of some running a similar criminal enterprise tied to real estate in the Florida Keys.

Hector says, "And the other three?"

"I've heard Mister Krutch fleetingly took up with the widow Cove—very fleetingly. Soon after her husband's suicide by shotgun, she appeared to still be sufficiently distraught from loss to throw herself down a crevasse in a tourist cave across the street from Krutch's place. Her body was never recovered, but I think we can presume she is surely dead."

The priest takes a breath, contemplating the bleeding figure hanging from the cross on the distant wall.

"The third was a teenage girl. Very pretty. Very kind. Came from a wonderful family. Then she suddenly was with child. Whom the child's father was I'm sure is your next question. One for which I have no answer. She drowned herself. Left a note. But her family resists the notion it was an act of suicide. The letter's authenticity they also doubt, of course. Candidly? So do I."

Hector crosses one leg over the other, asks, "And the fourth I suppose is—?"

"Thomas, of course."

"Of course. Have you met Usher Krutch?"

"Three or four times," the priest says. "I believe he's truly wicked. Actually evil. Yet I have no concrete proof or reason for thinking any of that. It's all drawn from instinct, and Krutch's elephantine condescension toward me. And I like to think I have a certain knack for reading people. It's hard for me to find the right words to describe it in Krutch's case. There's something about that man that doesn't seem quite human, and I mean that in a tangible way. Something almost elemental in what I perceive to be Mister Krutch's thinly concealed malignancy. He strikes me as the kind of man who'd derive elemental delight, almost nourishment, from others' suffering."

Hector has no idea what to make of that—it's almost like the priest is ascribing to Usher Krutch some sort of mystical quality of menace. Hector instinctively thrusts out a big hand. "Here we are, having this frank and frankly rather odd discussion, and you have me at a disadvantage. Never got your handle, Padre."

A smile. "James Patrick McCullough."

They shake hands. The priest's hand is strong and warm.

Contemplating the figure of Christ suffering on His cross, Hector asks, "How exactly do you think he does it? How does Krutch talk or finesse them into killing themselves? If that's indeed what he's doing?"

Father McCullough thinks more on that. He flicks stray cigarette ash from his cassock with yellowed fingernails.

Hector takes the hint and offers up his pack of Pall Malls.

The priest checks behind to ensure they're still alone, then accepts. "Thank you, Mr. Lassiter."

"Hector, Padre." He strikes a match and they both get their coffin nails going.

"To your question," Father McCullough says, long streams of smoke trailing from either nostril, "I think few of us are prepared to acknowledge how tenuously others around us are tethered to this world. I must think Mister

Krutch has a talent for sharply assessing character and divining human weakness. I think that perhaps Krutch unerringly seizes upon those barely clinging to life, and he has a facility for giving them just the right push to sever their last, fragile ties."

Another long stream of smoke is expelled toward the vaulted ceiling from his lips. The priest says, "In other cases, I think Mister Krutch covets, then kills to possess, as I've described in the case of his present property."

Hector says, "Neither of those explanations would cover Tommy. How to explain Tommy's death?"

"Thomas' perhaps crossed this demon ... recognized him for what he was and what he is doing? Perhaps that was enough?"

The word demon gives Hector unexpected pause. Probably because Krutch has his own underground, stench-filled cavern. Krutch seems to actually possess his own mini-Tophet.

Father McCullough shrugs, says, "Perhaps Thomas found Krutch out? Saw him for what he is. And, so, Thomas had to die before he perhaps took matters in his own capable hands, as I sense you're possibly endeavoring to do?"

That's the explanation that seems soundest to Hector regarding Tommy's death. It most coheres and appeals to him in view of Tommy's character.

The priest says, "Good reason for you, Booth and I to stay in close touch and keep still-closer counsel in the uncertain days ahead, don't you agree?"

Hector smiles and rises. They shake hands again. "Let's make that our very plan, Father."

"How best to reach you, Hector?"

"There's a woman—a trusted friend who also knows of Krutch and what he appears to be. She works at the Park Hotel. Her name is Verity Chisholm. She can find me fairly fast. Certainly, the most reliably."

"You're a guest at that hotel?"

Hector opts for a white lie. "Was a guest. Moving around now. For my health. Moving targets bein' harder to hit, as the saying goes?"

"Hopefully an axiom that bears out for your sake, then. But that seems untenable to endure for long. Also, there aren't terribly many places to hide on this island."

Hector smiles. "I don't know. Until quite recently, Usher Krutch seemed to pull it off pretty well."

The priest snubs out the remains of his cigarette on the sole of his shoe. "There's an old saying a Jesuit who mentored me was fond of repeating. 'There are rare times when it is the proper tactic to retaliate first.'"

Hector scowls. "What are you saying, Padre?"

"I'm not saying anything. Not suggesting some order or direction, if that's what you're sensing. I'm merely presenting you with . . . food for thought."

Pointing again at Hector's torso, Father McCullough asks, "Might I see your gun a moment? I really am a kind of antique weapons hobbyist. Firearms, swords. I've never seen a classic Peacemaker in person."

Hector's a little thrown by that request, but draws his Colt and passes it to the priest. It's hammer presently sits on an empty chamber.

"Truly exquisite," the priest says. "And it has a quality about it, something I'd call charisma in a person. Not sure what I'd call it in a gun. But it is a noble weapon."

Then Father McCullough places a hand over the long barrel of the Peacemaker and says a few words of Latin that Hector doesn't quite make out.

"Pardon me, Father, but did you just bless my Colt?"

"Something like that." A thin smile. "What could it hurt, after all? We bless people. Even animals on certain days of the year. I've even blessed anchors and fishing poles, upon request, mind you. A gun in the right hand? Just another tool."

Hector taps on the fogged window and Verity unlocks the door.

She says, "Maybe next time you leave me alone like this you should do that with something more than just a six-shooter. The driver of every car that went by seemed to have Krutch's silhouette."

"I'm sorry." He pauses, says, "But I did invite you in."

"Never mind. So, you met the priest?"

"I did." Hector describes their conversation.

Verity says, "Sounds like he almost urged you to kill Krutch."

"That's my stubborn sense, too. Seems there's somethin' in the wind encouraging vigilante strikes at crazy old Usher."

Verity gets the engine going. She and Hector wipe at the fogged window glass with hands and elbows. She says, "Did the priest promise you dispensation for playing holy assassin?"

"Didn't go that far down that peculiar and bloody conversational road," Hector says curtly. A smile. "He did bless my gun, though."

"Really? How very odd."

"Feel like now I could maybe slay vampires or witches with the thing," he jokes. "Maybe even a demon."

She bites her lip, says, "I've been thinking more about it, frankly. If you thought your conscience could sustain against it—and with a priest and the police chief apparently squarely in your corner—then it almost becomes what you described to me earlier. A community sanctioned action."

Hector's taken aback by her sudden embracing of the notion of him having been given permission to do what he'd impulsively put out a while back—his musing about committing a justifiable murder at which she had balked.

Verity gets the Ford in gear, steers through the puddle-potted parking lot and back onto the road into town.

She veers on him, so to speak, seemingly playing devil's advocate in the opposite direction. "Of course, Krutch just might be innocent of the murders, and then …?"

And then?

Yes.

No drawing a bullet back into his newly-blessed Colt, not after it is fired.

No un-ringing that bloody bell. And so …?

Run.

Every instinct in Hector is to take Verity, flee Krutch and let the devil take the hindmost.

Or,

Kill Krutch.

Go ahead and kill him dead.

Do that today.

Studying him in glances as they drive on, Verity says, "What are you thinking? Unless you're hungry—and I'm not—I'm really not sure what to do next. Don't know where to go."

"Not hungry, either," Hector says. "Let's hit the docks. Chat up some more old salts. See what they predict now for last ferry runs?"

The lake men's collective wisdom points toward another very unseasonable weather day to come, then maybe two final days of navigable weather—Hector's escape weather, as he now thinks of it.

Then the end of ferry season will surely have arrived.

15
THE UNDERTAKER

Rather than another tourist joint, they settle on what Verity touts as a local favorite for lake-caught perch, creamy coleslaw and big, fresh cut steak fries, all of it washed down with icy cold Canadian beer.

After a couple of bottles, Hector rises to relieve himself. Verity says, "My loaner gun is in the car. Leave me your sanctified Colt until you get back?"

Hector briefly sits back down and says, "Surely," surreptitiously passing her the Peacemaker under the table.

When he gets back, she returns his gun.

More overheard weather talk as they continue dining. And more overheard suicide talk.

Rumors now have it a tourist drunk on bathtub gin might have fallen off a pier and drowned.

Search teams are reportedly quietly combing the banks near the ruins of the burned-down Hotel Victory—one of the largest hotels in America until it was torched and robbed while heavily occupied in 1919.

A drunken tourist going off a pier in a storm doesn't seem to Hector like something Krutch would be behind. Verity agrees.

More whispers: Someone broke into the airport overnight. They sabotaged every accessible aircraft. Repairs will be impossible without critical parts that can only be flown in by other planes or delivered by boat.

This act of destruction seems very much to speak to Krutch's hand at work, to Hector's beleaguered mind. It's further strategy, perhaps, on Krutch's part, to keep his pool of victims—and Hector, particularly—firmly in place for a long winter's bloody sport.

What might Krutch also do about the last of the boats that should steam in soon?

Burn all the docks?

Krutch's ultimate aims are still so inscrutable and potentially bizarre to Hector that almost anything seems possible.

Nearly all crazy options seemed very much on the table to the novelist.

Her thoughts again seeming to track his, Verity says, "So, we won't be flying out. So far as boats go, short of controlling the weather, I can't imagine what he can do to stop those coming."

"Mine the harbor, maybe?"

The thermometer's dropping again. Hector thinks he scents snow. A couple old salts think so, too. One says, "Get a good snow, water's will calm. Maybe we'll get one last supply run or a ferry over and back before day's end, yet."

Just that faint prospect perks Hector up. But his mind is also on Tommy, again. He dwells on what the priest said about *Thomas.*

Hector says to Verity, "You said there's no coroner on this island. No real medical examiner, right?"

"That's right," Verity says, arching an eyebrow. "Why?"

"Grasping for new angles of attack or investigation," Hector says. "Who plays that part? Some kindly old island sawbones? Please tell me it's not just a damn dentist or a middling veterinarian."

"The mortician," Verity says. "The island's only funeral director."

"Got it." Hector shakes his head. Jesus Christ. Perfect.

That reality somehow actually exceeds his lowest expectations. Yet he tries to make a joke of it. "Kind of all-in-one shopping sort is he, this old boy?"

Verity says, "Life is rarely perfect, Hector."

They drive to the funeral home. Verity says, "Rather than loitering outside like a sitting duck for Krutch or some minion this time, I'm just going to drive. See you in half-an-hour?"

"Should be plenty of time," he says.

Another passionate kiss, then Hector slips out into the lashing sleet.

Sheltered from the icy rain by the funeral parlor's generous front porch, Hector rings the doorbell a second time. He blows into his cupped hands to warm them while he waits.

The sound of approaching footsteps inside. A window curtain is pulled aside a smidge. A thin, withered male face peers out at Hector. The novelist registers round-rimmed glasses, a high forehead and gray-brown widow's peak.

The door opens and a slender man a few inches shorter than Hector introduces himself as Grafton Keeler, island mortician, medical examiner and Boy Scout master.

"My name is Hector Lassiter, and I—"

Hector falters as the funeral director reacts to that admission. The novelist can't believe his writing reputation—such as it is—could have also reached this man. The island's too small and he's too early in his career to have so many fans in one remote, ill-populated place. Hector says, "I was—"

"A close friend of Tom's," Keeler finishes for him. "I know. I actually have something for you. A letter left you by Tom. Come in, won't you, please?"

Hector enters. The ground floor is the public working space for the funeral parlor. It looks just like any funeral home after the somber ritual has climaxed. It also smells strongly of fresh flowers and incense, likely to cover the whiff of early decomposition or embalming fluids from elsewhere.

The mortician leads Hector through the viewing parlor and back into his office. Its walls are covered in dark paneling; the clubby chairs sport red leather upholstery.

The view from two of the office's windows looks out across a back garden with a lakeside vista. It's snowing now, big and fast-falling flakes.

Keeler says, "When your friend's body came to me, I found two letters stashed in the boot he wore over his artificial leg. One letter was addressed to you, Mr. Lassiter. It was, and remains, sealed. The other letter was addressed to me and contained instructions for what I was to do with the letter to you."

The man settles in behind his big desk. The table's top bears a heavy glass sheet protecting a red leather laminate. Keeler says, "It's no exaggeration on my part to say your simply wandering in here today is going to give me back hours of my life on a weekly basis."

Hector holds up his pack of coffin nails, gets an approving nod and the mortician reaches for his own box of cigarettes. Keeler lights both with an ornate, tabletop lighter.

Through a curtain of smoke, Hector says, "How exactly am I giving you so much time back?"

The mortician deposits an envelope on his desk. "Tom was quite firm in his instructions that I shouldn't simply presume to mail his letter for you to your home address in Key West. He made it quite clear home isn't a home for you as most would think of it."

A polite smile dies on the funeral director's lips. "You do move around, a lot. My my, I'd no sooner find you were seemingly in Paris or in Venice, only to learn you'd pressed on to other parts. I could never quite locate you to wire you directly to stay put so I might get this letter to you. Which, parenthetically, your friend Tom was adamant should reach you as soon as possible."

Hector's heart is racing. What the hell is in this letter Tommy left for him? What was so urgent and personal it required delivery directly into Hector's hands? But he says, "I'm surprised the chief of police didn't presume to confiscate that letter. Even to open it."

Keeler shakes his head. "With Tom gone, only you and I know this letter exists. I should volunteer now, that before I took up this trade, I also studied law. Still maintain a small, quiet little law operation, as well. Your letter—and Tom knew enough to emphasize this—is a matter of attorney-client privilege. Or so he insisted in that other letter left me, along with my retainer."

Mortician, medical examiner and lawyer.

This widely credentialed islander truly is a one-man band, Hector thinks. He asks, "Before I trip over another, any other occupations you'd like to confess to up front?"

"I dabble in real estate a bit. That's a small, grim joke, actually. It mostly just involves selling plots in the local cemeteries."

A grim and small joke, indeed, Hector thinks sourly. But he says, "Did you talk much to Chief Booth Parker about Tom's death? Maybe about the possibility it might have been something other than apparent suicide?"

"Surely," Keeler says, fiddling with a key and his center desk drawer. "Tom's missing leg absolutely precludes his death being suicide, particularly as performed. I'll say here to you, right now, I'm certain it took no less than two, and more likely, a minimum of three people to hang Tom in that manner."

Keeler taps the envelope on the desk between them. The envelope is heavily taped and its flap redundantly sealed with wax, like some medieval emperor's formal correspondence to an opposing potentate, or maybe even to the goddamn Pope.

Eyeing the letter, Hector squeezes in a last question. "Any revelations that might shed light on all that in the letter Tom left you?"

"None at all," Keeler says. "My letter contained just the instructions I've shared with you regarding your letter."

With much drama, he slowly pushes the letter across the desk to Hector.

Keeler then inhales deeply, releases a long stream of smoke through prim lips. "I can't expect you to share the contents of your letter with me, either, of course, but I have my curiosity…."

Hector makes no promises. He accepts a bronze letter opener and cuts his way through the tape, the waxen seal and adhesive flap.

Tommy's familiar scrawl pierces him.

Hector reads on, very aware of the way Keeler is studying his face, assaying his face for some reaction. Perhaps a look of shock or the like.

Hector reads:

> Heck:
>
> If you're reading this, Hoss, things took a very nasty turn for me, as you'll know by the time this likely finds you, pard.
>
> Kid, if you're reading this, things have sorted out a bit like I last hinted to you.
>
> I can only figure that the man I mentioned—named Usher Krutch by the by—has killed me. He probably did it in his usual way and I probably look like a yellow coward who went off his head and offed himself. Ain't crazy about that standing as my coda, but dead's dead and what do I care what those left behind really think? I don't have a "legacy" or "brand," like you, old kid, to nurture and protect.
>
> I have still fewer old true friends.
>
> I'm writing this because things are coming to a head, and because Krutch seems to have an interest

in you now, Heck. I'll get to the whys for that soon enough, kiddo.

Don't skip ahead, please. Like a wise and trusting horse, I need to lead you to this impossible water hole, distant. If you jump to the end, you're just going think I'm a loon who probably really did kill himself in whatever wicked way Krutch has come up with to stand for my suicide.

Krutch knows I'm onto him. About an hour ago, deep in his cups, the son of a bitch called me on the phone. I guess you might call what followed a crazy-ass confession.

Heck, a few lines up, I boasted I was going to deftly lead you like a reluctant horse to these crazy waters. Faced with the need to do that now—hell, I ain't no writer like you, as we both know, old kid. I find now I'm not up to the task at hand. So, I'm gonna just put it out there. You know, like old Armand Ellroy down there in the Mexican desert used to put it around the campfire. This'll be "the naked lunch at the end of the fork."

We've both faced more than our share of devils in our time. Truly wicked and evil, black-ass sons of bitches. Killers of every stripe, from Villa to that fuckin', leg-stealing Kaiser's minions.

They were terrible devils in their own ways, of course. But this man Usher Krutch? He actually claims to be the real deal—The Devil.

Lucifer himself.

You heard me.

Hoss, this man is surely what I've seen you refer to in your stories and books as a "pattern killer." Like

Jack the Ripper or that crazy kraut Fritz Haarmann, the so-called Butcher of Hanover.

At the very least, Krutch is the equal to those sorts of sick sons of bitches.

But it's much more, buddy.

Much, much crazier.

Krutch insists he's really The Devil. He says each of his victims will become his slaves in his own eventual afterlife. None of this makes a damn bit of sense, I confess that up front, Heck.

But Krutch believes it well enough. And he kills for his beliefs. And really, what is there to say or do after you know that? Krutch quoted someone named de Sade to me (had to hit the library books to figure that one out, because you know I only ready Zane Grey and you, kid. P.S. Have you read Tales of Swordfish and Tuna yet? It's great!).

Anyway, this quote Krutch threw at me went like this, I think:

"It is an article of faith on the island of Borneo that all those persons a man kills will be his slaves in the next world; and as a result, the better a man wishes to be served after his death, the more he kills during life."

Or something like that.

Krutch rambled on about how making his kills look like suicides foxes God and the church and so traps his slaves in a kind of special limbo or purgatory increasing Krutch's power. Also, something about how the quality of the person killed gives him extra power, too. Crazy, Hoss.

But then he talked about <u>you</u>, Heck. He knows we're acquainted. Said how he needs his own "scribe." Says he needs one "who writes clearer and who reaches more in this world than goddamn John Milton or Bill Blake and their too-few egghead readers."

Krutch says he sees you as his "pulp-lit apostle" whatever the hell <u>that</u> means.

Swear to God, he said all this, kid.

I don't believe it of course, this stuff about him being the Devil. It's all just bloody craziness. But Krutch <u>is</u> killing people, Heck, no doubt there.

And he's focused on you now, for the reasons said.

Kid, he's given me twenty-four hours to kill myself, or says he'll come and do the deed for me.

So, I'm seeing to this letter, to a couple of other loose ends, and a few other goodbyes owed if things do go off the rails in the next few hours.

See, before night's end, I'm going to this bastard's house (address below) and I'm putting Krutch down like the mad dog he is.

Or maybe he <u>will</u> get me.

It occurs to me you'll maybe want to see right done by me if I go down. Avenge me in some way?

No need for that, of course. But you being you, and me knowing you for the loyal friend and reluctant but driven crusader you are?

Here are a couple of critical things you need to know:

Krutch has at least two partners. One's male. He's a ferry worker, what I suspect your Grandpa Beau would call a "roper." His name is Coyne.

The other, who is also a roper, but far prettier (never judge a book by its cover, am I right, my kid author?) is a dame. Twist currently goes by Natasha Shale. Anyhow, that's the name she gave *me*. Skirt's real name, I think, is Augusta Krutch. As implied, she's Usher's daughter. Again, I think.

Whatever her name, she is very pretty, very appealing.

But her hands are bloody, too, I'm sure.

For a helpless horndog like you, kid, she might even be more the threat than her old man.

A snapshot of the Devil's Daughter—one I took on the sly—is in here too. She's fond of aliases but she can't do much to change that pretty pug of hers.

But please don't go after them, Hector.

I'd ask you hand this all over to the local lawman. He seems honest if not so effective in chasing this "Devil" to ground.

Best you steer well-clear of the Krutch family.

Let some others take them down.

They surely can't kill like this forever, not with impunity.

But knowin' you Heck, I expect you'll want to try and throw this Devil back into Hell, yourself.

All good luck if you take it on as a mission, Hoss.

Just don't forget to close off the family trade by seeing the wicked daughter's put down, too.

See you on the other side, Heck.

(If you're even let into heaven!)

Vaya con dios, my one true brother!

T

Hector's forgotten cigarette has reduced to a long conical ash.

It burns his fingers. Cursing, Hector drops it on the glass tabletop, then apologizes.

Keeler waves a hand. Says, "Anything you care to share?"

Rubbing his burned fingertips, Hector says, "Far less here than would be compelling to you than I'm sure you think. Having said that, do you know a woman by the name of Natasha Shale?"

"No."

"How about Augusta Krutch?"

"Not her, either. You look like a man who could use a drink. Whiskey? Water? On the rocks?"

"Whiskey would be wonderful," Hector says. "Neat, please."

"I prefer it that way, too."

As the mortician rises and moves to a sideboard laden with crystal glasses and an impressive array of sparkling decanters, Hector searches the envelope again.

His scorched fingertips feel the photo inside.

He slides it out, turns it over, then clinches up inside.

Those lips, those eyes.

Verity.

16
THE LAST FERRY

Standing on the porch, stomach warm with not enough whiskey and now smoking another Pall Mall, Hector stares out through the snow flurries falling heavily all across the island.

He supposes this must be what they call "lake-effect snow"—it's not just sticking, but has already accumulated to more than half-an-inch.

And *Verity* hasn't returned for him yet.

Just as well, as he's not sure how he'll handle seeing her; how he'll fake being flirty with her until he decides on a final course of action against her and her wicked old man.

That word, final, rings in Hector's head.

This woman whom he's been enthusiastically coupling with may have at very least helped to murder his dear friend.

Verity may well have helped hoist Tom up to the top of that beam to choke to death.

In his last letter, Tommy referenced Hector's grandfather, Beau Stryder, venerable Texas gentleman and secret bunko artist supreme. A man who remains the acknowledged North American master of the Big Store con.

Much of what Verity and Krutch has done indeed echoes just such an enterprise: Ropers, false identities.... And a prime mark in the person of a gullible Hector.

Verity's position at the only operating hotel on the island? The perfect place to make Hector's acquaintance, just as she did. Now he wonders if desk clerk "Lou" was ever really his fan, let alone a recipient of that signed copy of Hector's first novel.

Roped by a pretty face and a sexy chassis.

Grandpa Beau would never let him live it down, if he knew.

Hector curses and flicks his cigarette into the snow. It lands with a sizzle. He strikes a fresh match and sets fire to Tommy's letter. The sneak photograph of Verity he retains.

Cursing again, Hector turns up his collar, thrusts his hands into his coat pockets and with a hurting leg, begins slogging through snow, on a beam for the downtown commercial strip. His Great War wounds fast have him limping, one foot cocked out to the right—not quite qualifying as a club-foot gait, but close enough.

Chances are, he'll walk—or rather limp—right into *Verity*.

Otherwise, if she's quick enough before more snow erases them, she can just follow his damn footprints in the snow from the funeral home to wherever he winds up—he is the only pedestrian in sight.

Hector reaches the strip. He stalks into the police station. His lonely footprints mark his unmistakable passage all the way from funeral home to police station.

The chief looks up, says, "No offense, but you look like hell, Hec."

"Funny you should say, Chief. Ever hear the name Augusta Krutch?"

"Nope. Some kind of kin to Usher, I take it?"

"Daughter, I hear. Also likely an accomplice."

"Jesus Christ!"

"Yeah. She has at least one other alias. That would be Natasha Shale. Does that handle ring any bells?"

"Huh-uh, Hec."

Frowning, the island's top cop opens a bottom drawer, pull out two shot glasses and a bottle filled with something amber.

Amber is always tasty.

He pours two glasses. They tap tumblers. Hector downs his. The chief immediately fills him up again. Hector weighs the risks, says, "You know Verity Chisholm of course."

"That name also rings no bells, Hec. Another alias of this Krutch woman?"

Hector feels sick inside. He downs another shot, accepts another refill. He's already starting to feel mildly drunk. He's starting to think he's embracing jiffy intoxication as a means toward some particularly bloody end.

He reaches in his jacket pocket, passes the photo of Verity to Booth. "You *do* know the face at least?"

"Sure," the chief says. "That's that new round heels waitress over at the Park Hotel. Her latest gig. Gets around a lot, I hear. In every sense. Not just waitressing jobs. Making time with men. Maybe with a woman, now and then. To be fair, maybe it's just lot of rumors because she so welcoming to so many tourists, if you get the dirty drift. But my professional instinct? Probably not just rumors."

Well, Goddamn.

Hector says, "That's Verity Chisholm. The handle I know her by, least ways. And I have to confess I'm one of those tourists, Booth. Have been for a couple of days."

"I see . . . ." The chief shakes his head; rubs his stubbled chin. "So, this woman. She's also Augusta Krutch?

"Tommy thought so. She's Natasha Shale, too." His voice growing thicker, Hector says, "Gonna throw an address at you now."

Eyes narrowing, the chief says, "Do it, Hec."

Hector shares Verity's home address.

"I do know that place. Derelict presently. Was the home of Don and Margie Turner. They ran an ice cream shop, until they hit a rough patch. Defaulted on a loan. They found them in that house, in the kitchen, about two months ago. They put their heads in the oven together, embracing. Or so it appeared. Asphyxiation. No realtor on record, yet. Think the place, furnishings and all, is still tangled up in probate court."

Hector realizes his head is in his hands.

Booth is somehow already up, palm pressed to Hector's back.

"You okay, Hec?"

"Just need a second to get some traction on reality."

The chief says gently, "I need to know more, you know."

"Of course you do. Can tell you on the way. Need you to drive me to that house. At very least, I need to pick up some personal effects I left there. Seems I've been trespassing on a crime scene these past few nights. Thought it was her inheritance. Guess, in her way, maybe she wasn't lying when she told me that."

Verity coveted the house, Hector figures, and simply killed—or had the owners killed—and took it over. The same strategy evidently favored by her monstrous old man.

Booth sighs and rises. "Hector, I'm getting the drift in spades. And I'm goddamn sorry, buddy."

On the ride over, Hector lays the rest out. He fills in most of the details of Tommy's letter.

He weathers a tart tongue-lashing from the chief for having burned that piece of evidence.

"It might have been used against the bastard, you know," the chief says.

But a bit later Booth relents and says, "But as the source is claiming his killer is Satan himself? Jesus Christ, probably would have backfired in court. Hell, how couldn't it? Obvious grease for an insanity defense."

Chief Parker also tells Hector that the ferryman, Coyne, "Ate a gun, about a week back."

Rumor is, Coyne got a nasty diagnosis from an island sawbones.

Rumor is.

The private drive back to Verity's supposed lakeside cottage is presently covered over by a virgin layer of snow.

The chief presumes to force the door and they find the place unoccupied.

Hector bitterly gathers his things, slinging his bags into Booth's back seat.

As Booth turns around to head back down the private drive in the other direction, they see it at the same time: Their tire tracks in the snow are now overlaid with more sets of tracks—a car has come in behind them, then retreated.

Verity, surely.

She probably followed them here. Logically, she would have followed Hector's footprints to the police station, and then followed the top cop's lonely tire tracks from the station to her house. Those stops representing clear indications Hector now knows all and has turned on her.

Hector makes another logical leap and decides she now knows that he knows precisely who she is.

The chief says, "All things considered, you're too compromised to help me usefully going forward, Hector. So, I'm going to tell you now, buddy. I got official word a couple hours ago, there is a ferry leaving the dock in an hour. The snow has settled conditions on the lake, but there's also an Alberta Clipper bearing down on us that could well shut down further ferry service this season after this afternoon's single run. I'm saying this is quite likely your only chance off the island until a few months distant. The fact you instinctively gathered your luggage strikes me as an omen. Much as I'd like to have you by my side to end all this, should I drop you at the goddamn ferry station, Hec?"

Hector searches the top cop's eyes. "For Christ's sake, yes. By all means, please do. And thank you for this, Booth. Best figure months more here would surely be the death of me."

Hector buys his ticket and surrenders his luggage to the new ferryman, an immensely tall, intense-gazed man with feverish black eyes and gold front teeth. The ferryman says, "You're safely booked and I'll get your stuff loaded on. You've got about half-an-hour's wait if there's anything you need to handle before we shove off.'

Hector thanks him, buys a cup of piping hot coffee. He settles on a bench with a newspaper someone's left behind. He checks his pocket watch: twenty-five minutes until scheduled departure.

Hector tries to focus on the headlines of the day, but all he can think about is Verity.

A door opens and cold wind stirs Hector's dark cowlick.

Usher Krutch smiles, holds his hands out, palms up, showing he's unarmed. He carefully pulls out pocket linings, then opens his coat as further evidence of no hidden weapons.

Krutch says, "Sadly looks like you'll evade a winter with me, after all. But surely, we can't leave without some last discussion, my scribe. Some attempt to resolve matters between us?"

Hector's hand drifts to his coat pocket where his big old priest-blessed Colt presently resides. He says evenly, "I've got a few more minutes before I get the hell off this rock, Usher. So sure. Let's have us that last talk."

17
THE DEVIL'S DAUGHTER

Walking slowly along the lakeside, some distance from the ferry and any ears, Hector keeps his hand on his hidden gun.

He's covered the sound of its tell-tale cock and roll onto a live cylinder with the squeak of the ferry station door as they stepped back out into the still heavy-falling snow.

Hector doesn't have much time before the final ferry departs, so he cuts to the chase.

Hector says, "Tommy left me a letter that just came into my possession a bit ago. It's all there about you. Also about Verity and your interest in me. You're clearly mad, thinking yourself the Devil. All of this you've done is fucking insane. Even you must see it."

"So, you know who I really am. You should also know, I can't be killed, not by you, nor by any mere man… or woman."

Hector shakes his head, declares, "The next world awaiting you is either Hell, or oblivion. Either way, nobody's going to be playing your slave in any fairytale afterlife, Usher. And I don't want to hear your crazy arguments to the contrary. There are just precisely two things I require from you. First, how'd you compel Tommy to write that damn suicide letter? I just can't see Tom not brassing it out, even with a gun to his head."

Krutch clips the end of a cigar with his little guillotine and gets his smoke going. "Oh, Tommy had precious little in this world but your friendship. And that of a beloved dog. A one-eyed spaniel he called... yes, *Hector.* I gather you were a sort of surrogate son or maybe a kind of kid-brother to Thomas? An honorary baby brother? Either way, I promised to spare his dog. And to see doggie placed in a good home."

Hector takes a deep breath. Raw-voiced, he demands, "What happened to Tommy's dog, Krutch?"

"Ah. I promptly slit its throat. I did that while Tommy was dangling from that beam by the rope around his neck, kicking and strangling to death... But watching the pooch—this other Hector—bleed out."

It's a real act of will not to shoot Krutch, here and now.

Hector says thinly, "So you fucking lied. Again."

Krutch smiles back. "I am the Father of All Lies, after all."

"Horseshit. You're not the Devil. And your daughter—Verity, or Augusta?"

"Her given name is Lilith."

"More lies. Whatever her goddamn name, did she kill with you?"

"Countless times, Hector. Groomed for it, from infancy. She is also the consummate seductress. The epitome of the phrase, 'the womb and the tomb.' She's the one who actually put the noose around your dear Tommy's neck, you should know. I think Lil enjoys the actual act of killing far more than I do these years. I'm more focused on the endgame—my growing army of slaves for my own far-distant afterlife. I'm more eager in swelling the ranks of my dark angels I'll eventually range against Our Father. In my own good time. But my lovely Lil? She relishes a fine kill. So much so, that I've made it a project, even a crusade, to confine her to this island. If this entire world was her oyster? Then I fancy this world would fast become still more a charnel house than humanity manages to make it on its own."

Enough of your lunatic babbling, Hector thinks. He says, "Far be it for me to reject a reader, but, no, Usher. I'm going to end you now. This is your judgment day. Welcome to Hell, Mister Krutch."

In a single motion, Hector draws his Peacemaker from his pocket, presses it between Krutch's eyes and immediately pulls the trigger.

A dry fire.

Desperate, Hector tugs the trigger again and gets another empty-chambered click.

Krutch grins and claps his hands. "Delicious irony, thrown back in the writer's face! Looks like you were also foolish enough to neglect your gun in my daughter's proximity, Hector. Though I'm sure she didn't take your bullets out to save my life. She increasingly craves me dead, and has for some time, now. But she fears she can't bring it off; knows like no other how hard I am to kill. No mere gun can do that job!"

Smiling, Krutch says, "She's complained for longer than I can calculate that I've been holding her back. Restraining her from her self-decided destiny. So, she was probably looking out for her own safety, depriving you of those bullets. Unintended consequences are vexing, eh? Anyway, no gun on earth made by man can kill me, just as I've said."

With a snarl, Krutch knocks aside Hector's Colt and draws his own derringer.

"Mine has bullets," Krutch says, beaming.

Hector flings down his Colt and clutches at Krutch's wrist; one of Krutch's derringer's two shots is fired into the air.

Hector reaches back into his pocket with his other hand. He draws his recently purchased fishing knife and drives it deep and hard into Krutch's inner, upper thigh.

Eyes widening, Krutch stammers. Then he screams and spastically fires his second and last shot, again into the air.

Drooling, Krutch drops his empty sleeve gun.

Krutch clutches at his leg but Hector has already twisted the knife embedded there. Hector drags the blade up and then down, then shoves it left to right and back again, filleting Krutch's femoral artery.

Hector quickly steps back to avoid the arterial spray that fast stains the snow in scarlet gushes.

Krutch claimed to have been in Paris during the time of the Nada cult.

Mister Krutch claimed to have read Hector's first novel in French translation. Hector takes him at his word about having facility with the French tongue and points with his bloodied knife at all the blood in the snow and, declares, "*La neige rouge, eh, bâtard?*"

Hector then retrieves his Colt and the sleeve gun.

Krutch, wild-eyed, holds tight to his thigh, struggling to stop the sluice of blood pumping from his ruined leg with each increasingly frantic heartbeat, staining his straining fingers red with each fresh, precious surge.

Hector tosses the sleeve gun far out into the lake. He then fishes his pockets for spare bullets and loads two into the Colt. "Not just any gun, Krutch. Not this one. This gun was originally the possession of an Ohio writer who wrote—wait for it—*The Devil's Dictionary*. And a priest actually blessed her a few short hours ago. Reckon we'll see what, if any, difference that makes for one like you now, yeah? This is for all your dead, but especially for

Tommy, you sorry son of a bitch. Oh, and for Tommy's dog!"

Hector kicks Krutch in the chest, propelling him back into the icy lake. The chill lake water would be plenty sufficient to kill in just minutes, all on its own, Hector figures.

The novelist casts a last look around—still no witnesses in sight.

He wipes off its handle and tosses the knife far out into the water.

The mounting wind howls like a banshee. The ferry is almost invisible now in the white-out snow.

Hector takes aim and pulls twice on the Peacemaker's trigger.

One to the heart, one to the head.

The sound of the each shot is buried by the sound of the winter wind.

Contrary to Krutch's claims, the Colt seems to do its job plenty fine, priest's blessing or no.

Eyes open and mouth gaping, Krutch is very still in the water, arms outstretched, blood billowing around his body.

Hector takes a last look around, then kicks fresh white snow over the scarlet stains on the ground, hiding all the blood spilled there.

Then he gets another cigarette going and returns to await his ferry off the island.

Chances are, he'll be safely ashore long before Krutch's body is discovered.

Either way, he's gambling Booth Parker will never ever chase him down for this slaying committed for the good of all the presumed-innocent folk about to weather this winter on the Great Lakes island.

The Peacemaker repeatedly bumps Hector's thigh as he wades through drifting snow. He thinks of his Colt's original owner. What was Ambrose Bierce's noted quip on killing published in his *Devil's Dictionary*? Ah, yes:

"There are four kinds of homicide: felonious, excusable, justifiable and praiseworthy."

Hector figures his slaying of Ktch represents at least three of the four.

And Verity?

Hector reckons she'll be a lone fugitive on this postage stamp island, a presumably far much easier get for Parker and Company than her bloody and crafty old man.

Hell, on this car-starved island it should be as simple as following her Ford's tire tracks through the still-accumulating snow.

In a way, Hector doesn't envy the cunning bitch the hunt for her to come on this tiny, terrible and soon to be ice-bound patch of hollowed-out rock.

There's surely no place to hide. Not ultimately.

Not even in all those myriad caves and gem caverns lurking underfoot.

Not trapped on a winter-isolated dab of an island for months with a small but fierce army of devoted hunters focused on running you to ground to avenge their lost ones.

With a lonely last horn blast, the ferry pulls away from the Put-in-Bay docks.

Perry's monument slowly subsides into the curve of the Great Lake, then it disappears entirely in the fog of hard-falling, lake-effect snow.

Hector sips the last of his precious Highland whisky from his flask. He's eager to bolster his dulling rye and bourbon buzz.

He thinks of Krutch's stunned and crazed expression as he struggled in the frigid lake waters, bleeding out before those two kill shots from Bierce's priest-blessed Peacemaker secured the self-declared *Devil's* certain death.

So much for "baleful gazes" and "Devil's parties" and all that Miltonic horseshit.

And so much for absurd demonic invulnerability from any gun "made by man."

Hector broods again on Ambrose Bierce and another definition—one for Satan—in Bierce's cynical and wry, *Devil's Dictionary*, a book that swiftly became a favorite of Grandpa Beau Stryder, via Hector:

DEVIL, n. The author of all our woes and proprietor of all the good things of this world. He was made by the Almighty, but brought into the world by woman.

Hector assures himself he would never have played scribe to Usher Krutch—real Devil, or no.

Not on his most desperate day poised before his typewriter or some defiantly barren notepad would Hector ever descend to that.

At last sighting Ohio's northernmost shoreline, Hector fights this crazy urge to kiss the mainland ground of the Buckeye State when he finally plants foot off this damned, final ferry.

The snow is also picking up on the mainland, turning to thick squalls in the mounting, icy Canadian wind.

As he's waiting for his luggage, a voice calls out to the smattering of departing passengers, "Mr. Hector Lassiter? I have a phone call for you. Is there a Hector Lassiter out there?"

It could be Booth.

Hector flinches. He thinks, *Jesus, maybe they've already found Krutch's corpse!*

Then, *But just as likely not.*

And Hector is still convinced Booth will never bring him to book for Krutch's demise.

So Hector rolls the dice; accepts the phone call.

Verity says, "I'm truly sorry it ended this way, Hector. I'm sorry for your friend, Tommy. But I correctly sensed you were the one who could and would at last somehow put my father down, for all time. He was long past needing killing, well and true. And the so-called law surely couldn't do that job. I also needed bait and father was already focused on you. Tommy was a lucky break in that way. Lucky for me, anyway."

A moment's silence, then, "I saw you kill him. Father, I mean. I adore you all the more for doing it the way that you did. Engaging him in close, with steel at first, like olden, truer and better days."

A beat, then she says, "Blades are so intimate, after all. The bliss of penetration. He killed my mother that way when she turned on him, you should know. He correctly sensed I was turning on him, too. Father knew things were fast coming to last blood between us. But I needed a worthy champion. I chose you. And I chose well. I love you with all my heart and every other inch of me, Hector. Please never doubt that, my best and eternal darling."

Hector sighs. "So, it is really true, at least in this much. You are Krutch's daughter and you were his partner in these and probably only God knows how many other killings? I know you're a manufactured monster. But you're every bit as sick and bloody as your old man. You must recognize that."

An edge comes into his voice, and Hector snarls, "Are you really deluded enough to believe you're the Devil's daughter?"

She thinks about it for long seconds, then says at last, "I think I am what my birth condemned me to be, as you just said, Hector. There was only ever my father and his sickness. I didn't make my own key decisions. Not ever. Not until you. Father made all my other choices for me. Contained me on the island, a doomed prisoner as much as any of his victims. As to what Father was or wasn't in some grander sense, I'll just leave you with a proverb, of sorts, my dearest darling."

Verity says, "Someone once remarked, 'There is no Devil. Only God when he's drunk.' But I'd put it to you, Hec. What if there was a Devil? And what if He got drunk? I think if that could happen, it might look something like what was going on with Father as his end drew closer at your hand. Father was wholly out of control with his vices. They'd all but swamped him. Then Father got obsessed with you, but in a deliciously blind and wholly self-destructive way. I admired you from afar, in my way, so I set out to acquire you."

Seething, Hector says, "Acquire me? Like hell. You don't own me! You're just more unfinished bloody business, now. Merely a sick filly who also needs putting down."

"Know that I do love you, Hector. If it matters, I really was going to tour Europe with you, Hec. If I could bring it off without detection. I was going to try and change out there on the road with you. I really am wholly taken with you. You've been my savior, in several ways."

"Your savior? Jesus Christ."

"Maybe we can still have Europe," she races on. "You could try to help me change, couldn't you? All the way, and forever? Or, given what you write, I could perhaps be your muse?"

He recoils even as she swiftly warms to that notion. "Yes. Yes! I quite like that idea! I do the deed, however wrong the tribe might think it, then you write about it!"

Hector says coldly, "Nix. I'm not in the market for a murdering muse. And I've told Parker all about you, darlin'. Alerted the chief and some others. You should know that Tommy left a note and photo of you, fingering you beyond question, Augusta. Lilith. Natasha or whomever. You're soon enough going to find South Bass a very hard place upon or even *in* which to hide for very long, Verity. Hell, I even gave 'em that photo of you gifted me by Tommy, you heartless murdering witch."

A soft sad sigh. "Oh, but Hec, you poor dear! I just rode over on the boat with you! Rode right off that cursed island, and did it on the last ferry with you, lover man! I was stowed in the hold. Slid out at docking to find a safe place from which to make this last phone call. So you see, you've freed me! Now, thanks to you, I'm without boundary. You've granted me the world . . . ."

Startled, Hector looks around—seeking other phones, any phone booths.

But he sees nothing through the thickening curtain of fast-falling snow.

She says, "I also took the liberty of borrowing your Melville novel, along with those bullets in your gun. I took the latter because I sensed somehow, we were in danger of reaching the end of our so-sexy game. I've always had a sort of second-sight, you should at last know.

"As to the borrowed book," Verity concludes, "I needed something to pass the time on the passage over in the ferry's berth. So, I skimmed your Melville novel, darling Hector. Melville's book? It ends on a resonant and very cautionary line. Perhaps one for you to take to heart. You know—in case you recklessly dare to press your luck with me? Melville wrote, *Something further may follow of this masquerade.* I think we both know we're not fated to cross paths again. Not unless you force me to find you. So please don't come looking for me, Hec. I couldn't bear the outcome for you. *Je t'aime*, Hector Lassiter."

Verity hangs up first.

Shaken, Hector collects his bags and stalks off to the ferry's fenced parking lot to reclaim his long languishing, Chevrolet AA Capitol Roadster.

The plunging mercury and rising humidity soon make old war wounds ache and Hector begins to freshly limp.

He lets her engine warm up as he works to clear his Chevy's windows of snow, and under that, a thin but stubborn layer of ice.

At last underway, he gives his roadster a little more gas to get that extra, faster distance from the Great Lakes island he vows he'll never visit again.

In the middle of same-as-nowhere Ohio, some place where the fast whitening fields are plowed of corn and the gravestones outnumber the rooftops, Hector takes a deep breath of chill air through his car's slitted driver's side window.

Despite everything, he's thrilled to at least be off cursed South Bass—increasingly farther away from "The Devil's Lake" as winter barrels in.

It isn't going to be the carnal idyll in Key West with Verity he'd envisioned.

But thank God, he learned the truth about her in time.

Hunt her?

Maybe he will.

Or maybe not.

Either way, Hector is already starting to toy with the opening lines of a new novel that in his mind, at least for now, he's titling *Satan's Daughter*.

"I see him always in a lonely street, in lonely rooms,
puzzled but never quite defeated."
—Raymond Chandler

"The puzzle isn't so interesting to me
as the behavior of the detective attacking it."
—Dashiell Hammett

BLACK MASK BOYS: PART I

(LOS ANGELES: JANUARY 11, 1936)

Stooped and scarecrow skinny, Dashiell Hammett says, "C'mon, Lassiter. Don't be coy. You are not an effective cock tease. Get your ass up and into this photo."

Hector smiles over the rim of his cocktail glass, spying fellow "hardboiled" scribe Raymond Chandler surreptitiously and swiftly skidding off white gloves. Chandler does so for posterity's sake and personal brand protection—the crime writer frequently requires those gloves owing to a rare skin condition.

A fey and thinly clandestine Anglophile, Chandler is also improbably *the* 800-pound gorilla amongst active *Black Mask* pulp magazine writers.

Chandler adjusts his glasses, jabs his pipe point at Hector and chimes in, "Dash is right! Don't be a prig, Hec. You and Dash go back with the *Black Mask* farthest of any of us."

Curling his lip, Chandler growls at a bald, slightly taller man to his right. "Jesus, Moffatt. Has the *Black Mask* even published you? I think not. For sheer number of stories printed under his own or a pen name, only Raoul Whitfield has out-published Hec in *Black Mask*. Give Lassiter your place!"

Sitting out of camera range and nursing an Old Fashioned, despite his boozy brain fog, Hector credits Chandler's grasp of pulp-lit, "literary" history.

Hammett and Hector both indeed cracked *Black Mask* publication around '23.

Tubercular Hammett made his *Black Mask* bones while stateside.

But Hector scored his first several stories in the hard-boiled crime pulp magazine from abroad.

Stories pounded out late nights and typically the bolder for the good but cheap wine its high school drop-out author inhaled at the time—all while living and learning the fiction writing craft in Paris, France.

The first stories Hector published in *Black Mask* were convincingly set against edgy American backdrops, yet clandestinely penned while Hector prowled the romantic cafés of the Parisian Latin Quarter.

Hector's were white-knuckle tales knocked out after long – if not-always-fruitful days spent trying to compose *more serious* works, ones he hoped would be regarded of *literary* quality.

Stories that might be declared *edifying*, to use a word favored by his prime Parisian mentor, Miss Gertrude Stein.

It was much the same for Hammett, Hector knew. At least so in those heady, delusional early days, when Roaring Twenties pulp writing, although lucrative, then seemed to both fledgling authors and former Great War ambulance drivers more like whoring.

Hammett was, at least in the early going of his pulp-fiction career, a frustrated but still-secretly striving poet.

But Dash's crime novels—staccato, razor's edge works suggesting a near-enough Hemingwayesque terseness that critics frequently seized on it, some even rating Dash better than Hem—earned Hammett his not-inconsiderable lunch money.

Hector sips his highball, waves a big hand. "I'm not even a Left Coaster. If I attach myself to any American city these years in terms of the pulps, reckon she'd be New York. Anyhow, ya'll know I hate everything about this town other than easy studio money for script work or dialogue doctoring. All that aside? Old war wound's actin' up. Fiercely. Torture to stand. So please, have at it boys. Me? Gonna stay put and drink."

For Hector's money, the Nikobob Café mixes a world-class cocktail.

Or, Hector revises his estimation, maybe the bartender's canny enough to know that when serving a bunch of crime fiction authors, a heavy pour's not only expected—it's compulsory.

Hector drains his tumbler and raises it, signaling for another cocktail.

As he does that, the attendees of the first-ever "West Coast Black Mask Get-Together" crowd closer at the other end of the table to fit themselves within frame.

They include Raymond Moffatt, Chandler, Herbert Stinson, Dwight Babcock, Eric Taylor, Hammett, Arthur Banes, John K. Butler, W.T. Ballart, Horace McCoy and Norbert Davis.

Hammett and Chandler, both standing, seem from Hector's point of view to entirely ignore the camera, looking at one another as the photographer snaps away.

Both authors are relatively snazzy dressers ('though Hector privately thinks Chandler's necktie more than a tad frantic).

But Hammett is easily the more charismatic of the pair.

Dash's bushy shock of very-prematurely white hair surely doesn't dim his presence. Quite the contrary.

Only because six-foot-two, huskier Hector declines the group portrait, rail-thin but six-foot-one Hammett towers over his fellow *Black Mask* scribes as they strain to strike poses for the photographer.

Hector smiles to himself. If Hammett's simple height didn't irresistibly draw one's eye first to Dash, the fact Hammett is the only writer who's chosen to pose in profile would easily do the same.

Then there's Hammett's palpable, *Fuck this* attitude.

Or at least what Hector takes for laudable disinterest on the part of the creator of Sam Spade and the Thin Man in posing for a photograph with some otherwise fine fictioneers and a smattering of pulp fiction also-rans.

Returning to the matter of height?

Hammett towers over his posturing *Black Mask* peers—including Chandler—this despite the fact Dash isn't even standing up straight.

Meanwhile Moffatt—the ringer in the *Black Mask* authorial assembly—stays firmly put, stubbornly standing shoulder-to-shoulder with Chandler.

Horace McCoy, bouncer-turned-actor then turned-author, says to Moffatt, "You going to invite yourself to the burlesque joint after this too, Raymond Moffatt?"

Horace winks at Hector.

Just last week, Hector finished reading a darkly sublime novel by McCoy called *They Shoot Horses, Don't They?*

With reddening cheeks, Moffatt says, "It's Saturday and I have a date. In fact, my best gal is meeting me here in a few minutes. So, no. I won't be joining you all in slumming at that skin dive."

The other "Raymond" in the room—the comparatively prim Chandler, who is married to a woman seventeen years his senior—quickly volunteers, "'Fraid I have to skip that joint, too, fellas. Have to leg it as soon as we get this picture wrapped up."

Hammett says to Hector, "Gimp stem or no, you are sticking around, eh, Hector? I need somebody to really drink and talk with in that dump while the other guys gape and gawk."

Caught in mid-swallow, Hector flashes Dash a thumbs up with his empty left hand. He finishes swallowing, says smiling, "Sure, Dash. You, me and plenty of *charla profunda*.

Then the room falls eerily silent.

If the other writers weren't all looking at the camera at the same time for that photo that will eventually decades-hence prove a minor-historic artifact for *noir* crime fiction fans, the authors' gazes are now precisely locked on the same spot—at least for the moment.

All authors' eyes but Hector's.

Hector is facing his fellow writers, who are now all staring not back at him, but well past Hector.

One of the gaping writers wolf whistles.

Suddenly beaming, Moffatt says, "Ah, my date arrives! Fellas, meet my best gal, Miss Natasha Shale."

One of the other crime writers mutters, "Christ, the luscious tomato must be fuckin' blind."

It takes a moment for that name to sink in with Hector.

When it does, despite himself, Hector twists in his chair.

Hector's pale blue eyes lock with those of the striking blonde woman poised there in a tightly tailored jacket and skirt; swaying in high-gloss stiletto heels.

Even behind her black mesh veil, Hector can see it is indeed her.

Everyone else in the room instantly intuits that Hector and this stunning blonde are acquainted.

The duo are also palpably and equally shocked to see one another again.

Moffatt's "best gal"?

Verity Chisolm, of course.

From very low on a radio, Fred Astaire croons. "A Fine Romance."

Verity finds her voice first.

"So delicious to see you again, Hector," Verity says with a smile. "Oh, and happy belated birthday, darling Hec!"

Unarmed, and with his intermittently bum leg throbbing, Hector has made no attempt to immediately trail a fast-departed Verity and Raymond Moffatt.

Hell, Hector reckons they could be halfway to Bel Air or Beverly Hills before he could reach the street with his leg aching as it is.

Instead, Hector remains at the now largely empty, long table in the Nikobob Café, bracketed by a suddenly available-to-linger Raymond Chandler seated just to his left, and nattily dressed Dashiell Hammett to Hector's right.

Hector has moved on in his drink of the moment to an old Prohibition favorite called "The Four Horsemen." It consists of a half-ounce of Scotch whisky, a half-ounce of Tennessee whiskey, a half-ounce of bourbon and a half-ounce of Irish whiskey.

Over a steadily mounting array of empty tumblers, the increasingly tight trio talk as Hector massages his throbbing leg. An ancient shard of German shrapnel is making its final passage to break the skin. Hector recognizes this from past, bloody and painful experience.

Wincing now and then, Hector continues to knead his leg even as he gives a heavily edited account of his brushes with Verity, AKA *Natasha Shale*, on that Lake Erie island almost a decade past.

Afterward, Hammett says, "This woman, Verity, or whatever alias she goes by now—Natasha is it? She said meeting you again was *so delicious*. You had to register it, Hector. It was not subtle. It was not remotely sparing of Ray Moffatt's feelings. Am I indeed safe in assuming you and this gal got horizontal at least once?"

"At least," Hector confesses laconically, staring into his half-empty glass.

Hammett weighs that, presses, "Whatever became of the frail's murderous old man?"

Hector sips his drink. He craves a cigarette, but foregoes it for the sake of Hammett's TB-ravaged lungs.

Carefully choosing his words, Hector says, "Oh, the father died not too very long after I last saw him. Homicide. They found Krutch's body in Lake Erie after a fleeting thaw just around Christmas."

Tapping out his pipe, Chandler raises his gimlet with a re-gloved hand. "And the dishy daughter with eyes like strange sins is still ducking the law and living high on the hog from the looks of those threads shellacked to her like skin on a grape."

"So it would seem," Hector says dully. He repositions his aching leg on an adjacent chair. "I really should go after her."

Hammett snorts softly. "Your bum leg says otherwise. Anyway, that boat has sailed. Almost literally. Besides, what would you really do if you confronted her again?" A crooked smile. "What?"

Dash makes a pretend gun with thumb and forefinger that he proceeds to fire. "Would you whack her? Really, Hector?" Then Dashiell Hammett laughs and growls, "Bullshit!"

Hammett drains his latest glass and shakes his head.

"Extinguishing her is a thought," Hector says, trying to do so with the same darkly humorous tone Hammett used in putting that last loaded question to Hector.

Suddenly frowning, Hector demands, "Dash, what do you mean—that boat has sailed?"

But it's Chandler who answers. "Before you got here, before we knew what trouble this dame is, Moffatt was going on and on about how the pair are hopping a train tonight. From Los Angeles, they are rolling east to jump a liner to Europe for a winter idyll."

Hammett cuffs Hector's shoulder. "So you see, it's looking to be a long chase, Hec. That's if you're really—and stupidly—intent on making it."

Shrugging, Hector says. "Right . . . And I'm not necessarily sold on this as my necessary crusade, taken in that light."

But then Hector hesitates. "How much do you two like—and so, maybe correspondingly, how much do you fear for—Mr. Moffatt?"

Hammett produces a cigarette, affording Hector the tacit greenlight to do the same.

After shaking out his own Pall Mall, Hector fires them both up with his Hemingway-gifted, engraved Zippo.

Dashiell Hammett confesses from behind a curtain of smoke, “I met Moffatt today. Just like you, Hec. As for the lady and her maybe having taken on her wicked old man’s bloody work? Who the hell’s to say? Still, she’s a dish, and that’s for certain. But again, like Moffatt, the cooze is a stranger to me, ’til just a bit ago.”

Attention shifts to Chandler, who’s puffing away at his freshened pipe. Ray Chandler seems to Hector at least to enjoy building up the moment.

After a couple more draws, Chandler says, “I know Moffatt a bit. Don’t particularly care for him. Not based on that little I do know.”

Stroking gloved fingertips across the equally white table cloth, Chandler continues, “As to fearing for Moffatt—or as to any real threat this woman might pose to him—I’ll only say Moffatt told me he took his ‘best gal’ off the hands of another writer. Did that a couple of months ago. Some sorry hack published in something called *Weird Tales*.”

Hammett laughs. “Given Moffatt’s looks, the fantasy writer he cuckolded must have somehow been even more formidable the misfit. Jesus, that would take some doing.”

Adjusting his glasses, Chandler says, “Oh, it wasn’t like that. At least not as Moffatt confided it. No. Moffatt met, then picked-up Hector’s Verity or Natasha at her deceased boyfriend’s wake. Reportedly, tragic stuff. Moffatt said the boyfriend died just two days after dedicating his first novel to this twist named Natasha.”

Hector drains his drink.

Their server is suddenly right there. The bar guy inquires if sir desires another? Hector declines.

Pressing Chandler, Hector demands, "This dead fantasy writer—?"

"Alan Phillip Hott—"

"Sucker's name doesn't matter," Hector cuts off Chandler. "What does count, is how did this *Weird Tales* writer cash-out?"

"Suicide," Chandler says.

Hammett, an ex-Pinkerton, shoots back, "Really? How exactly? Pills? Rope? Was it a head in the oven, or maybe a swan dive off some bridge?"

Chandler shakes his head. "Total exsanguination."

Hammett arches darkly bushy eyebrows. "I'm sorry. What does that mean?"

"Means he bled out, all the way," Hector says. He then pounds the table with a fist and discarded cutlery and soiled place-settings jump. "Goddammit! Maybe I do need to chase their sorry asses to Europe."

The bartender is standing close by again. He positions a phone with a long cord in front of Hector. Rather redundantly, he says, "Phone call for you, Mr. Lassiter."

Hammett begins to rise to grant Hector privacy. Yet Chandler, closely eyeing Hector, doesn't stir.

Hector says, "Please, both of you, do stay." Then to the bartender he says, "I will have another drink, thanks. Make it a double, buddy."

Then Hector raises the candlestick phone's receiver to ear, but turned well-outward so Hammett and Chandler, leaning in close, can also hear.

Without a hello, Hector says, "Is this to forever be our pattern, Verity? Revelation, then a threatening phone call cowardly placed by you from hiding?"

"Safer for you, safer for me," Verity says, "so don't be insulting, darling. Still, it was pleasing to see you this afternoon. You're still such a handsome man. Still a man's man, and a lady's man."

"But also an older if not a wiser man," Hector says. "Yet, strangely, you haven't aged a day. And I take it Mr. Moffatt isn't close by? Or is he already—you know—not so longer with us?"

"Ray-Ray is safely seeing to our luggage if you must be such a paranoid beast about me," Verity says. "And Ray-Ray will stay safe. As will you. So long as you don't hunt us."

Hector says, "Right. If I don't. And yet? Can't help but to reckon old Ray-Ray suddenly only has got one book left him with you in his life."

He can hear the bewitching smile in Verity's voice. Hector remembers that smile up close—lolling in her bed before he grasped her true nature.

Verity teases, "Could be."

Hector grips the phone harder. "You're really pursuing this, aren't you? This insane obsession of playing dark muse to fiction writers, then offing 'em when they get a book out of knowing you? Should I reckon it's only a matter of time 'til you get round to trying it with me?"

A husky chuckle. "Don't sound so hopeful, lover man. I already got my book out of you. And you didn't even have to die to do it. So shows you how much you know. *Satan's Daughter*. You wrote it without my prodding. I quite love it. Cherish it the most so far, frankly. It's surely the best-written, so far. It has become for me, well, yes, my *Gospel of Hector*! But now be a good boy, and be missing from my life, Hec. Let's just consider tonight a piece of bad luck that fortunately didn't take a bloody turn."

Just like the last time, Verity hangs up first. She does it again without a goodbye.

Hector racks the phone as Chandler whistles lowly.

The bartender delivers Hector his fresh drink. Hector takes a deep swallow, savoring the burn all the way to his belly.

Raw-voiced, Hector says to his fellow *Black Mask* boys, "Don't suppose Moffatt mentioned where their European tour's to begin?"

Hammett shrugs; Chandler shakes his head.

Carefully, Dash says, "Depending on how prolific—how fast Moffatt doesn't write—you may have another chance at crossing paths with this tigress again. But only if you're crazy as that witch clearly is. Personally, I hesitate to raise this because I hope you'll evade any future encounters with the loopy bitch."

Hector demands, "What do you mean by another chance, Dash?"

Hammett looks to Chandler, says, "No. Goddammit, just no. I haven't the stomach or the heart." Hammett smiles at Hector. "Just too fond of you, Hec."

Chandler chews on his pipe stem, deciding. He says finally to Hector, "Before you arrived late, it was announced an East Coast version of this *Black Mask* get-together is planned in December. In New York City. Moffatt announced he plans to also be there 'With my best gal,' as he put it."

Hammett says, "Seriously, Hector. Swear to me you'll give that get-together a wide berth, won't you? Confine yourself safely to Key West? To Paris or Spain? Maybe Christmas and New Years in Florence or Venice? Or hell, you and I can just go on a pub crawl across Frisco. Pad out our respective rap sheets for drunk and disorderly conduct citations?"

Hector doesn't commit. He further contemplates his drink.

At last Hector observes, "As fiction writers, I think you two must agree. Starting a story *in medias res* is one thing."

With a furrowed brow, Hammett says, "Sure. Done right, starting in the middle of a tale can stoke tension."

Stubbing out his cigarette, Hector raises his eyebrows.

Hector says softly, "Exactly. But ending a story in its middle . . . ?"

"Everybody thought I was crazy.
A writer, you know—he's just a sort of crackpot."
—Lester Dent

"I found an article by a successful writer of
mystery stories.
It told how the source of inspiration, or what have you,
can go dead or latent, leaving a writer more or
less helpless
until it returns. My agreement changed to horror."
—Walter B. Gibson

BLACK MASK BOYS: PART II

(NEW YORK CITY, DECEMBER 20, 1936)

The bustling streets of Chinatown glisten beneath a thundering December rain.

Hector is huddled in a cozy booth of a Chinese joint he last ate in as a child with his maternal grandfather, Beau Stryder.

But tonight?

Grown-up Hector's dining with fellow crime fiction writers Lester Dent and Walter B. Gibson.

Respectively, "Les" and "Gib "are at the moment the penultimate and ultimately most-prolific and highly-compensated pulp fiction writers in America.

Until quite recently, Walter has been pounding out two Shadow pulp magazine novels a month—a Herculean literary feat typically prolific Hector simply can't fathom.

A new but less prolific writer, Theodore Tinsley—another *Black Mask* Boy—has recently been brought into help Gibson keep *The Shadow* gravy train rolling on the best-selling pulp magazine focused on Gibson's chuckling, black-clad vigilante who totes twin automatics he isn't at all bashful about using.

The Shadow series also frequently benefits from Gibson's considerable skills as an avid magician and noted ghost-writer for a host of top magicians, ranging from Thurston, to Blackstone, to the late Great Houdini.

Tinsley's been brought on board to mix things up with more hardboiled menace, blood and thunder violence, and, yes, increased sex appeal aimed at luring readers over from *Saucy Romantic Adventures, Spicy Detective Stories* and their ilk.

In an effort to equal the Shadow's market success, lanky and adventurous Les Dent was recruited to write the currently monthly adventures of strapping, brilliant globe-trotting adventurer and do-gooder Clark "Doc" Savage, Jr.

And Hector?

Hector is currently doing okay on the writing income front.

But that's only thanks to strong royalties and recent success in placing some older, previously unsold yarns.

Otherwise, for some alarming reason, as a working fiction writer, Hector's currently and completely blocked.

The trio of crime authors are nearing the end of a light-lunch-for-three in the venerable Port Arthur Chinese Restaurant on Mott Street.

Their shared meal consists of Won Ton and Chinese vegetable soups, egg rolls, shrimp and lobster sauce, roast pork, chicken chow mein, broiled rice, almond cakes and too much hot tea that has all three already-edgy authors' frayed nerves further jumping.

Dressed for an event later in the evening, the chain smoking trio are attention-getters.

Where Les is tall and laconic in a western way—very much in the same mold as Hector in that sense—Gib is shorter and significantly graying. An ex-newspaperman who worked the crime beat, Gib speaks like a Philly-born-hard case-turned-New York detective.

Something about Gib always suggests to Hector a salty owl.

Gib growls, "Let me try and sort this. Verity seems not to have aged since the mid-twenties. She's also hell bent upon having a host of crime fiction writers immortalize her in print. Now, Hec, there's this thing called a *tulpa* and—"

This groan. Les cries out, "Christ on a crutch! Please, no, Walt! You've already made me crazy with that goddamn nonsense about strongly imagined creative concepts miraculously come to life—"

Hector quickly raises a hand. "Please, both of you! Time's getting' short. Tonight's *Black Mask* shindig? Just four hours off. So let's please talk about what I might do now to stop Verity from killing again." A bitter smile. "And, also, I hope about what you two might do to help afford me some cover for whatever I might have to do to indeed stop this black, black witch for keeps."

Gib says, "Me? Came up a cropper regarding useful dope on this dame, Hec. So sorry. I hit up every connection I had from my Philly newspaper days. What did I dig up? Zilch. All I can confirm is Verity was still going by Natasha Shale when she came back from Europe—apparently alone—in late April."

Walt fires up his latest cigarette. "As to this writer Moffatt? Nothing on that gent. No death certificate. Hell,

I can't even find a bibliography for this author. No editors hereabouts seem to have heard of Moffatt. Other than making the scene back in Los Angeles at the gathering you were a part of, and then nosing into that noted photo with Hammett, Chandler and the rest, Raymond Moffatt, so far as I can ascertain, has left no literary footprint."

A moment's hesitation, then, with a squirm, 'Gib' amends, "Unless Moffatt writes under a pulp house name…."

That last statement elicits a wince from Les.

Despite Les and Gib's titanic success in the hero series pulps, Gibson publishes his wildly popular Shadow novels under the house name of "Maxwell Grant."

Dent's equally best-selling Doc Savage yarns are published under the company by-line "Kenneth Robeson."

Gib checks his notes again. He exhales twin streams of smoke from flaring nostrils, suggesting one of the countless Chinese dragon illustrations adorning the restaurant's tapestries and tri-panel dividers.

Gib continues, "As to any other pulp writers who've died between April and now? I've found just one. Robert E. Howard. Believed dead by his own hand in Cross Plains, Texas. Yet, based on all I've learned about Howard's death, there's no way Verity's fingerprints are on that gun. Not figuratively, not literally."

"But of course," Hector grumbles, topping off their tea cups.

The three writers have their corner of the Chinese restaurant nearly to themselves.

There's just one Asian male close by, dining alone. This man is strikingly tall and jaw-droppingly strapping, despite his hunch-shouldered posture as he slurps at his egg drop soup.

The three writers heard the big man order his meal in what passed to them for Chinese.

As Hector surveils the behemoth in studied glances, the giant exchanges his empty bowl for a plate containing several egg rolls that he proceeds to slather with hot mustard and duck sauce.

Searching his fellow authors' eyes, Hector says, "Strategy, brothers! That's what I most need your help on." A pause, then, "And I may require an alibi. I've also worked some of my own sources, Gib. Raymond Moffatt? I also can't tell you if he's dead. But I am confident that at least seven other crime fiction writers and pulp hacks are in fact deceased because of this woman."

Les Dent strokes his moustache. "If Moffatt is disappeared at the least, then what makes you think Natasha—Verity if you prefer—will even show up tonight at the *Black Mask* party without Ray Moffatt?"

Hector shrugs. "Hell, I'm not sure even if Moffatt shows later he won't be barred at the door by the organizers. He still has no known record of ever publishing in *Mask*."

Gib shakes his head, says, "Jesus. Neither do I."

Hector laughs, bumping elbows with Gib. "But you're my date tonight."

Les, having published or at least contracted for two new and very fine hardboiled stories in *Black Mask* in this soon-to-close calendar year is assured admission alongside Hector, who is still recognized as a pioneering *Black Mask* alum. Hector remains a fictioneer held in fond regard by *Black Mask's* editors and eager readers.

Surreptitiously spiking their ginseng tea from individual flasks variously containing single malt, Irish Whiskey and gin, the three pulp fiction writers spark off one another, pitching "plots."

But increasingly, Hector realizes for Les and Gib, their plotting is at best an intellectual exercise, coming from a predisposition more concerned with page-turning than the prospect of any of them—chiefly, Hector—remaining unprosecuted in a real-world rather than a pulp-lit judicial setting.

Dejected, Hector claims the check when it arrives on a plate with a scattering of fortune cookies.

Hector notices as that happens, the strapping Asian man at the next table settles his own tab.

Something is off about this immense man, Hector inchoately senses. Also something vaguely familiar. The man is immensely tall, and intense-gazed, with feverish black eyes.

Gib cracks his fortune cookie first. He snorts, reads aloud, "No snowflake feels responsible in an avalanche."

Hector mutters to Les, "You next, brother."

Lester Dent plucks out the narrow sheet of paper, groans.

"Jesus," Les laments. He also shares his fortune aloud. "You will die alone and poorly dressed."

Eager to move on to possibly more useful interaction with this fellow fiction writers on their way to the New York-edition *Black Mask soiree*, Hector is reaching for his cookie to get the silly tradition behind them when a shadow falls across their table.

An attractive Asian woman with a Louise Brooks-style raven bob stands there, smiling.

Behind the woman now stands the giant Asian. He's grinning with two gold front teeth. With a massive walnut-stained hand, he pulls back his overcoat to reveal the butt of a big revolver.

The woman claims the fortune cookie Hector was reaching for. She smashes it in her hand, then flings its crumbs onto the floor. She says aloud in a not particularly convincing attempt at broken-English, sing-song Chinese, "So sorry, but now my turn!"

Then, switching to English, in a fully American accent, the woman reads aloud, "The world may be your oyster, but it doesn't mean you'll get its pearl."

That seems to put a pout on her pretty mug.

Hector searches the woman's face, thinks, *It could be her*. He says, "You should probably brood on that warning, you know. Truly take it to heart."

The woman is about to respond when the waiter approaches, apparently sensing electricity in the air. The waiter inquires in English—presumably for the sake of the three Westerners, "Miss Dwan! Everything is okay?"

The woman quickly reverts to her singsong American-Chinese, "Yes. Okay. Perfectly Okey-Dokey."

When the waiter is again out of earshot, in her American accent, and in a far huskier voice that Hector certainly knows, the woman says, "Your server miscounted. There is a fourth cookie left for you, Hector."

Smiling thinly, Hector says, "You sure that King Kong behind you—who I now take for a former Lake Erie ferry-man—wouldn't prefer to have it?"

She smiles. Now he is certain.

Just like her voice, Hector certainly knows her natural smile.

He says, "This big fella is obviously in disguise, too. Why is it I feel like he's probably the muscle behind the act of hoisting my buddy Tommy to his death on that Lake Erie island?"

A disguised Verity says, "You feel all that because you can be clever. Eventually. As to my fortune? The oyster that is this world may or may not be mine in the end. But that fortune cookie now laying all alone there is definitely yours, Hector. Be a good boy. Be a man. Share its message, just like your prose-writing peers did. Just as I did. After all, what are we without our self-delusional tiny rituals? And anyway, it's well past time you began to walk with the future."

Never breaking eye contact with her, Hector crushes the last fortune cookie in his hand, mirroring Verity's actions.

Unlike Verity, Hector doesn't just drop the crumbs on the table or cast them aside. He retains the cookie fragments in his left hand.

Quickly glancing sidewise at Gib, who is seated on the same bench but to Hector's left—seated closest the wall—Hector sees that Gib notes the retaining of the cookie crumbs.

Beneath the table, hidden mostly by far taller, huskier Hector's torso, Gib taps Hector's foot under the table with his own.

Having caught Hector's attention again, Gib subtly straightens his right arm, simultaneously cupping his fingers as if to receive something from his coat sleeve. The knuckles of those grasping fingers brush Hector's thigh, giving him a glimpse of the black ebony stick that has dropped from Walter Gibson's sleeve.

Hector smiles inwardly, *Good old prestidigitating Gib!*

Les faces Hector from the opposite side of the booth.

Consequently Les' face remains in profile to the woman and the armed giant looming behind her.

Les arches an inquiring eyebrow not visible to the woman or the giant.

It's Les' way of asking Hector for instruction.

Hector raises a foot under the table; taps toe to Lester Dent's right kneecap.

Hector then glances at the giant. Then Hector says to the woman, putting stress on certain words, "Reckon, then, I *right*ly *nee*d to comply."

Les smiles thinly; winks his understanding with that eye Verity and her flunky can't see.

Hector's heart soars a second time. *Good old Les!*

With his right hand, Hector holds up the slim strip of paper containing his fortune. He reads it first to himself, smiles.

It's a queerly appropriate fortune for a career writer.

Hector reads aloud, "A conclusion is simply the place where you got tired of thinking."

Hector again looks to Gib, then to Les.

Smiling encouragingly, Hector says, "Brothers? Shall we?"

From there, things literally explode as the three thriller writers take chain-lightning action.

With his left hand, Hector hurls those sharp and crisp fortune cookie crumbs into Verity's face. She squeals, momentarily blinded.

As the giant reaches for his gun, Gib is already raising his right hand. He holds a magician's wand in that hand, which he raises above his head.

Even as Gib's arm rises, Hector reaches out with *his* right hand, grasping Verity's trim waist. Hector hurls her rightward and downward toward the floor.

Gib also snaps his magician's wand downward at the same time.

The special magician's wand Gib grips is called a "firing wand" and it goes off like a starter's pistol.

A blinding white flash temporarily blinds Hector in one eye.

Crying out, blinded in *both eyes*, the disguised giant stops his reach for his gun and grinds both palms to his stinging eyes, crying out in agony.

Now it's Lester Dent's turn.

With Verity out of the way, Les lashes out with his left foot at the blinded giant's exposed right kneecap.

The sound as the giant's leg breaks is wince-inducing.

The breaking bones also elicit louder, still-more frantic screams from the big man.

Those screams, Hector notes with some surprise, are disarmingly shrill—so very high-pitched.

Even as he thinks that, Hector is hauling himself out of their booth. With a taped roll of nickels clutched tightly in his hand, Hector swings with everything he owns.

Hector's fist collides with the giant's windpipe.

Goliath drops to the floor like a bomb-toppled church steeple.

It occurs to Hector the giant might well be dead, even before the big head bounces twice against the tiled floor.

Swept up in the adrenaline-surging moment, Hector couldn't care less if he has slain the stranger.

His Peacemaker is back at his hotel room, under his pillow and three-floors above the small ballroom of the

Knickerbocker Hotel where the *Black Mask* writers are scheduled to gather in a few hours.

Unarmed, Hector is reaching for the now exposed butt of the giant's shoulder-holstered gun when he feels another gun's barrel knowingly pressed to the worst of Hector's scars from his Great War-era leg injury.

The gun is cocked as Verity brushes the last of the stinging fortune cookie crumbs from her eyes with her free hand.

"I suppose," Hector says, slowly rising with hands raised, "those colored contact lenses and glued-on rubber eyelids you're wearing to look more Asian helped protect those green orbs of yours from all the cookie crumbs."

She says, "So, you have seen through my disguise."

"Hardly takes a Lamont Cranston, or a Doc Savage—let alone a Sherlock Holmes—to do that," Hector says. "Besides, you've seen my leg and so know where that bullet would do precisely the worst damage, Verity."

"Regardless, keep those hands up, Hector," she says.

To Les and Gib, Verity orders, "And you two—keep your hands flat on the table." She nods at Walter's spent explosive wand. Snarls, "Very cute, that. Cute for fake magic."

The waiter again dashes in, about to inquire if anything is wrong when he clearly realizes everything is wrong. He instinctively raises his hands.

"Chun," Verity says in her own voice, "Do be missing. Do that now. I'd truly hate to hurt you."

Chun does that.

Hector says, "I trust my friends are going to be safe?"

"You can trust, Hector," she says. "Verity Chisholm is long presumed dead. Killed when her car was run over at a train crossing in Bakersfield, California in the late 1920s."

Hector nods, smiling thinly. "*Her* body mangled beyond recognition, no doubt."

"Just so," Verity says, as Les and Gib study her with equal parts fascination and fear.

"Natasha Shale has passed, too," she said. "More recently, of course."

Gib risks interjecting, "Also on the list of those with little time remaining, I suppose is . . ." Gib nods at her present disguise.

"*Ming Dwan*," Verity says with a slight bow.

Shaking his head, Gib says, "Whatever you call yourself in that Oriental get-up, your feet are a dead give-away. American feet. Feet made for pumps; high heels. But feet that have never been bound."

Les smiles, chips in, "Then's there's also that All-American rump."

Frowning, Verity says, "Bid farewell to your writer buddies now, Hector. If you behave, Hec, there's still just a slim chance you might live to see them again."

Hector smiles at his friends. "In the spirit of the lady's pledge that I may yet continue to draw air, I won't say goodbye, brothers. Rather, *au revoir*."

Retrieving his gun from the very-still giant's shoulder holster so it can't be used against her by the two seated pulp authors, Verity says, "Start walking, Hector. Stay at least six-feet in front of me."

To Les and Gib she warns, "Wait ten minutes before you stand up. Do otherwise? I swear I will kill Hector."

Pausing in the vestibule, still pointing a gun at Hector, with her free hand, Verity whips off her black-banged wig and false eyelids and thrusts them in a coat pocket.

Her blonde hair is scraped tightly back and secured in a bun above the base of her skull.

Verity deftly extracts her colored contact lenses, revealing distinctive green eyes.

Hector shivers, seeing how this seemingly means to go.

The armed woman who will walk Hector out onto the street—and possibly even kill him there?—she will appear very different from the one with whom he left the restaurant and to whom at least English-fluent Mister Chun will surely describe to police.

Verity finishes buttoning up her coat to cover her Asian-style tunic beneath.

Back inside the restaurant, Les and Gib debate whether to immediately follow Hector and Verity.

The more intrepid of the pair, Les is rising when Gib takes his arm and says, "Whoa, just one more second, pal!"

Gib nods at a fast-moving woman dashing to the door, asks, "Les, who is that leggy redhead leaving now, and why does she also have a gun?"

The rain has transitioned to sleet that stings the eyes.

"I've been rethinking things between us of late," Verity says, squinting. "I've decided I think I do want another book from you about me."

A pause, then she amends, "Partly, because I'd enjoy another book from you about me, Hec. But also because I want another book from you regardless of whether I appear in it. You seem not to have published anything substantial in a while. You frankly have me worried. As an avid fan, I mean."

Hector, also squinting against the icy rain, wishing he had sunglasses, says, "I can't deny you haven't in some dark way inspired me here or there in the past. Yet that's hardly the point. Besides, you're not the first fiend to claim to have somehow fired my work. Candidly, I fear you're far from the last who will presume to do so."

A soft chuckle. Verity says, "As to anymore perhaps being behind me in the role of muse, that's going to hinge on what's said between us in the next few minutes."

But any such conversation never comes.

There's a blast from behind that sets Hector's ear ringing.

For just an instant, Hector figures it's wild Walt Gibson, charging after with his ballistic magic wand.

But then Hector flinches again, as something wets his eye. This time, it's not icy rain, but something warm.

Reaching for his face, Hector's fingertips come away bloody.

Verity falls against him, then pitches forward, striking the pavement with the right side of her head. She rolls onto her back.

Her face is in bloody ruins.

Another woman, pale-skinned, red-headed, steps over Verity's body. She levels an automatic and fires another bullet between Verity's breasts.

The redhead's second shot is a gratuitous, at best, Hector knows, wiping Verity's blood and brain tissue from his eyes with a display handkerchief.

The redhead with a gun says in a near-frantic, breathy voice, "Someday, believe me, you'll thank me for doing that, sir!"

"Hell, I'm likely grateful already," Hector says softly back, so only Verity's slayer can hear.

"That thing killed my brother," the redhead sobs.

"Shut up, please," Hector snarls at the stranger. "Because the less I know, the less I have to share with the homicide dicks."

As a crime writer, Hector realizes the role he must fast begin to play for street witnesses or simple gawkers that will soon be gathering around them.

For the moment, those looking on are locals, and Hector's wagering few if any are fluent in English—not as a first or a mastered language.

Hector whispers urgently again to the redhead, "Before I kneel down and act aggrieved, two things! She has a gun in her right hand, and another in her right pocket. In that same pocket, is a black wig that could aid your flight. Take all three. Put on the wig in that alley a block to your left. The guns? Pitch them down some storm-water catch basin, but at least four blocks from here. If you can, hit a shop and get a new coat and sample some perfume, *a lot* of perfume, on your right hand and forearm. That will muck with any gun-fire paraffin tests if you're identified and arrested."

The woman ducks down, scooping up guns and wig as Hector blocks all that from the view of fast-gathering witnesses.

Hector locks eyes with hers, says, "Now, run for your life!"

The redhead does that, fast turning the corner into that alley.

As she's running from him, Hector falls to his knees, pointing at the obviously dead woman at his feet. He cries out, "Somebody call an ambulance!"

He suddenly realizes Les and Gib are huddled close behind. Les asks urgently, "You didn't—?"

"Lord no," Hector whispers back. "Some woman I don't know did this."

Gib says, "Then what's the play, Hec? And by the way, that shot of yours to the throat left that giant back in the restaurant a croaker."

Hector's mind is moving a thousand miles an hour. He focuses, slowing his train of thought, weighing possible implications or unintended complications or readings that might possibly spin out of the false scenario he's tending toward.

Hector says at last, "We didn't know any of the three. The three of us are in black-tie for tonight's *Black Mask* event. Let's hew to the claim they were grifters or thugs who mistakenly thought because of our threads we were well-heeled in these hard times. Mine was a kidnapping for ransom gone very bad."

Les says, "And the woman who shot this woman dead?"

Hector shrugs. "Hell if I have an explanation for that. Let the cops figure that out. That's their trade, after all."

There are plenty of potential pitfalls in all this, Hector knows.

Particularly if the redhead doesn't evade capture.

But if she is apprehended, anything said between them will be he-said versus she-said, and as a fiction writer and well-paid fabulist, Hector knows he enjoys plenty of unfair advantages as a liar.

Hector rises slowly, wincing as his bad leg and knee crack with the cold and icy rain. He shoves his hands deep into his pockets, awaiting arrival of the homicide boys he's sure somebody must have by now summoned to the scene of this strange, Chinatown-at-Christmastime murder.

Lighting a Pall Mall while contemplating Verity's apparent corpse, Hector recalls his priest-blessed Peacemaker he used to put down Verity's allegedly demonic old man.

Exhaling smoke from his nostrils like a blue-eyed dragon, Hector supposes it's far too much to hope the unnamed, ginger assassin at least took the trouble to use silver bullets to end Verity, their mutual *bête noire*.

THROUGH THE VALLEY OF THE SHADOW OF ROOSEVELT'S NOSE

(SOUTH DAKOTA, 1953)

This one is as bad as that other the so-called Misfit recently put down.

That pious old bitty in Georgia who'd yapped her family right into an early grave.

Old woman was a talker, okay. She said more than plenty, but didn't really say anythin' in the end. Mostly, she seemed to the Misfit in love with the sound of her own shrill voice.

This one, the tall, handsome man with the mutedly graying brown hair and pale blue eyes, seems still more chatty. It is almost like the man enjoys their dialogue. Like the fool doesn't sense how this means to end.

Bobby is losing patience with the man, too, he can see. Bobby's finger softly rubs the trigger of his automatic.

Just a moment ago, they learned the handsome man is something more than a talker.

Other than a talker…?

Maybe that is how to put it. Cussed words. Either way. Hell, they are probably all the same thing, in the end, the Misfit assures himself.

Anyway, the man is a writer. An author. A writer known, or so Bobby says, as "the man who writes what he lives and lives what he writes."

A man named Hector Lassiter.

Lassiter isn't alone. Hector has a woman with him. A pretty woman. More than pretty, most would likely say. But tarted up fetchin'. Perfumed and painted like some Whore of Babylon. And they have a kid with 'em, too. A tow-headed boy-child of less than eight.

The boy, Tommy Lee, has this thick cowlick up front that won't be tamed. There are wide, scared eyes on the boy. So, they'll take care of that tyke first, as is custom. Bobby will see to that, of course. Get it over fast-like for the child. They always put down the youngest first. The so-called innocent.

Then it will be the woman's turn.

The man—Lassiter—will be the last to go.

Let Lassiter see it all, first. Wrench the challenge out of those pale blue eyes.

Though I walk through the valley of the shadow of death... I will *fear no...*

Shaking his head, snorting softly, the killer looks down the barrel of his gun at the man in his sights. He says to the writer, "An author, eh? And I thought I was a misfit. Ya'll just an artsy coward. A fool rewritin' the world 'cause he's got no stomach for this one. Mister, I don't see need durin' these mean times for any more writers. Not no need since the prophets. And ain't them prophets proven themselves to be sorry liars, anyhow? It's a mean old world. A good man is hard to find, and anyway, what would you do with a good man if you did find him?"

The killer cocks the hammer back on his revolver; cylinders roll.

"And I can tell you just this much for certain, sir. This is one part of your life you will not be writin' about. Not never. Reckon you just had the bad luck to wander into *my* story."

The killer looks at the writer's natty sports jacket, says, "Could use me a new coat."

With two fingers, the killer pushes his silver-rimmed glasses back up his nose. "Ain't no pleasure in this, mister. Not for me, despite what you might be thinkin'. But you will all be at peace."

Glancing up at the granite heads of the presidents staring sightlessly forward into the void, he says, "Like the Lord, them faces are. Right there and yet not there. Not at all."

He spits into the dust. "Look at them—lookin' but not seein'. Starin' off to where it don't none matter."

The killer shakes his head, spits again. "Ain't no carin' in this world."

It started as a simple film gig.

Hector was to come up with some suspense stuff for a thriller Alfred Hitchcock was just beginning to fiddle with.

Hitch had this notion of setting a climactic chase scene across the faces of Mount Rushmore. He'd paid Hector, novelist and sometimes screenwriter, to come out to South Dakota and wander around the national monument. See what the soaring scenery might stir in the crime novelist.

Hector had swiftly taken up with this local woman from the F. O'Connor ("The *F* is for *Friendly*!") car rental agency. A comely divorcee named Emmy Thorp. Emmy is all legs and pouty lips.

At first the woman resisted. "I subscribe to *Confidential.* You have a reputation, Mr. Lassiter. As a kind of high-tone tomcat, I hear tell of you. An adventurer and a lady's man? A scrapper. A hard man."

Hector just smiled and said, "Don't believe all that loose and low talk, darlin'. That's just to sell books and movie tickets. Hell, I'm gentle as kittens."

He'd taken Emmy and her son, Tommy Lee, out for a picnic around the monument; aimed to squeeze in a little film scouting expedition.

Down here in the basin—the scrublands of the Black Hills—in the shadow of all those massive historical heads, they promptly ran afoul of this bespectacled killer and his bloodthirsty friend, Bobby.

The writer's rental car's radiator took a stone along the unpaved road while snaking below the monument.

As Hector was standing there, staring at the smoke roiling from under the hood, an old black heap suggesting a hearse rolled up. Two men had climbed out.

One, somber and bespectacled, said, "Lend a hand, mister?"

Hector had heard radio reports about the men. He'd heard they were believed to be in the area. He'd seen some newsreel footage and read the newspaper reports of their cross-country killing spree.

Sure. Hector knew this man and his partner's fearsome reputations well enough. Hector also made them, like that.

But Hector had also known enough not to show any signs of having recognized them. He'd played it casual.

Or so he thought.

Somehow, the man with the glasses and gray hair had in some way correctly intuited Hector knew exactly who he was.

As they stood there, considering one another with dawning realization of recognition, a meadowlark trilled.

The shadow of a still-winged, high-gliding turkey vulture swept silently over them.

The stranger suddenly pulled his revolver.

He pointed it at Hector's face and said, "This is unfortunate."

They are faced off now in the shadows of those giant granite heads; standing in the dust, staring at one another.

Low and steady voiced, Hector says, "Get in your car and drive off, now. Not as if I can chase you or go phone ahead to the police with my car broken down as it is. You'll have more than a fair head start. And you won't have any more murders stacked against you in court."

The killer shakes his head and says, "Ain't no sense in any of that. You can't know the future any more than me, mister. We've gone this long without police catchin' us. I reckon we can go on for as long as there is left us, and that might just be plenty." He shakes his head and says, "And you're in no spot to be sendin' us along and leavin' you here. That's not our way. If you know anythin' about me, and I suspicion you do, then you know that."

Hector wets his lips, looked around; he stares a moment up at Teddy Roosevelt. Well, looks up Teddy's nose, really. The writer doesn't fear much for himself. Not yet. But the woman and the boy? The boy, particularly? They shouldn't have to feel this flavor of fear. They also shouldn't have to see what is likely to come.

"You boys really best be movin' on," Hector says. "This road's not lightly traveled, by all accounts. Someone's apt to happen by and soon."

"We was on this path a long ways and didn't see more than y'all," the killer says. He points at the dusty road in its opposing direction, says, "Don't see any tracks headed out that a-way you all were goin', neither. I'd say we are plenty alone." He rubs his jaw, says, "We're always alone. Even in company."

Hector frowns. Tommy Lee is shaking now, teeth chattering despite the heat. The boy's knees are knocking.

This needs to be wrapped up, pronto.

Hector says, "Just shut your goddamn mouth, pal. You're nothin' more than a blood-simple jackal. Your buddy here? Even more, maybe. But you're just as low and mean and bad as this psycho you truck with."

A little flare there in the killer's eyes; much more of one in Bobby's.

The one with glasses, the leader, says, "Can't much argue with you about Bobby here. He can be a handful, and he does like the work. Maybe too much. Takes pleasure in it. But there ain't no real pleasure in life. That's what makes me different."

"No, that's what makes you more pathetic—more the monster," Hector says. "Your buddy here has at least found his sorry love. He's bloodthirsty. You are, too. But you pretend not to be. That's what makes you the lower creature on the totem pole."

Bobby convulses into this donkey bray of a laugh and says, "Thet's perfect, mister! Thet's *ex*-actly right! He kills like me, but kids his conscience by saying t'ain't no pleasure! Hell, way I see it, he's just trying to keep options open in case he's got it wrong and he does have to face the judgment."

Hector says, "Didn't I read there used to be three of you?"

The one called Bobby said, "Was a misunderstandin'." He flashes an accusing glare at the bespectacled, older man. "Guess it's true what they say. Never go off jawin' 'bout politics or religion." A beat, then, "'Specially not religion, eh, Boss? One cross word and Boss here put down poor Hi like he was some rabid cur."

So, the man with glasses—the Misfit—has a temper. Hector smiles inwardly. Good. And so much for honor among thieves… Or killers.

Hector says, "Best close your eyes, Tommy Lee. Emmylou, you too."

The gray-haired man swivels his gun at Bobby's head. "You keep them eyes open," he orders Emmylou and her son. "And you, Bobby Lee, you commence to apologizin', and askin' me for forgiveness, right now! Soon as you do that, Bobby, then you can walk them two into the woods yonder and finish business."

Bobby said, "You turn thet goddamn gun away from me! You've got no right in hell to—"

"Have me every right," the gray-haired killer says. "Got me every right 'xactly 'cause there ain't no rights in this world. In a world with no rules, it falls to them who can and them who dare to lay down the law. Restore balance."

Hector says again, more softly, "Close your eyes Tommy and Emmy. Keep 'em tight-closed, 'til I say."

The killers are ignoring Hector, the woman and the child for the moment.

Bobby, clearly flustered now, says, "You cow-simple son of a bitch! You sorry-ass—"

A crack makes the others flinch and Bobby's right eye and most of his forehead dissolve into pink and white spray.

Even as Bobby sways, already dead on his feet, the gray-haired killer is swiveling his gun back toward the writer, aiming to get Hector Lassiter back in his sights.

But there is another crack.

The killer's gun hand is enveloped in another spray of blood and bone chips; the killer's wrecked revolver tumbles to the dust.

Uncomprehending, the gray-haired killer stares at his ruined hand. All but his pinky finger are now severed to bleeding stumps.

The man, Lassiter—this writer—has an old Peacemaker pointed at the killer's head. The wicked-long, antique Colt looks like a museum piece.

The writer's pale blue eyes are mocking now. He says, "Personally? I choose to think this is the price you pay for not bein' a reader. That silly phrase they attach to me? 'The man who lives what he writes and writes what he lives'? I don't have much patience for it. But I suppose there is a kernel of truth nested in there. Enough so that had you ever read a story or book of mine, you'd have known to frisk me."

Hector checks to see the woman and the child still have their eyes tightly shut. He says, "Keep those peepers closed you two, but please don't worry. I've got the only gun, now. You're perfectly safe."

Emmylou says, softly, “Thank God!”

It comes as a snarl from the killer with the badly bleeding hand: “Ain’t no God!” He tries to bind his shirttails around his bleeding hand.

“Don’t bother with that,” Hector says. “You’re not going to bleed to death. Not from that hand. Use that good paw to get a hold of old Bobby’s belt. You’re going to drag what’s left of him into that glade, yonder, where you meant for him to take mine.”

Huffing, struggling to drag his dead partner into the trees, the killer says, “This is in no way right. My story, it wasn’t meant to end. Not this way.”

Following behind, his Colt trained at the killer’s head, Hector says, “These things are a matter of perspective. Sometimes, I think the wrong point of view makes for much of this world’s misery. Take you for instance. Take now and here.”

They reach and then enter the copse of pine trees, out of sight of the woman and her child.

His teeth chattering, his knees threatening to fail him, the killer says, “I don’t understan’.”

Hector shrugs. “Your story. You wrongly said your story isn’t meant to end this way. That’s your whole problem. One of perspective. Point of view. This isn’t your story. It never was.”

Hector says, “Way I see it, you stumbled into my story.”

The killer falls to his knees, like he might beg or pray for mercy. He says, “Mister, you don’t believe in anythin’ any more than I do. I can tell! You’re no different than me. Ain’t no God, and you know it! You’re—”

“Oh, I am wholly different from you,” Hector says. “Fella said, if you gaze into the abyss, the abyss also gazes into you. You and me? We maybe looked into that same black hole. Difference between us? You flinched."

Emmylou hears a single gunshot.

She grabs Tommy Lee and hides among the trees on the other side of the road, terrified something has gone wrong.

Hector wanders out from among the distant pines.

Emmylou runs to meet him. She hugs Hector, hard.

Emmy says, "It's over?"

The writer smiles. "It's over. The end."

She holds him close, murmurs promisingly in his ear, "A hard man is good to find."

FIRST DRAFT

(NEW MEXICO, 1957)

Marita is dead, no question.

"Writing these books that you do, Héctor," the big, damp Mexican madam says, fanning herself, "you see now why I sent for you, yes?"

Hector Lassiter squats down next to the murdered prostitute, hams on heels and head on side, examining her body.

The girl's own head has been nearly twisted off.

She's sprawled on her belly, a rare enough position for a woman in her line of work, and rarer still for one with such a rack.

Spread-eagle on her belly as she is, Hector shouldn't be able to see luckless Marita's lolling tongue and bulging eyes—the blood vessels all ruptured.

But now the dead girl's head is turned 180-degrees, like she's checking out her own backside and understandably not appreciating her impossible view.

She was called "Marita," at least in this house.

Like so many in her trade, her real name may have be far from that one. Stories have it she was one of the very rare ones who seemed to actually relish her work, making it at least seem to those who paid to be with her that such time together was something not like the filthiest of commerce.

Anyway, given the sorry way she had to make her living, she certainly didn't deserve to die for it.

So, goddamn someone, anyway.

As he always does under intense pressure, Hector slips outside himself to see how he's handling it. He seeks out what's sticking in his mind for later description. Grasping for that single telling detail that will lend that undeniable sense of verisimilitude that will later sell it to his readers.

Clutched in the dead girl's hand is her locket, torn from her ruined neck.

Hector coaxes the locket and broken chain from the dead girl's hand. He opens it to reveal a picture of an older woman who resembles the dead girl around the mouth and eyes.

Surely her mother.

Hopeless, facing death, Hector figures Marita reached out for her mama—like a doomed little girl reaching for her mother's protective and loving hand.

He rises, wincing as his knees crack. He fishes his sports jacket's pocket for his Zippo and pack of Pall Malls. Hector doesn't really want a smoke just now. It just seems the thing he should do. Possibly calm his nerves by putting his shaking hands through the calm routines of muscle memory? And he always plots his stories best when smoking, or behind the wheel of his Chevrolet.

Hector slits the virgin pack with a yellowed-thumbnail and shakes one loose. Firing it up, he turns to Madam Ruiz. He blows smoke, asks, "Where's the kid?"

"In another room," the old and big boss whore says, curling her hairy lip.

It's been twelve hours since Hector last shaved, yet the shadow on Luisa Ruiz's upper lip already shames his. "He's passed out, stinking drunk," she says.

Hector nods. "The boy talk much after…?" He gestures at Marita's body with his cigarette.

"No, Héctor. We found her like this when the kid went twenty minutes past his paid-for time. Marita—" the madam pauses to cross herself "—was found just like this. He was laying on the bed, like I say, passed out, drunk and snoring. The pig."

"And, so, you sent Manuel to find me," Hector says, suddenly feeling a headache coming on. He squeezes the bridge of his nose.

Manuel found Hector easily enough. The madam's errand boy put the arm on the pulp magazine writer/crime novelist/screenwriter in the Pale Fire Cantina, just a few blocks from Hector's La Mesilla hacienda.

The madam squeezes Hector's arm. She says, "Your books, the stories about you and what you do and how it's later written about by you? Well, I knew you could help me, Héctor, like nobody else can. And we go back. And that boy, his poison family? They are well known, as you well know. And this other man? Stephen Walker, who is running for mayor? He's a moral crusader, yes? He's already trying to shut down operators like me. This obscenity—this killing in my house by this kid, well, you know what will happen, yes?"

Hector nods. He surely knows.

Walker is a Bible-thumping madman and a hypocrite of heroic proportions. A scripture quoting politician and a leading light of the local Catholic Church.

But Hector Lassiter, "poet of the gutters, borderlands and bawdy houses," as Anthony Boucher once described him, sometimes moves in twilight circles—the better to gather source material for the kinds of books he writes.

Hector has heard the stories of Walker's border crossings.

He's heard tales of the politician's visits to Juarez brothels that offer children up to rich pervert gringos.

The couple of times Hector has met Walker, the politician has stunk of breath mints, as if they could ever mask the stench of fifty-five years of never-ending gin-swilling.

And the passed-out boy in the other room?

He is Joseph Newton, son of Evan Newton, New Mexico oil tycoon.

Hector half-smiles, thinking to himself, *Quite a cast of characters.*

The madam wrings her pudgy hands, searching Hector's palest of blue eyes. "I don't know what I can offer you to make you help me with this mess, Héctor."

Currently, Hector is between books, going through a rare dry writing spell.

He's been unable to get even a short story going, though he owes one to *Stag*.

And he's looking for something bigger, something that he might expand into his next novel.

Lately, he's been thinking it's time to take his swing at Hammett's *Red Harvest*.

Hector tells himself that perhaps tonight's sordid and bloody escapade will prime his writing pump.

As the madam noted, gritty events like this have done that very thing in the past.

For Hector, life has imitated art, has imitated life, and so on—and for so long—that the writer himself now increasingly confuses his memories for his stories, and vice versa.

A few weeks ago, a baritone busker passing through the borderlands sang a song that put it more succinctly: "We live what we write and we write what we live . . . is that wrong?"

Whatever else this house peddles, it offers a hell of a fine bowl of chili. At last Hector says, "How about house credit on booze and grub, through the New Year?"

In two days, it will be Cinco de Mayo: Months of no-pay liquor and some low-end meals seems just compensation to the author's own admittedly rarefied mind.

The brothel matron nods vigorously. "Done. But what should we do?"

Hector grinds out his cigarette on the bottom of his boot. He tosses the stub aside. "Get a big rug or something we can roll poor Marita up inside, *por favor*."

As an afterthought, he asks, "Marita got family 'round here?"

The oldest whore shakes her head. "No, not here. They're on the other side, somewhere in the Yucatan, I think."

Hector nods. Somehow that makes it a little easier to take liberties with the girl's already decimated reputation. And it's pretty tough to libel the dead. "While you do that," Hector says, "Manuel and any others needed should carry the boy down and put him in the back seat of my car. It's the blue Chevy Bel Air convertible, parked out back."

The other working girls help Hector roll their fallen sister up in the tassel-ended rug and Hector shoulders the load.

He gently lays Marita out in the trunk of his Bel Air and softly slams shut the lid, thinking, *Poor little bitch: Dead and* still *you have a busy night ahead.*

"What else?" the big madam asks, fanning herself more vigorously in the sultry New Mexico night.

"Fetch me three bottles of whatever young Joe was drinking before he evidently decided to murder your girl."

The madam gestures at one of her other girls—a topless and sullen white girl with bad teeth and a horse face—who trudges inside to do her madam's bidding.

Hector shakes his head. If he ever writes of any of this, he's going to have to write that one prettier than she is in life. As she truly is, she's detracting from the scenery—bringing a more sordid and even a seedy air to affairs.

She returns with the three bottles of tequila and Hector stows them under the front passenger seat. He tells Manuel to squeeze into the back seat with the boy murderer.

Turning to Luisa Ruiz a last time, Hector says, "I need to know you'll all never talk about this, of course. Not *ev-er*. Regardless of any pressure thrown your way. Not you, and especially not your girls. I wasn't here tonight, right? Marita wasn't working here tonight, right? That boy never reached here tonight, understand? If this ever goes public, I will tell the real tale to save my ass, even it if sinks you. Got that?"

Luisa Ruiz crosses herself again. "You have my word."

Hector really doesn't want to dwell too deeply on what a boss whore's pledge might or might not be worth, push comes to shove.

"All right then," Hector says. "Just threaten your girls within an inch of their lives if they ever let slip any of this."

Then the author slides behind the wheel of his Chevy and sets off for the "better" side of town.

Manuel asks, "What first? We drop the *pendejo* off at his home?"

Hector shakes his head. "No damn way. I love my car, and it's still eighty degrees in the dark and poor Marita surely won't keep."

Hector passes a bottle of tequila over his shoulder to Manuel. "See if you can get some more of this into the boy in his sleep—every drop you can."

"I get it," Manuel says. "Keep him drunk and passed out, yes, Mr. Lassiter?"

Actually, Hector is shooting for a fatal dose of alcohol poisoning, playing to a dark hunch.

Well, maybe not so much a hunch, as much as it is an urge for this all to go in a certain direction for Joe.

But, for now, Hector says, "Sure."

Hector palms the wheel, drifting into a filling station lot and steering over next to a phone booth. Hector climbs out, fishing change from his pants pocket, then pulling out and shaking loose his display handkerchief. He slips a dime between his front teeth and bites down on it. Talking through those clenched and blocked teeth will change the cadence and tone of his voice. The layers of handkerchief over the phone receiver will do more of the same. The other coins go into the pay phone.

Presumptive mayor Stephen Walker answers.

Hectors says, "This is the very call you've surely long feared, asshole. And don't you try and hang up on me. See, I have pictures of you, snapshots of you screwing kids."

Terrible and telling silence.

Hector lets it hang there a few moments more, then asks, "Your family home?"

This quaver: "*No* . . ."

"Good," Hector says. "Get in your damn car. Then drive to where I am. Just across the bridge at Rosie's. I'll be the well-dressed gringo with the camera. *And* a stack of photos. And, yes, the negatives, too. And here's the good news. I'm relatively cheap. Five hundred dollars, and it all goes away."

Hector hangs up, not waiting for an answer.

Then the author slides back behind the wheel. He cracks the seal on a bottle of tequila and takes a deep swig.

He's fully committed now, and he has got to steer her into port.

He's never been one to start something and not at least carry it to its end, even if it proves not to be a keeper.

And this far in, he surely can't bin this story.

Fortunately, there aren't many roads in La Mesilla.

Stephen Walker has to drive by this parking lot to make his border crossing. Walker drives a brand-new, black Cadillac with big red-white-and-blue magnetic campaign signs mounted on both front doors.

Hector figures, flustered as Walker's apt to be, he'll be foolish enough to leave them in place on his way to his rendezvous with his presumed blackmailer.

Less than five minutes later, the favorite to be the town's next mayor indeed goes rolling by at speed in his impossible-to-miss Caddy-cum-billboard.

Hector gets his Chevy in gear and drives in the opposite direction, to Walker's posh pad.

Manuel starts getting fidgety as they roll up before the big house.

Hector hands his sidekick the open bottle of tequila he's been drinking from and says, "Finish her off, old pal."

While the Manuel goes at the bottle, Hector slides out of his car and scopes the Walker house. Its front door looks impregnable. He walks around back and finds a screen door.

Hector slips out a library card and wedges it in the too-wide crack and easily pops the catch-and-eye hook securing the rickety door.

Then he goes back around the house, and helps Manuel pull Marita's body from the trunk.

Huffing, they lug the carpet and its contents inside and up the stairs. They roll the dead prostitute's nude body out of the carpet and onto the mayoral hopeful's big bed.

Manuel rolls the carpet up again and heads back to the Bel Air as Hector slips another dime between his teeth and, using the handkerchief again, scoops up the mayor's phone and dials the police.

Disgusted to have to wait through nine rings, Hector at last gets a cop and lays out his confession in-persona as Stephen Walker. Hector goes for something breathless and psychotic sounding—really getting into it.

As Walker, Hector admits to killing a prostitute he paid to visit him in his home. "Walker" says he's running for the border and will never be back. He says he hopes the cops will make his wife and kids understand how it was.

Pleased with how he has put it, how he's laid it out, Hector hangs up the phone, then trots down the steps and slides into to his Chevy.

The night is full of sirens already.

It's a heady thing, shaping the face of a city to your idiosyncratic, and maybe even darkly just designs.

Manuel, now in the front seat next to Hector, truly flying on tequila, says dreamily, "What now, *Jefe*?"

Hector takes the empty bottle from the young Mexican and says, "I have a few more calls to make."

There are three other significant houses of ill repute in La Mesilla. Hector makes inquiries and finds his worst suspicions about Joe Newton are on target.

To Hector's mind, a near-cherry boy doesn't just get drunk, get off, then decide to break a woman's neck and simply sleep it off.

Hector drops dimes and quickly learns at least five local working girls have died recently, just as Marita has.

The girls were presumably killed by Joseph Newton.

In most cases, the boy's father paid money to cover up Joe's crimes. In a couple of instances, the madams or the pimps, in the manner of Luisa Ruiz, elected to undertake their own cover-ups.

The crime writer hangs up the phone and slides back behind the wheel. Manuel has drunk himself unconscious. His head is pressed to the passenger's side door and he's snoring, this drool-trail sliding down toward his collar. Not a pretty image.

But it's just as well that Manuel's out cold, just like murderous Joe.

Hector drives out of town and into the desert—just far enough away to avoid anyone seeing, but close enough to be within plausible walking distance of town—at least by Hector's estimation. These sorts of things are always a matter of intuition and extrapolation, in his admittedly rarified experience.

From years of writing fiction, Hector has learned this: not everything can be told as it truly was.

Some things are simply too true to be good; to be boiled down to effective prose.

With his handkerchief, Hector wipes down the three bottles of tequila, then presses each bottle several times into still-unconscious Joe Newton's hand.

He then hauls the boy out into the desert scrub.

He spreads Joe out across an anthill. Grasping their necks with the handkerchief, Lassiter arranges the three tequila bottles around snoring Joe, just so.

This is what Hector's going for:

Joe got legless drunk, went off his head, then wandered off into the desert night to his doom.

The temperature is predicted to drop into the twenties by midnight.

There is already a fierce, west-to-east wind.

All the liquor, the ants, the rattlesnakes, scorpions and the cold—one or all of them—will have their way with Joe, Hector figures.

If not, there'll be surely be another time, and maybe that will yield another story. But no more working girls will fall prey to Joe's strangling hands, not on Hector's watch.

Hector breaks off a branch of rotted scrub oak and wipes away his footprints and heel marks from Joe's body back to the Chevy from which he was dragged.

Driving back to the Ruiz whorehouse, the writer surveys the scenarios he's fashioned on the fly these past hours.

There are plenty of potential pitfalls.

What if Joe has told someone where he was bound this night?

What if Joe has paid for Marita's favors before and told someone of those times? If so, Joe and Marita dying on the same night could raise serious questions, even in the minds of the lackluster, local law.

Hector rolls down the window and runs his hand back through his graying-brown hair.

Yes, there are potential holes in his improvised plot that could spell trouble, later.

But this is just a first draft, Hector assures himself.

He tells himself he'll fix it all later, if or when he ever gets 'round to putting it all down on paper for posterity.

Midnight. Hector is smoking at her bar when the madam returns, a fresh bottle of tequila and some ham sandwiches wrapped in wax paper arranged on the tray in her hands.

"They've arrested Stephen Walker for murder," she says happily. "It's on the radio. Even if it never sticks, he'll never be mayor now, and that's not nothing, you know."

Hector, who knows, nods as he accepts the tray from Luisa Ruiz.

The fat madam smiles and asks, "Think you'll ever write about this, Héctor?"

The writer smiles and shrugs. "Rather hard to say, honey. Sometimes they maybe live better than they read."

THE LAST INTERVIEW
(NEW MEXICO, 1967)

More than a thousand miles from Lake Michigan to the borderlands—this hellhole of red dust and terra-cotta tile roofs.

The Las Cruces sun tumbles down legless drunk behind Picacho Mountain, making the reporter squint. Jug-eared LBJ is yammering on through the radio's static: more lies about Vietnam.

The last three hundred miles are a shock-absorber punishing, pothole-peppered agony. The sixty-five Ford Galaxie's been making new noises since somewhere south of Santa Fe. Expensive-sounding noises.

The rolled-down windows and strategically angled wings do little but push around the fidgeting journalist's beads of sweat.

But the struggling Ford delivers the interviewer to his destination: A posh hacienda in La Mesilla—two stories of stucco with a wrap-around second floor porch, hard by the Rio Grande.

The author's English wife greets the journalist... leads him to a first-floor guest room. "Sleep," she says. "Tomorrow you two talk."

Hector Lassiter, burly, unshaven, brindle hair askew, lays in his deathbed, contemplating the stinging stump of his truncated right leg. The leg was lost last month to gangrene borne of diabetes ... diabetes borne of alcoholism ... alcoholism borne of living the life that feeds the books that pay for the life, and the liquor, that cost him the leg.

The doctor has lately eyed Hector's tingling left leg with intent.

Or so the dying novelist believes.

Hector's also taken to sleeping with a loaded antique Colt '73 Peacemaker hidden under his pillow, preparing to take himself out—do it before they can amputate his throbbing hands ... take those critical, increasingly-tingling trigger fingers.

The doomed author listens to his caretaker, or fifth "wife," as she regards herself, reading this likely last-journalist-come-to-interview-him the riot act: no smuggling in liquor, no loaning of cigarettes.

A promise she'll be back in three hours' time. She tells the reporter she means to take advantage of her husband's company to venture out with Carmelita, their long-suffering Tarahumara-born servant for some goddamned misbegotten, budget-busting shopping spree.

Now the door opens, and the reporter—gaunt, straw-haired and bespectacled ... perhaps vaguely tubercular—shoulders in, lugging a big black leather bag. Can't be more than twenty-two. He's sporting thick-lensed glasses that probably spared the poor bastard the draft.

Hector spreads his arms, smiles ... those famous dimples, nearly buried under his hoary beard. "Holy Jesus," the last of the first-wave *Black Mask* writers says out of the side of his mouth, in full Texas drawl, "a thousand fucking miles to record the last ruminations of a fitfully lucid, one-legged hack writer. How empty must your life be, eh lad? Fuck on a bicycle: Hope I live down to expectations. Who's this one for?"

The reporter smiles crookedly, revealing crooked teeth. "*Esquire*." He plugs his reel-to-reel recorder in and lays the microphone on the pillow by Hector Lassiter's head. He presses the "record" button with a nicotine-stained thumb.

"If you don't mind, thought we'd start with some impressions regarding your peers," the reporter says, extra loud for the recorder.

"*Peers*? Yeah, shoot," Hector says, already disappointed.

"Right: Dashiell Hammett?"

"Pussy-whipped communist."

"Raymond Chandler?"

"Unwitting homosexual."

"Cornell Woolrich?"

"Overtly queer." Hector winks. "But I feel a gimpy affinity with old Corny. He's a fellow cripple now, same circumstances. Or so I hear."

"Agatha Christie?"

The writer's brows knit. "Faker. Fucking *mystery* writer."

The reporter scratches his head. "You're a mystery writer."

"I'm a crime writer. She's a 'mystery' writer. It's different."

"You sound resentful."

Hector smiles, shakes his head. "I outearn her. And her stuff is shit… stupid puzzles solved by a daffy old bitch or an effete fucking Belgian. Fuck that. Ever meet a loveable old bitch or effete fucking Belgian who could do more than rub you the wrong way? They'll still be reading me long after the worms have done with Dame Christie. Her audience is nearly as old as her."

Hector Lassiter gestures at his side table with a hairy, shaking hand, pointing to a haphazard stack of hardcovers and softbound galleys in danger of falling. "Look at those damned things. Pretty high pile, eh? Cocksuckers all still crave jacket comments from me. Crap, most all of it. Fucking book about a detective cat in there somewhere. No shit, an actual fucking pussy detective. Holy pleading bleeding Jesus. It'll probably win the Edgar. If I'm not dead when it happens, some dipshit will come after me to write an introduction for the reprint for the Limited Editions Club. Mark my words."

The reporter smiles; crosses one leg over the other. Hector thinks, *Six weeks ago, I could do that, too.*

The reporter tugs at his shirt's sleeves. Hector thinks he sees needle scars, just peeking under the cuffs. He frowns. Hector thinks, *Another fucking junkie.*

The reporter says, "How about Rex Stout?"

"Another lefty."

"Estelle Quartermain?"

"Fucking *mystery* hack of the first water. Bad as Christie. Hell, worse—her stupid 'locked room mysteries.'" Hector waves a hand. "Ever hear of anyone really getting whacked in a locked room?"

The reporter shrugs... he's got those telltale nervous hands and feet. And he's sweating out of proportion to the undeniable heat. Hector knows the signs. He thinks, certain now, *Junkie.*

Hector snorts. "Exactly. No damned way. People die over a ten-dollar drug deal. They kill over a dumpy woman in some peanut-shell-strewn, cigarette smoke-laden cantina. They cuff their wife 'cause she won't shut up during Carson's monologue. Her head hits the bedpost, and she falls to the floor, her neck at some impossible angle. I've written those scenes. Scenes I've lived or witnessed. Fucking Dame Quartermain dismisses me for those scenes. Says I only write about whores, drunkards and bottom-feeders. Of course, she doesn't use those terms. But I know what she means. Says I'm sordid. Says I'm seedy. All because I don't have some humpbacked dowager with some shaking, beloved Chihuahua solving murder cases in vicarages ... murders involving exotic poisons. All that dainty dialogue and 'action' in service to some fretted-over puzzle plot. Know what, scribe of mine? When you have to run to the reference books, you're not writing. Use that windy passage as a pull-quote, eh lad?"

Bouncing one leg, the wired reporter says, "I interviewed Estelle Quartermain a couple of months ago. She's a nice lady."

Hector grunts and says, "And that should matter to me—her being 'nice'—that should matter to me as a reader? Why should that be, exactly? There's a letter on the nightstand over there from her somewhere. Arrived last week. She's still nursing a grudge over something I said to her at a party ten years ago. Writes religiously, about once a month, stubbornly pushing for an apology to her husband. I said something in my cups, or so she says ... I don't remember what. Her husband left early. Do remember that. Ruined her night, or so the purple-haired bitch says, stewing under that fucking beehive. Estelle says I hurt her man's pride, in a 'lingering' way." The writer waves it away with a thick-fingered hand. "She says I 'don't have the brains' to write the kinds of books she writes. The point is, I have the brains not to write the kinds of shitty books she writes."

The old writer's big bed is bracketed by double-doors. The doors open onto the upper porch. There is heat lightning on the horizon now. Black clouds roil either side of Hector Lassiter's head. The old writer smiles crookedly, says, "My witchy warden's words of warning aside, got some smokes?"

The reporter smiles and roots around in his jacket pocket; passes Hector a virgin pack of Pall Malls. The crime writer slits the pack with a long, yellow thumbnail and the reporter fires him up with a battered silver Zippo. Hector's cheeks hollow once, twice. He blows some smoke rings, says, "Who do you read, son? When you read for yourself, I mean."

"Some Hesse. Burroughs."

"Skinny Billy. Junkie. Fucker shot and killed his wife playing William Tell, ya know. And Hesse? He's a fuckin' kraut. What about crime fiction, who do you read?"

"Uh, been reading some Kenneth Robeson."

"Kenneth Robeson? Ain't no such beast, boy. You reading those fuckin' *Doc Savage* paperback reprints?"

The reporter squirms. "A few here and there … good camp. And Robeson's stuff is—"

Hector draws deep and blows smoke out both nostrils, like some paunchy, mutilated dragon. "'Robeson' was a house pen name, invented by Street & Smith so they could fire the real hard-working pulp writer on a whim if need be. Same shitty kind of outfit that published *Black Mask*. 'Maxwell Grant,' who wrote the bulk of *The Shadow* novels, he was really a guy named Walt Gibson. Buddy of Houdini's. Wrote two novels a month for more than a decade for old

S&S. Had a battery of typewriters, the keys all stained with blood. No shit, Old Walt typed his fingers bloody. All the time. Let's see your affable Mrs. Quartermain match *that*."

Hector turns his mouth down. "Anyway, nine times out of ten, your 'Ken Robeson' was a fella name of Lester Dent. Great guy. Born out west, like me. Lonely childhood to stoke that imagination. Just like me. Used to hang with him in Florida. Good as Hammett and funny to boot—when he wrote his own stuff. Look for the books under his own name, sonny. Look for a short story, 'Sail.' Good as anything the best of us have done."

The reporter nods and smiles. "Will do. Florida: You lived there for a few years, in the Keys. Knew Hemingway. You two had a falling out."

"Old news, boy. Put it this way, my Florida P.I. novel, *Wandering Eye*, was ten times the novel *To Have and Have Not* was... and published the same year. Outsold Papa, in those early Depression days. Hemingway dismissed me as a 'mystery' writer. Still, he knew his shit in the 1920s, those great short stories. His notion of 'one true sentence.' Too bad he forgot all he knew, down there on Bone Key."

Hector chews his lip, considering the junkie journalist. He weighs angles. Decides to play with a notion, just a bit... probably never go the whole course... just flirt with it a bit. Keep himself interested.

Hector reaches over to the side table for a legal pad and pen. He hands them to the reporter. "Game I used to play with Hemingway. We'd challenge each other to top one another's one true sentence. Write this down, eh?" Hector recites:

"I killed him because..."

He says, "Okay kiddo, finish it. Make it the truest sentence you can, but keep it fucking short."

Smiling crookedly, the reporter nervously bounces the point of the pen on the paper. He weighs the words: "I killed him because..."

"... he was bitter and used up"?

No. Might piss the old man off.

"... of what he said to me"?

No. Too weak.

The reporter searches, sensing the old man's eyes on him... on his wrists, sending him off, tugging down his sleeves. He thinks of what Hector Lassiter has said about Estelle Quartermain. He remembers what Estelle told him about the used-up old one-legged man laying before him now. With his left hand, the reporter writes:

"I killed him because of what he did to her."

Hector Lassiter takes the notebook back, reads. He beams. Still has a pretty solid set of teeth. "Good, son. Perfect, really. Short, simple, evocative. And it's gotta all come down to a woman in the end, eh? Always does. Even for Woolrich, at least in his books. *Cherchez la femme.*" He hands the notepad back to the reporter. He says, "I feel like a proud teacher. Sign your work for the old man, huh?"

The reporter smiles crookedly again. Under his "one true sentence" he scrawls "Andrew Nagel." He passes the legal pad back to the old writer. Hector looks at it again and smiles, shaking his head approvingly. "Good fucking start,

Andrew. You get back to Chicago you write what comes after, yeah? Send it to me. Deal?"

"Sure, Mr. Lassiter."

"Hector. We're fellow writers now, Andy."

The old author is seized by a thought. He abruptly asks: "Andy, what have you read of mine, huh, kid?"

"Read *Rooster of Heaven*. And I really loved the film."

"That was a novelization, sonny, not a novel. I wrote a straight-to-paperback treatment just to put back the parts of my story that that one-eyed fucker Sam Ford tore out for his fucking waste of a film. In the land of the blind, the one-eyed man might be king, but in the land of the two, or, even the three-eyed? Well, he's just another myopic dumbass. What else of mine have you read? Anything? Tell the truth."

The reporter shrugs. "*Inside Job*."

"Famously—some would say infamously—done for money. I had a daughter born with a hole in her heart. Needed the cash for a surgery that killed her. My baby girl was named Dolores. She hung in until the age of three. Her first—and last—word, was 'Daddy.' Quote that, Andrew."

The reporter searches the old man's filmy blue eyes. Hector's cataracts look like some inept impressionist painter's notion of drunkenly dispersing clouds.

Well, it's a line Andy is toying with … maybe needs work.

Hector grunts and points a shaking finger at the reporter. "You drew this assignment, didn't you boy? You didn't come all this way because *Rhapsody in Black* rocked your world? Never read *The Shortest Story*, and so experienced no revelations, right?"

The reporter straightens his shoulders; feels his sweaty shirt peel loose in a few places from his acne-dappled back. He says softly, "I drew the assignment, sir… like you said."

Hector credits the reporter's candor. At least the scrawny fucker has that going for him. "Hell, doesn't matter," Hector says, resigned now… sadly settling on his scheme. "What do you want from me, Andy?"

"There was a hotel in El Paso. It was May 13, 1956."

The old writer tips his head on side. And so it comes. As it always does.

The eternal question.

The one he has never answered.

Hector Lassiter says, "Now that's a locked room, boy. That's my private mystery. The pain too private to trot out."

"You might never get another chance to go on record, Mr. Lassiter."

Hector bites his lip, sighs. "'There was a ship.'"

The reporter catches that one on the first bounce. "Coleridge… right?"

"Just so. So, you do read more than just bad pulp fiction and my toss-offs."

"It's a classic."

"Sure it is, Andrew." The bearded writer puffs his cigarette and gestures at his missing leg. "'It was that accursed white whale that razed me; made a poor pegging lubber of me for ever and a day.'"

"Ahab," the reporter smiles.

"Like old Melville, do you?"

The reporter shrugs again. With two fingers, Andy stabs his slipping glasses back up the bridge of his damp nose. "So long as you don't start regarding me as your Moby Dick… sure, why not?"

Hector winks and shakes his head. He reaches to the side table for a box. "Only 'Moby Dick' I regard lately is the one between my one-and-a-half legs, and he's not breaking surface much these days." The old writer roots through the box, pulls out a hypodermic and a little vial of liquid. "Insulin," Hector explains. "You'd think three years of heroin addiction back in the late 1950s,"—a damnable lie—"would have given me some facility with this damned rig." He looks for a reaction from the reporter and doesn't get much … the kid licks his lips and averts his eyes. "Don't suppose you'd be able to help me out with this, huh Andrew?"

The reporter says, with little conviction, "Wouldn't know how." He shoots his sleeves again.

Hector snorts and spikes his remaining leg and grimaces. He sits back and retrieves his Pall Mall. He feels himself leaning harder into his dark notion. "Don't suppose," Hector says, "you smuggled in anything to drink?"

"Couldn't be good for you, Hector."

"Think I'm going to bounce back from this? Nah. We enjoy the moments left us. Solid advice, Andrew."

The reporter grins and reaches in his bag. He holds up the Jim Beam bottle. Andy Nagel smiles wider—meaner—at the dying writer's hungry smile and cracks the seal. Hector points to a sideboard across the room. Five glasses sit on a serving tray there, gathering dust. The reporter rubs clean two glasses on the untucked tails of his shirt and pours two generous doses. He passes one to the dying novelist.

Hector savors the delicious bite and burn. He sighs: That warmth infusing his chest … fucking sublime. He settles back into his pillows.

"Now," the reporter says. "It's 1956. Your wife dies, some say suspiciously. You're a fleeting suspect before it's reluctantly ruled a heroin overdose. The case remains ... inconclusive. What really happened, Hector?"

The old writer stubs out the butt of his cigarette. He snags the soft pack and shakes out another; leans in for the reporter to light him up again. "No. Not like that Andy. You want the story? The story nobody has ever had? Well, a couple of favors, Andy my boy. 'Cause, ya know, I have to go on living this shitty excuse for a life after you've gone on to your next 'assignment.'"

There's a languishing writing desk in the northwest corner of the room. Hector gestures at a straight-back wooden chair. "For starters, tuck that sucker up under the doorknob," he says "— can't have the she-bitch and her taco-bending sidekick finding us with the booze and coffin nails, can we?"

The reporter winks and rises. He wedges the chair's back up under the brass knob and nudges it tight with his toe.

The old man gestures at the windows next. It's raining now, and the rain is blowing in. "Best close and lock the windows, too," Hector says. "Won't be able to do much about the scent of the cigarette smoke, but wet walls and floors—*très* more suspicious. And the heat? Well, it's a dry heat, right?"

The sweating reporter closes and secures the doors on either side of the author's bed. He sheds his jacket and is about to sit down when the old man says, "Last favor. Grab another glass over there, eh? Might need to go two-fisted for this ... dark waters my boy, dark fucking waters."

The reporter sets the spare glass down on the nightstand and then holds up a finger. "Hold on a minute—need to flip the tape." The reporter plays with the spools; tightens them. He hits "record" again. "Okay. It's 1956. It's your wife's last day on earth."

How do you tell a man why you murdered a woman you loved?

How to start?

How do you give it context? Not to alibi yourself or excuse what you did. How do you show why you were driven to do that *bad evil thing to her?*

Your baby's Mexican mother's secret drug addiction, that's at the dark heart of it all.

Your woman's heroin Jones: it weakened your unborn daughter's frail body, condemning her to death before she was even born.

It was an addiction that was well hidden by Maria. She injected through the soles of her callused feet. She kept it hidden through your courtship... a year of marriage... and through nine months of pregnancy.

She hid it well, through three years of your daughter's short life.

Then it comes: These perplexed words from a doctor, chewing his lip over your daughter's death bed... hints of congenital birth defects perhaps goosed by... well... perhaps some narcotic influence. For there were other things wrong with your little girl... things only just being discovered... or suspected. A welter of birth defects.

Dolores dies in your arms, whispering "Daddy."

Unable to face your house, or your daughter's empty bedroom, her absent voice and laugh, you booked yourselves into a hotel room—paid up two weeks in advance.

You feel sorry for Maria for a time, until when, confronted, she confesses her addiction a week after your daughter's funeral. Drunk, scaring yourself with your thoughts about killing this woman who bore/murdered your child, you reluctantly let her shoot you up.

Once.

It's shitty strategy on Maria's part... drug monkey logic. She stares at you with the addled echo of your dead daughter's dark eyes, lips parted, watching for signs of your capitulation to the heroin.

But the drug that mellows her makes you go dark and cold. *You let the resentment fester—let the poison stoke your darkest impulses. Let it build on the hate you feel for Maria for letting her worthless devotion to this wired short ride cost you your black-haired, black-eyed baby girl.*

Maria condemned your little girl to a slow death that dragged on for three years—three years to let you grow to achingly love the poor little girl born with no future. Three years of hollow hoping that age will grant her frail body the strength to swamp her damaged heart—render that fierce fucking hole irrelevant.

But your love and hope, your fame and talent, can't fill the hole in your baby girl's heart.

Little Dolores dies whispering "Daddy."

You ride that one and only heroin high—free-associating. Plotting.

You scope the room... assess angles.

In the end, you go the easy route.

As Maria lays naked on the bed, black hair spread on the pillow, luxuriating in her high, begging you to fuck her—to make a new baby—you instead berate her... leave her alone to her tingling trip. Soon enough, she's asleep. You grab the hotel ice bucket… twenty-five trips… and the tub is sufficiently full of cold cubes.

Holding it through a handkerchief, you pick up her hypodermic, surveying the bottoms of her feet. Their soles are covered with scabbed-over punctures, like the scars of a thousand scorpions' stings.

Fuck it—go for her arm. Three shots… of air. *Give the junkie bitch an embolism of epic proportions. You follow that with a massive injection of heroin.*

You carry her naked body into the bathroom and drop her in the ice, spreading it over her. You lay the needle on the closed toilet lid by the bathtub, next to the empty vial.

You write an angry note to her… all the expected words. You lay out in the letter your disgusted discovery of her drug addiction… what it did to your dead daughter. Now you're leaving her… and you wish your wife in hell. You date it yesterday. You stick the note in her dead hand, flung out strategically over the side of the tub.

You pack your stuff, and, still using a handkerchief, drop the Do-Not-Disturb sign on the doorknob. The air conditioner is full up: May take twelve, fifteen hours for the ice to melt. You'll be buying drinks and slapping backs—conspicuously—*in Ciudad Juárez in less than two.*

Tell this junkie reporter the truth?

You do. Baldly.

Andrew Nagel stares out at the storm raging on the horizon, says, "Jesus, this could make me."

It could indeed. Hector says, "That's your last one true sentence, Andrew."

Then Hector Lassiter reaches under his pillow, grasps the well-worn butt of the Peacemaker, and, cocking, reaches over and presses the barrel to the reporter's left temple. He tugs the hair trigger.

Adios Andrew.

Alone again … as he always seems to be.

Alone at the typewriter.

Alone in his own head.

Only time Hector didn't feel alone—those scant moments spent with his baby girl.

Two more shots—fired through each spool of tape … reduced to magnetized confetti. The ruined recorder kicks twice.

Andrew Nagel was a southpaw—Hector was careful to note that when Andrew wrote his first true sentence. Using the edge of the bedsheet, Hector grabs the legal pad from the bedside table and tears off the top sheet of paper with its signed, unwitting confession. He slips the note into Andrew's dead right hand. He gingerly raises the reporter's sleeve—a welter of needle scars; several of them look fresh. *Worthless junkie.*

The old one-legged writer grabs a pen and Estelle Quartermain's languishing letter. Hector annotates it with lies. He scrawls vile notes in the margins—a punched up version of that night of the supposed big slight he can't recall. At the top of her letter, Hector Lassiter writes, "Estelle, you clapped up cunt, I'm *so* fucking grateful I slept with you that night. Fond fucking memories … so to speak."

The crime writer—the last of the first wave *Black Mask* writers—surveys the room. It's a plausible enough murder-suicide scene for these backwater environs.

But now for the vexing nuance—drive that old mystery writing bitch up a wall.

Fox those cops.

Reaching to the other side of the bed, Hector Lassiter picks up a tube of his wife's lipstick. He applies it to his dry lips, careful to avoid the stray hairs of his moustache and beard. He picks up the derelict bottle of whiskey and the virgin glass, pours four fingers and downs it, leaving a glass rimmed with lipstick. Then he smokes two cigarettes, stubbing out the lipstick-smeared butts in the empty tumbler.

Enter the mystery woman.

He rubs the lipstick from his mouth with his fingers and licks those clean, washing away the taste with swigs of whiskey straight from the bottle.

Now, reaching again to the side table on his wife's side of the bed, Hector Lassiter grabs a bottle of perfume. He breaks it on the edge of the table and slathers perfume on his gun hand and arm—voiding any possibility of a paraffin test that could reveal Hector fired a weapon. He tosses his arm across his wife's side table—feigning the spastically flung arm of a dying man. Glass breaks, costly cosmetics fly.

Satisfied with the effect, Hector wedges the Peacemaker in Andrew Nagel's dead left hand, finger on the hair trigger, barrel pointed at a one-legged pulp novelist. Hector reaches for the never-used cane that his fifth "wife" has hopefully placed by the headboard. He positions Andrew's dead hand . . . scoots himself in place. With the rubber stopper of the cane, he pushes the dead reporter's dead index finger back against the hair trigger.

Jesus fucking Christ.

That burn.

Like a thousand shots of whiskey, received at once.

That sound.

The Peacemaker tumbles to the tile floor.

Groaning, Hector returns the cane to its former position.

Gut shot.

A bad way to go.

Call it half-assed penitence.

And his remaining leg… there's no feeling left. Must have nicked his spinal chord. Maybe severed it.

So: Paralysis to boot.

Dipping his finger in his own wound, light-headed now, Hector grimaces and twists, reaching up over his headboard. He writes above his bed, wincing with the pain:

FOR

EQ

For a moment, he frets, thinking of pillow-biting Cornell Woolrich, fearing the "EQ" might be misconstrued—suspected of standing for "Ellery Queen"… hinting of sodomistic shenanigans.

Then he remembers Estelle's newly annotated letter.

Hector gingerly rubs a little blood from his gut on Andrew's dead trigger finger.

Hector sucks his blood from his own finger. Then the dying crime writer lays back for a last time on his pillow.

Hector lets that old whore death settle in with him, warm and slow.

Death with imagery: scenes from his books in montage. A melodramatic mélange the punchy pulp writer confuses for his own memories:

His lonely office.

Guttering light from a neon sign pulses through slanted shades.

A slow-turning ceiling fan stirs old dust.

Enter the woman: at first, just a busty silhouette through stenciled pebbled glass. Then, she's standing before him in silk stockings with seams up the back. Raven hair and ruby lips. He'll learn she likes to bite his shoulder while peaking. Betrayed, tricked, played for a fool, he'll shoot her during a last shared orgasm…

Mean streets: It's Chicago. It's 1936. He's sent to settle a union strike. He settles that strike. But there are casualties. Talk about a killing floor…

A sibilant homosexual lackey (Street & Smith will balk at that…so call him "a Nancy boy") comes calling. Nancy boy is in thrall to an endomorphic European of indeterminate origin (adapted for film, the part will be played by Sydney Greenstreet). The pair slays his partner, seeking some elusive bronze statue of a wolf with a treasure map stowed inside. A man owes his partner, even if he is banging his dead partner's dipsomaniacal wife. So he sets off again down those mean streets…

From his far-off place, Hector can dimly hear screams now, screams from somewhere. Fists pounding on a door.

The screams grow closer and he thinks he hears breaking glass in the distance someone shouting for him. But it's too late…and now drowned out by music…some march maybe, played on a hammer dulcimer… drums, tiple and accordion… "Tramps & Hawkers."

Hector reaches out his hand and the little girl takes it and smiles. He towers above Dolores, beaming, standing there on his two solid legs.

They march up the side of the hill somewhere near Creel, half-walking half-running through prickly pear, maguey… sage and heather.

There's a dark-haired woman at the top of that hill, astride a strawberry roan, silhouetted against some bloody sunset.

F FOR FAKE

(PARIS, 1974)

Hector Lassiter sits with his wife in the rear of Le Select, two drinks in, and for once at total peace in the City of Light, when Orson Welles lumbers up to their table out of nowhere and wraps a meaty hand around his neck and squeezes.

The big, bearded actor gets his face down close into Hector's and bellows, "Well, goddamn you for the cruelest of fakers, *Hec*tor! Curse you for a traitorous cur!"

The gargantuan actor's breath reeks of cigars and wine. Orson is far larger than Hector remembers ever seeing his younger friend.

And yet Orson is in the improbable company of beautiful and exotic-looking brunette—willowy and very, very young.

Uninvited, Orson and his female friend pull up chairs: Orson's groans under his considerable weight. He carefully leans his cane against the table and smiles at Alicia, Hector's wife of a few years. Orson says to her, his breath still coming hard, "I know that I *know* you, lovely, but I can't quite place you in time, my dear."

Alicia looks to Hector—looks to see if he is going to try and rebut his identity—but Hector just smiles awkwardly, sadly, and nods for her to go ahead.

"We met many years ago," Alicia says to the bearded, bloated and physically overtaxed actor-director. "It was on the set of your picture, *Touch of Evil.* I was a background player. That is also," she nods at Hector, still being careful not to invoke that name, "where he and I first met. I thank you for, that."

"Well, I'm delighted to have played matchmaker," Orson booms. He then introduces his own companion, so slender, pretty and dark—a woman magnetically attractive to Hector—as Oja Kodar, "an artist in more than her own right. And also, an actress of no small promise."

Oja smiles at Alicia, sizing her up rather nakedly. She says, "And you are from . . . ?"

Alicia smiles and extends a hand. "Los Angeles. But my parents were from Mexico. And you . . . ?"

"Croatia," Oja says, shaking hands, curtly.

Almost immediately, Orson's tone changes. "All very nice. But now there's the matter of my wrath, and of your unthinkable betrayal, Hector!"

Glowering at him, Orson rumbles, "How dare you not bring me into the circle of knowing the truth about you? I should think you would trust me, if anyone. Dammit, I carried your coffin!"

The novelist—presumed dead for more than half-a-decade—tries like hell to find the proper words to explain, to defend his deception to Orson, but he falls desperately, even pathetically short.

Hector ends up red-faced and shrugging. He says, "I am truly sorry, Orson. You're surely right. I should have let you know, and right away. Even before I took that crazy plunge in officially offing myself, so to speak."

Orson chews his lip. He says, "Clearly Marlene doesn't know what you've done, for she'd have already killed you for real in retaliation if she did. Miss Dietrich still mourns like hell after you! You should know that! And you should feel even more terrible about that! But then Marlene doesn't have a sense of your feet of clay, and your callousness. Not like I do. Joe Cotton and Rita are still quite sad at your passing, too, the poor devils."

Hector smooths a hand across the tablecloth, says, "Orson, the simple fact is, if I hadn't killed myself, pretend-like, I really believe I'd already be quite truly dead. After Hem and all that happened with him, and Ian Fleming, too, I thought long and hard about running the risk of letting that same artistic albatross drag me down. That albatross being my infernal public persona. I didn't want my god-damn so-called larger-than-life reputation to destroy me like it did Hem or Ian. It sells books, I reckon, but what it takes in the years and your quality of life? Simply not worth it."

Hector suddenly realizes "Hem" might be confused with "him," by Oja, at least, and so clarifies to her with, "You know, the way Hemingway's persona ultimately destroyed Ernest? The way having to play 007 burned out and destroyed good old Ian?"

Still seething, Orson says, "I understood exactly what you meant, Hector. I understand probably more than you can fathom. I have something of the same larger-than-life sort of persona bedeviling me, after all."

Indeed.

Orson closes a big meaty hand over Hector's, says, "I forgive you, old friend. Only because it's not yet too awful many years since you *died.* I choose to think in a few months—in a year at most—you'd have reached out to me. That you would at last let me know that you are, to use one of your pungent habitual phrases, still north of the dirt. So, we go forward from here, yes? With me gratefully on board regarding your happy continued and two-legged existence?"

"Yes," Hector said carefully, "of course we do. Emphatically so. It'll be good to have an old friend from the old days to talk with .... One who gets all my references and a kind of kid-brother with whom I've shared so many wild and frequently wonderful times."

Hector orders a fresh bottle of dry Spanish red wine, then listens as Orson explains more precisely whom his lissome companion is and exactly what she means to him.

Hector is fascinated by the woman, and physically drawn to her.

Lucky Orson, to have found this remarkable woman at just this fraught point in his life. And one who will accept him in his current, severely obese condition. Carrying so much girth, Orson strikes Hector as a massive heart attack waiting to happen—a textbook "widow-maker."

And yet, there is also something almost majestic about the big, bearded actor—a kind of air of a noble ruin or grand half-collapsed abbey.

Something of the leviathan in the man.

And my God, that incredible, unmistakable voice of Orson's has only deepened with age and only the Lord could declare how many cigars.

Still, Hector finds himself sizing up Oja and trying to figure how Orson won such a beauty at this stage of his life, living legend or not.

But then Hector has Alicia, a marvel in her own right and the woman Hector is determined to die loving.

A younger woman Hector feels he hardly deserves.

Hector is finally showing his last wife the Paris of his long-lost youth, the city where he apprenticed and found his voice as a fiction writer. With nearly all of his friends from the old day's quite dead, *Le Select* seemed a safe enough haunt to return to for just a couple of drinks.

And he was intent upon making new Parisian memories, sweet ones with Alicia to offset the bittersweet ghosts of Brinke, Molly, Sylvia, Gertrude and Ernest, and so many others from the 1920s who otherwise define the Paris that still looms so large and vividly in his memories and dreams.

As they murder a bottle of wine together, Orson speaks about a new film he has just finished, "Something radically new in form, Hector. A new kind of cinematic format, old friend. It's nonfiction, yet fictional nonfiction, so to speak. You of all people, Hector, should grasp what that could portend."

More goblets of wine stretch into dinner in a bistro just around the corner.

Dinner leads to a shared cab ride back to Orson's and Oja's place for a private screening of what will prove to be Orson's last, fully realized, yet wholly independently produced film.

Hector finds himself utterly captivated by the very strange, idiosyncratic piece of cinema spooling out before him.

Alicia says she also quite enjoys it, radical as it is in comparison to what she normally regards as a "film."

From Hector's perspective, the work is impossible to summarize or even to classify, just as Orson has cautioned.

It spins on confidence games, hoaxes.

On a forger-painter and on a fiction writer who has penned a suddenly notorious, recently revealed to be phony autobiography allegedly penned by a bizarrely reclusive Howard Hughes.

The damned movie is a beguiling house of mirrors and almost a kind of genre unto itself, Hector thinks.

When his film is at last over, Orson turns off the projector and pours fresh wine for himself, and then one for Hector, whom he leads out onto a smallish balcony.

Looking out over a quiet Parisian street, watching insect-gorging bats flit above them in the summer night, Orson heedlessly, even rather gruffly dives headlong into a harrowing pitch that sets Hector's teeth on edge and his heart to racing.

"It came to me as a powerful epiphany, watching my film with you, the one man on this sorry earth who might truly grasp the message of this film at its darkest core," Orson says.

Orson rushes on, "'The man who lived what he wrote and wrote what he lived,' must surely appreciate *F*."

"I surely do," Hector says sincerely, but carefully. "I goddamn love it. It's the most confounding, brilliant thing I've seen in a long time thrown up onto a screen."

Having said that, Hector reminds himself the movie isn't remotely commercial.

Hector is somewhat sure the film will be critical darling among European *cineastes*, but it will surely bomb back in the States where the mass audiences is still so goddamn provincial.

So goddamn narrow in the worst of ways when it comes to confronting and processing honest art, be it on the canvas, on the printed page, or on the silver screen.

The American popular audience won't ever sit still for Welles' new film, no more than audiences back in the day embraced Orson's *Citizen Kane* upon original release, Hector figures.

No more than anyone appreciated Orson's *The Lady from Shanghai* or *Touch of Evil,* back when they were fresh even if mauled by interfering producers—works challenging contemporary cinematic conventions and thwarting audience expectations.

Yet in polls, *Kane* is increasingly routinely regarded by film critics as the finest American movie ever made. *Touch of Evil* is increasingly being viewed as perhaps the last, great gasp of classic film noir.

But Hector already fears Orson will be long in the ground before the American public comes around to—if it ever does come around to—the genius and charms of *F for Fake.*

"I must confess, out of earshot of Oja, that times are terribly hard, Hector. Money is harrowingly tight."

Orson confesses that quite ominously. He continues, "Even tonight, as I watched my film again with you—the smartest and best audience who I know for my picture—I think of that line from Kipling: 'It's pretty, but is it art?' More to the point, as things stand for me more immediately, is it remotely bankable? I got lucky with all that stuff with one of my so-called stars as it were. You know—with Cliff Irving, and the scandal since it's become known he utterly faked the Howard Hughes autobiography."

Toasting one of the flitting bats, Orson says, "I didn't know any of that was the case when we were filming, I swear it's so. But it is a potential windfall, in that sense. But I need something more even than that, I think. Something that will really seize the public's imagination and give *Fake* that extra boost it needs and deserves with a last wild, twist in the tale. And now, suddenly, here you are, Hector! Miraculously restored to me, my old friend. You're like another gift from the Gods, an even better and more remarkable gift than Cliff Irving."

Hector's radar is instantly and fully up. He lies, "You've lost me, buddy...."

Orson says, "If you were to allow me to fold your own confidence game into my film about hucksterism and fakery? My God! If I could announce through my film that Hector Lassiter still walks the earth on both legs and more vibrant and vigorous than ever? If I could say you're still with us, and entertaining us, despite that horrid alleged end in an invalid's bed in New Mexico, allegedly killed by some junkie journalist?"

Orson gives Hector a vast smile. "Why, it would be like what you were doing in 1938, when you at last told the world the truth about Brinke Devlin and her various pen-names in order to extend what you charmingly termed her 'literary long game,' far into the future, in your romantic and laudable passion to keep her works in print."

Holding up a fat hand as Hector beings to balk, Orson rushes on:

"Your resurrection in my film could change both our fortunes. Forever and for the better, my dear Hector! Change our very lives and the lives of those we love, too. Surely, you can always use more money, old man. I can even grant you points in the film, if you insist."

Hector feels like he's been dealt a gut punch. He also almost feels as if a panic attack is coming on. His heart is racing even harder; his palms and forehead are damp and he's seeing spots. Hector suddenly has to hold tight to the iron balcony's railing just to keep his footing.

At his best, Orson has always been wildly unpredictable and a very high-maintenance sort of acquaintance.

Orson also has a raging, ego-maniac's tunnel vision and utter lack of empathy in life regarding others, if not in his actual art.

Hector strongly fears that even if he says no, Orson might well simply thunder on with this crazy plan to reveal Hector's 1967 staged murder-suicide a hoax.

It would be very Orson in that way—consistent with his burly and berserker's nature.

From an apartment below, Sinatra is crooning "As Time Goes By," to a lush, Nelson Riddle orchestration.

Hector says firmly, "I'm never going back to the man I was. I can't ever do that, Orson. It would be …." He falters, then says nakedly, "It would be the very real death of me, Orson. I know it would be."

"You're saying no to me might be the death of me, old friend," Orson says, holding his ground. "After the years of grief that you've dealt me with your ruse, you certainly owe me more than a bottle of wine and some kinds words about my film you're now threatening to sink."

"You simply can't put that guilt and weight on me," Hector lashes back. "This time yesterday, you were happily following your vision, and I was at best dust in your mind, just as you say. Please, in a public sense, please keep me that way, buddy! I'm Beau Devlin, now. I'm writing the books I want to write—that I'm driven to write—just as you follow your own maverick vision as a filmmaker. Hector Lassiter became little more than a brand, a yoke I simply can't ever put back on. Not in this, or in any other lifetime. I can't do that and continue as an artist in my own right. That you surely have to understand. You, the man who heroically thumbed his nose at every film studio on earth."

Seeing it requires still more, Hector bites his lip and says, "And too many of my enemies are all still too active, too. There are even still those surrealists, from back in the day who nearly sank you when you were making *Lady from Shanghai*. There's still the ghost of goddamn J. Edgar Hoover, same as running his Fascist, witch-hunting version of the FBI through his flunkies. Many of my enemies are also still your enemies, Orson. If you kick me back out into the limelight and open those old closet doors again, you sow the wind, old pal. Do you really want to stir up either of those hornets' nests? The crazy daughter of that art collector who nearly successfully framed you for the Black Dahlia murder is still very much in the wind, old friend. And the FBI is still running like Hoover isn't safely two years' at room temperature.

"My loved ones need me to stay dead to keep those devils at bay, and to keep them from potentially knocking on your door to get to me, Orson," Hector races on. "Do you really want to put Oja at that kind of risk? Remember what happened to that would-be young actress Elizabeth Short on your watch? What you are asking of me? It's not just everything. It's actually same as asking me to burn down my life and the lives of my wife and my children."

Orson smiles sadly, looking defeated.

Raw-voiced, he finally says, "I surely wouldn't take your happiness from you, much less threaten your family's safety, regardless how it might turn the tide for me. You surely know that in your heart of hearts, my oldest and best friend. I'd never do that, of course. It was rude and thoughtless—downright selfish of me to ask, Hector. And as if I'd ever do anything to harm you, or that you'd ever presume to do something that would harm me...."

Something in that last sentence stirs uneasy memories in Hector he can't lay useful hand to in the moment.

They awkwardly embrace there on that balcony overlooking a little slice of twilight Paris, once Hector's favorite city in the world, as bats continue to dip and dart overhead.

Hector prays he can take Orson at his word—just this one time—without eventual or even catastrophic disappointment.

Hell, if Orson really wanted to use Hector to pull himself out of his current dire straits, he would surely try to follow Hector's example and dramatically change his way of living.

Orson would get healthy, and more urgently, Welles would step back from his reputation as a swaggering, blustering auteur who has spent years starting and stopping promising projects before they are ever fully brought to fruition.

From Hector's point of view, for too long, Orson's vision has smothered under the anchor that is the public's perception of this strange creature that has never really existed—this alternately shadowy presence and portly bon vivant known as "Orson Welles."

Just as an aging Hemingway was crushed under the weight of his own hype—Ernest's own crazily constructed macho persona destroying its creator—"George Orson Welles" has been equally undone by the simple and lethal trap of embracing and embodying an idealized self that has become a kind of all-subsuming piece of performance art.

Staring down at the dark street, Orson begins to quote from his latest movie's narration in his wonderous voice:

"Our works in stone, in paint, in print, are spared, some of them, for a few decades or a millennium or two. But everything must finally fall in war, or wear away in the ultimate and universal ash.... We are going to die, Hector. Our songs will all be silenced. But what of it? Go on singing."

Searching Hector's pale blue eyes, Orson says, sounding only half-doubtful, "Seen in that light, maybe an artist's real name doesn't matter at all, nor in the end."

EXIT 'THE MUSE' (BALTIMORE, 1986)

The ancient author by all accounts opened the mystery convention's hotel bar.

Some with him think he might close it, too.

It is one day before the official kick-off of the annual "Bouchercon" convention and more attendees have begun checking in as planes arrive and the afternoon gets on.

Increasing numbers of crime and mystery writers are also crowding the lounge. A handful have found their way to the old author's table.

The stranger claims to be over eighty, although he looks somewhat younger. He wears no nametag like the ones many others are wearing.

He certainly seems like a crime writer, and evidently a venerable one.

But the authors sitting with him are too polite—or perhaps too embarrassed by their own ignorance—to press the man for his name. None remember ever seeing this man at any previous North American mystery conventions.

Perhaps he writes under a penname?

Anyway, the old writer doesn't invite that flavor of inquiry.

He simply is, and he is, well, pretty charming.

He also has this presence.

If William Holden hadn't hit the bottle too hard and accidently killed himself falling down drunk in his apartment at age sixty-three, he might now look more than a bit like this old writer does: a full head of white hair brushed back from a bronzed forehead and falling a bit long at the collar; pale blue eyes and Golden Age Hollywood-style charisma.

"Dashing" is the word that comes to mind for the youngest writer at the table, Natalie, seated to his right.

The old writer has dimples when he smiles and traces of a stubbornly clinging Texas accent. He wears an open collar white shirt and checked sports jacket, despite the increasing mugginess of the bar as more readers and writers pack in tighter.

A song of moment on bar's sound-system: Berlin, "Take My Breath Away."

By the old writer's right hand, next to his double dram of single malt, is an unopened pack of Pall Malls with an ancient Zippo balanced atop. He storms along, "Last time I came to one of these sorts of gigs? An Edgar Award banquet in New York. Hell, you couldn't see the hacking hack P.I. novelist sitting across from you for all the coffin nail haze in the banquet hall that year."

If the old man is arguably the eldest writer at the convention, Natalie is likely the youngest.

She is twenty-two and her debut novel is scheduled to be published in early November. Softcover galleys of her slim noir have been thrust into gift bags given attendees.

With no finished hardcover out there yet, Natalie feels more than out of place sitting with the established crime writers also sharing the old man's table.

Cheryl, petite, brunette and a last-year Edgar winner, smiles and says, "Golly, when was that Edgar event, sir?"

"Must have been about sixty-three," the old man says. He smiles at the young woman. "Some dotty cat-mystery writer spilled her gimlet on me. Holy Jesus, but that dame could put 'em away. If they gave a special Edgar for being lushed-up, that bitty would have been a lock."

An Irish crime writer, struggling against jet-lag, says, "Jesus wept! You're saying it took nearly a quarter century to steel yourself for another one of these gigs? Fuck on a bicycle!"

"But I'm here this time for a worthy reason," the old man says. "*Cherchez la femme*. Lookin' for a very particular woman."

Natalie spies Cheryl checking out the old man's left hand. There is a gold band on the third finger of his left hand. He might be a sentimental widower? Cheryl smiles, lifting her beer for a sip, says, "Looking for a woman? Shucks, but you already seem to be spoken for."

The elder author follows Cheryl's now more direct gaze to his wedding band; shakes his head, then pats the young woman's hand. "No, darlin'. No. My skirt-chasing days are well behind me. I'm lookin' for this woman with a very different breed of intent."

Sitting next to the Irish crime writer is a nattily dressed, balding man with a brushy moustache and intense brown eyes. He guzzles his latest in a chain of black coffees; his other hand rests on a copy of his newest novel.

The old man picks up his battered old Zippo and turns it to consider something seemingly engraved there. He flicks it open with a one-handed jerk and spins the wheel.

He eyes the sputtering blue-orange flame before closing it with a click.

Natalie scents the butane after-scent. It makes her crave a cigarette. There's definitely something engraved on the lighter, but she couldn't quite make it out.

The old author says, "Given our shared trade, you're surely all acutely acquainted with the concept of the femme fatale? Well, the skirt I'm lookin' for? She's that treacherous model of female, but of the first water. What an old writer friend of mine from Paris days might call, "*a world-class bitch, complete with handles.*"

The old man drains his single malt. He checks the others' glasses for depth. He signals the waitress, holds up four fingers, then points at himself. He says, "You four will have heard of a promising young crime writer named Jesse Chapman?"

Even Natalie knows that name.

Jesse won a best-first-novel competition sponsored by one of the major New York publishers. He'd summarily racked up some key award nominations, then, aged thirty, he'd shot himself in his hotel room while attending a mystery writing convention in the Windy City a few months ago.

"Chapman was a kind of a protégé of a friend of mine," the old man says. "I think there was a bit more to his death than meets the eye. Me? I blame this particular woman."

The old writer frowns, eyeing the bartender. He suddenly says, "And that bastard's reaching for the wrong brand of whisky, goddamn him!" The elder author briefly excuses himself, quickly as he can making his way to the bar.

Curious, Natalie reaches over and scoops up the old man's Zippo, turning it in the low lounge light to read the engraving there. Some of it had been nearly rubbed away from years of use, but she makes out:

'One true sentence.'
— E.H.
Key West,
1932

She carefully places the ancient lighter back atop the Pall Mall soft pack, engraved side down, just as the old novelist left it.

He settles back into his chair alongside Natalie. The old writer growls in a deep baritone, "Damned bartender nearly served me up a blended, the sorry son of a bitch!"

The old man points at a muscular man in a tight-fitting black T-shirt standing at the bar. The man towers out at least six-five, maybe six-six. His head is shaven, and he has a black moustache and goatee. The old man says, "Who the hell is that?"

Natalie says, "That's Jacob 'Jackpot' Potts. He's ex-CIA, ex-Special Forces. Ex-cop. At least his program guide biography claims that's all so. He writes that series of men's adventure novels. You know the books I mean? *The Iron Avenger* series?"

"Nah," I don't know 'em, the old man says, "But this Jackpot sounds like a real piece of work." The old man smiles at the auburn-haired young writer, says, "Darlin', I don't think I caught your name."

She smiles, says shyly, "Natalie Napoli. I feel a little out of place with you all here. My first book isn't even out. Not officially."

The old writer winks. "Nonsense. You're right where you should be. We're all just folks, here."

She is about to say, *And* your *name, sir*...?

But another writer cuts in. The balding author says, "You were telling us about the Chapman kid's death? About this woman you're hunting?"

"Right," the old writer says. "They found a copy of Jesse's own novel in the kid's room, inscribed to this seemingly comely young thing. It read, 'To hot Verity! Hope you dig this tale! Always, JC.'"

The Irish crime writer growls, "Sounds like the lad hooked up with a fan before he took himself out."

"Surely looks that way," the old author allows. "Or was meant to look that way. You remember another crime writer, Robert Lange?"

Everyone knows that story.

Two years earlier, the brooding, withdrawn and famously self-destructive crime novelist was found dangling outside his office window in downtown Los Angeles, hanged from a length of clothesline lashed around the leg of his desk.

In Lange's coat pocket, they found a gun and floppy disc containing the unfinished manuscript of his next novel.

Everyone regarded it as another suicide.

"What wasn't made public," the old author says, "is the bound copy of one of his own novels that was in Bob's other coat pocket. It was a paperback inscribed, "'To Verity, who turned off the gas ... for a time.'"

Natalie shivers despite the closeness of the barroom. "That's for certain?"

"Absolutely," the old man says. He moves his arms from the table and sits back as the waitress places their fresh round of drinks before them.

The old author says, "There are two more crime writers' deaths I've poked around these past few months. One of 'em was a woman. Mind you, these are the ones I know of. There could be others writers' bodies strewn in *Verity's* wake. But in each case that I've identified, the writers' bodies were found with copies of their own books signed to Verity."

Guzzling his fresh coffee, the balding author, evidently "James" *Something* based on his book's partly obscured byline, says, "If the police know about this, why haven't they—?"

"Nah, they don't know," the old writer cuts in. "Different jurisdictions. I'm talking states—sometimes even international borders—apart. And nobody's tipped the Feds. It's just a few old-timers like me who've compared notes and stumbled onto this. Made the connections. She seems to work these conventions mostly, this Verity. Some kind of serial killer-cum-groupie or maybe a kind of anti-muse. Either way, I'm the only one of the old guard who's clued in and who's still got the wheels—who's still reasonably ambulatory, to say—to hunt around after this twisted bitch. Well, me and a slightly younger writer pal or two."

He sips his single malt, adds, "Verity's got raven hair these days. Wears it in a kind of Louise Brooks-style bob," he says with a strange tone Natalie almost takes for resentment. Staring into his glass, he adds, "She has 'striking green eyes' and a 'charming personality,' according to a female pourer in a lounge down Music Row way."

The elder crime writer smiles and winks at the other authors. "So, I'm keeping an eye peeled for this dishy, deadly young green-eyed thing."

Incredulous, the Irish writer says, "And what will you do if you find her?"

"Figure I'll figure that out in the moment," the old man says. "In writing, and in life, I reckon, I've always been what they call, 'a pantser.' Tend to improvise. Make it up as I go along. Character drives plot, and plot informs characters. Outlined books? Suckers always read as outlined books to me, not like character-driven stories. Instead, heavily plotted whodunnits and the like—these too-fretted-over, too-detailed mysteries always are thick with stock characters I can't be moved to care about."

Natalie is struck by the tone of contempt the old scribe ladles over the words "whodunnits" and "mysteries."

The elder author rants quietly on, "In all such written-to-outline books, the folks in 'em are littler better than pack animals—only put down on the page to advance preconceived mystery outlines. They are what I call plot donkeys."

Natalie notes that the big, bald writers squirms in his seat at that, then drains the latest in his long line of black coffees.

The old writer's hand drifts to the left lapel of his sports jacket. He pulls it a bit closer across his chest. From Natalie's perspective, it looked like the old man might have something bulky under there, hanging under his left armpit.

She wonders, *Something in a holster? Hm.*

Natalie's distracted then by a boisterous, fortyish crime novelist loudly making his way toward their table; he slaps male backs and trades hugs with several female mystery writers along his way.

This new man presently shakes hands with a short and bespectacled writer who has long, lank black hair and a prognathic jaw. After a few words with the longhaired crime writer, the exuberant, flirty fiction writer finally reaches their table.

This author's name is Porter Dover, Natalie knows. He has a couple of novels under his belt about a licensed private eye named Troy Umbrage.

Natalie is about to introduce Dover to the ancient author, figuring in this way to maybe at last pry the old author's name from him, but the elderly crime writer says, "No need sweetie. Already know of this son of a bitch. Sorry reputation precedes him."

Then the old writer says to the new arrival, "Well, Dover—your series seems to be gaining traction. And that frankly stuns me. 'Fraid I tend to put P.I. novels in the same low-tier, too-hard-to-take-for-real bracket as cozies. You know? All that crap featuring sleuthing pussycats and dowager detectives? Annoyed and prissy sleuthing clerics? Tarnished knights and mean streets…? For my money, all that had already descended into sentimental slop even before Old Ray Chandler crossed south of the sod."

Dover frowns, even as he pumps the old man's big bronzed hand. "Well, tastes vary, I guess, Mr. Devlin."

"First, you have to have taste."

The old man—Devlin?—waits until the private-eye writer sits down, then he scoops up his packet of cigarettes and lighter and drops them in his coat pocket. He says to the four authors he's been talking to, "Folks, gangrene has now set into our conversation. I'm gonna amble."

Devlin rises. He kisses the petite female author Cheryl on the top of her head. He shakes hands with balding James and the Irish crime novelist.

Ignoring Porter Dover's offered hand, Devlin says, "It was a pleasure meeting you four. Maybe we'll meet you again somewhere else down life's road."

Then Devlin lavishes the most attention on the table's neophyte novelist. He bear hugs Natalie and rasps in her ear, "Good luck, kiddo. You're coming into the business at a crazy time! Hang tough, sweetheart."

Devlin waves an arm at the room. "And now the 'legacy' writers set in like a generational infection. Now we get the tag-alongs and coattail riders. Writing wives and children and kid-brothers coasting on aging or already-dead established author's names. Christ's sake!" He smiles ruefully, again revealing those deeply-etched dimples. "But hell, book publishing's never been a meritocracy."

The old man smiles again at Natalie, says, "Know I'll be watching you particularly, darlin'. Be followin' your progress with sincere interest, Nat'. My advice to you? Embrace the Bushido Code, kiddo."

Natalie, completely charmed says, "I'm sorry—the Bushido Code? I don't know it... Mr. Devlin is it?"

The old man smiles, says, "Go into each battle expecting to die and you'll survive." He kisses her hand, says, "I'm Beau Devlin, by-the-by." He jacks a thumb at his breastbone. "That's my handle."

Natalie watches as Beau Devlin meanders to the bar to settle the table's tab before Dover can order.

Natalie continues to study the allegedly octogenarian author as he spritely makes his way through the tangle of other writers and their fans increasingly clotting the lounge. Something about old Beau Devlin fascinates Natalie, draws her to him.

She tells herself maybe she's staggered into an actual mentor in this elder crime novelist.

There is a tall and thin, gray-haired man with prominent ears loitering at the entrance to the lounge. The man sports a black eye-patch. Natalie vaguely registered him lurking there a few minutes back.

The one-eyed man claps Devlin's back and they wander together toward the lobby, soon enough far from Natalie's line of sight.

The opening hour of the opening day of North America's biggest annual mystery and crime fiction convention:

Natalie savors her first coffee, browsing in the book dealer's room before heading to the suite where she is scheduled to appear on one of the day's first panels.

Porter Dover stands at the opposite side of the dealer's room, chatting up a raven-haired young woman.

The woman's hair is cut short like a blue-black helmet and she's wearing a tight-fitting little black dress, very slinky.

The young woman is—how would the hardboiled old author she met yesterday put it, back-in-the-day?

Maybe, *dishy*? *A tomato*?

Quite the twist?"

In her head, Natalie hears the old crime writer growling those words in his whisky – and cigarette-stoked Texas baritone.

Yet, none seem right for him. She remembers another phrase Beau Devlin has used in her presence: *Cherchez la femme.*

Natalie moves around the table to study the woman in profile.

The stranger's black hair is indeed cut in a severe bob reminiscent of silent film siren Louise Brook's trademark 'do.

The woman has penetrating green eyes. She clutches a copy of Porter Dover's debut novel to her breast.

Fishing around in her backpack, Natalie finds and raises a point-and-shoot disposable camera she brought along to maybe get some shots of herself with some favorite authors.

She snaps a picture of the striking, black-haired woman.

Natalie is thinking of approaching the pair, trying to think of something to say to interpose herself, when someone takes her by the arm.

An older woman with a mauve beehive says to Natalie, "What luck finding you! I'm moderating the 'First-Timers' panel and I have the others gathered in the hospitality room just across the hall."

The older woman is the author of a long-running mystery series aimed at latch-hook enthusiasts. She says, "I want us all to chat a bit before we begin our panel! Get some chemistry flowing, because we both know, staying in print is all about selling yourself... We must entertain in person in these settings!"

The older female mystery writer takes Natalie firmly by the arm, steering her out of the book dealer's room.

But Natalie keeps stealing glances back at the striking young raven-haired woman now leaning closer into Porter Dover.

Natalie sees Porter accept the copy of his own novel, then he reaches into his leather coat's pocket. He pulls out a Sharpie to inscribe Verity's copy of his book.

Natalie moves through the convention hall in a kind of delirious state of delight: Her first panel went really well, she thinks. She found she has a gift for comedic presence she'd previously never known lay within her.

Her first book-signing went equally well—countless copies of her advance reader copies were thrust in front of her by smiling readers seeking autographs.

Yet Natalie remains very much alone at this, her first convention, so she beelines for the bar, hoping to maybe spot at least one of those four authors from yesterday's table she might latch onto—an excuse to join *another* table of established authors to build rapport with toward hanging out during future such events.

In a corner booth, far as can be found from the bar-room chatter and sound system speakers sits striking old Beau Devlin.

Natalie sets course for him, but then sees someone is seated opposite him. The bare elbow looks distinctly feminine.

The old man's pale blue eyes are fixed firmly on his companion; he takes no note of Natalie.

As she draws even with Beau Devlin's booth, Natalie sees there is indeed a woman seated opposite Beau—raven haired, green-eyed *Verity*.

Natalie gets quite lucky: the quartet in the booth at Beau Devlin's back are leaving. Despite glares from loitering, standing groups hoping to claim the booth, Natalie darts in, her back to Beau Devlin's, the better to hopefully hear him.

A server promptly appears to clear the empty array of countless beer bottles and wine goblets.

As she does that, Natalie decides to treat herself—she has about $400 in mad money provided by her publisher for expenses—and so orders what she heard Beau Devlin order for himself the day before: "A double dram of Glenmorangie."

Natalie's a bit of a default Scotch drinker anyway, but has never had a proper single malt.

Alone, at her clean table and awaiting her drink, she's delighted to hear not just Beau Devlin's side of the rather heated and intense conversation going down in the booth at her back, but also the words of the woman … Verity.

Verity says in a honeyed tone, "Just accept it, Hector! When it comes to me, everything old is new again. Here's an idea to convince you I'm all that I claim! I will describe—in Dickensian detail—every move of our first night in bed together back on that storm-swept tiny island. Understand, this will be a blow-for-blow reminiscence of the first time we were one person. Our first time as the beast with two backs?"

Natalie detects a soft snort from the elderly writer whose back is to her own.

Beau—actually *Hector*?—says, "Whoever you are, you can talk that nonsense all day. But I expect you'd only be quoting from some long-dead and quite mad woman's diary, at best. Bottom line? I don't buy you're some ageless entity. No eternal muse of destruction. Oh, you look much like the Verity I knew back in the Flapper era, I admit. But I've seen plenty times how stubbornly strong genes can be in working their wonders across generations at this point of my surprisingly long life. You are not that Verity."

Verity says, "Oh, please Hector! You're going to end up hurt trying to twist yourself into these positions of impossible denial. Face facts."

"Facts?" The old author contemptuously echoes the word. "Please. You're surely at best a grand-daughter? Maybe even a great-granddaughter? It's something like that."

Verity snaps back, "Okay, let's pretend that's how it is. If so, how do you know we're not blood? Because, I know how reckless things were that first night back on the island. No precautions were taken."

Beau-Hector says dully, "Off the point, even if it were so. And you seemingly put much more of a premium on blood than I do. Family? In my bloody experience, family is a concept that far more often fucks up than fixes anything."

Natalie's waiter brings her glass of Highland single malt and a bowl of pub Chex Mix. Natalie continues eavesdropping, ignoring the bar snacks so as not to miss a word under the sound of crunching and chewing.

The Scotch, however, Natalie sips and fast savors: *Beau Stryder*, or *Hector Whatever*? He certainly shares her taste in hard spirits.

Natalie bites her lip at the sound of a deep and husky female sigh; she next overhears: "Hector, whatever you think about what is or isn't the reality of me, why do you still pursue me like this? Why this, well, let's call it what it is, this decades-long vendetta against me and mine?"

"I reckon this craziness is a kind of family business for you all," the old man accuses. "But it always ends with people murdered. Whatever the case, you're unfinished business. An unpunished killer."

A soft chuckle and Verity says, "Admit it, you're captivated by the mystery of me."

"Not at all," Beau-Hector immediately rebuts her. "I've not an inkling of interest in any of that. Best believe, I'm well-past such vexing nuances and my own time is ever-shorter. Hell, I don't even buy green bananas these days. Point is, like I warned you, or rather, warned one of your look-alikes, I am going to end you, too, and end everything you value before you or others like you can hurt anymore people. I will end you like I ended Usher Krutch—well and truly and for all-time!"

Verity snarls back, "Not if I end you first, and face it Hec—you're not the man you were in the 1920s, or even the 1930s."

Natalie hears fast retreating heels on tile. She glances around her booth and sees Verity stalking off.

Her waitress is suddenly at Natalie's shoulder, nodding at Verity's empty glass. "Another?"

"Yes, please."

Natalie figures she'll presume to finish that drink seated across from old Beau (Hector?) Devlin.

When her fresh whisky arrives, Natalie half rises to shift booths, but sees the old author has somehow quite silently also vacated the booth behind her: a new party of four is in the process of claiming it.

Having settled her tab, to her mild relief, Natalie spots Porter Dover at the bar-proper, chatting up a struggling mid-list author who recently abandoned his own series to continue that of a more noted but recently deceased private eye novelist.

Natalie waits until the other writer drifts on, then she approaches Porter Dover. She says, "Porter! We met briefly yesterday."

Beaming, he says, "Natalie, right? I remember."

"This morning I saw you with a woman," Natalie said. "I think she and I might have gone to school together. She has black hair, green eyes. Very pretty."

"Yeah, Verity something or other," Porter says. "Yeah, she was . . . interesting. Unfortunately, some other writer interrupted. Some guy who actually calls himself Jackpot, or something like that. He took her away to some restaurant, I guess."

Natalie deftly brushes off Porter; nearly dashes to the convention sign-in desk. This is staffed by writer volunteers. A youngish woman with spiky, dirty-blond hair sits behind the table. She's going bra-less under a black T-shirt that reads, "The Butler *Didn't* Do It."

Natalie says to the T-shirt wearing woman, "I'm looking for another attendee I met this morning and was supposed to meet by the front desk for lunch," Natalie says. "I only have her first name. Verity."

The other mystery writer flips through pages on a clipboard. "Not seeing any Verity's here," she says.

Remembering, Natalie gets out the photo she'd taken of the raven-haired woman. On a chance, she shows it to the spikey-haired mystery writer.

The established author looks from the picture to Natalie and back again.

"Not Verity," the mystery writer behind the desk says. "But I do recognize her." The mystery writer picks back up the clipboard, finger trailing down the list of names. "Not Verity," she says again. "No, she's Desiree Thorp. At least on paper."

Natalie goes to the hotel front desk, then. She hands the desk clerk an improvised story. Natalie wangles herself a room number for Desiree Thorp.

Natalie, checking room numbers, realizes she's close to her destination.

The she stutter-steps.

An old man with his back to Natalie is chatting in flawless, unhesitating Spanish with an elderly and portly Latina housekeeper.

The old man points a big thumb at Verity's—or Desiree Thorp's—room. He holds up a leatherette wallet Natalie sees holds a silver badge.

The elderly housekeeper appears to think about it, then nods and gets out a keycard, opening the door for what would surely have to be America's eldest law enforcement officer.

It's actually old Beau Devlin, of course.

Smiling at the woman, Natalie calls out, "Hey there, please! I'm the officer's intern!"

To the old man, she says, "Hey, partner, wait up!"

Natalie slides through the closing door, squeezing in just behind the old writer.

The perturbed old author frowns at Natalie. He says, "You being here is a calamitous mistake, darlin'. You shouldn't be pokin' around after this wicked witch, Nat! Please believe me!"

"Then what are you doing here, mister?"

The charismatic codger says, "Tying off a too-long-dangling loose end. And looking for a certain letter."

The old man thinks about it, then strokes her auburn hair behind Natalie's right ear. "God save us all from beguiling young sleuths. Jesus, I feel like I've staggered into a Nancy Drew novel."

Then his robin's egg blue eyes swiftly scope the room. His gazes seizes on a slip of paper on the nightstand. He moves toward it.

Nimble Natalie almost gets there first.

He says, "Too late for this epistle," moving the note behind his back, out of Natalie's sight and reach.

"Writing is my default weapon of choice," he says. "Often as not, it gets the job done plenty fine. But not this time. Been overtaken by events, I fear."

He crams the letter in his pocket. He scans the room a last time, then uses a handkerchief to wipe down some spots where Natalie has recklessly left fingerprints.

Next he seizes on a souvenir convention bag of the sort handed out to every registered author and reader. He pulls out one volume, leafs through it and shivers. He replaces the book in the bag and slings that over his right shoulder.

"This is going to be a crime scene, soon. We need to clear out, pronto. And anyway, I need a cigarette."

"Me too," Natalie says.

He smiles. "My kind of vice-ridden crime fiction writer. So let's get downstairs, pronto, kiddo. We'll finish talking over smokes. Then we both need to leave this hotel and go separate ways, and I mean for keeps. If that housekeeper should identify us having been in here … and being a pair?"

The old man and the young woman smoke together on the hotel's concrete exterior deck.

The patio area has become a kind of de-facto gathering spot for nicotine-addicted authors. The old novelist leads Natalie to the far, shaded-end of the patio, well away from other cigarette fiends.

Natalie says, "You said it's going to be a crime scene up there in that room. And the letter you took from there?"

Smoke streams from his nostrils as he contemplates the view of downtown Baltimore. "I was angling to force a confrontation or compel the murderous little maniac to flight, well away from this hotel and all these peeping mystery and crime writers, yes," he says. "But events overtook me, just as I confessed to you. Overtook my message. Overtook Verity, too. Seems she picked the wrong next victim."

"You mean Porter Dover?"

"Nah, I fouled that one up for her," the old man says. "And I'll probably soon enough regret that. He's an execrable excuse for a writer. But no, Verity next set sights on that strapping body Nazi from yesterday, the so-called 'Iron Avenger'. Things got nasty and Verity finally came out on the short end of her own bloody game for once. This Jackpot fella and an old crony of mine are taking care of disposing of her body now."

"This doesn't seem remotely right," Natalie says, pole-armed. "The police—"

"Would never buy the truth and old Jackpot would probably go down for a homicide rap, justifiable though Verity's killing surely was. No. We writers best clean up our own mess, this 'round. Besides, kiddo, that woman came here with multiple targets."

The old man holds up the souvenir Bouchercon book bag he took from Verity's room.

"This was the murderous muse's, of course," he says. "Verity culled the usual junk stuff we all got in our bags along with the decent stuff, all the amateur bookmarks and lackluster, straight-to-self-published paperback titles and the like."

He reaches in and pulls out a stack of books. "These particular volumes? Verity gathered these with criminal intent."

Natalie recognizes the spine of her debut's galley. The old man pulls it from the stack, passes it to Natalie.

She shrugs and says, "There must have been a couple of hundred of these shoved into all those attendee gift bags."

The old man lights up a fresh Pall Mall with his Zippo; shakes his head. "Sure. But did the others galleys come complete with an inserted piece of paper with your room number on it? Did they come with copious notes about you on the inside of the rear cover? *Likes, dislikes…*? Did those other advance reader copies come stuffed with print-outs of your profiles from your publisher? A cut-out of an instamatic photo Verity snapped of you and I together, talking yesterday?"

Natalie realizes she's shaking.

The old man catches it; smiles sadly.

"Sorry, darlin'. It's a lot to take in on the fly, I know. But Verity was coming for you. You got very lucky."

Natalie nods, shivering. The old man wraps an arm around her shoulders. "You dodged a strange bullet, darlin', that's all. Shrug and move on. Hell, groupies are bad enough. But to have to deal with one like Verity? That's asking too bloody much of any author."

Natalie nods, trying to wrap her mind around it. But she's also trying to wheedle at least a certain flavor of admission from the old storyteller. She says, "I feel I still don't know your real name, sir."

"Doesn't matter a lick," he insists. "And I have to be shoving off in just a bit. So, I'll just leave you with a last piece of advice, writer-to-writer. If you're open to an old scribe's counsel?"

"Of course!"

"You're just starting off, dear Nat. We writers usually accumulate reputations. It either just evolves around us, or we shape a persona for ourselves. Either way, that persona can draw some strange flavors of attention from readers and the like. Verity's a very extreme example, of course."

The old man lights a fresh cigarette for Natalie with his old Zippo.

He says, "Just please step careful and don't build a brand you can't live with, later. By brand, I speak of your writer's persona. I say this from bitter personal experience. I've endured several versions or spins on Verity and her ilk down through the years. It's one of the reasons I contrived to check out of this crazy genre game, at least by real name, back in sixty-seven. Killed myself off on paper, then wrote my way into a new life, you might say."

Natalie cups his chin between thumb and forefinger. With sloe eyes, she searches his strangely pale blue eyes.

"I've been doing my own sleuthing, sir, mostly around the rare book room downstairs. May I at last call you Hector Lassiter?"

The old man takes her hand in his and squeezes. "Only if it stays our secret. Otherwise, I'm already safely dead to the world."

Natalie smiles. "Right. Of course. Secret-sharers forever."

Hector smiles, says, "How long have you wanted to be a novelist, kid?"

"Since as long as I can remember," Natalie says.

"Exactly. Same for me. You dream a dream for a long time, then it starts to come true. But next thing you know, your dreams can start dreaming you."

"I'm not sure I understand what you mean," Natalie said.

The old writer said, "Honestly, darlin'? I hope like hell you never do. You've been researching me, you said. You possibly know I picked up this tagline: 'The man who lives what he writes and writes what he lives'?"

Natalie searches his pale blue eyes. "Must confess, it did come up in the process of my crash course on all things you.... It did that, a lot."

She gives him a funny smile. "But it also got phrased the other way, here and there—*the man who writes what he lives and lives what he writes.*"

"Right," Hector says. "Speaking from long and bitter experience, however you chicken and egg all that, it's a plenty bloody way to approach art and life."

Also from Betimes Books

Dimitri Bortnikov
Soul Catcher ISBN 978-1-9161565-2-4

Fionnuala Brennan
The Painter's Women: Goya in Light and Shade ISBN 978-0-9929674-8-2

Hadley Colt
Permanent Fatal Error ISBN 978-0-9926552-6-6
The Red-Handed League ISBN 978-0-9934331-2-2

Les Edgerton
The Death of Tarpons ISBN 978-0-9934331-4-6

Sam Hawken
La Frontera ISBN 978-0-9926552-2-8

David Hogan
The Last Island ISBN 978-0-9926552-1-1
Hear Us Fade ISBN 978-1-9161565-7-9

Kim Hood
They All Fall Down ISBN 978-1-9161565-1-7

Richard Kalich
Central Park West Trilogy ISBN 978-0-9926552-7-3

The Assisted Living Facility Library	ISBN 978-0-9934331-9-1
A Man Made Long Ago	ISBN 978-

Robert Kalich

David Lazar	ISBN 978-1-9161565-0-0
A Man Divided	ISBN 978-1-9161565-6-2

Patricia Ketola

Dirty Pictures	ISBN 978-0-9934331-3-9

Jackie Mallon

Silk for the Feed Dogs	ISBN 978-0-9926552-0-4

Donald Finnaeus Mayo

Francesca	ISBN 978-0-9926552-3-5
The Insider's Guide to Betrayal	ISBN 978-0-9934331-6-0

Craig McDonald

One True Sentence	ISBN 978-0-9926552-8-0
Forever's Just Pretend	ISBN 978-0-9926552-9-7
Toros & Torsos	ISBN 978-0-9929674-0-6
Roll the Credits	ISBN 978-0-9929674-1-3
The Great Pretender	ISBN 978-0-9929674-2-0
The Running Kind	ISBN 978-0-9929674-3-7
Head Games	ISBN 978-0-9929674-5-1
Print the Legend	ISBN 978-0-9929674-7-5
Death in the Face	ISBN 978-0-9934331-0-8
Three Chords & the Truth	ISBN 978-0-9934331-1-5
Borderland Noir (editor)	ISBN 978-0-9929674-9-9

Sean Moncrieff
The Angel of the Streetlamps ISBN 978-0-9929674-6-8

Colin O'Sullivan
Killarney Blues ISBN 978-0-9926552-4-2
The Starved Lover Sings ISBN 978-0-9934331-5-3
The Dark Manual ISBN 978-0-9934331-7-7
My Perfect Cousin ISBN 978-0-9934331-8-4
Marshmallows ISBN 978-1-9161565-4-8

Gérard Ramon
In Love with Paris ISBN 978-2-7466-8421-8

Kevin Stevens
Reach the Shining River ISBN 978-0-9926552-5-9

Betimes Books is a non-profit literary publisher based in Dublin, Ireland.

For more information please visit www.betimesbooks.com

www.ingramcontent.com/pod-product-compliance
Lightning Source LLC
LaVergne TN
LVHW050928080826
845145LV00001B/255

* 9 7 8 1 9 1 6 1 5 6 5 9 3 *